Simon Raven was born in London in 1927. He was educated at Charterhouse and King's College, Cambridge where he read Classics. After university, he joined the army as a regular officer in the King's Shropshire Light Infantry and saw service in Germany and Kenya where he commanded a Rifle Company. In 1957 he resigned his commission and took up book reviewing. His first novel, *The Feathers of Death*, was published in 1959. Since then he has written many reviews, general essays, plays for radio and television as well as the scripts for a number of successful television series including *Edward and Mrs Simpson* and *Love in a Cold Climate* plus a host of novels. The highly acclaimed ALMS FOR OBLIVION sequence is published by Grafton Books in chronological order. The sequence takes its title from a passage in Shakespeare's *Troilus and Cressida*, has been referred to as 'a latter-day Waugh report on another generation of Bright Young Things', and has been compared favourably with the *romans fleuves* of Anthony Powell and C. P. Snow. With the publication in 1984 of *Morning Star* he began a new novel series under the title THE FIRST-BORN OF EGYPT. It is a sequel to ALMS FOR OBLIVION. Simon Raven lives and works in Deal, Kent.

D0255770

SIMON RAVEN

Before the Cock Crow

The First-born of Egypt: Volume III

GRAFTON BOOKS
A Division of the Collins Publishing Group

LONDON GLASGOW
TORONTO SYDNEY AUCKLAND

Grafton Books
A Division of the Collins Publishing Group
8 Grafton Street, London W1X 3LA

Published by Grafton Books 1988

First published in Great Britain by
Muller, Blond & White Ltd 1986

Copyright © Simon Raven 1986

ISBN 0-586-06353-6

Printed and bound in Great Britain by
Collins, Glasgow

Set in Times

List of Characters in Order
of Appearance

Captain the Most Honourable Marquess Canteloupe of the Aestuary of the Severn

Major Fielding Gray, a novelist

Major Giles Glastonbury

Leonard Percival, secretary to the Marquess Canteloupe, a Jermyn Street man

The Marchioness Canteloupe (Baby): *née* Llewyllyn; niece to Isobel Stern and cousin to Rosie and Marius

Daisy, Lord Sarum's nurse

Tullius Fielding d'Azincourt Llewyllyn Gregory Jean-Josephine Maximin Sarum Detterling, called by courtesy Baron Sarum of Old Sarum, son and heir to Lord and Lady Canteloupe

Jo-Jo (Josephine) Guiscard *née* Pelham

Theodosia Salinger (Thea), an undergraduate of Lancaster College; Carmilla's twin

Teresa (Tessa) Malcolm, Maisie's 'niece'

Rosie Stern

Jakki Blessington

Caroline Blessington

'Mrs' Maisie Malcolm, Proprietress (with Fielding Gray) of Buttock's Hotel

Jeremy Morrison, an undergraduate of Lancaster College; younger son of Peter Morrison

Ptolemaeos Tunne, an amateur scholar; uncle, through his dead sister, to Jo-Jo Guiscard

Piero Caspar, an undergraduate of Lancaster College

Carmilla Salinger, an undergraduate of Lancaster College; Theodosia's twin

Sir Thomas Llewyllyn, kt, D Lit. & Litt D, Provost of Lancaster College, Cambridge, father of lady (Baby) Canteloupe, brother-in-law of Isobel Stern, being married to her sister Patricia

Len, his secretary

Isobel Stern: *née* Turbot, mother of Rosie and Marius

Milo Hedley, a schoolboy

Raisley Conyngham, a schoolmaster

Palairet, a schoolboy

The 'Chamberlain', Peter Morrison's manservant at Luffham; formerly manservant to Canteloupe

Peter Morrison, MP, 'Squire of Luffham

Betty Blessington

Colonel Ivan Blessington, her husband, a stockbroker

Ivan ('Greco') Barraclough, an anthropologist; Fellow of Lancaster College

Nicos Pandouros, indentured page to Barraclough after the Maniot custom; undergraduate of Lancaster College

Jude Holbrook

Alfie Schroeder, a journalist

Jack Lamprey, an ex-officer of Cavalry

Ashley Dexterside, a designer

Myles Glastonbury

Gat-Toothed Jenny, a stable lass

Oenone, a daughter to Jo-Jo

Don Simone Fontanelli

Jimmy Pitts, a jockey

Mrs Statch, servant to Ptolemaeos Tunne

Corporal-Major Chead, an old soldier

Aunt Flo

PART ONE

In the Shade of the
Old Judas Tree

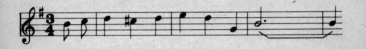

'Time for "Absent Friends",' announced Captain the Marquess Canteloupe of the Aestuary of the Severn, and rose to his feet.

Everyone else round the table rose after him: Major Fielding Gray and Major Giles Glastonbury (both formerly of the same regiment as Lord Canteloupe, the 49th Earl Hamilton's Light Dragoons, commonly known as Hamilton's Horse); Leonard Percival (formerly of the Wessex Fusiliers, with whom Hamilton's Horse had a close connection, and of what may loosely be called the Secret Service); and the Marchioness Canteloupe (formerly Miss Theodosia Salinger). Also upstanding was Daisy the Nurse, who lifted her little charge, the thirty-four month old Tullius, Lord Sarum of Old Sarum, heir to Canteloupe and step-son to my lady, from his chair beside her, stood him up on the seat of it, and gave him a glass of well watered Montrachet with which to honour the coming toast.

'Absent Friends,' intoned Lord Canteloupe. He drank off his glass and threw it over his left shoulder to shatter against the wainscot.

'Absent Friends,' all the company repeated after him – all, that was, except Lord Sarum of Old Sarum, who gave a crow of excitement and struck with the rim of his glass at the face of his step-mother, who was sitting on the other side of him from his nurse.

'A good thing that girl Daisy was on the ball,' said Leonard Percival to Fielding Gray and Giles Glastonbury as the three of them walked in the bare Rose Garden. 'If that glass had got home on her ladyship's face – '

' – Thea would have caught his wrist if Daisy hadn't,' said Fielding Gray. 'She has very quick reactions. Have you ever seen her in a tennis court? Always there to guard the galleries or the dedans a tenth of a second before the fastest ball.'

'Still, it's not the sort of show one wants at Christmas luncheon,' said Glastonbury; 'it very much upset my process of intake. Not a good thing when there'll only be cold supper.'

'The whole thing was thoroughly *mal à propos*,' agreed Fielding, 'quite apart from any damage to the digestion. It was a major boob by Canteloupe. Such a toast, coming when and where it did, was almost certain to put Theodosia in mind – painfully in mind – of Canteloupe's first wife, Baby. And in the event, it did even worse. It somehow sparked young Tullius off to make a kind of protest at Theodosia's sitting in the place of his mother.'

'Whoa there,' said Percival. 'Nobody's going to tell me that Tully understands anything about that . . . at his age.'

'Nearly three,' said Fielding. 'Who was it – John Stuart Mill or Macualay – who'd read the whole of Gibbon before he was two and a half?'

'But nobody has actually *told* Tully anything,' Percival said, 'so how could he be making protests?'

'Unless that ginger nurse of his – '

' – But even if she had, how could he understand? He can't even talk yet. Not a single word. The boy's potty,' said Giles Glastonbury.

'Language, language,' said Percival. 'You'll be talking about niggers next.'

'Imbecile then,'

'Still not allowed,' said Percival. 'Worse than the first, in fact, because even more contemptuous.'

'Backward, for Christ's sake, or whatever mealy-mouthed piece of unction is current. There's something deeply amiss with that child. You've only got to look into his eyes.'

Glastonbury and Percival, both of whom, as very old friends of Canteloupe, knew that the child was Fieldings's, begot on the previous Marchioness at Canteloupe's own request, now had the grace to look embarrassed.

'I didn't want the job,' said Fielding, knowing what they were thinking; 'don't blame me.'

'Oh, we don't, my dear fellow. But what,' said Glastonbury, 'do we think ought now to be done?'

'That's hardly for me to say.'

'No good having a potty heir. Better none at all. I speak,' said Glastonbury, 'without malice and as one of Canteloupe's oldest chums, anxious to consult two others.'

The three men filed out of the Rose Garden through a tunnel of yew. When they debouched into open ground, they formed a line of three and proceeded, at a stately military saunter, over the wide lawn in front of them towards a distant copse of lady birch. At last, as they

11

converged with a stream that was also heading for the copse:

'The decision must clearly be for Detterling,' Leonard Percival said.

'Detterling?' said Glastonbury.

'That is what I call him.'

'To his face?'

'Let us say . . . that it is the privilege of a long established ally. I have been in his service as private secretary ever since the year in which he first . . . acquired his title; and before that I was intimately involved with him in one affair and another . . . when, of course, he was still known as Detterling. So that, to remind us both of the dear old days, is what I call him.'

'I've often wondered why he engaged you,' Glastonbury said, his voice rustling with irritation.

'So have others. Baby Canteloupe couldn't stand me. Theodosia has to make a great effort, almost successful, bless her heart, to conceal her distaste. Daisy loathes me outright. I conclude,' said Leonard Percival, 'that I do not appeal to women. But that is beside the point . . . which is that Detterling, he alone, must decide what to do about his heir.'

'Has he asked your advice?' said Fielding, partly to annoy Glastonbury, and partly because he knew that Canteloupe would almost certainly have asked Percival's advice and he was very anxious to know what Leonard had counselled.

'Hypothetically,' said Leonard. ' "What," he remarked to me a few weeks ago, "should we do if something happened to Tully?" I suggested, as I think he expected I would, that a child would have to be fathered on Theodosia in the same fashion – though not, I thought, by the same person – as a child had been fathered on Baby.

"The trouble is," he said, "that Theodosia married me on the absolute agreement that there should be no sex. None at all of any kind whatever." Still, he seemed to think he might find a way of persuading her. He is exceedingly keen, you see, that the marquessate should continue.'

They came, with the stream, to the edge of the copse. The silver trunks grew from the verges of the stream and thronged impenetrably for at least twenty yards on either side of it.

'This is not the way in,' said Percival.

'Do you know it?' asked Fielding.

'Theodosia could have as many brats as you like,' grumbled Glastonbury, 'but that still leaves Canteloupe with a potty heir.'

'Unless, as Detterling himself put it, "something happened to Tully." To get in, we go round the edge this way,' said Leonard Percival leading off to the right.

'What did you mean just now,' said Glastonbury, 'about something happening to Tully?'

'I should have thought it was clear enough. Even these days children get childhood diseases. Even these days,' said Percival, as he parted two bramble-bushes and led the way down a narrow path, 'there can be unexpected variants or complications, which lead to early death – or "tragedy" as the yellow press insists on miscalling it, not having read Aristotle's definition. Or again,' said Leonard, 'if a child is not quite normal, not quite happy in the head, it is often easy to persuade highly paid doctors and nurses to exercise what is known as "benign neglect" . . . particularly if their charge shows signs of turning vicious. Detterling's old friend Doctor La Soeur,' smiled Leonard, 'will be an expert, I think you would find, in the theory and practice of "benign neglect". And then, in this appalling world, there are myriad types of accident.'

They stepped off the path through the birch trees on to the green margin of a pool, round the entire circumference of which were massed more birches, leaving only two or three yards between themselves and the grey waters.

'Why have you brought us here?' said Glastonbury.

'We simply came. A casual walk on Christmas afternoon . . . has led us, by chance, to Baby's private copse. "Absent Friends."'

A chill breeze briefly ruffled the pool's surface. Five or six flakes of snow spiralled down from a platinum sky.

'I'm going in, damn it,' Glastonbury said.

He disappeared, shivering jerkily, down the tiny path that had brought them into the copse.

'That summer,' said Percival to Fielding, 'that summer after Baby Canteloupe had borne Tullius, she used to sit here with Jo-Jo Guiscard, herself by then heavily pregnant. I used to eavesdrop. Some very peculiar things were said. Jo-Jo was fierce to bear a boy, with whom she was already dangerously infatuated: she was going to play with his little prick, she said, and seduce him as soon as he had hairs. All healthy boys want to fuck their mothers, she said; and since boys ought to be instructed by older and experienced women, what better and more economic arrangement could you have than letting them learn with mummy?'

'Poor Jo-Jo,' said Fielding. 'Such entertaining plans – and she had to go and have a girl.'

'But perhaps the oddest thing,' said Percival, 'was what *wasn't* said. There was very little talk about the baby Sarum. Tully. Tullius. Plenty of talk about how he came to be born, but none, or almost none, about the finished product. Baby told Jo-Jo the full tale of how you were chosen as father, how reluctant you were at first, how versatile and amusing you were in bed after you'd at last consented . . . though you weren't too hot on straight fucking, she said, which was rather a worry – '

' – I remember. She handled that very cleverly – '

' – Oh yes indeed, and now here was little Tully to prove it. Here he was, with the right number of limbs and eyes and balls, all set up with his pram and his Nanny – here he was, and not a damn thing was said about him. She didn't want to talk about him, even when Jo-Jo encouraged her. She didn't hate him, she didn't dislike him, not particularly, she just didn't want to know about him. You see, she'd spotted, or so I think now, that something was wrong. And her response to this? Just cut your losses, girl, and forget the whole damn thing.'

'Yet she fed the child herself.'

'Yes. Because she knew it pleased Detterling, and she knew that Jo-Jo liked watching her. And she liked being watched. They were very happy together that summer; they adored each other, took care of each other, entertained and gambled with each other. They didn't want it to end.'

'But of course it had to.'

'Yes,' said Leonard Percival: 'with Jo-Jo giving birth to a girl she didn't want, and Baby left lumbered with a boy she didn't want – '

' – What a pity,' said Fielding, 'that my one excursion into parenthood turned out such a disastrous flop. I knew no good would come of it, and so I said both loud and clear, but neither Baby nor Canteloupe would listen.'

'Never mind that now,' said Leonard. 'Whatever had happened, Baby would have got bored in the end . . . bored with her silly title, and with her pantaloon of a husband, and with rearing the little heir – the teething and the wet knickers and the chicken pox and the prep school carol service and the best friend from Worthing or Sunningdale coming to stay for the summer holidays – she'd have got bored with all that, though she might just have put up with it for a time if Tully had been beautiful or clever. But Tully wasn't. He was just a moron. Not all there. Twelve annas in the rupee. "Backward" at best. And she knew what was going to happen. The special tutors, the special school, the sickening pretence. So she took the first good excuse that offered and went her ways. Good riddance. Let her not come back,' Percival called across the pool in the manner, half propitiatory and half denunciatory, of an unconfident exorcist.

'Why should she come back?'

'Because this is where she was happy. There is a smell here, a smell particularly appetizing to revenants, of decayed happiness. Glastonbury caught a sudden whiff of it just now and didn't like it. That's why he left in such bad order.'

'But why "decayed" happiness, Leonard? It came to an end, as it had to, but nothing happened to turn it sour at any stage. After a time, after quite a long time, it simply ceased in the natural and necessary and long foreseen progression of events. While it lasted it was unspoiled – or so you seemed to be telling me just now. So I repeat, Leonard: why "*decayed*" happiness?'

The platinum sky had changed to dirty copper. There was a second and rather thicker descent of whirling snowflakes, which stopped as suddenly as the first.

'Time to go in,' said Fielding Gray.

'No. Stay here with me and I shall answer your question. I'll tell you what poisoned Baby's happiness that summer and also helped, with several other factors, to send her packing. You know that Baby used to have . . . special perceptions . . . to dream dreams and hear voices.'

'Like her Aunt Isobel. I thought all that went for good when she bore Tullius.'

'So she said, and so she wished. But one afternoon by this pool, Fielding, one afternoon of that summer two and a half years ago, I was listening among the birches, and this is what I heard. . . . .

'"Some few years ago now," Baby had said to Jo-Jo in the summer's afternoon by their pool, "when I was about thirteen or fourteen, I went one September with Poppa to Venice.

'"It was a happy time in some ways; the first time I'd ever really had Poppa to myself, the first time I really got to know Canty – for he was there too, in fact it was while we were all in Venice that he heard he'd inherited his title. And Fielding Gray was there, very successful at that time and being rather cross and funny about it, and even funnier about the PEN Club, which was meeting in Venice just then, and all those huge tipsy cupidinous ladies who belong to it. All very entertaining. But there was a lot of sadness too. Poppa was looking for lodgings in which to spend the winter with his friend, Daniel Mond, who was probably going to die. Eventually Poppa found a little tower, a sort of two-storeyed summer-house, a casino they call it in Italy, in the garden of a place called the Palazzo Albani, which was being hired by an old friend of Canty's. Well, *that* was right enough: it was a pretty tower in a pretty garden (and of course gardens are rather special in Venice) and they had people they knew in the Palazzo if they wanted anything.

'"But there were other things in the Palazzo too. To start with, this friend of Canty's – Max de Freville, it was – had a Greek partner called Lykiadopoulos, and Lykiadopoulos had a little Sicilian boy called Piero, a dear little boy with a club foot, whom and which I fancied like all get out – but that's by the way. One evening when I was dining there, just before I had to go back to school in England, Piero showed me some rooms up on the roof, in a kind of penthouse. There was a very curious shrine, and also an old nursery with some lovely eighteenth-century rocking-horses. At the time I didn't think too much about these because I was thinking of delicious Piero, but it came to me afterwards that there was some terrible sadness about the nursery, about the rocking-horses and the little uniforms hanging there and the children who had once been playing in it, about what had happened to them and their parents later on – there was some really horrible secret which had poisoned the whole past, which was still infecting the house, even the garden and the casino, though no one seemed to have noticed this except me, and come to that I'd only noticed it long after I got home, when I dreamed one night at school about the nursery.

'"Anyway, the years went on and I forgot about all this, more or less – though there was some novel of Fielding's which Poppa said was based on something he had found out about the Albani family and their Palazzo. I never read it, because Fielding's stuff bores me stupid, but I remember thinking to myself, 'So there was something peculiar about the Albani, I must ask Fielding when I see him', but when at last I got round to asking, which was while we were in bed in Saint Tropez one morning trying to make Tully, he brushed it all aside and said, 'All that's best forgotten now, let sleeping dogs lie', and not a word more would he say. So then I started to be even more inquisitive and tried to reach back to that nursery, but I couldn't, I couldn't see anything, so I gave up – rather thankfully in a way – until suddenly, just a few days after I'd had Tully, there it all was again, as clear as morning, the nursery and the two rocking-horses with a sabretache hanging from one of them . . . and a tremendous feeling of anguish over all of it, anguish and hatred and, unmistakeably, lust, not just the straightforward kind but tormented and twisted lust, the skilled and deliberate corruption of trust and affection, the smooth mockery of deep taboo."

'"Don't get too heavy about all that stuff, darling," Jo-Jo had said, tapping her belly; "remember what I'm planning in that line."

'"Are you?" said Baby shortly. "In this case it ended in the most macabre misery for several people. I could feel that. But somehow this mattered less than another element which was beginning to come through: an element of straight physical violence, far less sinister but very powerful, not unconnected with sex but connected with it only at two or three removes. A revenge killing. A lynching perhaps. Not in Venice any more. The scene had shifted. There were marshes. An eighteenth-century church. Sudden death and speedy burial. And a figure, slowly emerging from the coffin as it was carried by shambling peasants towards the church. A figure, not the corpse of the murdered man, that was still in the coffin, but a bright and beautiful boy of sixteen or seventeen, who came up out of the coffin and stood on top of it, naked, then fondled his tool, went back on his hunkers, and pissed a great swooshing arc into the air, right between my eyes – "

'" – Christ, darling. Talk about twisted lust – "

'" – Right at my forehead," Baby had said, "bang between my eyes . . . in *accusation*. There was no lust in any of this. There was arraignment, and it was me – me and mine – that were being arraigned."

'And of course,' said Percival to Fielding Gray, as they lingered by the pool among the birches, 'we know where all that came from. Somehow she'd slipped into a net with the Albani children, just as she had done, briefly, years before, after that September in Venice; and through the Albani she'd got on to fitzAvon, the special envoy to Venice . . . the stranger who was befriended by the Albani family, and whose real name was Lord Rollesden-in-Silvis, only son and heir apparent of the first Marquess Canteloupe – '

' – Who had managed to have him sent abroad,' Fielding took up the tale, 'with a specially contrived mission and under an alias, to escape the results of a murderous little frolic in a London bordello . . .'

'. . . Lord Rollesden-in-Silvis,' mused Percival, 'who married a peasant girl in the marshes near Oriago and started an unknown and virtually undiscovered but absolutely legitimate line of Sarums, which continues to this day and offers, as its latest male issue, Paolo Filavoni, the rightful Marquess Canteloupe . . . Filavoni, an Italian version of fitzAvon, licitly and officially adopted by the family . . . Paolo Filavoni, direct descendant of the first Lord Canteloupe's only son, and thus himself Lord Canteloupe by right of primogeniture, who lives a bare, dank, distressful life with his only surviving relative in the swamps near the Laguna Veneta – '

' – And is much given, understandably perhaps, to pissing at passers by . . . or that's what he did when I last saw him. For Baby's benefit too,' Fielding said, 'in this dream of hers or whatever.'

'And then at last,' said Percival, 'and then at last, she told Jo-Jo as they sat by this pool that summer, Baby remembered something else. Now, you probably recall that she came out to Venice for Daniel Mond's funeral. Tom hadn't wanted her there, it was all Detterling's idea. I expect he just wanted an excuse to see her. Anyway, out she came and very soon after she'd overheard, as she told Jo-Jo, overheard on one of the boats which followed the barge carrying Daniel's coffin, a lot of sudden and violent talk about Detterling's new title being false or fraudulently assumed. Something about some wretched child whom he had unjustly superseded, about some recent discovery which by rights ought for ever to unseat him. For any number of reasons she was highly wrought up and in great confusion at the time; the circumstances were highly peculiar and the talk, from her point of view, fragmentary; and so she subsequently muddled or jumbled or thought she must have imagined what she'd seen or heard, until it all seemed too indefinite, too dreamlike, in the end too *distant*, to be worth heeding. Everything had reverted to normal and was going along quite happily: why bother about nightmares which had come – and gone – at time of stress? So she thought no more of it and married Canteloupe, became "my lady" and courted Fielding Gray . . .'

'With what results we know,' said Fielding Gray.

'But *now*,' said Percival, 'now that she'd borne Sarum and was sitting by this pool with Jo-Jo . . . *now that she'd had her vision of the boy from the coffin who pissed his accusation at her* . . . she began to think again of the angry discussion on the way to Daniel's funeral service, of the peasant child in the marshes who was being denied the wealth and splendour that was his by right. She knew . . . or thought she knew . . . that she and Canteloupe and even Tully, were somehow inculpated: that they had done somebody, the naked boy on the coffin perhaps, a dreadful injury.'

'But she had no knowledge of the details necessary to support such a belief . . . and now she'll never know them. Why bring this up again, Leonard?'

Suddenly the grove flared white with snowflakes.

'Because although Baby will not be making trouble on this account, I have a feeling that somebody else is about to.'

'Very few people know of it. All of them, good friends of Canteloupe.'

'Wasn't there an Englishman on the spot when you went to that village in the marshes? Name of Holbrook?'

'I don't think he knows much. We did our best not to let on to what we were up to when we went there – pretended we were doing academic research into social conditions in Italy in the late eighteenth century.'

'He must have thought your researches were very specialized. He may well have smelt something peculiar.'

'But he wouldn't dare show his face,' said Fielding, 'anywhere where he might do damage. After what he's been up to – drug running and protection rackets and God knows what else – he's stuck in those marshes for ever.'

Already the snow had made a halo of Fielding's hair and a Hebrew cap on Percival's pate.

'There is,' said Percival, 'in practice at any rate, a statute of limitations in situations such as Holbrook's. After a certain time, his type of misdemeanour becomes – well – of academic interest only. Organizations like the police or my own former Department in Jermyn Street, are happy to extend truce in return for confession.'

'Is there any reason to suppose this has been done in Holbrook's case?'

'None that I know of. I am only indulging a little general but educated speculation . . . in order to convey to you that this Mr Holbrook may not be quite so strictly and conveniently exiled as you appear to think.'

'I'm sorry, Theodosia,' said Giles Glastonbury; 'but I must leave to-morrow.'

'Boxing Day?' said Canteloupe sadly. 'I thought you'd stay at least till the 31st. There'll be a little shooting later . . . racing at Wincanton and Taunton – Cheltenham, too, if you stay on into the New Year. And if the bloody snow doesn't hang about.'

'Sorry, Canteloupe. I . . . I had a message earlier this afternoon. I must go.'

'Very well,' said Canteloupe petulantly, and helped himself to a muffin. 'Where's Nurse with Tully?' he snapped at Theodosia.

'Tully has indigestion after his Christmas dinner. He won't be down this evening. I'm sorry you must go,

Giles,' Theodosia said to Glastonbury. 'But if you must . . . ?'

'I must.'

So you really were put out by what you felt in that copse, thought Fielding Gray, and exchanged a split-second glance with Leonard Percival: a hard-bitten old soldier like you, torturer and executioner at the Viceregal Court (though unofficial of course) in the last days of the Raj; swordsman and blackmailer; the man who shot one of his troopers out of hand for sleeping on sentry duty; who poisoned statesmen and assassinated princes – you, of all people, to get upset by a breeze in the birch trees.

'At least,' said Theodosia to Fielding, 'I hope that *you* won't desert us so quickly.'

'I'd like to stay as long as you'll have me. Twelfth Night . . . ?'

'*Or What You Will*. More tea? But won't they be wanting you in London? Mrs Malcolm and those girls?'

'Not Maisie Malcolm. Maisie wants me out of the way,' said Fielding, 'until her niece Tessa is back at school. She thinks . . . that Tessa has an adolescent crush on me which I encourage.'

'And do you?'

'The whole thing's chimerical. There's no crush to encourage. Trouble with Maisie is, she's having the change of life – for the third or fourth time at that – and it's making her crabby and jealous. If she could only see straight, she'd know that Tessa has eyes only for Master Marius Stern.'

Which should be quite enough to keep her from worrying about anything else of the kind, he thought. Perhaps that's why she refuses to see it. Easier to face up to the image of an old goat (me) than the Great God Pan in person.

'Then how nice,' Theodosia was saying, 'for Tessa to be at school with Marius.'

'God knows what the bloody place is like now,' grumbled Canteloupe. 'Little girls of thirteen prinking about.'

'Most public schools have girls these days,' said Theodosia.

'Yes. Big ones in the Sixth Form being coached for the Universities. Not troops of Brownies. I wonder his mother sent Marius there – wasn't he entered for Eton?'

'His mother had second thoughts,' said Fielding. 'Besides, Marius wanted to go where he's gone because Jeremy Morrison went there. His hero.'

'And yours, they tell me,' said Canteloupe nastily, still riled by Glastonbury's defection, 'I thought,' he went on, 'that you and young Jeremy were going on some trip just after Christmas. His father mentioned it when I last saw him in the House. Now,' said Lord Canteloupe, 'I shall be delighted, my dear Fielding, if you choose to stay here not only for Cheltenham at the New Year but right through to the Gold Cup in March. We have, after all, plenty of room, and with your studious habits you are not a difficult guest. But,' said Canteloupe, 'I don't quite see how you can both be here with us and abroad with Jeremy Morrison at the same time . . . if you take me.'

'Don't be so nosy, Canteloupe,' said Theodosia, half sister, half Nanny.

'Not nosy at all. Perfectly logical question. Fielding here says he wants to stay with us till Twelfth Night, while Jeremy Morrison's father – Luffham of Whereham, or whatever ridiculous name he now gives himself – says that Jeremy and Fielding are off on a tour within a week of Christmas. That was what Luffham said – within a – '

'Granted,' said Fielding; 'and among old friends I shall return a true explanation. My expedition with Jeremy

Morrison is now uncertain. He is dragging his feet. He is tired of me. He is getting ready to cry off. So when he does, I wish to be in a position to say, "Very well, I have another excellent engagement, in Wiltshire." The only thing is,' said Fielding, 'that I'm such a fool about him that if he *were* still on for the trip I'd be out of here the moment he beckoned.'

'Not very flattering to us,' Theodosia said, 'but Jeremy does have that effect on people. It is something to do with that huge round face. It compels one towards it, as if it had gravitational powers. I am, you see, by way of being an expert, at least a former expert, on Jeremy. Don't bother with him any more, Fielding. Oh, he's fine and great fun with it – just so long as he's getting what he wants out of you and still sees more blood worth the tapping. But once he's had all the blood there is to have – or rather, all of it that he wants, for he is very discriminating and does not drink the dregs – he just glides away. To judge from what you've been saying, he is gliding away from you now. Let him go, Fielding; and get yourself a crucifix and a wreath of garlic in case he should come back.'

'Good-bye, Giles,' said Fielding.

'Good-bye, Glastonbury,' said Leonard Percival.

'Good-bye, Fielding. Good-bye, Percival. Let me know, one of you, if anything . . . worthy of notice . . . should occur on the precincts.'

Major Glastonbury stooped almost to the ground,

inserted himself into his Porsche, and rolled with vigour and *éclat* down the straight mile of the drive.

'I bet he wouldn't have driven so fast if Canteloupe had been here,' said Fielding. 'Where is he, by the way?'

'He decided to pay a few neighbourly calls with her ladyship. Customary at this season, and a good opportunity since the frost has fucked up the racing. Detterling,' said Percival, 'likes a bit of old-fashioned etiquette. He still keeps cards, you know, and leaves them on people when the London season begins and ends. *Pour prendre congé.* That sort of a thing.'

'He was always broadly conventional in outlook but totally opportunist in his own particular motives and actions. "Detterlings," he once said to me, *à propos* of the Army, "Detterlings do not serve: it might be our family motto. Graceful and ingenious shirking is what we Detterlings are bred to." So he's out doing the right thing now – but only because he's got nothing better on. Why, Leonard, does a man who sees through pretence and humbug so clearly take all this trouble to produce heirs to his title – when he knows that the title belongs elsewhere and that any scion of his house will be spurious? Why does he bother with it? I can see that he likes the money and the estate, and wants to hang on to them for his lifetime; but beyond that . . . why does he want to perpetuate a falsely inherited peerage through further doubly false inheritors who are not even the heirs of his body?'

'I think,' said Leonard, 'that he enjoys deceiving the public and the establishment – as a way of gratifying his contempt for both – but also feels that he has some kind of duty to them, because they are, after all, his world and all that is therein. So he wants to keep the show going, for their benefit and his pleasure.'

27

'Does face . . . or sentiment . . . play any part in all this?'

'Not a great deal. It's a matter of *approval*, Fielding. You said just now that Detterling was "broadly conventional in outlook". So of course he broadly approves of a properly managed and assigned marquessate, if only because it is more seemly than an improperly managed one. He approves of continuity in such matters.'

'But the whole pont is that there is no genuine continuity or propriety in any of this. The marquessate belongs to someone else – and has done for the last hundred and eighty odd years – and its present official heir apparent is the product of collusive cuckoldry.'

'You also said just now,' said Leonard, 'that he is an opportunist in his motives and actions. "Detterlings do not serve," you quoted him as saying. Then what could be more appropriate in such a man, or more enjoyable to him, than passing off a House of Sand, the shifting chambers of which are crammed with lies and squalors and illusions, as a Castle of Rock from whose battlements the banners and blazons of honour fly boldly to delight his friends, dismay his foes and defy all challengers? He approves convention, Fielding, he derives much comfort and benefit from it; but he also sees through it, is rather contemptuous of it, and eludes it if it thwarts his pleasure or purpose. What could be more natural than that he should combine all these feelings into one supreme act of public celebration and private mockery?'

During a long and thoughtful silence, they walked across the Great Court to the Fives Court.

'So . . . if little Tullius proved useless in his role of Sarum,' said Fielding, 'you think that Canteloupe would dispose of him?'

'In the most tasteful and conventional manner. He

would send him to Doctor La Soeur's nursing home rather, so to speak, than the Tower.'

'And he would expect Theodosia to get herself pregnant?'

'He already does. Any man – gentleman – of her choice, he says.'

'And if she refuses?'

'She will be replaced,' said Leonard; 'with taste and tact, of course. What Doctor La Soeur will do for Tullius, "young" John Groves of Groves & Groves, Solicitors, will do for Theodosia.'

'She adores Canteloupe. It would kill her.'

'In that case,' said Leonard, 'she had better – much better, don't you think? – do what she is told.'

'Marius is restless,' said Tessa Malcolm at lunch on Boxing Day in Buttock's Hotel.

'Yes,' agreed Marius's younger sister, Rosie Stern: 'but he has no reasonable excuse for being so, and even if he had, he should not have left us on Christmas afternoon.'

'He stayed with you for Christmas dinner,' said Jakki Blessington, and furtively looked down at her tiny new breasts, something she did when she felt truculent.

'But he should have stayed on until to-day,' said Jakki's sister, Caroline, glancing down in the same manner as Jakki, though having as yet no new breasts for inspection, 'if only because he knew that old friends – you and me, Jakki – were coming to luncheon.'

'It's my belief,' said Tessa's Auntie Maisie Malcolm (as

the girls all knew her), 'that he wouldn't even have stayed for Christmas dinner if we hadn't had it at lunch time.' She lowered down the table at all the four girls over whom she presided, as if it were they, and not Marius, whom she was arraigning. 'He was that fierce to go with that Jeremy Morrison,' she rumbled, 'that he'd have gone as soon as whistled for, Christmas dinner or no.'

'I can't say I blame him,' said Jakki. 'I've always fancied Jeremy Morrison myself.'

'That's enough of that, Missie.'

'Of course,' said Caroline Blessington, 'Jeremy's father is a lord now. Which means Jeremy is The Hon.'

'The Honourable,' said Rosie: 'it is vulgar to abbreviate. To be fair to my brother, I don't think *that* makes any difference to him. After all, Jeremy's father is only a life peer, which is not very impressive when you think of some of the others . . . like Hugh Thomas or Ted Willis. No; I don't think Marius went because of Jeremy's new blue blood: I think he went for the *esprit*.'

'Which is a polite way of saying,' said Jakki, 'that he got fed up with being surrounded by bloody women.'

'Mind your tongue, Missie,' said Maisie, the dutiful martinet. (My God, she thought, if some of my old clients could see me now, wouldn't they just laugh their balls off . . . and wouldn't their cocks go stiff as staves for Tessa, like I know Fielding's does, dirty pig.)

'That wasn't very kind,' said Tessa, 'to me and Rosie and Auntie Maisie.'

'Auntie Maisie, Rosie and me,' clacked Maisie.

'Even if life peerages aren't very impressive,' said Caroline, 'it's quite flattering to Marius that the son of Lord Morrison – '

' – Lord Luffham of Whereham is what he calls himself,' said Rosie.

' – That the son of Lord Luffham of Whereham should be prepared to spend half of Christmas Day driving from Luffham to London and back, just to fetch him. Marius, I mean.'

'Jeremy Morrison has always favoured Marius,' said Rosie Stern, rather primly.

'It started the other way round,' said Jakki: 'Marius had a hero worship thing about Jeremy. That's why he agreed to come to our school instead of Eton. Jeremy had been at our school, and his father before him, so Marius wanted to go there too.'

'He shouldn't have. Marius's father was at Eton,' said Maisie with peculiar tenderness, looking long on Tessa: 'Tessa would have gone to Eton and not your school, only Eton don't take girls.'

'That it does,' said Jakki.

'Not under a certain age, it doesn't. But at your school they've started taking 'em from thirteen, which is why you and Tessa go there –'

' – And why Caroline and I will be coming next autumn,' announced Rosie. 'I long for it. It's very lonely here when Tessa's away.'

'She's only a weekly boarder, ducks. You have her for weekends.'

'I'm somehow not sure,' said Rosie, in a measured tone, 'that I have her properly, even at weekends.'

An ample silence fell over the table.

'Don't be ungrateful,' huffed Maisie, trying to draw a red herring. 'You know you *asked* to stay here at Buttock's for as long as your mother went on living in France.'

'I do know that, Mrs Malcolm, and I love being here with you, and I'm very comfortable, and I'm not ungrateful at all,' said Rosie, rising and going to kiss Maisie's cherubic mandibles. 'All I'm saying, is that I miss Tessa

31

when she's away during the week, and I don't think that quite all of her comes back for the weekend when she does. Which is a disappointing thing to happen when you love somebody and have been looking forward – oh, for such a long time, it seems – to being with her again.'

'Milo Hedley,' said Jakki darkly.

'Who's Milo Hedley?' her sister asked.

'Nobody,' said Tessa, who had gone very shiny in the face. 'Nobody at all,' she said, her husky little voice crackling with insistence: 'just a friend of Marius's. He's in the school fencing team, and Marius wants to learn the sabre, so once I went to watch them.'

'*Beau Sabreur,*' said Rosie sadly, as she slipped back into her place between Jakki and Caroline.

'Darling Rosie,' said Tessa: 'it's only that after five days at school, it takes time to get used to everything here again, more than just the weekend.' She leaned across Caroline, lifted Rosie's black wavy hair with both her hands, and kissed her on her left ear. 'That's why I may have seemed different.'

'I doubt it,' said Rosie. 'You've had plenty of time to get used to me again during these holidays, yet you're still different, some of you is still not here.'

'All of me will be soon. I promise.'

'And by then,' said Rosie, 'Marius and I will have to go to France to pay our visit to Mummy. It'll be too late.'

'Well, I'm a weekly boarder like Tessa,' said Jakki, seeking in her turn to draw a red herring, 'and all I can say is that I hate coming home at weekends.'

'Jakki, how horrid of you,' said Caroline.

'Marius says,' persisted Jakki, who knew that her sister was only being ironical but that Rosie was bitterly wounded and must at any cost be distracted from further discussion of Tessa's seeming failure in love, 'Marius says

32

that all the most exciting things happen at weekends, all the intrigue and the infighting and the assignations –'

' – Fine goings on,' said Maisie. 'I'm glad my Tessa comes home when she does. I won't have her mixed up in that sort of a circus. But I dare say it's all fancy. With respect to you, Missie,' she said to Rosie, 'that handsome brother of yours always was a champion liar. So we'll have no more of this silly chatter, you girls, and we'll all take a good stump round Hyde Park. Nothing like fresh air to blow away *notions*.'

'Bugger,' said Marius, as his golf ball hopped twenty paces and into waist-high marsh reed. He banged the heel of his driver on the bank of the tee.

'Careful,' said Jeremy Morrison; 'with the ground as hard as this, you'll break it.'

Marius broke it. He looked down on the severed head of the club, then reached down for it and chucked it into the reeds.

'I can do very well without a fucking driver,' he said, and propelled the shaft after the head in the manner of a javelin.

'Pity to do that to a hickory club,' said Jeremy; 'there aren't so many left.'

'Aren't there? Steel shafts are miles better anyway.'

'I dare say. But that driver was my mother's. It was her set I lent you.'

'Oh. I'm sorry, Jeremy. Would you like me to fetch the bits back?'

'No. There's no one left nowadays who could mend it.'

'What a shame. I *am* sorry I lost my temper, Jeremy. It ought to be easy to hit a stationary ball and I get furious when I can't.'

'So do I. Perhaps we should stick to cricket. My turn to try.'

Jeremy's drive ballooned away to the right and landed in a stream.

'I think,' Jeremy said, 'that this hole is ill-starred for both of us. Let's go to the next tee and make a fresh start.'

'Why don't we just stop?'

'We've driven all the way over from Luffham,' Jeremy said. 'We must persist.'

'We've persisted for eight holes. I've lost four balls and you've lost three. Don't tell me you're enjoying it any more than I am.'

'I can't think what made me suggest it. A vague notion that you were good at ball games, I suppose. Bloody nuisance they cancelled the Boxing Day meeting at Huntingdon. Lover Pie was running.'

'That horse we backed at Newmarket? In some very long flat race, I remember.'

'That was over two years ago. Lover Pie don't run on the flat any more. But he'll keep on over fences for ever. That's Fielding Gray's house – over there to the right.'

'Oh. Yes. Of course he sometimes lives here in Broughton Staithe, doesn't he? It must be very lonely, out here at the end of the golf course.'

'He doesn't mind that when he's working. He goes walking in the sand dunes. The first time that I came here, he took me for a walk in the sand dunes.'

'What a common little house,' Marius said.

'It belonged to Major Gray's parents,' said Jeremy, in

a voice which implied that that was all that needed saying.

'Did you know them?'

'Certainly not. I'm not yet a hundred and ten, you know. But my father did. He rather liked Fielding's mother. We'll leave our clubs in their garden,' Jeremy continued, 'what's left of our clubs, that is, and I'll show you where Fielding took me.'

He led Marius over some frosty rough to a gate in a wire fence. Beyond the fence was a garden of weeds and marine grasses, up the centre of which a narrow path conducted them to the foot of the steps that led up to the wooden veranda of Fielding's common little house.

'Under the steps,' said Jeremy.

They deposited their clubs.

'You'll be seeing Major Gray before you leave for France with Rosie?' said Jeremy.

'No. Mrs Malcolm won't have him in the house when Tessa's there. She thinks they fancy each other.'

'Dear God . . . I want a message delivered to Fielding.' They went out through the gate at the bottom of the garden. 'I want you,' said Jeremy, 'to find ways and means of delivering it.'

'Why me?'

'Because I think you will make a very suitable messenger.'

They struck across a fairway, then up a slope of rough grass towards the dunes. Beyond the dunes was the low sound of the Wash as it beat sullenly at the distant mud.

'We know each other well,' said Jeremy. 'I come to you at school and you come to me at Luffham. When you were discontented at Buttock's on Christmas Eve, you applied to me to rescue you, because you understood me well enough to know that your request would not be refused by me. I repeat: you understand me; so if I give you a message for Fielding Gray, you will understand exactly what is meant by it, and you will therefore deliver it in a manner to convince him.'

'I shan't be seeing him. Mrs Malcolm won't let him come near Buttock's until Tessa and I have gone back to school.'

'Telephone him. Arrange a meeting before you go to France.'

'If you will tell me the message,' said Marius, 'I shall see what is to be done.'

Green eyes, fair hair, down on cheek and upper lip, slightly overgrown for his age, loose but not shambling: delectable and most surely desirable, but not, thought Jeremy, for me; never, thank God, for me. As they came towards the first of the rotting brick and concrete ammunition bays left over from the war, Jeremy began to explain:

There were a lot of things, he said, that Marius had to understand before he would be able to grasp the nature of Jeremy's message for Fielding well enough to have any hope of delivering it correctly and tactfully. What Jeremy was now about to tell Marius was an essential preliminary to his being entrusted with the message.

'If I consent to be,' Marius said.

To begin with, Marius should know that Jeremy had decided to stay up at Lancaster College, Cambridge, for a fourth year, beginning last October. This was largely in order to have a firm base from which to insinuate himself into the world of polite letters and reputable allies (literary dons) who would assist him with introductions. Sir Thomas Llewyllyn, Provost of Lancaster, though not the man he was, might be very useful on that front, to say nothing of Ivan ('the Greco') Barraclough, the Hellenist; Sir Jacquiz Helmutt, the Archaeologist and Essayist; and other 'odds and sods', in which category Jeremy included

Fielding Gray. Fielding was not a Lancastrian, or indeed a Cambridge man at all, but he made frequent visits to his friends in the College, and somehow the atmosphere and ambiance brought out the best elements in him – by which Jeremy meant, as he candidly admitted, those elements which best prompted him to urgent effort in the interest of Jeremy Morrison. Jeremy at Lancaster was the kind of privileged and graceful fantasy-Edwardian ephebe whom Fielding delighted to assist. Jeremy removed to London, say, or to Paris, would have had far less appeal: no doubt Fielding would still have done something for him (if only for the sake of his *beaux yeux*, so to speak) but far less than if he (Jeremy) were still loitering in a kind of perpetual Lancastrian autumn on the willowed banks of Father Cam.

For this kind of reason, then, Jeremy had returned from Luffham to Lancaster last October. After shameless wheedling of the Provost and his Private Secretary, Len, this backed by the promise of a colossal contribution to the fund for replacing the deceased College elms (Marius should remember that Jeremy was now very rich), he had been allowed back in his old rooms by the river; and here he sat doing a course of dainty reading and giving frequent dainty entertainments, waiting for Fielding's and Sir Tom's literary acquaintance to gather him into their fold and arrange his agreeable employment.

'What,' enquired Marius at this stage, 'did you hope to write? Novels? Poetry? Plays?'

'Anything,' said Jeremy, 'which would bring my name before the public.'

'Weren't you perhaps . . . putting the cart before the horse?'

'Don't be a little prig.'

'Let me remind you,' said Marius, 'that it is *you* who

37

are asking a favour of *me*, and that I must therefore be allowed the right of comment.'

'If I erred, I was certainly punished, as you shall now hear . . .'

The Literary Editor of *Sackcloth,* the first to whom Jeremy was introduced by Fielding, took him to a cinema near Victoria Station and started caressing his *privata*. Jeremy, aware that occasional concessions had to be made by literary or theatrical aspirants, permitted the hideous old gentleman's endeavour and indeed achieved a creditable (in all the circumstances) erection . . .

'By thinking of somebody else, I expect. Who?'

'Never you mind.'

'Me?'

'Absolutely not. One of the under-matrons at Oudenarde, if you must know, who used to play with me in my bath when I was a little boy.'

'Very erotic.'

'Very . . .'

But even so Jeremy could not manage ejaculation into the horny old hands, and after a while the Literary Editor excused himself ('for a pee') and reappeared neither in the cinema nor in Jeremy's career.

A publisher recommended by the Provost was prepared to 'commission' an account of a bicycle journey from Alexandria to the Cape. 'Splendid opportunity for a fit young man. Get you away from that frowsty College of yours.' But the 'commission' apparently carried no advance, not even the price of a second-hand bicycle, and on learning from *Private Eye* that the firm offering it was already three months late in payment of the last half-year's royalties, Jeremy withdrew.

'Why,' said Marius, 'didn't you try my father's old firm? Stern & Detterling? Fielding Gray has a lot of pull there.'

'Stern & Detterling,' said Jeremy, 'turned out to have amalgamated with a firm of printers called Salinger & Holbrook. Canteloupe arranged it after your father Gregory died. Now, the two chief shareholders of Salinger & Holbrook were the Salinger twins, Carmilla and Theodosia.'

'I know. Grand girls.'

'Grand girls . . . who wouldn't be at all gratified to see my name on the list of publications.'

'Oh come, Jeremy. Whatever you did to either of 'em, they're too big to bear a grudge.'

'It's I that bear the grudge. They've helped me so often – and been cheated for their efforts. Oh, I don't actually *owe* them any more, but I would have done, and been quite happy to welsh on them altogether, had it not been for my father's sudden decision to pass a lot of land and money over to me. I've cheated them in other ways too . . . emotionally. So they make me feel ashamed, Marius, and I bear them a grude for it, and work for them or for their firm I shall not, now nor ever.'

'Beggars can't be choosers. Only, of course, you're not exactly a beggar.'

They walked down the beach, across firm, wet sand towards the distant sea, but paused when the sand turned into grey, smelly mud.

'I was prepared to beg for work, but not from them.'

Jeremy's third introduction, and the second arranged by Fielding Gray, was to the Arts Editor of *The Connaught Muse* (published from a house in Connaught Mews, ha, ha). He was a spare and sibilant Scot who took him to lunch at a restaurant called The Meat and Two Veg Ad Lib, and chomped like a bulldozer through huge quantities of all three.

'My wife,' he said, 'used to be a brilliant cook. People

39

like Fielding Gray begged me to ask them to dinner. Then she got socialism – the extreme kind, I mean. She had always been pretty left wing, like me, but now she went crazy with it. First of all her meals were reduced to peasant dishes full of beans, bones and potatoes: then there was only rice and seaweed: then there was nothing. She was too busy shaking her fist in Downing Street or outside American air bases, even to put maize into the pot. So do you wonder I like a bit of a blow-out here? The old mag has an arrangement with the place at a twenty per cent discount: otherwise we shouldn't be able to afford even this.'

'All very trying, I do see,' Jeremy had said. And then, a few minutes later, after his host had demolished a mountain of mash, 'Fielding Gray was saying that you might need an occasional article . . .'

'It's broke we are, as ever,' the Arts Editor had countered; 'but of course if Fielding recommends you, I'd like to give you a trial. Five pieces without payment, and if we like 'em we'll start you off at the minimum rate for the sixth.'

'The minimum rate?'

'Forty pence a hundred words.'

'Oh.'

When the first book had arrived from *The Connaught Muse* (a closely printed Goliath on the Portuguese Epic), Jeremy had sent it back with a polite plea of indisposition, and this, thank God, had been the end of that connection.

'You could have given it a chance,' Marius said now, as they turned left along the line which divided sand from mud. 'After all, you didn't need a fee and you did have a chance to get published.'

'Magazines that don't make an effort to pay properly – with the partial exception of school and university magazines – are not to be taken seriously. No good being published in a journal that no one takes seriously.'

'So by now,' said Marius, 'you were pretty fed up with the world of letters? You felt you were not appreciated at your true worth?'

'Yes,' said Jeremy, who failed to detect any irony in Marius's remark. 'I thought perhaps the so-called media – television and that kind of thing – might suit me better. So Fielding arranged for me to meet a man called Jacobson, a director he'd once worked with who was now in a firm which specialized in up-market TV serials. He wore short silk socks,' said Jeremy, 'which hardly even covered his skinny ankles.'

'So of course that put you right off him straight away.'

'No. I gave him the benefit of the doubt because he was Jewish and Jews have their heads screwed on where the entertainment world is concerned.'

'Thank you for your graceful compliment to my people.'

'You,' said Jeremy, 'are about as Jewish as golden tressed Apollo.'

Very lightly, he pressed Marius's blond hair with the palm of one hand.

'My father was a Jew,' Marius said.

'Precisely. To be a proper Jew, you must have a Jewish mother.'

'I may not be a proper Jew,' said Marius, swivelling his green eyes out over the sea and back, 'but I have my father's Hebrew blood. And this Mr Jacobson – how did he turn out?'

'A mocker. He told me that he'd started work at the age of thirteen as a clapper-boy to his uncle, who made dirty films in his garden in Epping. He had no time for la-di-da young men, he said, unless they were prepared to forget their university education and come and do like-wise. I said that I could hardly make thirteen any more but I'd happily be clapper-boy to sex films in Epping . . . under his direction, I presumed? Like all mockers, he was extremely self-important and would not take his own turn at being mocked. The idea that he, the great Jules Jacobson who directed the *Odyssey* and the *Idylls of the King*, should go back to directing porn shows, was too much for him. No sense of humour or proportion, you see. So I was sharply shown the door.'

'And which was the next one you knocked on?'

'I didn't. I was finally through with all that. I didn't, you see, have to suit anyone except myself. I certainly didn't have to suit Tom Llewyllyn and Fielding Gray any more.'

Jeremy turned briskly away from the Wash and walked up the beach towards the remains of a semaphore tower that was perched on an unusually high dune.

'Isn't that rather unfair to them?' said Marius, bringing up the rear. 'They arranged those interviews at your request. You mucked them up because you wouldn't give the people a fair chance – '

' – A fair chance, I ask you. Who sat in that cinema having his cock rubbed raw?'

'Well, you didn't give any of the others much of a chance. Anyhow, what I mean is that just because they all came to nothing, those interviews, that's no reason for turning on the Provost and Major Gray. They did their best for you – and you say you're done with them.'

'I associate them . . . particularly Fielding . . . with failure.'

'So what are you going to do now?' Marius said.

'Withdraw from Lancaster and begin a new and serious endeavour. To do with the land, my land, at Luffham. A proper task, a proper purpose, for any man of intelligence and vision. And now we come to the message that I want you to pass on to Fielding. For some time he has been pressing me to go on another of our journeys. The Provost has said I can have leave of absence – not that *he* matters now I've withdrawn – and Fielding wants me to go with him to Italy, Greece and Turkey.'

'How very nice. Do you remember, you and Fielding once promised to take me on one of those trips? I'm still hoping.'

'There aren't going to be any more. That's my message for Fielding. From now on that sort of thing's over . . . for a long time at least, and as far as Fielding is concerned, for ever. Please tell him.'

'No. I shan't have a chance. He won't be there, as I told you, when I get back to Buttock's, and immediately after that Rosie and I are going to Mummy in France. And after *that* I shall be back at school.'

'You promised you'd find a way.'

'I said that if you told me your message to Fielding, I would see what was to be done. About such a horrible message nothing is to be done. Or not by me. You do your own dirty work.'

'You must understand that I have come to a crucial stage in my life. Firm decision is now necessary; I must drift no longer, Marius. So a firm decision I have now made – to set a new and definite course that will take me ever further from Fielding Gray.'

'You are leaving him. He has come to need you – you have encouraged him to come to need you – and now you are deliberately going away from him. Why should I be the one to tell him this?'

'Because you would do it so charmingly.'

'Ugh. How can anyone trust you, Jeremy? How can I

43

be sure that you will not go away from me?'

'Come to that, I don't suppose you can be.'

'Oh, Jeremy.'

They passed the semaphore tower, at the top of which the stumps of the maimed arms signalled a sloppy 'N', and started down the reverse slope of the dunes back towards the golf course.

'At least I never encouraged *you* to need me, Marius,' said Jeremy. 'You made all the running, remember?'

'Yes. I was desperate. But after that, I thought you had come to like me.'

'Well enough. I hope that I shan't leave *you*.'

'Then why are you leaving Major Gray?'

'Because I have now had my fill of everything he has to offer. His knowledge, insight, philosophy, talent, experience and technique – all of them, such as they ever were, are for me stale and nearly exhausted. Nor do I need his money – of which I suspect there is now much less – since I have many times as much of my own.'

'You could still be kind to him,' Marius said, as they marched over the fairway towards Fielding's house. 'You could remember what he has done for you and show your gratitude by being with him, even travelling with him, from time to time.'

They collected their clubs from under Fielding's veranda and went back down the jungly path to the end of his garden.

'Fielding Gray takes up too much room in my life,' said Jeremy. 'You will come across the same thing pretty soon in your own. Someone you have loved suddenly becomes a boring, importunate nuisance.' Jeremy shut Fielding's gate behind them. 'This person may be the same as ever he was but he will now be distasteful to you nevertheless. He asks no more than he ever did, but this will now be too much for you. For you yourself will have changed, Marius, as I have changed, and what you once held precious will suddenly have been changed to lumber of which you wish only to be quit, so that you can go on unburdened towards your new goal.'

'What you are leaving behind is not lumber,' Marius said: 'it is somebody who has a right to expect your care. You are indecent, Jeremy.'

'You will find, Marius, that when the struggle is between decency and convenience, convenience has a way of winning, and that is the way of it here. Quite simply, Fielding Gray has become *inconvenient* to me, an embarrassing feature of a life which I now forswear.'

'Oh, Jeremy, Jeremy,' said Marius as they climbed into Jeremy's car (no longer the little Morris that had been his mother's gift but a quivering Alfa Romeo): 'Oh, Jeremy,' Marius said, and was silent all the way back to Luffham by Whereham.

'Jeremy Morrison has withdrawn from the College,' said Len, the Private Secretary to the Provost of Lancaster: 'his letter arrived this morning, so it must have been posted just before Christmas Day.'

'Good riddance as far as you are concerned,' said Ptolemaeos Tunne, one of the Provost's guests for the Twelve Days.

The other guest, Piero Caspar, an undergraduate of Lancaster and a ward (in a complicated way) of Ptolemaeos, considered this remark in silence, then turned to

45

Carmilla Salinger (a Fellow of the College, who was spending her Christmas there) as if to invite the comment of someone better qualified than himself.

'Jeremy is such a horrible cheat,' said Carmilla, cocking her enormous arse in order to scratch the seat of her corduroy trousers. 'He made both Theodosia and me love him, though in very different ways, then just turned and vanished into thin air . . . only to emerge from it as solid as ever when there was something he really wanted. Usually money.'

'Did you let him have it?' said Len, knowing the answer.

'Yes. On one occasion we both gave him money to pay the same debt . . . without knowing it, of course. He juggled his affairs very cleverly.'

'He's settled up with you now, I dare say?'

'Oh yes. Now his father's handed over half Norfolk at three grand an acre . . . to say nothing of the house and some liquid money . . . he has seen his way to settling up with us.'

Sir Thomas Llewyllyn rose from his chair and shuffled across the chamber to a glass door which led into the Provost's walled garden. How old he looks, thought Carmilla: he can't be sixty yet, but he's creeping about on a stick, with his head awry like a weeping chancel. What has done this to him? Death, she thought: too much death; and now the desertion of Jeremy Morrison.

'Tullia never liked that Morrison boy,' the Provost said, looking out over the garden.

'Tullia' had been his daughter, commonly known as 'Baby', formerly married to Lord Canteloupe.

'You all remember the day we christened Tullia's son, Sarum,' said the Provost, turning back to face into the chamber. 'It was in the spring of the year in which the elms died. But they were not yet dead when we christened Sarum, christened him in the Chapel and then came in here, into this room, to drink his health. You were all here, except you, Piero' – he pointed his stick at Caspar – 'it was before you exhumed yourself from that convent of yours. But apart from Piero, you were all here,' he said, 'and a great many more people, and young Jeremy Morrison among them.'

'Yes,' said Carmilla. 'I remember. He made up to Thea and me in front of our Da. A very smooth performance.'

'And he tried another smooth performance,' said Tom Llewyllyn, 'on Tullia. She set his nose quivering, I could tell. But I didn't mind, because I saw the way she sent him about his business. Like throwing a bucket of cold water on a randy mongrel. I was pleased with her and almost sorry for him. I had a soft spot for him, you see. It was after Tullia snubbed him that he came and made up to Carmilla and her sister.'

'As you observe, Provost, I was not here,' said Piero; 'but it is clear, in general, that something about Jeremy affected your daughter with nothing less than sheer revulsion . . . in the end with extreme and hysterical revulsion.'

'Which sent her bolting off to Africa,' said Ptolemaeos.

'Surely . . . it was what happened in Burano that did that,' said Carmilla. 'Gregory Stern's crucifixion, and that weird picture underneath the cross.'

'The picture,' said Piero, 'was that of a woman who is about to alleviate suffering by loving attention. To be more precise, a woman who is about to give sexual consolation to boys who are already far gone with the plague. Like Gregory Stern's death on the cross, it taught her that the way to salvation must be by compelling herself to love that which repelled her.'

47

'You say Jeremy Morrison repelled her,' said Len; 'she didn't start loving him.'

'No. But she forgave him, and then went out to Africa in order to bring love, to give pleasure, to beings infinitely more repulsive than Jeremy could ever have been. All sorts and conditions of men, black and white, who were dying . . . of leprosy, yaws, bilharzia, elephantiasis . . . of anything, no matter how horrible . . . these she loved and comforted. And she did so, we are clearly told by a missionary who knew and admired her, by giving whatever sexual pleasure she could to anyone who was still capable of response. It was, she said, her only gift.'

'Thank you, Piero . . . for being so accurate about my daughter,' said Tom, turning back towards the garden. 'It was, I suppose, high time I learnt the exact truth. How did she die? Of a rare tropical disease, they told me. Presumably contracted in the course of her charitable works.'

'No,' said Ptolemaeos. 'Canteloupe told me that was a cover-up. She was murdered on the order of a powerful African official who was jealous of her exclusive preference for the diseased.'

'And so now my sister is wife and Marchioness to Canteloupe,' said Carmilla, 'and has care of Baby's son.'

'How's all *that* going on?' said Len, in case there were some hot item which he hadn't yet heard.

'Thea seems very contented,' said her sister lightly. (Too lightly, thought Len.) 'She always had a sort of uncle-worship thing about Canteloupe.'

'And the baby?' said Len. 'Tullius?'

Carmilla turned her head and pretended not to hear.

'Sarum of Old Sarum?' persisted Len. 'Canteloupe's heir?'

'Not right,' said Carmilla.

'In what respect wrong?' said Ptolemaeos Tunne.

'Mentally. Extent of damage as yet uncertain, but abnormality, of some kind, definite.'

'Not a good thing,' said Len, 'that an important peerage should pass to someone who is . . . mentally deficient.'

How can they all be so unkind? thought Tom. How can they talk about Tullia's son like this, in front of me, in my own Lodging? But I suppose they know I can no longer defend myself, have been unable to stand up like a man for these two years now, ever since the elms in the Avenue died.

'What does it matter,' he now said aloud, 'what does it matter who inherits this peerage?' His bitterness and grief that his grandson, all he had left of Tullia, should be spoiled, sent him to seek release in despair and destruction. 'At least two of us in this room know that the whole thing is a fraud. The real heir belongs to a line got out of a peasant girl, a raped peasant girl just old enough to be fertile, one hundred and eighty odd years ago, in a marsh village near Oriago. Samuele, the village is called. I was there when we proved it, proved it from the Church Register. So was Piero.'

'Yes,' said Piero, 'you and I and Fielding. A long time ago. Before I went to my convent.'

'And who else,' said Len, 'got to hear about this?'

'Canteloupe and his secretary, Leonard Percival,' said Piero.

'Both safe, one would have thought.'

'My old master, Lykiadopoulos, and his partner, Max de Freville.'

'Both dead, beyond dispute.'

'Baby Canteloupe.'

'Also dead.'

'She may well have told her friend, Jo-Jo Guiscard,

49

who keeps very little from her husband, Jean-Marie, or her lover, Mrs Isobel Stern.'

'My niece, Jo-Jo, and her *ménage*, now live very remotely,' said Ptolemaeos Tunne, 'but these days easy communications corrupt good security. And even though several privy to the secret are now dead, it does leave a disquieting number who are quick.'

'What you have to remember, Ptolemaeos,' said Tom Llewyllyn, who was now rather calmer, 'is this: although the thing was proved to my satisfaction, and Fielding's and Piero's, the actual process of proving it in law would be tantamount, these days, to impossible. The expenses would be cosmic, and there are certain necessary documents – quite apart from the Church Register at Samuele – which are extremely difficult to interpret and may in any case by now be unobtainable.'

'But if we take the proof for granted,' said Ptolemaeos, 'who is this rightful heir now dwelling in Samuele?'

'He is an orphan from the floods of sixty-six,' Piero said. 'He lives – or did live, in 1973 – with his spinster aunt, apparently his only relation. In return for a small sum of money, she consented to introduce us.

'I can still see it,' he said, 'there he is in his aunt's garden, digging; a handsome little boy of about ten, strong and broad-shouldered for his age, wearing shorts which show classically formed bare legs. Paolo Filavoni, legitimate heir to Rollesden-in-Silvis in the direct line, and so now the rightful Marquess Canteloupe. Look at him, all of you. He stops digging. He sticks his spade in the mud. He smiles at us all, pleasantly enough . . . and then down with his shorts, skipping and cackling for glee, he waves his already quite sizeable penis at his audience. "*Paolo*," shouts his aunt, as well she may, and rushes into the vegetable patch to put a stop to these goings on . . . whereupon, believe it or not, he flexes his knees, points his piece, and pisses up most powerfully into her flustered face.'

'Hmm,' said Ptolemaeos, after a short silence. 'And that was the scene in 1973?'

'It was,' said Piero, and turned for confirmation to Tom, who nodded.

'And this engaging imbecile is now a ripe seventeen or more,' said Ptolemaeos. 'Are there any brothers or male cousins? Or uncles, perhaps?'

'I think not,' said Tom: 'though of course we were not at leisure to spend as long as we might have wished with the Register.'

'Why not?'

'A crooked Englishman who lives in the place was hanging about and sniffing. Name of Holbrook. A chum of your Dad's,' said Tom to Carmilla, 'the original Holbrook of Salinger & Holbrook.'

'But he disappeared many years ago, Da told us.'

'Yes. To Samuele in the marshes, where he took refuge from his iniquities with his ageing mother. Not the sort of chap we wanted to let in on this affair,' said Tom, 'so we tried to keep him from knowing what we were up to.'

'Luckily, he had some kind of an attack,' said Piero, 'and lost interest. Though it may have revived after we had gone . . .'

'But such a fascinating field for investigation,' Ptolemaeos said. 'From an academic, a genealogical, an historical or humanist point of view – from any point of view you like, except of course with any practical intention of upsetting poor old Canteloupe. That would never do, and in any case, as Tom says, could probably never be done. But as a story to be studied and cherished it has everything. The events leading up to the rape; all those generations between the rape and the discovery of Paolo

51

of the penis; even that wretched Englishman, Holbrook, lurking in the village. Fascination. An interest for my old age.'

'I dare say,' said Carmilla. 'But if you do anything, anything at all to upset Canteloupe – '

' – I've just said I shouldn't dream of it – '

' – If you do anything, even by accident or inadvertence, to upset Canteloupe, Theodosia and I will come to your lair in your Fenland kingdom, cut off your balls and throw them to those two old witches you employ in your kitchen.'

'Darling Carmilla,' said Ptolemaeos; and to Piero: 'where do we begin?'

'Good-bye, Jeremy,' said Marius.

'Good-bye, old thing. Don't worry about this business of Fielding Gray. I'll handle it myself.'

'I've no doubt you will.'

Jeremy's Alfa Romeo was parked just off the Cromwell Road, more or less licitly provided he didn't linger more than thirty seconds, a stone's throw from Buttock's Hotel. Marius got out, bent his seat forward and hoicked his suitcase (rather a large and elaborate one, thought Jeremy, for a boy not yet fifteen) out of the back.

'I'll miss you,' said Jeremy.

'Don't.'

'Don't what? Don't miss you?'

'You know I always want to cry when you say that. So don't.'

'All right. How soon is your plane?'

'Five o'clock. Rosie and I will have to go straight to the airport.'

'Then I'll run you there.'

'No. You'd have to come in and see Mrs Malcolm first. Neither of you would care for that.'

'Nor we would. How thoughtful of you. You'd better run along then. Go well to Navarre, Marius – or is it Béarn?'

'I'm not sure. It might even be Gascony.'

'Navarre sounds the grandest of the three. Henry of Navarre, and all that. So go well to Navarre, Marius, and go with God.'

'Did Fielding Gray teach you that?'

'No. My father. He had it from some Indian he knew.'

'Go well to Luffham, Jeremy; and go with God.'

At the same time as Marius and Jeremy were exchanging this ancient courtesy, Piero and Len were walking down the Avenue of Lancaster College.

'I still can't get used to it without the elms,' said Len.

'They were removed very shortly after I came, so it's not the same for me. I wish it were, in a way.'

'Look,' said Len, warmed by this remark, 'you like the place, and the place likes you. You did brilliantly in your Tripos last summer. You are expected to do brilliantly again next. We want you here. Stay.'

'I might *not* do so brilliantly next summer.'

'We shall still want you. Lancaster has never made too

big a thing of exam results. Even if you did pee your pants a bit, the College would still fix you up with a Research Studentship. As Tom's Secretary, I'd see to that.'

They crossed the Queen's Road and went into the Fellows' Garden.

'I know you would,' said Piero. 'You are one of the least moral people I have ever met but you keep absolutely to your spoken word. You could fix it, and you would.'

'And then a Fellowship. Unfortunately they don't give 'em out for life any more, but we could manage quite ample tenure.'

'From the gutters of Syracuse to the High Table of Lancaster College. A very happy issue, I must say. Unfortunately I must also say "no".'

'Why?'

As always when crossed, Len began to walk faster.

'Wait for me, Len. My foot – '

' – Sorry. Forgot. Why are you saying "no"?'

'I have given my word that when my third and last year as an undergraduate is over next June, I shall go back, as full time secretary and companion, to Ptolemaeos Tunne.'

'God, how dreary. Doing things like investigating Canteloupe's marquessate.'

'I think,' said Piero, as he limped over the croquet lawn, 'that the matter of Canteloupe's marquessate is rather intriguing. I was in on the ground floor, remember – and I have no reason at all to suppose that this particular *histoire* is finished yet. But even if I were bored stiff by it, my dear Len, the fact remains that I have given my word to Ptolemaeos. He found me a new and much needed identity and sent me here to Lancaster. "Nay, more and more of all,"' quoted Piero, 'it was he, a stranger, who took me in when I arrived, a ratty, runty, lame little friar in his filthy habit.'

'We took you in too.'

'Only after Ptolemaeos had – and at his persuasion.'

'You must not sacrifice a splendid future to that fat old fucker in the Fens.'

'Mustn't I? Were it not dark, Len, I should be able to point to the Judas Tree. It grows near here, I think.'

'You are not made to spend your life looking after old men.'

'Perhaps that's exactly what I am made for. It seems I have a taste for it. I served, remember, a very long apprenticeship. At least I shall now be a secretary and no longer a whore. Not that Lykiadopoulos ever touched me, but I was still his whore . . .'

'Expand.'

'That is another story for another day. For to-day, Len, you have my best thanks for a most civil offer, which I must refuse for reasons which you understand as well as any man living.'

'Your whole life wasted – on a point of honour.'

'You yourself, as I have just remarked, always keep to your word. So must I, in this matter at least. Besides, it will not be my whole life. Ptolemaeos Tunne will not live for ever, and he will leave me a lot of money.'

'In pig's arse. How much did Lykiadopoulos leave you?'

'He gave much money, at my request, to the Good Brothers of San Francesco del Deserto, so that I might retire among them.'

'That'll be about all you're fit to do when you've finished running errands for Ptolemaeos Tunne.'

'Please, Len, my friend,' said Piero, 'do not be so ill-tempered. I shall stay here with you until June, and then go back to my patron in the Fens. But the Fens are not far from here, if we should want each other's company and love, and I do not think that Ptolemaeos will ever again move from the Fens for long.'

Fielding Gray and Leonard Percival walked by a river which formed the southern border of Canteloupe's demesne.

'Still no word from Jeremy Morrison,' said Fielding. 'If he were serious about this expedition of ours, he'd have been in touch by now.'

'You were going to Italy?'

'*En route* for Greece and Turkey.'

'Through the Veneto and Yugoslavia?'

'Perhaps. It was one of the things,' said Fielding, 'that we were to discuss.'

'I was going to ask a favour of you, if you went that way. I was going to ask you,' said Leonard Percival, 'to go to Samuele by the Laguna Veneta . . . and inspect Paolo Filavoni.'

'You seem to have that child on the brain.'

'A child no longer.'

'He was a simpleton, Leonard. Well made, physically, but otherwise – merely the village idiot.'

'Might he not be of more . . . import . . . now that he's grown up?'

'Why should he be?'

'I never saw him myself,' said Leonard. 'But from all accounts he was not only well made, as you have just observed, but very handsome. Now, idiots who are habitually engaged in simple manual tasks – which must surely be his lot – grow up to be of prodigious size and strength. If one adds to this that he is also handsome and well proportioned, one might find something – somebody, I suppose I should say – really rather remarkable.'

'But what . . . so to speak . . . would one *do* with him?'

'Ah, that I can't say. All I know is that the whole story haunts me, and that I should like to hear some account of the anti-marquess – '

' – Of the *real* marquess – '

' – Of Paolo Filavoni, now he is a man. Indeed, I should very much like to see him for myself, only to make a special journey for the purpose would seem somehow disloyal to Detterling. I *was* in the area about two years ago, but there were too many preoccupations for a visit to Paolo.'

Fielding gave a short laugh out of his pinched little mouth and directed his round red eye straight between Percival's.

'What is this yearning,' he said, 'to see a mindless hulk?'

'A sight of him would make the story live for me. As I say, I am fascinated by it, but I shall not feel it is quite real until I have actually seen Paolo.'

'Did you ever read that novel, which I based on the business?'

'I did, and much enjoyed it,' said Leonard quite sincerely. 'But I need flesh and blood, for once in a way, not shadows.'

'Shadows they may have been, but very profitable. I haven't made money like I made from that book for a good many years now. Shadows, yes, but they had their own vitality. There's been nothing like them since. That's my trouble, Leonard. I've lost my vitality. My work is stale. Now Gregory Stern is dead, there's no one in the firm to write for.'

'Surely Detterling takes an interest?'

'Not any more. He used to, very much so, but now he's so obsessed with his estate and its transmission that the whole thing is left to the Managing Director. Ashley Dexterside. When Gregory died and Canteloupe fixed up this amalgamation with Salinger & Holbrook, Ashley came with S. & H. as a production man, a bloody good one too. But somehow . . . everything else has got pushed on to him, so that he's now in charge of the literary side as well. *He doesn't understand writing*, Leonard: it's no pleasure to work for him. The only man there now who does partly understand what I'm trying to do is Ivan Blessington, who also came with Salinger & Holbrook. Ivan may be the girls' nominee but he has nothing to do with editing.'

'I wonder those Salinger twins don't take an interest. Carmilla and her ladyship.'

'If only they would,' said Fielding. 'The trouble is, they were brought up simply as *shareholders* of Salinger & Holbrook, and firmly discouraged from having anything to do with it. Don't interfere, their father Donald would have said, when lucid. Don't you worry your pretty little heads, the Board would have told them when he wasn't – and after his death. So they didn't, on the whole, except to beg the occasional favour for a chum; and now it's become a habit of mind with them – "leave the firm alone, it's a boring old business at best' – even though the whole thing has changed and might now, since the addition of the publishing side, be of considerable interest to them.'

'Can't they see that for themselves?' Leonard said.

'Childhood habits die hard. All I know,' said Fielding, 'is that they don't take an interest, and neither does anyone else, not an *intelligent* one, and all I seem to be writing for Ashley Dexterside is absolute slop, and my royalty cheques for the last eighteen months have been merely *squalid*. So perhaps it'll be as well if Jeremy does back out of this trip. I can't really afford it anyhow.'

'But he can. Now his father's handed so much over.'

'But he wouldn't,' Fielding said.

'Why not? You've given him enough treats. Really generous ones.'

'He wouldn't think it worth it. Leave aside the fact that he's extremely *mean* with money, except when spending it on himself, he just would not see any point in paying for somebody who no longer has anything new to teach him or amuse him with.'

'But . . . He could enjoy your company for its own familiar sake. At his age he can't expect something *new* the whole time. And he certainly doesn't need a travelling tutor any more.'

'With Jeremy, what is familiar is boring. He is too shallow to understand or enjoy the pleasures of recognition. I once proposed a visit to Holkham, which is not very far from Luffham – only to be told that he had no need to go there again, as he had been taken when still a child. You see what I mean?'

'Leaving all that aside,' said Leonard, 'there comes a question of reciprocity: he *owes* you.'

'He doesn't think like that. All those treats you say I gave him – that was in another world, he'd say. What counts is where we are now. I failed to do any good for him last autumn, when he was trying to get into the plush end of Grub Street, and so now I'm pretty certain he's going to give all that up and move on to the next thing – and whatever that is, it won't include me.'

For some time they had been walking through a wood

which grew on both banks of the river. Now they emerged into a meadow.

'There is a legend about this meadow,' said Fielding. 'Six knights in black armour murdered Geoffery the Troubadour here. He'd been singing too sweetly to their wives and daughters. His grave is in a churchyard near Salisbury. A . . . very old friend once took me there.'

Leonard considered this. His scimitar nose seemed suddenly to grow another inch out of his forehead, and its tip to curve downward and inward until it almost pierced his chin.

'Six to one is unfair odds, of course, but as we know, the wages of sin is, in one form or another, death. If you are short of money,' said Leonard, as a result of some crooked process of association, 'why not sell your half of Buttock's Hotel?'

'The only buyers would be the developers. They'd simply flatten the place, and so I am bound not to sell it to them as a condition of Tessie Buttock's will. That wouldn't stop me if I were desperate enough, as it is binding in honour only, but it would stop Maisie selling her half, without which mine is of no value.'

'Honour,' said Leonard Percival: 'an attractive word but what a nuisance it can be. Tell me: those documents you discovered in Venice in 1973 . . . the ones which led you to Samuele in the marshes and so to the discovery of the true reigning line of the Sarums, with Paolo at the end of it . . . Have you still got them?'

'I used them for my novel. Then I put them away in the bank.'

'How very prudent. And would your honour prevent you from disposing of them for cash?'

'You mean . . . Canteloupe might like to have them for safe keeping . . . in his bank rather than mine? I once thought of that before. Luckily, I was saved by the proverbial outsider at sixty-six to one. Money came in from elsewhere.'

'And now?'

'Blackmail is an ugly thing.'

'So is poverty. After all, if you were not extortionate . . .'

'I am not desperate yet, Leonard . . . though I will admit, I should very much like to be in a position to offer Jeremy this journey to Greece and Turkey as an entire and total gift. My gift. There would be something rather grand about that . . . to say nothing of how I yearn . . . yearn, Leonard . . . for his company as I used to know it.'

'From what you have just been saying, his company will obviously never be "as you used to know it" again. Now then. Six black knights against one troubadour, you said: in this very meadow. Wasn't he unarmed, this troubadour, and attended only by a page boy? Wasn't he playing and singing to the boy as they rode?'

'Yes. You've heard the story before. From Canteloupe, I suppose. The family has always revelled in it.'

'No. I did not hear it from Detterling. From somebody else. I shall remember presently.'

In the distance, a cathedral suddenly rose off a ridge like a cardboard cut-out from the centre pages of a Christmas Annual.

'Saint-Bertrand-de-Comminges,' said Marius to his sister.

'Ah,' said Rosie. 'It looks pleasant enough, doesn't it? But whenever we come here I always remember that M. R. James wrote the most horrible ghost story about it: *Canon Alberic's Scrapebook*.'

The taxi passed into a narrow lane with high-hedged banks. The cut-out collapsed into the annual.

'M. R. James had a diseased mind,' said Marius. 'Glinter Parkes at Oudenarde House told us, after reading us his story about the schoolboy who was drowned in a well and kept on crawling up out of it. It was one more good reason for not going to Eton, he told me later. Imagine being at a school where they would put up with M. R. James as Provost.'

'How very silly of Mr Parkes,' said Rosie. 'To start with, the Provost of Eton is *not* the Headmaster and stays almost entirely in the background, so that no one knows he is there; and in the second place it happened many years ago. No reason at all for not going to Eton now.'

'He also told me that M. R. James had read a story of his to the Eton Boy Scouts in camp one year, about a Boy Scout who had all his blood sucked out by a vampire. The Scout Master threw the body over his shoulder like a rag doll.'

'Still no reason for not going to Eton now.'

'Glinter was quite desperate that I shouldn't. Mummy had turned against Eton and was putting on the pressure, and he'd begun to be afraid that I wouldn't quite get into College, whereas I was almost certain to get a school, to *our* school, which would be one up to Oudenarde instead of one down, so in the end . . . what with all of them . . . and what with Jeremy . . . I gave in.'

'Why call it *our* school? I'm not there yet.'

'Tessa is, and Jakki. And you and Caroline are coming next autumn.'

'So Mummy had her way,' said Rosie. The cathedral, now definitely made of stone and not of cardboard, reappeared in the windscreen of the taxi.

'Ah,' said Rosie, assessing the quality of its appearance: 'We're nearly there.' Then, 'Why can't Mummy find a proper *man*,' she said crossly, 'instead of that tiresome girl, Jo-Jo?'

'I expect Daddy's death upset her.'

'She'd started carrying on with Jo-Jo *before* Daddy died,' Rosie said.

'Jo-Jo is a conceited bitch,' said Marius.

'I like her husband.'

'He lets her wear the trousers.'

'She didn't want little Oenone, you know. She wanted a boy. I think it's Mummy that mostly takes care of Oenone.'

The taxi stopped by the entrance to the graveyard of a Romanesque church, that stood in a meadow just under the southern ramparts of Saint-Bertrand. The nave and the transept were in ruins. The chancel still had a roof and some appearance of stability.

'I hope they've made the place more comfortable than it was in the summer,' said Marius: 'all that money Mummy's got – and she has to live in a deconsecrated chancel.'

Leonard Percival remembered how he had originally come to hear the story of the black knights and the troubadour. The story had been passed down in the

Sarum family, until some time in the 1940s it had been told by the previous Marquess Canteloupe (the present one's distant cousin) to his son, the Earl of Muscateer (a title which had become extinct when the marquessate passed, by an elaborate instance of female remainder, from the family of the Sarums to that of their cousins Detterling). Lord Muscateer, while an Officer Cadet in India in 1946, had told the legend to a crowd of fellow cadets gathered round his deathbed. One of the cadets, Peter Morrison (now Lord Luffham of Whereham) had told it to his son Jeremy; and Jeremy had told it to his friend, Piero Caspar, who had told it, along with its provenance as detailed above, to Leonard.

This had happened while Leonard was on a visit to Piero's guardian, Ptolemaeos Tunne, who wished to examine an irregular edition of Valerius Flaccus, which was in Detterling's library, and had been too lazy or debilitated to travel to Wiltshire to do so. Since Detterling had been too busy with lawyers (discretionary trusts for Sarum) to go to Ptoly's home in the Fens, he had despatched Leonard with the book; and one evening, while Ptolemaeos was poring over Valerius' tenth rate hexameters, Piero had told Leonard the story of the black knights and the unarmed troubadour, Lord Geoffery of Underavon. Thinking of all this now, and thinking also of the manifold and polymath investigations which Ptolemaeos conducted from his Fenland lair, Leonard suddenly conceived an idea which might appeal to the rotund savant, and went to the telephone to ring up Piero, who, as he knew, was still sitting out the Twelve Days of Christmas, along with his guardian, in the Provost's Lodging at Lancaster.

'A taxi?' said Isobel to Rosie and Marius, as the three of them sat in a row on the sedilia behind the south choir stalls. 'A *hotel* for the night in Toulouse? Do you think that we're made of money?'

'Pretty well,' said Marius. 'Anyway, what else were we meant to do? Walk here in the dark, carrying our luggage?'

'I told you in my letter. Wait in the airport waiting room until daylight, get a bus to Toulouse Railway Station, a train from Toulouse to Saint-Gaudens, and then a bus from Saint-Gaudens to Saint-Bertrand.'

'Which would have taken so long,' said Marius, 'that we'd have had to go home as soon as we got here. Though come to think of it,' he said, eyeing the choir stalls and the steel spiral stairway that led up to the improvised first floor under the barrel vaulting, 'that might not have been too bad a thing.'

'Don't be unkind,' said Isobel. 'I've been looking forward so much.'

'Oh, mummy . . .'

Both children rose from the sedilia and stood before Isobel. To Marius she gave her throat to kiss. To Rosie she gave both hands, stretching her arms out on either side of the nuzzling Marius.

'Oenone is upstairs,' she said, 'having her mid-morning nap. Jo-Jo and Jean-Marie have gone away to make room for both of you.'

'Why didn't they take Oenone?' said Rosie. 'She's theirs, after all.'

'I think she is almost more mine. I would like,' she said, 'to have a child out of Jo-Jo, that was actually by me.'

Marius giggled into her bosom. 'Don't be silly, Mummy,' he said. 'Thank God you're so nice and warm. It's freezing in this place.'

'I've turned the oil stove off to save money.'

'What is all this about saving money?' said Marius. 'Daddy left plenty. You explained to me at the time how it had all been arranged, and so did the lawyers, and I *know* that we have at least three quarters of a million pounds between us – not counting the value of the firm.'

'We must try to pretend we haven't, darling,' said Isobel. 'We must try to be like everybody else, like Jo-Jo and Jean-Marie, for example, and live on very little.'

'But Jo-Jo,' said Marius, 'is loaded. Everyone in her family was killed in a car crash, which left her and her Uncle Ptoly to scoop the entire kitty – much more than we're worth. It comes from lavatory pans,' he said.

'You haven't understood, darling. Jo-Jo has to pretend to be poor in order not to offend Jean-Marie.'

'Jean-Marie's books have been doing extremely well,' said Rosie, 'and one of them has been serialized by the BBC. Canteloupe came to lunch with Mrs Malcolm one day and told us all about it. Jean-Marie is making more money than almost any of his authors, he told us.'

'But that still leaves him poorer than Jo-Jo, poorer than us. Our money is an insult to Jean-Marie, just as Jean-Marie's money is an insult to those even poorer. We must all try to pretend we have nothing, behave as if we had nothing.'

'Don't you see,' said Marius to his mother, 'how stupid,

how *dishonest* that is? To have all the money you need, but to pretend to have none – making everyone round you thoroughly miserable when they might be having a very nice time. It's worse than dishonest: it's diseased.'

Rosie came down the metal stairway with the happily babbling Oenone.

'Marius doesn't like me any more,' said Isobel to Rosie. 'Just as well you are only staying a very few days. I do not think Marius will come at Easter: he will go to the lawyers, and will amuse himself in London, in Buttock's Hotel.'

'Or elsewhere,' Marius said, remembering Milo Hedley's invitation on the last day of school before the Christmas holidays. 'Raisley Conyngham has a place in Somerset,' Milo had said: 'very comfortable with lots of servants – he is rich for a schoolmaster, you see. And horses, beautiful horses, which he races. You ride, don't you, Marius? The Riding Master at Oudenarde said you were the best horseman he'd ever seen, even better than your father, with whom he'd ridden in the Household Cavalry. He knows Raisley, this Riding Master of yours, and when he knew you were coming here and not to Eton, he told Raisley about you when he met him one day at Cheltenham Races. So Raisley wants to meet you. He hasn't gone out of his way so far, because it is bad if a master is seen to seek out a small boy in his first year. But now you are in your second year, Marius, and Raisley wants to meet you very soon. Raisley will invite you for Easter, Marius. You're not quite sure? Your mother in France? Well, let's see how things go on. You can leave it all – except of course your mother – to me.'

'Elsewhere,' Marius said.

'And you, Rosie?' said Isobel. 'Shall you want to come at Easter?'

67

'For Oenone,' said Rosie.

'As good a motive as any, I suppose. But what about Tessa? Won't she miss you? Especially if Marius is not at Buttock's.'

'I do not think,' said Rosie coolly, 'that Tessa is going to miss me much any more. Besides, she has already hinted that at Easter she will have a special invitation.'

'What invitation?' Marius said.

'She was not candid. She was guilty, you see. The one thing which I absolutely realize is that the invitation will not include me.'

'Poor Rosie,' said Marius, clasping the inside of her elbow with one hand. 'It's a wretched business, being dumped. I hope I never am.'

'You would do better to hope,' said Rosie, 'that you never do any dumping. Being dumped is horrible, yet it can be endured. But to do the dumping is to dishonour the past – to poison all that has been between you and the other person – to murder your own soul.'

Piero telephoned from the Provost's Lodging in Lancaster to Leonard Percival in Wiltshire.

'That idea of yours for Ptoly's entertainment,' he said: 'the Canteloupe inheritance. I've been discussing it with him. Now as it happens, the idea had already been put into his head by the Provost, who was going on about the thing a day or two ago. Ptoly got quite inquisitive then, and now your suggestion – that he might be able to buy the documents that started it all off – has really hooked him. How much would Major Gray want for those manuscripts?'

'Nothing that Ptolemaeos couldn't afford. But both he and I,' said Percival, 'will want a promise as well . . . a promise that the whole thing is to be treated strictly as a matter of scholarship . . . that any further investigations are to be conducted only for Ptoly Tunne's private interest and entertainment.'

'In short,' said Piero Caspar: 'no spiteful tricks to disturb the *status quo*. Why should Ptoly want to upset Canteloupe?'

'He might feel like having fun and games with the real heir. Do you remember that chap during the Regency who brought an orang-utang to London, and bought it a baronetcy and a seat in the Commons? Ptoly might find it funny to play some similar joke with the idiot Paolo Filavoni.'

'No, Leonard. You spent too many years of your life spying before you went to Canteloupe. You're corroded with mistrust. Any trick of the kind you mention is strictly not Ptolemaeos's style. He is an analyst, not an impresario. He'll take an enormous interest in the background and history of the thing – all those pranks in the garden of the Palazzo Albani, he'll just love those – and he'll probably cast a sharp eye at the actual pedigree of Paolo-in-the-marshes. He will want to check everything that actually happened – a privilege he'll be paying for. But he won't be getting up a Paolo-for-Marquess movement, I promise you that.'

'Right,' said Leonard: 'what shall I tell Fielding?'

'Tell him to get the manuscripts out of his bank and come down to the Fens any day after to-morrow – when Ptoly and I are going back there – giving two hours' notice for the benefit of the domestics. Then we'll see.'

'See what?'

'The manuscripts and what they're worth.'

'Be generous, Piero,' Leonard said. 'Fielding is rather low, what with one thing and the other.'

'Personally, as you may know, I am exceedingly mean. Once a kept boy, always a kept boy: we expect to be treated and fêted and never to spend a penny of our own even if we get rich – least of all on those who were open-handed with us when we were poor. It was our due, we tell ourselves, so it is a point of honour not to repay it. But I digress. Since we shall be spending Ptolemaeos's money, I dare say I can afford to be . . . not illiberal.'

'What will Ptolemaeos think about it?'

'More and more,' said Piero Caspar, 'he is leaving such matters to me.'

At school, Marius was in the Fifth Form (Classical) and Tessa in the Fifth Form (History). Marius was in the Headmaster's House, Tessa in one of the *Domi Vestales* recently established to absorb the new females. They did not, therefore, meet very often, except at twice-weekly 'O' Level Art lectures, which were conducted for the paradoxical and salutary purpose of taking the 'O' Level candidates' minds, at least briefly, off their 'O' Levels.

Jakki Blessington, though only in her first year, was encouraged to attend the 'O' Level Art lectures on a voluntary basis. And so it came about that on the third Friday of January, the three of them met and sat together for the first time since well before Christmas. During the lecture, which was given by a retired master of enormous age, still known as the Senior Usher, having been the last 'beak' to hold this now obsolete office, the children held their peace: not only out of respect for their instructor but out of considerable interest in his witty, worldly and somewhat improper instruction. When the lecture was concluded, they remained companionably in place for a little gossip about the events of the holidays; but no sooner had Marius begun to describe the horror of dossing down in a sleeping bag on the planks of the improvised first floor of the Sanctuary at Saint-Bertrand, than they were interrupted by an ephebe two sizes (so to speak) bigger and taller than Marius, wearing his hair in a style which approximated to that of an Athenian *kouros* of the Archaic period, and smiling the beguiling yet faintly contemptuous smile which distinguished the sculpture of the same era. He mounted the lecturer's rostrum, and:

'I've got to lock the place, my darlings,' announced the ephebe. 'It's my week as Duty School Monitor. Sorry, but please go quietly.'

'Oh Milo,' said Marius and Tessa, and swayed in their seats.

Jakki sat still and closed her lips very tight.

'You can continue your discussion *al fresco*,' said Milo Hedley.

'Cold outside.'

'I see. Then if Miss Blessington will give me just a tiny smile instead of trying to impersonate a Gorgon, I will leave you all here for ten minutes more, while I make the rest of my rounds and then return.'

With difficulty, Jakki made herself smirk, for Tessa's and Marius's sake, not for her own she told herself; so that they could sit in the warm. Milo Hedley waved, sauntered down the steps of the rostrum and was gone.

71

'Now you've placed us under an obligation to him,' Jakki said. 'I'm off.'

'What have you got against him?' said Marius.

'He's too *got . . . up*,' said Jakki. 'I don't like him and I don't trust him and I can't bear watching you two writhing like hooked eels when you see him.'

'We do nothing of the kind.'

'I agree. You don't really. You just rub your thighs together as if you were trying not to piddle on the floor. See you next lecture.'

Red in the face and sniffing ominously, Jakki departed.

'What brought that on?' said Marius to Tessa. 'She always looks forward to our talks.'

'She didn't want to be beholden to Milo. She loathes him – that's clear enough. But come to think of it,' said Tessa, 'there's no reason why he should have interfered with us. This lecture hall is locked by the School Porter at six P.M., *not* by the Duty School Monitor at noon. No one has ever interrupted us like that before. It's something that Milo has thought up. Do you think he wanted to be rid of Jakki?'

'He was very scathing with her, certainly.'

A small man, in a tight, belted jacket worn with knickerbockers and green checked stockings, entered the room. He had crinkly brown hair and a very inviting smile which displayed brilliant rows of slightly oversized teeth. As this smile reached its climax, Milo Hedley came in and halted very close to the little man, just behind him, like a highly confidential equerry.

'Mr Conyngham,' muttered Marius to Tessa. 'So that's why Milo wanted Jakki out of the way.'

Uncertain what to do next, Tessa and Marius sat tight while Raisley Conyngham, with Milo still very close to him and just behind him, came up the aisle of shallow steps. He then stopped and turned to face down Tessa's and Marius's row of benches, and smiled again, this time more briefly and less theatrically.

'Teresa Malcolm,' he said, 'and Marius Stern. Niece of the celebrated hotelier – or should we say "*hotelière?*" – and son of the famous publisher. Well. I thought it was time we met, so I told Milo to arrange it. Though as it happens, you, Marius, have just been switched to me for special and individual instruction in Latin and Greek verse, so we shall meet again very soon in any case. It will be agreeable to teach someone who promises well (as I am told) in these civilized exercises.'

He looked, thought Tessa, rather like Dennis Price in a very old black and white film called *Kind Hearts and Coronets*, which she had seen with Rosie during the holidays, before Rosie had left with Marius for Saint-Bertrand. Rosie had said that it was a trivial film and had not been pleased by the cynical jokes. Tessa had loved every moment of it. She rather thought, now, that she was going to love every moment of Raisley Conyngham, but felt a slight chill in her stomach in anticipation of the absent Rosie's almost certain disapproval.

'If you don't mind,' said Conyngham to Tessa, 'I shall call you "Teresa", though I know most people call you "Tessa". Teresa has . . . a maturity . . . which Tessa does not. Now, come and shake hands with me, both of you.'

Tessa and Marius shuffled along the benches to meet him in the aisle. First he greeted Tessa; a brief, civil handshake, nothing more. Then:

'Have you kept up your riding?' he asked Marius, as he shook his hand with similar brevity. 'They say your father was the finest horseman, in his day, in the Household Cavalry. Too large a man to race, of course. So will you be, in another year's time. But I hope you are keeping it up.'

'I go out in the park during the holidays, sir.'

'Not enough. We must have you on horseback while you are here as well. The arrangements for riding at this school are quite damnable. But Milo will see to it.'

He glanced at Milo, who nodded acknowledgement of the order. Marius was called upon, he felt, to express neither gratitude (which he felt) nor reluctance (which he also felt, as riding might complicate an already complicated schedule) nor indeed any opinion of any kind whatever. He would do what he was told, it was already clear to him, or he would incur displeasure; and for some reason, a reason of the gut rather than of the heart or of the head, it was unthinkable to him to risk incurring Conyngham's displeasure.

Jakki, walking sadly away towards her *Domus Vestalis* (a different one from Tessa's) saw a boy who was loitering about with a yo-yo, some fifty yards from the door of the lecture room. This was a contemporary of Marius called Palairet, who was not bright enough to be taking his 'O' Levels that year nor sufficiently interested in art to go to art lectures. Although Jakki did not know him well, she had met him at Buttock's when he had come to stay with Marius some eighteen months before, while they were both on holiday before their last term at their prep school, Oudenarde House in Sandwich. She had also run across him quite often since, usually when he was with Marius.

So both good manners and a vague liking for Palairet, now made Jakki stop for a friendly word or two, though she knew she was not looking her best.

'Cold, hanging about,' she said.

'I'm waiting for Marius. Is he coming?'

'No. He's still in there with Tessa. If you wanted to see Marius, why didn't you come to the lecture?'

'And sit there for a whole hour before I can talk to him? When we first came here,' he said to Jakki, 'although we were in different houses, we used to meet every day . . . for the whole of our first year. Now he never comes near me unless I hunt him out.'

'He's very busy, you know. "O" Levels coming this summer. Under sixteen hockey and fives now, and then there was under sixteen footer before Christmas.'

'Yes, I know. I used to play in all the teams with him at Oudenarde, but somehow I haven't kept up with him here.'

'Stiffen up, you wreck,' said Jakki. 'You're nearly as bad as I am. *I* never see him either, except at those lectures.'

'*You* are a year junior to him.'

'That's not meant to count any more.'

'No. I was going to Eton, you know, where it still does, I think. I only switched when Marius told me he was coming here.'

'Why are you telling me that?'

'When I told Marius that I was coming here too,' Palairet said, ignoring Jakki's question because (his manner implied) the answer would be indelicate, 'he told me how glad he was. We'd always been friends at Oudenarde House – '

' – Didn't he beat you up there? – '

' – He hit me in the throat. An accident, of course. Not

his fault. So after that we were better friends than ever, all through our last year at Oudenarde – we used to go riding together as well as games – and all through our first year here. And now . . . he can't even find time for a game of squash.'

All this was uttered without self-pity, in a level tone of voice, as a matter of social fact. Palairet was behaving perfectly decently, thought Jakki, simply stating a case which in many ways resembled her own (for although never really close to Marius, she had known him pretty well for some years and was miserable at the way he ignored her) and which for that very reason (as he no doubt thought but was too tactful to declare) would be of some interest to her. The trouble with Palairet, thought Jakki, was that although he was a sensitive and considerate boy, he was also, in one word, dull: wholesome and unremarkable in looks, unsexy (rather like a picture of Harry Wharton her father had shown her in an ancient copy of *The Magnet*), faithful to the death, straight as a die, a real white man – Palairet was a walking cliché straight out of Dornford Yates or John Buchan, or rather, since Yates and Buchan were *not* boring (Jakki now thought), straight out of that super-bore, Henty. No wonder Marius avoided him – as indeed Marius avoided her. Well, perhaps she was dull too. 'A jolly girl' or 'a really good sort', a kind of female Palairet. God forbid, thought Jakki, and having nothing further to say either for Palairet's comfort or her own, she gave a kindly shrug of farewell and proceeded on her way to her Vestal House, there to have a wholesome and featureless lunch (a sort of *Palairet* of lunches, she thought) with sixty-seven other assumed and assorted Vestals.

'The trouble with you,' said Maisie Malcolm to Fielding Gray, 'is that you're a horny bastard, and that you've got the horn for my Tessa.'

'Rubbish,' said Fielding: 'the last time I had a horn was in bed three months ago – and by the time I'd got my hand down to test it, the damned thing had gone.'

Fielding, who was stopping in London to pick up his Venetian manuscripts *en route* for the Fens, was being allowed to stay at Buttock's because it was mid-week and Tessa was at school. Maisie had decided it would be a good opportunity to have a go at him about his lech for Tessa, which, she maintained, was unsettling Tessa to the verge of *oestrus*.

'You are imagining the whole thing,' said Fielding. 'I love Tessa, and I think and hope she loves me: we have a kiss and a pat whenever we meet, and there is an end of it.'

'She's sly, that Tessa. Though she's my own, I admit that. She fancies you and she'd do whatever you asked if she thought I wasn't looking.'

'I shan't ask anything,' said Fielding. 'What has got into you, Maisie?'

'That Christmas present you sent to her. That picture. It was worth a hundred pounds if it was worth a penny.'

'I thought she'd appreciate it.'

'Dirty pig. You thought you'd get yourself into her bedroom under pretence of seeing how she'd hung it, and then you'd start touching and peering and pawing – '

' – Maisie. We can't go on like this. We can't sell the hotel because of Tessie Buttock's will. Would you like to buy my half of it?'

'Can't afford. You may be able to fork out five hundred quid for pictures to corrupt little girls with, but I'm absolutely skint – '

' – No you're not. You may not be able to buy my share of the hotel,' said Fielding, 'but you're certainly not skint. You know the trouble with you, girl? You're having the change of life. You're imagining things, as I said. Like this ridiculous business of me and Tessa. It's so long since you've had it off yourself that *that's* making it even worse. What you need,' shouted Fielding, 'is a great big fuck, twenty great big fucks, and you'll begin to be sane again. The only trouble is, who can we get to fuck you? Well, I'll have a go, by God, yes I'll do what I can for you, you fat old whore. I've got an idea, by God it makes me feel quite young to think of it – so down with your knickers and up with the Curaçao bottle – just like the old days. That's it. You always did enjoy your work, didn't you? And Jesus Christ, you're sopping wet already.'

'There are two documents,' said Fielding Gray to Ptolemaeos Tunne. 'One is in the form of a Greek Reader for Children, which tells the story of the early life of Viscount Rollesden-in-Silvis, alias Humbert fitzAvon, in the guise of an animal fable.'

'And who wrote that?'

'It was written by a Venetian merchant called Fernando

Albani. Rollesden-in-Silvis had disgraced himself in England and had been spirited away, through his father's influence at Court, on a secret and pseudo-diplomatic mission to Venice under the alias of fitzAvon, one of the habitual family forenames. Some time after he reached Venice, he chanced to help Fernando's adolescent son – who was called Piero, by the way – to escape from a bordel which was being raided by agents of the Inquisition. Having thus put the family in his debt, he proceeded to claw it back with huge interest. The first document, the Greek fable, was written by Albani on the strength of what he came to know, later on, of Rollesden/fitzAvon's history up to the time of Piero's rescue from the cat house. The second document was written in French, correct but dull, and gave an account of what happened during the time between Piero's rescue and fitzAvon's death, some years later, while a refugee from the armies of Bonaparte in the marshes near Oriago, or to be more precise, in the village of Samuele some five kilometres from the Laguna Veneta.'

'I see,' said Ptolemaeos. They reached the end of his lawn, looked briefly over the hedge at the winter fens (a grey, Daliesque plane divided by an infinitely receding dyke), and turned back towards the house. 'Or rather, I don't see,' Ptolemaeos said. 'Why was the first instalment written in the form of a Greek fable?'

'So that Fernando could give it to his younger children as a disguised preparation for what was to come later. By the time he wrote the fable, the two elder children, Piero and his sister, had died, as had Rollesden/fitzAvon, in really fiendish circumstances, and Fernando felt that he should leave the family and perhaps the world some account of the affair, which was rich in moral lessons. He apparently hoped that the two younger children, the twins

Francesco and Francesca, would read the fable in the schoolroom, remember it until they were older, and then make the necessary connection and go back to it again. By this time they would be ready for the full horror of what was set out *en clair* in the second, the French, document, which they would easily be able to find if they took sufficient interest in the first to read carefully certain directions at the end of it.'

'But if they never reverted to the first after they were grown, if they'd just forgotten it, they would never have been able to find and read the second. Your Fernando seems to have left a lot to mere chance.'

'Yes. Deliberately. You see, he didn't particularly want to dish up the dirt about his family, but the action was so strong and had such terrible results and implications, that he felt it to be his duty to record the whole truth of the matter, yet in such a fashion that only those who were prepared to work hard and pay close attention would be able to get at it. He did not preclude or deprecate the possibility of a fortuitous and persistent outsider's coming on the code and cracking it. So he wrote what he wrote and disposed of it discreetly, and in his view it would be found and interpreted, by his children or others, if such was the will of God; if not, not. In any case he would have played his part by making the truth available – '.

' – If God wanted anyone to know it. Apparently,' said Ptolemaeos, 'He wanted you to know it. How did you come to find these documents?'

'That is a very long and fascinating story which I shall certainly tell you as part of the sale. But not to-night I think, or there will be no sleep for either of us.'

'One more thing to look forward to,' Ptolemaeos said. 'What happened to all the people in these manuscripts? Fernando and his children and the versatile Mr fitzAvon?'

'Death happened.'

'But how? What kind?'

'That is what you will be paying to find out. I am simply offering a trailer.'

Ptolemaeos chuckled.

'All right,' he said; 'I'll buy it. Or rather, *both*. Piero will settle the details with you. He knows far more about it all than I do and will make a fair price.'

'To avoid any nonsense about Capital Gains Tax,' said Peiro, 'I am going to pay you in a series of casual sums, varying between £130 and £1,145, that kind of thing, at irregular intervals. These can be lost or disguised or explained away quite easily in your accounts and ours, whereas the full £30,000, paid in a lump, might attract attention.'

'£30,000? Ptoly promised a fair sum, but this is munificent.'

'Not if you knew how much money Ptolemaeos has got. He could easily afford ten times the amount, but that would be ridiculous. The operative figure, as I hope you realize, is the *thirty*: in a sense, I am paying the traditional fee.'

'I don't deserve that crack, Piero. The agreement of sale is that these documents should be used for purposes of scholarship or entertainment only.'

'Nevertheless, you are selling the secret.'

'A lot of people know it already. Besides, those documents constitute no threat to Canteloupe or his title, even

if Ptoly chose to break his word about his use of them –
unless they are used in conjunction with the Church
Register at Samuele.'

'And why should they not be? Would you like to cancel
the sale before it's too late?'

A long silence.

'No,' said Fielding. 'I need the money, and I trust
Ptolemaeos.'

'You don't sound brim full of conviction about that,'
said Piero, who was beginning to write in an enormous
cheque book; 'but I don't think you need fret on Canteloupe's behalf. I should tell you, however, that an emissary *is* going to Samuele to check up on the Church
Register and see what's going on there . . . how, for
example, Paolo and his aunt are faring.'

'An emissary? You?'

'No. I have to go back to Lancaster in a day or two, to
resume my studies. You'll meet the emissary, whom you
know already, at dinner to-night.'

Dinner in the Fens that evening was informal and therefore eaten in Ptolemaeos's monolithic kitchen. The dishes
had been concocted that afternoon by Ptolemaeos's two
female attendants, who had departed, as usual, at sunset,
leaving instructions with Piero for heating up their crea-
tions. Those present were Ptolemaeos Tunne, Piero
Caspar and Fielding Gray; also Ivan ('the Greco') Barra-

clough, a Fellow of Lancaster and a very old friend of Ptolemaeos, and his page or esquire, Nicos, a young Greek from the Mani.

'First course,' said Piero: 'Fenland snails in Fen garlic butter. Fen garlic is twice as strong as the usual kind and wrongly reputed aphrodisiac.'

'Now then, Greco,' said Ptoly to his old chum, as the snails were served: 'I have a job for Nicos.'

'Nicos already has his job – for me.'

'Time that stopped, dear boy. You can't hang on to him for ever – too embarrassing for all of us, especially him. He's doing no good as an undergraduate – failed again last summer, I hear, and even Tom and Len between them won't be able to keep him on the College books much longer. He's getting too long in the tooth just to hang around being your study fag, and altogether a salutary change is called for. So I'm going to make Nicos independent of you – on probation at least. What do you say, Nico?'

'I owe much to the *kyrios* Barraclough,' said Nicos, as if by rote. He looked eagerly at Ptolemaeos, then dubiously at Barraclough.

'But by this time,' said Ptolemaeos, 'you owe even more to yourself. I'm going to send you off to Venice, Nicos, to make a little enquiry for me.'

'Ah,' said Nicos, eyes gleaming.

Greco Barraclough started drumming his fingers on the table.

'Details later,' said Ptoly; 'Piero will provide them. Basically, you have to examine some records in a church and take a look at the village cretin in a place called Samuele, not far from Oriago. I shall want to know how he looks, with whom he's living, whether he is properly cared for, all that kind of thing.'

'And what am I supposed to do,' snapped Greco, 'while all this is going on? Who is to keep my files in order? Who is to drive me?'

'You can do it all very well yourself. You're just pampered,' said Ptoly.

'It's all very well for you to talk. You have Piero.'

'Yes. And I pay him properly. You keep the wretched Nicos on baked beans and a shoe-lace.'

'He has sworn an oath – when he first came to me in the Mani.'

'Legally that oath was never of consequence,' said Ptoly, 'and morally it has long since expired. Right, Nico?'

'Right, *kyrie* Tunne.'

'So apply to Piero for details first thing in the morning,' said Ptoly, 'before you go back to Lancaster with the Greco.'

'If he applies to Piero,' said the Greco poutily, 'he will not be coming back to Lancaster with me.'

'Then he will be welcome to stay here until he goes to Venice,' said Ptolemaeos Tunne, 'or is well able to make such other arrangements as he may wish.'

Theodosia and Carmilla walked in the desolate Rose Garden; Theodosia pushed Sarum's pram, since it was Daisy the Nanny's day off, and Carmilla walked beside her, on her right.

'He's too big for a pram,' said Theodosia, 'but it provides a kind of camouflage.'

Sarum of Old Sarum mouthed at her from under the hood.

'Does Canteloupe know yet?'

'Oh yes,' said Theodosia. 'He wants another heir, though as yet he is not very clear about what will happen to this one. He just says there must be another boy . . . in case things go wrong.'

'I see. What is he proposing? Parthenogenesis?'

'The same as for Sarum. I am to choose the man.'

'*Not* what was promised.'

'He promised me there would be nothing of the kind with him. Nor could there be. He did not specifically preclude what he is now asking.'

'You had a right to presume – absolutely to presume – that such a thing was precluded.'

'I think so. But I do not wish to anger him. I love him, Carmilla.'

'What have you done so far?'

'I have told him I shall consider the matter.'

'Why not suggest artificial insemination?'

'Because Canteloupe wants the child to be conceived by a full and proper act of copulation. To Canteloupe a child born of injected sperm would be bogus, not the genuine article. And so, as I say, he has told me to choose a man. I can take as long as I like to look around . . . provided I am clear what the right true end of it must be. But it cannot be, Carmilla. Even with Jeremy, whom I loved so much, it could not be.'

'I know.'

'Then what shall I do?'

'Nothing. Just bear the matter in mind. If you keep it calmly and constantly before you,' said Carmilla, 'sooner or later a solution will present itself.'

'On guard,' said Milo Hedley to Tessa in the school gymnasium. 'Remember: the angle and poise of your whole sword arm must be such that it is protected by the hilt of your sabre.'

'Very uncomfortable,' said Tessa.

'Then take that.'

With a twist of his wrist he prised the bare steel button on his weapon all along her forearm to the elbow. Although Tessa's jacket protected her skin, the smart was vicious.

'Careful, Milo.'

'*You* be careful. You asked for lessons. I am doing you the compliment of assuming you really want to learn. *On guard.* That's better. Hold it for one . . . two . . . three . . . four . . . five seconds. Stomach in, knees flexed, right foot forward at a right angle – parallel with your sabre. You are to present as narrow a silhouette as possible. Not bad. That will do for now. And what,' said Milo as they removed their masks, 'did you make of Raisley Conyngham?'

'A very appealing gentleman.'

'Good. We need you, Raisley and I. We need you and Marius.'

'Need us?'

'You are the only two people in the whole school with anything which approaches distinction. Everyone else is dowdy.'

'You wait till Marius's sister, Rosie, comes.'

'She has not come yet. So we need you and Marius. The only two people fit to work with.'

'Work?'

'An exercise and an experiment in ingenuity. A demonstration of cerebral superiority. You'll see.'

'You sound rather like the young man in that movie *Rope*,' said Tessa. (Hitchcock's *Rope* was another film she had been to with Rosie in the holidays; it received a partial accolade from Rosie on the grounds that it did at least have serious thought behind it.)

Milo grinned. 'We do not have murder in mind. Something much more amusing.'

'Well, that's a relief. Tell me more.'

'It will also be an exercise in discipline. Do not ever let me catch you exposing your forearm again.'

'So I have money,' said Fielding to Jeremy; 'I can pay for it all; please come.'

The door of the Gun Room opened. A long, lugubrious but trimly moving figure came in with a tray on which were tea and muffins.

'Tea, Mr Jeremy,' intoned the figure. 'Good afternoon, Major Gray. I hope I see you in health.'

'Thank you, Corporal.'

'"Chamberlain" these days, sir, if you please. Chamberlain to my Lord Canteloupe, on loan to my Lord Luffham.'

'Of course, Chamberlain. A stupid slip of the tongue.'

'You were lucky he let you off so lightly,' said Jeremy

after the 'Chamberlain' had retired. 'He is very jealous of his title.'

'I suspect he gave me special treatment as a member of my old regiment. Loyal they are, that lot. Will you come with me, Jeremy? It won't cost you a penny. A marvellous trip, better than any we've done before. The Turkish part alone – '

' – All that's over, Fielding.' Jeremy pushed the muffins towards Fielding, not as one offering them to a guest but as one who rejects them for his own part. 'I thought you'd realize that when I didn't answer your letter. I thought you would understand . . . that all that was in another world. "Presume not that I am the thing I was."'

'What was the matter . . . "With the thing you was"?'

'Trivial. Light-minded. Travelling just to kill time. Amusing myself with – to be candid – frivolous and superficial companions. Immature.'

'You once came to me for a philosophy,' Fielding said. 'You seemed to think that my record, as a man and a writer, was rather impressive.'

'I know different now. I have seen something of your world . . . the world you inhabit both as a man *and* a writer . . . and I can measure the futility of your achievement. A lucky knack. Worthless. Of no importance whatever.'

'You were keen enough yourself to do well in that world,' said Fielding, stung. 'Only you failed utterly and didn't have the grit to go on with it.'

'I have found something which makes that world a total irrelevance, Fielding. The land; my land. I am not speaking now just as a farmer or a proprietor. I must become part of it, become absorbed by and in it, mingle myself with the genius of my land. You and I can no longer be companions as we have nothing in common now except the past. And the past itself must be forgotten, as a time of waste, a bitter insult to the spirit of the waiting land.'

Complacent, remorseless 'special', full of righteousness and excuse; self-loving, self-deceiving, unbalanced and extreme. I'm very well out of this, Fielding thought. If only I didn't love him so much, even now; if only the days didn't loom so lonely and so long.

'Very well, Jeremy,' he said. 'I'll count you out. But I'll stay the night, if I may. I'd like a word with your father.'

At dinner Jeremy drank no wine and left his father and Fielding *tête à tête* over the port.

'Mr Jeremy thinks that conspicuous abstinence makes him a person of consequence,' said the Chamberlain from his station under the portrait of Jeremy's mother: 'an unattractive delusion, my lord and Major Gray.'

'Thank you, Chamberlain,' said Peter Morrison, Lord Luffham of Whereham as now was; and when the Chamberlain had withdrawn and closed the double door behind him:

'In a grotesque way that poor booby gets saner every day. I think he's always rather taken the same view of Jeremy as I have, that he's a stumer. One should add,' Lord Luffham continued, 'that this business of a spiritual return to the soil has all come on very suddenly. Just after Christmas, Jeremy had young Marius Stern down to stay and there was none of that talk then. Oh, Jeremy was going to give up Lancaster and the arty world and you with them, because he was sick of you all and you hadn't

89

taken him at his own evaluation, but at this stage he simply seemed to see himself as becoming the genial 'squire', as taking a proper interest in his own acres and his own people; for the rest it was 'Heigh boy, and off to the races' – only the weather put paid to that. My point is, Fielding, that there was none of this mysticism, this religiosity, this fanaticism and self-righteousness that now seem to be going on. Or none, at least, until Master Marius departed to see Isobel in France.

'Now, one evening while Marius was here, Jeremy was running down the sort of trips he'd had with you, being snide about them and saying how glad he was not to be going on the next. Myself, I thought this was pretty mean of him; but since it's his house now, and I'm only here, when I am, on sufferance, I let it go by rather than quarrel. But young Marius wouldn't have any of it. He accused Jeremy of 'poisoning the past', not his own phrase, he said, but one he'd learnt from his sister, Rosie. There could be many kinds of treachery between friends, Marius said, but of them all the worst was poisoning the past, which was what Jeremy had just been doing *vis-à-vis* Fielding. Jeremy didn't care for that, I can tell you. So it's my belief that to defend himself against any more such charges, with reference to yourself or others, he's put out this spiritual smokescreen about the sanctity or whatnot of the land, hoping to obscure the meanness of his behaviour and present himself, through the vapour, as a chosen one who has been called. Quite a good way of preserving one's self-respect in shifty circumstances and airing one's consequence. To be fair, it's the kind of thing you might have done at his age, if you'd really needed to; but of course you didn't because you had a talent and were prepared to work at it, whereas Jeremy is all wind and piss. Shrewd, yes, particularly about money; but no real brains or intellect – and no tolerance of necessary grind. So if I were you, I'd now be thankful he's given you your cards.'

'Only I can't be, Peter. I adored him, you see.'

'The more fool you. You were always adoring someone or other that didn't suit.'

'I knew I had faults that bored or irritated him, we all do. So I tried to get rid of them – and I tried very hard, and successfully on the whole, to bear with *his*. He didn't seem to think it possible that he had any, Peter: Jeremy simply was not aware that it was even *possible* for him to be just as tiresome or *maladroit* or repetitious or spiteful as anyone else. But I bore with him, as I say, because I thought that one *did* bear with one's friends, that that was one of the obligations of friendship, that one did one's level best to keep things pleasant, that one overlooked their clumsiness or malice or parsimony if one possibly could. The trouble was that, latterly at least, he has not extended the same courtesy to me. The minute *I* committed some *sottise* he was on to me like a nest of vipers. So unforgiving, so cruel, so *violent*.'

'Physically?'

'That was lurking there, I think. But no: only oral.'

'Go away and forget him, Fielding. Leave here early to-morrow, having said a civil good-bye, and then go and do some work.'

'I haven't got any to do.'

'Find some. Make some. Surely Canteloupe will commission you to do something.'

'I'm not short of money.'

'What you need is work. Having something to do and knowing how to do it. It's the only thing that keeps a man sane. That's Jeremy's trouble: nothing to do, because he's never tried hard enough at anything to know how to do it. So now he's taking up silly, high-sounding fads, like the holiness of the soil. It'll be spiritualism next – no, even he can't be silly or dishonest enough for that – it'll be something which at least sounds right, like transcendental meditation.'

'The only Englishman who has ever written Latin Verse that might have taken in the Romans,' said Raisley Conyngham,' is A. E. Housman. Milton made quite a good effort with his Latin *Epitaph for Damon* – but produced a howling false quantity in the very first line. So Housman bears away the palm with the few elegiac couplets he wrote, as preface to his edition of Manilius. Who was he?'

'Manilius,' said Marius, 'was a Latin poet who wrote about astronomy.'

'All this is by the way,' said Raisley Conyngham. He examined the ceiling of the Addison & Steele Library, on which was painted rather an amusing mural of Addison helping the drunken Steele back into barracks when they were in the Horse Guards. '*You* are learning to write Latin verse: first because it will practise you in precision and flexibility of language; secondly, because it will help you get a scholarship at one of the two Universities; thirdly, because it is fun; and fourthly, because it is élite – not the sort of thing scruffy yobs do in comprehensives.'

'Surely they wouldn't want to?'

'No. But neither would they want you to. Have you not heard the modern slogan: if I can't, you mustn't; and even if I don't want to, you still mustn't, in case, unknown to me, I'm missing out on something. Why, Marius, do yobs savage buildings and pictures? Not because they want to understand them but can't – they don't give a damn about that – but because *someone else might understand them and take pleasure in them*, and the yobs and their socialist supporters couldn't possibly allow that. Enough of this. This version of yours of "When you shall hear the surly, sudden bell" is not a bad effort. *Quandocumque igitur* in the first line – too heavy and lifted straight out of Propertius. Pound, in his *Homage to Sextus Propertius,* translated it "When, when, when and whenever": rather overdone, but you see the point. For the simple "When" in Shakespeare's text, *quando* or *quandoquidem* or even *cum* would have been quite adequate.'

'I needed to fill up the line, sir.'

'That's honest.' Conyngham suddenly got bored. 'Alpha minus minus minus,' he said, tore Marius's verses across and threw them into the enormous fire. 'If the insurance people could see that fire,' he said, 'they'd have a fit and cancel the policy. An open fire in a library full of books. Faugh.' Once again he switched the subject. 'I thought you did rather well on that grey mare when we went out the other afternoon,' he said. 'I told Milo to choose a brute for you . . . and I was impressed with your performance.'

'Thank you, sir.'

'So sign these papers.'

'What are they, sir?'

'Part of the formalities we must go through if I'm to employ you as a stable lad over Easter.'

It was on the tip of Marius's tongue to enquire why Mr Conyngham should wish to employ him as a stable lad next Easter, when he remembered, or rather felt in the pit of his stomach, as he had in the lecture hall the other day, that Conyngham's orders were not to be questioned or commented upon. To ask what the papers were was permissible: further parley was impossible. If Marius so much as expressed surprise (even gratified surprise) Conyngham would raise an eyebrow, take up the papers, and go away, probably for ever. Marius passionately wanted him to stay; he signed the forms where Conyngham had marked them with pairs of crosses, and passed them across the table.

'Right. You're available for the whole of the Easter holidays?'

'Sir,' said Marius.

'No chance of complaints from your mother? Milo was saying something about her.'

'No, sir. I've had rather a disagreement with her, and as there isn't much room in her house in France, she'll be glad if I stay away.'

'Good. I think I can promise you an unusual Easter. Milo will be there, of course. And we rather hope to secure your chum, Tessa. You'd like that?'

'Sir,' said Marius heartily, though conscious of a flicker of jealousy, that Conyngham and Hedley should want Tessa as well as himself. At any rate, he comforted himself, she's not much good with horses. The one time she had been allowed a riding lesson in the Park had been sheer disaster. Whether Tessa had an allergy against horses, or horses had an allergy against Tessa, was uncertain. Whichever way it went, it was conclusive, one could almost say terminal.

'But that's at Easter,' said Conyngham: 'meanwhile we have ten weeks of stimulating studies before us. Greek verses next Thursday. I'm sick of those damned niminy-piminy ti-tom ti-tom iambics. Do the first twelve lines of Tennyson's *Morte d'Arthur* into Homeric hexameters. They include, incidentally, one of the most sinister lines in the English language.'

'Sir?'

'"A broken chancel with a broken cross." I shall be interested to see, my dear Marius, how you find an Homeric Greek equivalent for *that*.'

PART TWO
Queens' Pawns

The 'Queen', as we have her, betokens the Vizier, which was an Eastern Prince's most mighty minister.

ANON: *A Child's Manual of Chess*

Is it an echo of something
Read with a boy's delight
Viziers nodding together
In some Arabian night?

LORD TENNYSON: *Maud*; VII; iii

Theodosia Canteloupe, fearing lest she was growing sluggish, took to exercising in the Fives Court which was tucked away in one corner of the Great Court. She would taken two Fives balls with her and try to keep them both in play at the same time, a trick which required split-second calculation and absolute accuracy as to length.

It's high time I got back on to tennis, she told herself, Hampton Court or Queen's, instead of patting little balls about down here; but if I tell Canty I'm going to London to get some tennis practice, he may insist that I use the opportunity to look around for a mate with whom to do what he wants me to do. He's been silent about that since Christmas; but now that the guests (such as they were) are gone and the celebrations (such as they were) are done, I know that he may come back to the subject at any time. I cannot disappoint him, she thought, remembering Captain Detterling at Lord's that summer afternoon when she was fourteen: how gallantly he had lifted his panama hat, how kind and easy he had been with her, how pleased he had been to see her father and her father to see him. No, I cannot disappoint him; but I cannot do what he asks. I must just play for time, do as Carmilla says, keep the thing calmly and constantly before me until sooner or later a solution (but what solution?) presents itself.

One afternoon, when the early dusk forced her to discontinue her solitary game and she turned to leave the Fives Court, she saw Leonard Percival in wait at the far end of it.

Canty's jackal, she thought; but then she thought also of Leonard's age and ulcers, and a weary pity came over her.

'Good evening, Leonard,' she said, as pleasantly as she could.

'Good evening, my lady,' said Leonard, who often, and very greatly to her annoyance, addressed her in this form; 'taking the Christmas pudding off, I see.'

'Keeping in trim,' she said flatly, just restraining herself from telling this nasty old wreck (but Canty's friend, Canty's old friend) to be off and mind his business.

'Fielding Gray once told me,' said Leonard, 'how much he used to enjoy playing Eton Fives. At school . . . and later, whenever he could find a court and three other players . . . and so long as he still had two eyes.'

'He could have gone on playing with only one,' said Theodosia: 'simply a matter of adjustment.'

'But at that time, my lady, he had many other adjustments to make. As indeed he has now.'

'You mean . . . that he has to get over being dropped by Jeremy Morrison?'

'Among other things, yes. But what it comes down to, Lady Canteloupe, is that Fielding needs work. He has enough money, for the time, but he must have occupation.'

'Why are you telling me this?'

'Because you – and your sister – are important people these days in Stern & Detterling – *Salinger*, Stern & Detterling, that is. Or you could be if you wished, when one considers your shareholding. Now, Fielding has told me that he is out of sympathy in literary matters with Ashley Dexterside, the Managing Director – much as he respects and likes him in other ways. He also says that Detterling, your husband, no longer takes much interest.

Since Gregory Stern is dead, Fielding has no audience in the firm and has therefore become slack and indifferent about his work. Encouragement from you, and from Miss Carmilla Salinger, might be salutary, my lady. If he don't begin to work soon, he'll fret himself to pieces.'

'About Jeremy?'

'Yes. And his own decay. He decays neither quicker nor more evidently than any of the rest of us, but he is a fastidious man and therefore the more sensitive in this region. And, of course, in his case old age holds no prospects of dignity or serenity . . . merely those of boredom and neglect. Fielding likes movement, journeys, the pleasure of seeking out new sights and of recognizing and greeting old ones. As age comes on, he is less capable of travelling alone and (as he sees it) less able to find adequate and willing companions. From all thoughts such as these, he must be distracted – by work.'

'You want me to tell him that?'

'More than that.' Canteloupe was coming across the Great Court towards them. Courtesy compelled them to move to meet him. 'Persuade him that the firm needs books by him,' said Leonard hurriedly. 'Notions of loyalty, phrases like "the old firm", carry weight with him. And do you and your sister convince him that you will be the audience that Gregory Stern and Detterling – your husband – used to be. Then he will work.'

'Good evening, Thea, Leonard,' said Canteloupe. 'It's nice to know that old court is used again – if only just for knocking up.'

Knocking up, thought Thea; that's what they call it, in some circles, when a man gets you pregnant; he knocks you up. Was that a hint or a pun of Canty's? Surely not? Surely he couldn't have been as crude and indelicate as that? No, of course he couldn't. I'm imagining things; and until this solution of which Carmilla speaks 'presents itself', until something is settled, I shall go on imagining them. Well, at least Leonard Percival has given me something to think about other than myself. And an excuse to get away from here, if only for a day or two, without committing myself to Canty's horrible purpose. I shall telephone Carmilla at Lancaster this very evening.

After she had telephoned Carmilla, Theodosia went to Canteloupe's dressing room.

'Leonard has been telling me about Fielding Gray,' she said. 'He thinks Carmilla and I can help him.'

'How?' snapped Canteloupe.

'By giving him the encouragement . . . about his writing . . . which is no longer forthcoming from elsewhere.'

'Time he stopped. He's said all he has to say.'

'He must have work, Canty. He must have occupation.'

'So you and Carmilla are going to form a Fielding Gray Fan Club?'

'We are going to talk to him about his future books. I'm to pick up Carmilla in Cambridge the day after to-morrow, Saturday, and we shall go on to spend a night or two in the hotel at Broughton Staithe. Fielding is there and will be dining in the hotel.'

'Yes,' said Canteloupe. 'I remember that hotel. He dines there every night when he's at Broughton. I wonder his stomach hasn't disintegrated. You will not, Thea, even consider Fielding Gray for the role . . . of father. He's done enough damage already, from what I can see. Tully will never do as Sarum.'

'But Tully *is* Sarum. He will not just go away to suit you,' said Theodosia. God, she thought, how I loathe being with Canty when he gets on to this obsession. I can only endure it because I know that it will soon pass (for a time) and that I shall love being with him when he is himself again. 'Tully,' she continued, 'is as much your fault as Fielding's. Why did you insist? Why could you not let the thing take its natural course?'

'Because then it would simply have stopped. I want the thing to go on, Thea. Never mind about Tully just for now. Let us think of *your* child. *Not* to be by Fielding.'

'I couldn't bear to be touched by Fielding.' She did not add that she could not bear to be touched by any other man either, not even by Jeremy Morrison, whom she had loved so much. 'In any case,' she said, 'all that must wait. Until Carmilla and I have seen to Fielding. And for much longer. For what you are asking, Canty, you must allow me time.'

'Certainly. But time must have a stop. There now, my darling. Darling Thea. Smile your big, wide, lazy smile at me. You know, you surely know, how much I want this.'

'Yes, I know.'

'Let us say three months. I promise you I shall talk no more of this subject, or any aspect of it, providing you, for your part, promise to come and tell me . . . whom you will take as your lover . . . on or before 1 May. A very suitable date,' he said, 'and giving you much more than three months, nearly four.'

'Very well,' said Theodosia. 'But surely we could adopt? If enough money is spent, the birth could be fudged and the infant passed off as our own.'

'But it would not be our own. It would not be the child of our bodies.'

'Nor will it be . . . if I do what you ask.'

'*When* you do what I ask. But it will be the child of *your* body, Theodosia, and a fine body you have for the purpose. To that extent at least, it would be admissible as our heir.'

So what, she wanted to say: so bloody what? Do you really think that I don't know, or at least strongly suspect, the truth behind all this? Women, even ladies, love listening at doors, she longed to say: do you really think I haven't heard any of those conversations between you and your 'Secretary' Leonard about that child in Italy, those conversations which happen whenever (about once a month) you need reassurance that no one can or will actually prove anything, and Leonard earns his money by reassuring you? For that matter, she thought of saying, Carmilla too knows it all or most of it – she heard it straight from the mouth of Tom Llewyllyn. She told me when she was here the other day – not that I needed telling, but it was interesting to hear it from another angle. All this, and more, Thea yearned to tell Cante-loupe. But in the end she said none of it. It would do no good: it would only add one more complication to a situation already hideously complex. 'Why could you not let the thing take its natural course?' she had asked Canteloupe a few minutes earlier. There would have been none of this misery then, she thought, as she now repeated the question, again and again, in her head. But Cante-loupe had already supplied the answer, a very ample one: if he had let the thing take its natural course it would simply have stopped altogether, whereas he wanted it to go on. Of course he did, Theodosia thought. For then he would have some point in his life, he would have occupation: like Fielding Gray, like everybody else, he needed work, something to turn his hand to, lest his life be empty and himself as good as dead.

When Tessa arrived at Buttock's Hotel on Saturday afternoon, Rosie said:

'Well, I suppose it's nice to see you, even if it's not what it might have been.'

'Be friends, Rosie,' said Tessa. 'Even if things aren't what they were, let's make the best of it and enjoy ourselves as much as we can.'

'That's what I meant.'

'You had a very sour way of saying it.'

Rosie put a hand into her black hair, then started to reach, with the other hand, for the fair auburn wave over Tessa's forehead. Tessa sat quite still, neither aiding nor discouraging Rosie in this venture. Rosie hesitated a moment, then clasped both her hands together in her crutch, as if to keep them out of further mischief.

'Major Gray is allowed back here again,' said Rosie, changing the subject, 'even when you come. Something happened to stop your Aunt Maisie being suspicious.'

'What happened?'

'That's more than I know,' said Rosie, lying through her teeth, out of her respect for Tessa's respect for her aunt. 'All I know is that one evening, when they came to say good-night to me in my room, they were full of jolliness and jokes – the first time for many weeks that they hadn't just snapped and snarled at each other – and your Aunt Maisie said to Major Gray, "How nice it will be for Tessa to see you next weekend, it's been such a long time."'

'Is he here then? Major Gray?' said Tessa, in an oddly neutral way, Rosie thought, for someone who had always been so fond of him.

'Actually, no,' Rosie said. 'He had to go and see that Mr Tunne about something, in the Fens; then he went on to Jeremy Morrison's house in Norfolk. From there he rang up your Aunt Maisie to say that he would definitely *not* be going abroad with Jeremy and thought he had better try to start a new book instead. So he was going to his house in Broughton Staithe, which is where he prefers to do his work. Your aunt said, "Oh dear, what a pity, you'll miss Tessa, after all this time too," but Major Gray said he must keep out of London and get down to it. Are you sorry he's not here?'

'Oh, of course,' said Tessa; but her eyes were a long way away, thought Rosie; and when Tessa then started to smile, with great tenderness, Rosie knew that this was for somebody else, somebody alien to Buttock's and far away from it; not for her, Rosie Stern, who was here in the room, or even for Fielding Gray, who might very well have been.

'I've had an idea,' said Carmilla to Theodosia, as they drove towards Ely on their way from Cambridge to Broughton Staithe, 'about your little problem with Canteloupe. I assume he's still pestering?'

106

'Not exactly pestering. He's promised to say nothing more about it until the beginning of May – provided that I promise that some time not later than May Day I shall name the lucky father.'

'Quite a liberal allowance of time.'

'It'll run out fast enough.'

'Yes,' said Carmilla. 'Tell me with whom time gallops withal . . ." Do you remember,' she said as they sighted the roof of the cathedral, 'it seems only yesterday, Thea, but it was nearly three years ago – do you remember that afternoon we came here with Jeremy?' And he and I fingered each other off behind a screen in Bishop Alcocke's chantry, she reminded herself silently, before Thea joined us.

'I remember,' said Theodosia, whose memories of the occasion were less joyous. 'What is this idea of yours?'

'Well . . . that business I told you about when I came to Wiltshire the other day . . . that boy in the marshes near the Laguna Veneta, who has a claim to the marquessate.'

'The one supposed to be descended from the spy who was really the heir of the first marquess.'

'Right. I also told you, I think, that nobody could ever prove it without spending about a billion pounds and collating a lot of obscure and complicated documents. But for what it's worth, well, there it is.'

'For what it's worth, Carmilla darling, I already know about it – '

' – So you said. *Eavesdropping* – '

' – Though thank you for the tip. But where does any of that get us?'

'Couldn't it be your solution? Couldn't you tell Canteloupe straight out that if the real marquess is a boy in Italy, then that puts the kibosh on his whole endeavour –

because there's no point in rigging up an heir to a title which isn't even his?'

'No,' said Theodosia. 'He doesn't see it that way. We've never discussed it, because I'm not meant to know about that boy, but I just *know* that Canteloupe does not see the thing as you or I do. You see, Carmilla darling, Canteloupe is like an old trouper. Costume, greasepaint, trick lighting, transformation scenes – *theatrical illusion*, Carm – these things have become his life. All he cares about is that the show should go on, that his version of the Canteloupe Carnival should continue, regardless of effort or expense.'

'I think,' said Jakki Blessington, home for the weekend, to her sister Caroline, her mother Betty, and her father Ivan, 'that Marius Stern and Tessa Malcolm are being *spoiled*. There's an older boy, Milo Hedley – '

' – Ah, that name again,' said Caroline, remembering previous exegeses on this theme.

' – Milo Hedley,' repeated Jakki, and rattled her teeth like castanets, 'who flatters them with his attention – he's a School Monitor, you see – and there's also a smart alec beak who takes the classics and has a huge private income – he's in on it all somewhere – '

' – In on what?' said Betty with characteristic common sense. 'Are you suggesting something sexual?'

'No,' said Jakki, after some thought. 'Raisley Conyngham – that's the master – has a lot of charm which he turns on and off, but it doesn't at all suggest sex or seduction. As for Milo, he *is* rather sexy, but he gives me the impression that he doesn't care about it, at least not with Tessa or Marius, because there are far more interesting things he can be doing with them.'

'You seem to have studied up on this Milo all right,' said Caroline, giving her sister a jokey nudge.

'Of course I have. I want to find out what he's doing to Marius and Tessa.'

'And you conclude,' said her father, Colonel Ivan Blessington, 'that he is not taking them to bed?'

'I do.'

'Drugs?' said her mother.

'Absolutely not, I'd say,' said Jakki. 'You never saw four people who looked less as if they'd been doped. But they are all in cahoots. They look as if they've got some secret, or soon will have, which no one knows about except them and probably never will, but, boy oh boy, are they laughing their lights out behind everybody else's back.'

'It is entirely normal,' Ivan Blessington said, 'for younger pupils to fall under the influence of schoolmasters or older pupils. That is part of what education is about. Being influenced. If for good, good. If not, then the younger pupils will find out, in time, that they have been duped, and so will have had an early and useful lesson in the ways of a disagreeable world.'

'That's all very well,' said Jakki, 'but suppose they've been influenced for very, *very* bad? So bad, that it will turn out to be more than just a lesson in the ways of a disagreeable world, it'll turn out to be some horrible shame or desperation.'

'You are exaggerating,' said her mother comfortably. 'The Headmaster will be keeping an eye open, and would anticipate anything really harmful by dissolving the alliance. Right, Ivan?'

'Right,' Colonel Blessington said.

'The Headmaster,' said Jakki, 'has over six hundred boys and girls to keep an eye on and only two eyes.'

'He has others to help him.'

'Among them, Mr Conyngham. Mr Conyngham,' said Jakki, 'is rich and intensely respectable. He has been at the school many years, and has a marvellous record as a teacher. No one is ever going to suspect him of anything.'

'Then why,' said her mother, 'do you?'

'I just feel,' said Jakki helplessly, 'that in some odd and invisible way, Marius and Tessa are being made use of or betrayed. Or soon will be. I think they are the victims of obsession (their own and other people's) and I have made up my mind to warn them. I have arranged to travel back to school with Tessa to-morrow, and I can start on her in the train.'

'I shouldn't interfere, if I were you,' her father said. He hesitated a moment, then, 'Let me tell you a tale. A few years ago, when I was still working for the Corcyran Bank, I got wind of a very nasty piece of international mercantile intrigue. Now, it happened that at the time I was having a brief bout of religion – '

' – Male menopause,' said Betty cosily.

' – And although there was nothing actually criminal in the intrigue I had come across, it seemed to me to be immoral and dishonourable and above all un-Christian. And so I did something at the memory of which I have blushed, sweated and cringed with remorse ever since – '

' – You aren't blushing, sweating and cringing now,' said Caroline.

' – Time the healer,' her mother remarked.

' – I *peached*,' said Ivan. 'I knew someone who, I

thought, would resent the game which the Corcyran, among other banks, was playing . . . would resent it as much as I did and would see that an end was put to it.'

'And was it?' Jakki smiled eagerly. 'Was an end put to it?'

'The man to whom I took my information,' said Ivan, 'was a senior civil servant with whom I'd had frequent correspondence while I was Military Attaché in Washington. He heaved a very deep sigh, and explained politely that I was meddling with something which I did not and, given my mental outlook and limitations, never could understand. My interference would achieve nothing, he told me, except that on grounds of security certain highly inconvenient and expensive alterations would have to be made to certain current lines of planning (which would then, incidentally, become from my ingenuous point of view even nastier than before) in case I was imbecile enough to try to interfere any further. I was then removed from the Corcyran Bank – '

' – Pensioned off,' countered Betty.

' – At a rate that was a mockery and an insult. I was also given to understand that I had let down the side; imperilled the honour and prosperity of the nation; infuriated a lot of old chums who were in one way or another involved in this vital and intricate endeavour; and, for good measure, made of myself a cretinous, contemptible, self-righteous, po-faced, middle class, goody-goody prig. Ivan Blessington, the school sneak.'

'I wasn't going to sneak on anybody,' said Jakki in a small voice; 'I was only going to give a word of warning – '

'Worse, far worse,' her father said. 'Sneaking is merely delation: the telling of tales. Giving words of warning is *knowing better*, it is claiming moral superiority, an act of intolerable arrogance . . . particularly when you haven't the faintest idea, on your own showing, of what (if anything) is going on. So heed your old father, my darling Jakki – '

' – Who's giving words of warning now?' said Caroline gleefully.

'Don't be tiresome, Caroline,' said her mother.

' – Heed your poor old wounded and cast off father,' Ivan said, 'and learn from him, now, to mind your own moral business, and to leave Marius and Tessa and Milo Hedley and Mr Conyngham, and the whole bloody universe besides, to mind theirs.'

After dinner with Fielding on Saturday night in the L'Estrange Arms Hotel at Broughton, Theodosia and Carmilla felt like a walk.

'Otherwise that horrible food will congeal on my stomach and stay there for ever like a tombstone,' Carmilla said.

So all three stumped along the golf course to Fielding Gray's common little house, where Carmilla and Theodosia were given very long, but also very strong, whiskies and were invited (if not quite in so many words) to state their business in Broughton Staithe.

'We need your name on our list with a novel for next year,' Carmilla said.

'I wish you could have it, my dear. But I'm as dry as the Gobi. Written out.'

'Only because no one's been taking an interest. From now on Carm and I shall,' Theodosia said.

'The sexiest girl in the world cannot make an impotent man come,' said Fielding, who had had three large cognacs after dinner. 'Even the most intelligent readership, such as you two, my darlings, would provide, cannot rouse an extinct novelist to invention.'

After that it rather seemed as though the subject were closed. And so, to fill the silence:

'Who,' said Theodosia at last, 'is that beautiful man in the picture over the fireplace? And what on earth is he wearing?'

'That is my grandfather,' said Fielding, 'on my mother's side. He is wearing cross country running kit as worn in the mid-1890s. A very few years later, they allowed the drawers to end on, or even slightly above, the knees; but at that date they had to fit halfway down the calf. This portrait was done from a photograph taken on the day my grandfather broke the record in the East Anglian Cross Country Championship, otherwise known as the Grand Huntingdon Grind. In those days, the race was run over fifteen miles of fen, forest and wilderness, and finished on Huntingdon steeplechase course, of which those that survived had to make one complete round, somehow contriving to get themselves over all eight fences and the open water jump, before finishing at the post where they'd begun. Grandpa broke one arm falling,' said Fielding, his excitement and loyalty mounting, 'ripped open the palm of his hand on some brambles, sprained his ankle over the last fence, and still hobbled in to win by a nose from the reigning champion and cut ten seconds off the record. Fucking, bloody marvellous,' he shouted: 'I wish I could have been half the man he was.'

Both the girls raised their glasses to the picture and

drank a stout measure. Then Theodosia said, 'That portrait shows no signs of his injuries. I suppose the photo from which it was made was taken before the race?'

'After,' said Fielding, 'after. The photo showed everything – but when the picture was painted from it, Grandpa told the artist to leave his wounds out, in case he should later be asked about them and have to tell the full story. He was a modest man, you see. Not a gentleman. A grammar school boy who was apprenticed to the family baking firm in Cambridge. That was the bit my mother always left out, silly bitch. She was a real suburban snob – but she did love Grandpa and had wonderful tales to tell of him.'

'Now you tell them,' said Carmilla and Theodosia.

'His record for the Grand Huntingdon Grind stood for several years,' Fielding said, 'and was only broken while he was with the Yeomanry in South Africa. My mother always said he was "listed as a Gentleman Trooper", but in fact he was just a Yeoman like any of the rest of them, who'd saddled his own horse to follow the call. There's a photo of him somewhere, sitting on his grey with his sabre at the "carry", a plain Yeoman from his uniform and trappings if ever there was. But after he'd been in South Africa only a few months, a really grand thing happened. Grandpa was commissioned a Cornet "in the field",' said Fielding, 'like being made a knight in the old days – a proper knight at arms, not some greasy politician or alderman for his odious services rendered – and this was the way it came about . . .'

Having filled the girls' glasses, Fielding began the old story, heard so often from his mother: '. . . So when at last all the supplies were exhausted, my darling, and all the officers and non-commissioned officers of the squadron were mad or dead, your grandfather led the Forlorn

Hope from the stockade on the hill, out across the merciless veldt . . .'

Sitting in the Sunday night train from Waterloo to Farncombe, Jakki rememberd her father's story and refrained from offering Tessa warning or advice. Even if she discounted everything which Colonel Blessington had said, the fact remained that she was Tessa's junior, and at their school, to press advice on your senior (even in these days of equality and universal Christian names) simply was not the thing. After long cogitation, Jakki decided on a compromise; and at last, as the train left Guildford Station, she screwed up her courage to say:

'Lovely Tessa, why have you gone away from us? From Rosie and me? Why do you spend all your time with Milo Hedley and none of it with us?'

'I am with you now,' said Tessa, low and husky. 'I was with Rosie all last night – we still share a room – and all to-day.'

'Yet you are not with me and you were not with Rosie. In your heart you were, and are, with Milo Hedley and Raisley Conyngham.'

Tessa said nothing.

'Why do they fascinate you so much? Mummy asked whether they were giving you drugs, and I said no, never that.'

'Thank you,' said Tessa. 'Milo had an elder brother who was an addict – now dead from injecting bad heroin: it was mixed with Vim or baby powder or something.

People who take drugs are the most boring on earth, Milo says. Their only interest, their only subject of conversation, is their addiction and the methods of supplying it. They're so boring, Milo says, that they deserve to be dead and the sooner they die the better. He was glad when his brother died – quite apart from the fact that he will now inherit more money – because his brother was a disgrace to manhood – and to mankind. Here we are, I think.'

As they walked along the platform of Farncombe Station, Jakki reflected that Tessa, having deftly seized the opportunity offered for digression, had not made the slightest effort to answer the original question. Too late now to ask again. She could not say in front of the ticket collector, in front of the taxi-driver:

'Tessa, oh Tessa, why have you gone away?'

'Grandpa's third brother, Uncle Bill,' Fielding was saying to Carmilla and Theodosia on Sunday night in Broughton, 'was the black sheep of the family. The family baking firm had invented a new kind of meat pie, in honour of Grandpa's big race at Huntingdon, called the Brampton Grind, Brampton (once visited by Pepys) being one of the villages through which the contestants had to race – hopping on one foot (as I forgot to tell you last night) for the entire half mile between Brampton Church and Brampton Butts. Though "Brampton Grind" was not, one would have thought, a good name for sales (suggestive of everything which a pie should not be) the locals knew the history behind it and so bought a lot of it, being the men they were, and offered it around. Since it was made to a very special formula, it caught on all over Huntingdon-shire and Cambridgeshire, and later even further afield: in Hertfordshire to the south, in Suffolk, Norfolk and even Lincolnshire. A lot of money was made, and Uncle Bill's three plain daughters began to appear in furs. No harm in that, as they were fairly modest ones, but Bill overdid it in other ways. He got in with a fast-spending Newmarket set and in no time at all the duns were gathering. Whereupon he sold everything he had that was saleable for ready money – including his priciest asset of all, which was the secret formula for the filling of the Brampton Grind – and then he vanished to Australia.'

'What happened to the three plain daughters?' enquired Carmilla.

'They went too, as did Bill's wife, Aunt Effie. The girls were genteel and snooty and did not care for Oz at all, but Effie adored it. She'd always had a taste for the *rough* and had once openly avowed that her dream was to be raped by six navvies *coram populo*. How she got on about that no one ever established, but the legend was that anyone who came wooing the girls in Australia (attracted by the money which Bill was making by selling the Brampton Grind under another name in Melbourne), was first made to pleasure Aunt Effie in order to prove his sexual *bona fides*. On one occasion, the results were so spectacular that Effie expired of heart failure *in coitu secundo,* whereat Bill had a purple slab put up over her which proclaimed that her untimely death was a result of lifelong and unstinting labour in the Service of the God of Love.

'Of the three plain daughters, Clara, the eldest, married an Australian cricketer called Higgson, by whom she had a girl who was famous for her ugliness. The story is that one day when Higgson was battling at Adelaide for Australia versus England, he put up a dolly to Frank Woolley. 'You miss that catch, Frank,' called Higgson, 'and you can fuck my daughter.' Woolley laughed so much that he did miss the catch, but did not, so far as is known, claim his reward. The second of Uncle Bill's girls, Betsy Ann, became a Catholic convert and then a nun of exemplary peity . . . or so it was always thought, until one day the Mother Superior discovered her in the pantry with her skirts up and her arse parked on top of a milk churn. Her claim, that she was seeking to mortify the fleshly appetites of her sisters in the furtherance of their eternal salvation, was disallowed.'

'And there was one more,' said Theodosia. 'Did she stay with her father?'

'Wilhelmina May,' said Fielding. 'Yes, she stayed on with Uncle Bill as his housekeeper, until one day she took a drop too many of her home-made Marc de Melbourne and fell under a horse-drawn van in which the police went round arresting all whores that weren't on time with their protection money.'

'I shall be returning to London to-morrow, Monday,' said Lord Luffham of Whereham at dinner, to his son, Jeremy Morrison. 'Thank you for your hospitality.'

'This is your home, sir, whenever you wish it to be.'

'Then take a glass of wine with me, sir. Don't just sit there with your water like a one-man temperance meeting.'

'If you ask me, Father.'

'I do.'

The Chamberlain poured claret for them both.

'Now then,' said Lord Luffham: 'what exactly do you plan to do here? I've heard a great deal about your giving up a glittering but futile career in Cambridge or London, in order to come back to the land. Now you're back on it, what are you going to do with it that can't be done fifty times better by those who are already working it for you?'

'Honour my responsibilities to it.'

'What do you mean by that?'

'Understand it. Respond and relate to it. Respect its needs and harbour its powers of provision.'

'In practical terms,' said Jeremy's father, 'and as I have just remarked, all that is already being very well attended to by someone else. You yourself are woefully ignorant of the soil and everything to do with it, and if you're going to march round laying down the law to men who have spent their lives on it you will cause much offence. Even if you take yourself off to an agricultural college for a few years first, what you learn there will be worthless in the light of their long labour and experience. My question is, Jeremy: what function, of any import whatever, are you going to fulfil on the estate?'

'I am going to be Master of it.'

'In name, no doubt.'

'Master indeed. So first I must understand it. I know most of our people and have mixed with them since I was a boy. The trouble is that I have mixed with them only superficially, at festivals or cricket matches: I have played with them, Father, but not laboured with them. In order to understand them more deeply, and, even more important, in order to understand the soil on which they work, I shall lead the life of a farm labourer for as long as is necessary to bring me to proper consciousness of what the soil demands of those that work on it.'

'The drudgery will weary and bore you. The company will embarrass you and be embarrassed by you. You will be granted privilege and indulgence, whether you like it or not, and you will cause resentment by taking a poor man's bread.'

'I shall work for nothing, of course. No one shall be displaced,' said Jeremy, 'because of me.'

'If you do this work for nothing, if you do not do it from necessity, you will never really understand the nature of such work or of those that do it.'

'At least my old companions in Lancaster will have to take me seriously. They will be thinking and saying that I have deserted their world through idleness and pique; but if I demonstrate how hard and thoughtfully I am prepared to work in my own world, they will be put to shame.'

'They will simply say, "There is a young man who has inherited a very valuable estate and is now modishly trying to curry favour with his workmen." Listen boy: of course you are responsible to your *people*, and the more so as I myself have partly neglected them for many years because of my work in Parliament. So by all means care for your labourers, see to their welfare and give them justice. But don't go making a fool of yourself by playing at being a peasant. No good can come of your stepping out of your place.'

'I shall be showing Fielding Gray and the rest that I am a man of mettle and purpose, who despises and rejects all they have to offer.'

'Why are you so keen to reject them? You thought well enough of them once.'

'Because at bottom they are trivial,' said Jeremy.

'They seem to me . . . Tom Llewyllyn and Fielding Gray . . . to have devoted themselves very seriously to difficult and demanding occupations. What is trivial,' said Peter Morrison as was, a man who in his own estimation had done the same, 'about that?'

'Llewyllyn is an historian and an academic administrator: history, in the world as it is, is a useless luxury; and as for his administration, it is almost entirely done for him by his Secretary. Fielding Gray writes fiction,' said Jeremy, 'which is to say he invents lies. Hardly, my lord, a very serious form of endeavour.'

'What a howling prig I have for a son. I much preferred you when you were fooling with silly girls at Cambridge, spending my money – as it then was. A light-minded and light-fingered cad, but at least with a bit of sparkle and merriment about you.'

'Yes,' said Jeremy. 'They always say that Saul of Tarsus was a very jolly fellow in the days of the tavern and the garden. The trouble was, they say, that after he passed through Damascus and started calling himself Paul, he became boring, disagreeable and censorious. You will forgive me, sir, if I compare great things with small. My new course of life begins tomorrow – Monday. So I shall not see you again before you go, Father. Go well. Breakfast for me at six as from tomorrow,' he said to the Chamberlain; 'his lordship's, of course, at the usual time.'

He then rose and left the room though the pudding had yet to be served.

'Is he serious,' said Luffham, half to himself and half to the Chamberlain; 'or is this some very elaborate joke?'

'Let us put it like this, my lord,' said the Chamberlain. 'I know that Mister Jeremy has engaged himself to work under instruction at Pettifer's Hundred from tomorrow morning. I also know that he has telephoned to several leading newspapers in order to try to interest the editors of their feature pages or colour supplements in what he calls a "new form of social and spiritual enterprise on the land".'

'Have any of them bitten?'

'That's more than I can say, my lord. I can only hear what is said this end. But to judge from the tone of Mister Jeremy's voice, he did succeed in interesting a certain Mister Alfie Schroeder of the Billingsgate Press.'

'. . . And so when Grandpa got back from the Boer War,' Fielding was saying to Carmilla and Theodosia, 'he decided it was time to settle down. His wife, Gretel, was the daughter of a cooper from Saffron Walden, a woman of no particular interest except for her unlikely friendship with another woman, a certain Dolly Casters, who started out as an eleven year old housemaid in the cooper's house in Saffron Walden, and ended up as Mayoress of Cambridge. Soon after my grandmother Gretel had married Grandpa, she sent for Dolly saying that she had a good position in prospect for her. Indeed she managed to have her installed as a sales assistant in one of the leading draper's shops in Cambridge, the under-manager of which had been a beau of Gretel's when they were both children in Saffron Walden. Quite why Gretel should have taken such trouble over her father's housemaid, or exactly what was the bond between then, no one ever found out. What is known is that under my grandmother's tutelage, Dolly contrived to get herself knocked up, when she was still only fifteen and a half, by the draper in person (a distant cousin of Uncle Bill's wife, Effie) and blackmailed him into marriage. In the course of time, the draper became Mayor of Cambridge, while Auntie Doll (as she was known in my family by courtesy) was elevated accordingly. She always swore that she had made lavish provision in her will for my grandmother, as founder of her good fortune, but when the will was opened (after both the draper and Auntie Doll had deceased in a defective lift in a Railway Hotel in Staffordshire) it was found that my grandmother had been left precisely five pounds, 'as suitable recompense for her early services'. Granny took to bed and died of chagrin, while Grandpa died a year or so after, on the day of the 1939 Derby, having put up the entire four hundred quid which had been in Granny's Post Office account when she died (including Auntie Doll's fiver) at the very substantial ante-post odds available the previous autumn, on the winner, a horse called Blue Peter.

'Apart from my mother, the only other child of Grandpa's was Uncle Leslie, who became a tramp in 1950 and was last heard of – '

' – Getting too near to modern times,' said Carmilla as she and Theodosia rose. 'Stick to the dead, Fielding: they don't sue for libel. And now, if you'll excuse us, tomorrow is Monday and I have to give a tutorial at ten-thirty, which means an early start from the L'Estrange. We've very much enjoyed listening.'

'With material like that to hand,' said Theodosia, 'you won't need to invent much – now will you? A memoir, I think, not a novel. You might call it "Stranger than Fiction".'

'Too obvious,' said Carmilla. 'What about – yes, yes, it has to be – "The Grand Grinder"?'

When their taxi reached the School Arch at the end of the bridge, Tessa and Jakki paid it off, as regulations required. Since Jakki's *Domus Vestalis* was some way off and she was already (as a first year girl) several minutes late, she ran straight off towards it, leaving Tessa to proceed to *her Domus Vestalis* (where, being in her second year, she was not due for nearly half an hour) in the opposite direction.

On the way Tessa met Marius, who was with a gaggle of boys but somehow alone in the midst of it. He was obviously glad of the excuse to peel off and talk to Tessa.

'How silly they all are,' said Marius. 'We've been to the Sunday Film Club – which is another thing you miss by being only a weekly boarder – to see a revival of an old movie called *Kind Hearts and Coronets*. Very good and witty, I thought.'

'So did I, when I saw it in the holidays.'

'But not that lot I was with. They were saying just now that the plot was too "improbable". When I tried to explain that there is a convention, both for stage and screen, whereby that kind of "improbability" is permissible, they looked at me as if I were something rather distasteful, like an habitual liar or even a petty thief. 'It was untrue to life,' they said: 'a dishonest trick".'

'Rosie disapproved of it too, I remember.'

'I only hope she had some more intelligent reason. How was she over the weekend?'

'Reproachful.'

'I suppose she was. Thank God she's got this pash for Oenone. That may fix her up for a bit.'

'I hope so . . . Auntie Maisie was very cheerful and has forgiven Major Gray.'

'Interesting. Why?'

'Rosie didn't know. I expect she's just seen sense at last.'

'Was he there – Major Gray?'

'No. Working on a book in Norfolk. Or rather, trying to start a book. He's short of material, Auntie Maisie says.'

'He'll dredge up something. Like the man in that French story with the brain of gold. Every time his mistress wanted some money, he had to put his hand inside his scalp and scrape around for a nice yellow chunk.'

'But the point was, Marius, that in the end there wasn't any gold left. When he withdrew his hand, there were only a few specks of gold dust mixed with the blood in his fingernails.'

'Fielding's too old a pro to get caught like that. He probably took a lump out years ago and has kept it hidden ever since, in that horrid little house of his at Broughton.'

'I hope so,' said Tessa indifferently.

'You don't seem to care very much. I thought you were so fond of the old brute.'

'I was. I am. But it's the same with him as with Rosie . . . and Jakki. She was a real *pill* on the train this evening. Same as Rosie only more so. "Why have you gone away from us?" she said. What can one answer?'

'Nothing. I have the same sort of thing from Pally Palairet. Only he only *looks* it.'

'I suppose,' said Tessa in her small husky voice, compressing her two shoulders (as she tended to when in doubt or distress) so that she might feel, against the blade of one, the small lump which was on the blade of the other, 'I suppose that we've grown past them all. Jakki and Palairet are childish things, to be put away.'

She did not say, because she did not really think, that the reproachful Rosie also came into this category; for Rosie, though tiresome of late, was different from Jakki and Palairet, she suffered with some style, not like a neglected mongrel puppy: and even if this had not been so, Tessa would not have included her among 'childish things' for fear of hurting her brother.

'Rosie says,' said Marius, 'that one cannot put people away without destroying one's own soul. Although I think she exaggerates, I feel some truth in this. I feel, for example, that Jeremy, by deserting Major Gray, is at least belittling, besmirching himself. And yet . . . if, as you say, one grows past people, what is one to do? One cannot pretend that things are the same as they were before . . . no matter for how long they may formerly have been so. Indeed, the longer they have been so, the less easy it is to pretend they are the same when they start changing. And if one is caught out pretending, Tessa, one hurts people even more than by simply moving away from them.'

'Perhaps . . . if you have only loved someone *enough*, you *could* keep up a pretence that you still did.'

'What is the point? Why let people believe something that is false?'

'Because it may comfort them,' said Tessa: 'just as many Christians have been comforted, at the last, by a false belief in a life after death.'

'Once they are dead, they cannot know they have been tricked. But a live person will sooner or later see through any pretence . . . especially if it be a pretence of love. There is no answer to it, Tessa.'

'It seems not. It is bound to happen all the time, this "going away". Things must change: circumstances must shift: people must be hurt. Everything is in flux – which indeed brings some comfort, because if everything is in flux, so is the pain of being deserted and will itself be gone very soon, along with everything else.'

'Everything . . . is in flux? Who told you that?'

'Raisley Conyngham. It comes from a Greek philosopher called Heracleitos.'

'And yet one had heard,' said Marius, 'that some people sorrow to the end. Which do you believe, Teresa?'

'I think . . . that if one is to stay sane . . . one must believe Heracleitos and Raisley Conyngham.'

Fielding Gray sat at his desk in his common and horrid little house at Broughton and looked out across the golf course towards the sand dunes and the rotting gun emplacements. A sheet of white cloud drew itself over the sun and the snowflakes started skittering down on to the fairway, on to the rough just beyond his garden.

This is, at any rate, some sort of occupation, he thought, as he began to make notes of what he remembered of his mother's tales about his grandmother's relatives in Saffron Walden: Cousin Sue, who had opened the first fish and chip shop there; Auntie Jayne the suffragette; and Uncle Jeff the amateur rider, who had backed himself to win Ten Thousand (a hundred quid up at a hundred to one) and lost the race on an objection. His mother was at her best, telling these stories, he remembered: funny, animated, endowed with a happy turn of phrase which seemed to desert her completely once the tales were done – as indeed did all the fun and animation. Day to day, Mrs Gray had been an obstinate, narrow-minded, possessive and spiteful woman. Only when he had said, 'Mama, remind me about Auntie Lettice, the one who became fashion photographer for *The Stortford Mercury*' or something of the kind, did her eyes begin to glitter with jollity and not with malice, and her tongue to eschew the usual grizzling rebuke of his 'squandering', or low-bourgeois disapprobation of 'the silly ideas which he was getting at *that school*.' One must strike a balance, then: however shrill or dismal she usualy was, he thought, I must be grateful to her for providing matter and memories at this time of need. Uncle Goddart, who collected neck-ties and finally achieved twenty thousand different specimens (from one of which he hung himself when his wife ran away with a Ticket Inspector of the LNER) was, on the whole, fair exchange for many hours of nagging about those 'clever-clever friends you seem to have collected' – wait for it – 'at *that school*'.

The one friend of his whom she had always liked and who, for whatever reason, purported to like her, had been Peter Morrison, who sometimes came over from Luffham during the holidays. She liked, she said, Peter's 'solid common sense'. She knew, she said, that Peter, unlike most of Fielding's 'mucky and deceitful' companions, was 'on the level'. It was not without irony, Fielding now thought, that Peter's son, Jeremy, had behaved to him, Fielding, in such a particularly 'mucky and deceitful' way, quite definitely not 'on the square'. What, he thought, would Mama have made of Jeremy? Words and phrases like 'showy', 'pleased with Number One', 'devious' (no, 'devious' was too sophisticated for Mama), 'mouth crammed with lies', and 'clever enough to ambush himself', hovered in Fielding's mind. As usual, Mama would have been right and as usual, she would have missed the important points: the mountains of the moon smiling in the great round face; the huge, slow, lovable limbs; the lazy ironic asides; the easy, intelligent, soothing company. 'Cuckoo,' he thought, remembering the scholar Alcuin's elegy for his favourite pupil, who had simply gone away one mid-night and was seen by Alcuin no more, 'where art thou, cuckoo? Wilt not come again?' But did they have cuckoos, thought Fielding, where Alcuin was (Narbonne, was it, or even right down in Spain)? One cuckoo they had anyhow, one cuckoo whom they all loved and who went away one mid-night, leaving neither explanation nor forwarding address, pursued only by a futile lament:

'The old man Alcuin thinks long for thee.'

'A scholar?' said Raisley Conyngham, passing the port to Milo Hedley; 'Marius Stern a scholar?'

'Since you teach him individually, sir, I wondered how you assessed him in that line. One would wish to know . . . everything possible . . . about him.'

'Quite right. Well, in the real sense, Marius could never make a scholar. He is too restless; he must be cut out for a more active role in affairs. But in the sense of collecting a scholarship to Oxford or Cambridge, he may very well become one. He made a very shrewd effort, the other day, at turning the beginning of the *Morte d'Arthur* into

Greek hexameters. 'A broken chancel with a broken cross' – not easy to find a Greek equivalent. He used the word "τέμενος" or precinct, an inner precinct it often implies, and pictured the statue of the god as broken and mouldering with neglect:

αὐτίκα καί τέμενος πληγὲν πληγέν τε πρόσηλθον

εἶδος ἀποθνησκόν τ᾽ ἀπολειπομενοῖο θεοῖο.

'Forthwith they came to a ruined shrine and to the ruined and wasting image of the deserted god.' Too many "τέ"s hanging about the place, but *not* bad for a boy of fifteen or whatever.'

'I take it, sir, that for Marius to spend a few years at one of the better colleges would suit your purpose . . . whatever that may be.'

'Yes, it would, dear boy. Let's go and sit by the fire. Bring your port. There'll be coffee presently. What time do you have to get back to your House?'

'Any time, sir. I have the key.'

'You won't be wanted at Adsum? Or Prayers?'

'They no longer happen in our House, sir. We have progressed to a system of trust. No Evening Adsum, no Prayers other than private ones, no supervision of the younger boys' baths and ablutions, no formal Lights Out.'

'I strongly disapprove,' said Conyngham.

'So do I, sir. The older boys stay out in pubs, spending money their parents cannot afford. The younger ones stink, and chatter all night, and by day are as sullen as convicts.'

'That is what freedom does for boys of a certain age.'

'Agreed, sir, most heartily. They prefer – whether they know it or not – to obey. Perhaps we all do.'

'Well . . . at least I shall not be deprived of your company, Milo. A good thing, as what I have to say will not brook interruption. Now then. Where to begin? Ah, yes. Did I not tell you, a few days ago, that you should start reading Proust, as a remarkable study of a diseased mentality? The Foie Gras of Fiction, I think I said,' enunciated Raisley Conyngham primly, preening a little.

'You did, sir.'

'Well, I'm going to countermand the order. Don't read Proust yet. For one thing, there's a new and much better translation, by my old acquaintance Terry Kilmartin, due to be published in less than a year; and for another thing, I want you to read Balzac instead. Cruder, but in the end far more fascinating. Balzac is less concerned with mental disease (though there's a certain amount of it) than with mental deviance, deliberate mental deviance, often allied with great mental subtlety and both mental *and* physical endurance. Take the character of the arch-crook, Vautrin, who figures in several of Balzac's most important novels. Vautrin is a homosexual, and to that extent could be thought of, by some at least, as mentally diseased; but Balzac doesn't linger on that. Vautrin may or may not go to bed and commit "unnatural" acts with his young men – that is a matter of indifference. What Balzac concentrates on is how Vautrin *masters* his catamites (if such they be) and then takes total control of their lives and careers. These are so colourful, vigorous and complicated, that they would leave very little time for bedding with Vautrin – one good reason for supposing they probably didn't. By the time they'd seduced all the mistresses whom Vautrin prescribed – and through them conquered society up to the very throne; or by the time, on the other hand, that they'd explored the criminal hells to which he sent some of them to sweat and prosper; or by the time, yet again, that they'd struggled and triumphed in the professions to which he apprenticed not a few – they would not have had an ounce of energy left in them. Certainly not enough

131

for pleasuring the ugly old Vautrin who, to do him justice, never seems to force himself on any of them. He just picks them out of ditches and pilots them through the perils and intricacies of the World's Game until they finish up as the Champion Players.'

'He must have had a good eye for form, sir, to back so many winners.'

'Oh, he did. Even if you were up to your chin in a sewer, if you were winning material Vautrin knew at a glance. He hoicked you out and wiped you off and set you on the road up to social grandeur, or down to criminal empire, or simply across to professional dominance – in any case at all, to SUCCESS. Oh yes, he knew how to pick 'em, Vautrin did. I only hope our choices turn out half as well.'

'What have you in mind for them, sir? Up, down, or across?'

'Something rather different from any of those,' said Raisley Conyngham.

There was a knock on the door: a black-robed beldam entered, hunched over a service of coffee on a silver tray; she eyed Conyngham with split-second devotion, put the tray on a low table in front of him, and left.

'The last proper landlady in the world, I wouldn't wonder,' Raisley Conyngham said.

'What shall you when she ceases, sir?'

'Move into a hotel . . . no, Milo. I do not plan on moving Marius and Teresa either up, down or across. Round and round, perhaps; round and round, just under the surface. I want to make of them . . . perfect and unsuspected agents of subversion – unsuspected even by themselves, you understand?'

'Not very clearly, sir.'

'The nearest comparison I can muster is Raffles, the

gentleman cracksman . . . a thoroughly trivial and mis-
leading comparison, if only because Raffles obviously did
know what he was up to, whereas Marius and Teresa will
not. They will be fashioned so as to be totally acceptable
in almost any circle – just like Raffles, only with a far
wider range than he had. Theirs will comprehend not only
society (what's left of it) but also government depart-
ments, colleges of science, art and learning, industrial and
commercial federations, and so on and so forth. Now they
will, like Raffles, be well liked and respectable. Not just
apparently respectable, but, unlike Raffles, genuinely so.
When, as a result of these and other qualities, such as
personal beauty, intellectual ability, agreeable and co-
operative characters – when, I say, they are welcomed in
the various households or institutions for which they are
destined, they will *not* steal my lady's diamonds, as Raffles
would; nor will they purloin or memorize or photograph
the secret documents; nor will they drug, torture, blackmail or eliminate the Field Marshal or the Principal
Secretary; they will do none of these things, Milo, they
will simply and silently and effortlessly and unconsciously
subvert. Despite, or rather because of, their absolute
respectability, their good will, their innocence and their
outstanding abilities, they will act as the unsuspected
catalysts – unsuspected even, I repeat, by themselves – of
decay, disruption and disrepute, ultimately of total
dissolution.'

'An interesting notion, sir,' said Milo; 'but to whose
good, or ill, and for what purpose?'

'To the good, i.e. the enjoyment, of connoisseurs of
human vanity – '

' – You and me, sir? – '

' – To the ill, i.e. the frustration and fury, of self-
important jacks in office all round us. And as for the

purpose, if you wish one, the delight, dear to amateurs in every field, of proving that the thing can be done.'

'So . . . whereas Balzac's Vautrin was training winners of the World's Game, you, sir, propose to introduce . . . a new and secret element into the Game . . . which will eventually render it meaningless.'

'No. Just very much more complex and entertaining to watch. I am just putting in some Jokers.'

'I should have thought, sir, that God had already inserted enough of those.'

'Well, here are some of a new kind, albeit man-made. It will be interesting to see how soon the dedicated players spot them and what they decide to do about them. Black or white? Or with cream?'

'Black with sugar, if you will, sir. And what we are now planning for Easter is an elementary and preliminary exercise in the new subversion?'

'A trial manoeuvre, amusing in itself and from which much may be learnt.'

'And if the thing explodes in our faces?'

'There are too many safety devices, Milo. The key word in this whole conception is respectability – mine and yours as well as Marius's and Teresa's.'

'Safety devices, even of the most respectable manufacture, have been known to miscarry, sir.'

'If anything should go wrong, Milo, then it will seem, at the very worst, as if there has been an unlikely accident or a foolish misunderstanding. Nothing culpable – or if there should be any blame to be assigned, it will be such as to be easily assignable to God. As you aptly remarked just now, my dear Milo, most of the Jokers in the pack are indeed of his insertion.'

'There,' said Greco Barraclough: 'Paolo Filavoni, orphaned son and only issue of Giuseppe and Susanna Filavoni: taken into care, on his parents' death in the flood of sixty-six, by his mother's spinster sister, Anna Tomasino. Direct and last descendant of a line, clearly registered here all the way down, which started with Umberto and Caro fitzAvon (later, during her widow-hood, officially renamed Cara Filavoni) in 1797. That, I think is what Ptolemaeos Tunne wished you to establish.'

'That you, *kyrie*,' Nicos said.

Prompted by long affection and habit, and knowing that Nicos was too inept, in clerical matters, to see his way through even the simplest problem in that line, Greco Barraclough had accompanied Nicos on his expedition to Samuele in the marshes and was now checking the Church Register in the manner required of Nicos by Ptolemaeos Tunne. For his part, Nicos, also prompted by long affection and habit, accepted the Greco's attendance without objection, was grateful to him for deciphering the register, and was even apt, from time to time, to revert to former customs of address and obedience.

'Thank you, *kyrie*,' he now repeated.

When Nicos had reported at Heathrow for his flight to Venice, he had seen the *kyrios* ahead of him in the queue at the flight desk and had realized, more or less, what was happening. 'Hullo,' the *kyrios* had said: 'I hope you don't mind, but I thought I might come along too. For com-

135

pany, you know; and I think that I might be useful.' As indeed he had been, reflected Nicos now.

They loitered out of the church and into a small meadow. In the distance were some mean little houses of red brick ('bungalows', they would have been called in England, thought Nicos idly), then a small ridge, probably artificial in formation. Along the ridge was a row of dejected poplars, and above and beyond the tops of these the elegant eighteenth-century balustrade of one end of a flat roof.

'The villa which Samuele built,' said Barraclough, pointing. 'What's your next task?'

'To go and look at Paolo,' said Nicos; 'to see what kind of man he is and how he is living.'

'Very well. A few enquiries should find him out, him and his Aunt Anna Tomasino. We shall ask in one of these beastly little houses.'

As they walked across the slimy meadow, Barraclough went on:

'Have you any idea what all this is about?'

'Not really,' said Nicos. 'I do what I am told. It makes a change from studies for which I am not competent and from being your daily manservant. Not that you were ever unkind,' he said, 'just restricting. I was getting too old to be restricted. Yet for all that,' he said, 'I am very pleased that you have now come with me as my friend.'

He placed his hand lightly in the crook of Barraclough's arm.

Dear, bone-headed Nicos, thought the Greco: too unimaginative to take any interest; too loyal to question any orders; too thick to smell anything peculiar, and even if he did, too amiable and honest to wonder if there are any extras in it for him; just like a Boy Scout, sent on a simple mission and rather enjoying the ride.

A man with a scrawny body and a large imperial Roman

head (top heavy, thought the Greco, like a foetus) was walking from the red houses towards them. As he walked, he picked with the fingernails of one hand at the cuticles of the nails on the other.

'Can I help you?' he said in English.

'Yes,' said the Greco. 'We are looking for the *casa* of Anna Tomasino, who we believe to have care of her orphaned nephew, Paolo Filavoni.'

'And what do you want with them?'

'My old friend, Sir Thomas Llewyllyn,' said the Greco, 'Provost of Lancaster College, Cambridge, encountered Paolo and his aunt some years ago while he was here doing some historical and sociological research. Knowing that I was to be in this area, he asked me to visit the good lady and convey his respectful compliments, and also to report on the development of Paolo, of whom he has affectionate memories.'

Dear *kyrios*, thought Nicos, dear Greco, what would I have done without you?

'He does, does he?' said the scrawny man. 'I wonder whether he has affectionate memories of me? My name is Holbrook, Jude Holbrook.'

'It has been mentioned once or twice,' the Greco said. 'You live here with the lady your mother, I think?'

'Dead,' said Holbrook.

'I'm sorry to hear it.'

'I can't think why you should be. She wasn't your mother. I'll take you to Paolo. I shall be interested to hear what you make of him . . . Mister . . . Mister . . .?'

'Barraclough.'

'Ivan Barraclough? Author of *Maniot Customs* and *The Tombs of Areopolis*?'

'The same,' said the Greco, trying not to simper.

'My mother admired your work. She had it sent out by

137

the London Library. Remarkable institution – somehow it managed to despatch its parcels in such a way that they had immunity even from the malice of the Italian Post. The dear old London Library: I don't know what my mother would have done without it all these years.'

'Do they still send parcels for you, Mr Holbrook?'

'No. I am not a reading man.'

Holbrook's tone discouraged further enquiry into his pastimes. Without another word, he pushed in front of them and led them past several of the red brick houses, until they came to one which stood slightly apart, near a small, black pool. He knocked on the door of this, and was presently confronted by a large and slovenly woman with long, grey, greasy hair, who greeted Holbrook with respectful reluctance. Holbrook asked a brief question; the woman replied in some grotesque vernacular.

'He is, as usual, working in the old woman's garden,' said Holbrook. 'My mother took an interest in him and presented several sets of suitably educational toys, stating her hope that he might be allowed some relief from his labour to play with them. The notion was not approved by his Aunt Tomasino, who purported to think that the toys were some kind of witchcraft. They all disappeared without trace – into that pool, I imagine.'

Holbrook, disregarding the woman, led them across what seemed to be the only room in the house to a window which overlooked a sparse allotment.

'Sometimes he exhibits himself to strangers,' remarked Holbrook; 'I don't suppose you'd mind,' he said, looking obliquely at the Greco: 'it's his form of greeting.'

A very burly figure was bent over a shallow trench, preparing it (thought Nicos) for God knew what.

'Paolo,' called Holbrook, rapping on but not opening the window.

The figure straightened up. The face was handsome but jowly: the second imperial head this morning, the Greco thought; Holbrook's Caracalla and now this youth's Commodus. And there is someone else, thought the Greco, of whom he reminds me.

Paolo made a rude but amicable gesture at Holbrook with four filthy fingers spread above a filthy thumb, then returned to his task.

'He knows me quite well,' said Holbrook with evident affection: 'that is probably why he has not exposed himself after all. I am too familiar to disturb him. My mother used to say that he resembled a portrait she once saw in the National Portrait Gallery – some eighteenth-century nobleman who was a big wheel at Court and a well known patron in his day. She sent to the London Library for some book or other, and there it all was . . . with a reproduction of the portrait for good measure. Then,' said Holbrook, 'I remembered that Tom Llewyllyn and others had been nosing round here some time before . . . and began to wonder. You see, the man of whom Paolo reminded my mother, Lord High This, That and 'Tother, Marshal of Somerset, Commodore of the Avon (or something of the kind), President of half a dozen learned institutions, including the Philhellenic,' he said to the Greco, 'which might appeal to you – this man was a certain Earl of Muscateer, later promoted to Marquis Canteloupe.'

So that must be where I've seen Paolo's likeness before, thought the Greco: either in the National Portrait Gallery, or, more likely, in the chambers of the Philhellenic Society in London. 'At first,' Holbrook was saying, 'I thought this resemblance must be just a coincidence. Then I remembered Tom's visit again . . . and began to wonder once more. But shortly afterwards the book fell overdue and was returned to London, and a little later my mother fell ill and died, and I myself had a prolonged and horrible bout of a heart complaint that has bothered me on and off for many years . . . and so I lost interest. But it could be, it just could be, that your appearance might arouse it again. Perhaps *I* should start examining the ledgers in the church, which Tom Llewyllyn was so persistent about? And perhaps I should join the London Library and ask them to send out that book my mother had? It would make something to do. What do you think . . . Barraclough?'

'I think . . . that those ledgers in the church will make very dull and difficult reading . . . Holbrook . . . for someone who is not a reading man.'

'And *you*,' said Holbrook to Nicos: '*you* haven't said much yet. What is your concern with all this?'

'I am just here . . . for company,' said Nicos, effortlessly reversing (as indeed the event had reversed) the original roles of himself and the *kyrios*.

'So one would suppose,' sneered Holbrook, who much resented the quiet yet evident affection between Nicos and the Greco, the young man's hand in the crook of his elder's elbow.

'I think,' said the Greco, 'that we have seen all we came to see, Nico *mou*. Paolo seems quite contented.'

'He should be,' said Holbrook with an air of possession. 'My mother left an annuity to help feed him – and I always check with the lawyers to make sure it's promptly paid.'

'Well nourished he certainly is,' said Nicos, the first comment he had offered. 'How do you attend . . . to his other needs?'

'I suppose nature takes care of those,' said Holbrook with an old-fashioned schoolmasterly air, as if the subject were not one which decent fellows would willingly discuss. He looked contemptuously at Nicos and then, with a blend of speculation and concern, at Paolo in the allotment. Suddenly his look became prurient. 'Perhaps his aunt interests herself in her growing nephew,' he said. Prurience gave way to jealousy and spite. 'Why do you ask?' he said to Nicos. 'It's none of your business. But perhaps you wish it were. Want to take a hand yourself, do you?'

Nicos took his hand from the Greco's elbow and moved towards Holbrook.

'Nico,' quackered Barraclough in a hoarse, penetrating voice which he had used, when Nicos was still his page boy, to call him to heel.

Nicos came to heel.

'May I take your regards to Provost Llewyllyn?' said the Greco to Holbrook.

'Tell him . . . that I am most grateful to him for suggesting . . . first by his own visit and now by sending an emissary . . . so significant a line in sociological and historical research.'

When Maisie Malcolm received a letter from Raisley Conyngham in which he asked her permission to entertain her niece, Teresa, for the Easter holidays, at his house, Ullacote, near Timberscombe in Somerset, she was at first slightly reluctant to part with Tessa for the entire month of the holidays (which the invitation evidently comprised) and then slightly relieved to think that during that month Tessa would certainly see nothing of Fielding Gray. For although Fielding had been officially found not guilty of carnal intent towards Tessa, doubts still lingered in Maisie's mind lest one or the other or both of them might get 'carried away' or 'over-excited' one rainy afternoon, and she preferred to keep them apart except for short periods during which they could be closely supervised. What was on offer in Mr Conyngham's letter was country walks on Mr Conyngham's estate, tennis on Mr Conyngham's hard tennis court, swimming in Mr Conyngham's heated swimming-pool, much reading of improving works of literature ('In some sort,' Mr Conyngham had written, 'this will resemble an old-fashioned "reading party", which sounds pukka enough, thought Maisie, though why people should go to a party to read was more than she could see), and the company of Teresa's friend and Mr Conyngham's very promising pupil: Marius Stern. Well . . . all right . . . so long as they don't get too *fond* . . . thought Maisie; it does seem, when all is said, that after that wretched business two and a half years ago they *have* settled down just to be sensible and friendly; and in any case, I can't watch over them every hour of every day, leave alone when they're at school, I've just got to hope for the best, so I may as well hope for the best at this 'Ullacote' as well.

'He says there'll be horses too,' she said to Tessa at the weekend: 'racehorses which he trains on the moors.'

'Marius will like that,' said Tessa: 'I can't stand them, Auntie, as you well know.'

'Will they put you off? You don't have to go if you don't want.'

'Oh, I want, Auntie. I want. I shall miss you, miss you, miss you, darling Auntie, but I've always wanted to go to the country – the proper country – for a good long stay, and Mr Conyngham is such a super beak – '

' – Rich too by the sound of it – '

' – And it's always nice being with Marius – '

(– Nice? thought Maisie: well, all right, as harmless a word as any she knew –)

' – And then there'll be Milo Hedley.'

'Milo Hedley? Mr Conyngham doesn't mention him.'

'One of the senior boys, a School Monitor and School Fencing Pink. He teaches me the sabre, and I expect Mr Conyngham will put up a net so that we can all practise.'

'Fencing?'

'*Cricket*, Auntie. There are girls' Elevens as well as boys' at school, and I might get into the Girls' Under Sixteen next summer. I mean to try like anything,' said Tessa, meaning it.

'Well, God bless your heart then,' said Maisie, wanting both to cheer and to cry at the same time and half choking over the combination, 'and off you go to Somerset this Easter, as sure as God Almighty put salt in the Seven Seas.'

'Thanks be to God,' said Isobel Stern to Jo-Jo Guiscard as they walked up the hill to the *alimentation* in Saint-Bertrand-de-Comminges, 'that Marius is happily fixed up for the Easter holidays. Some master at his school has invited him to go to his house in Somerset where there are all sorts of lovely toys like swimming-pools and racehorses.'

'Who is this man?' said Jo-Jo. 'Rather rich for a dominee?'

'Name of Conyngham. Descended from that woman of George the Fourth's, I suppose.'

'*Raisley* Conyngham?'

'Right,' said Isobel. 'How clever of you.'

'Ptolemaeos used to talk about him. In the days when Uncle Ptoly still used to go racing, this Raisley Conyngham had an astonishing run of luck as an owner. Some three or four years ago . . .'

'An *honest* owner, I hope? According to Marius's Housemaster, who has written to me at Mr Conyngham's request, Mr Conyngham is entirely respectable . . . in every way fitted to have charge of Marius.'

'If Marius isn't coming for Easter,' said Jo-Jo, 'there'll be room for all of us. Not like at Christmas. Boys of that age take up so much space, somehow, but if it's only Rosie, she can be tucked in anywhere.'

'She can sleep on the camp-bed, next to Oenone,' said Isobel: 'she worships that child. She's been ditched by her friend, Tessa Malcolm, and Oenone was just the thing to fill the bill. A little girl of Oenone's age won't, you see, be easily able to escape her.'

'We'd better not let him see us,' said Jakki Blessington to Palairet.

Both had arrived independently to watch Marius play Eton Fives against Eton for the first of the School Under Sixteen Pairs.

'He'll hate it if he sees us hanging about,' Jakki said.

'But how are we to watch if we've got to hide?'

'Follow me,' said Jakki. She led the way up some wooden steps which had been built into a scrubby slope opposite the rear ends of the Junior Fives Courts. When they were about halfway up:

'Into the bushes,' Jakki said.

And there they were, cosily seated in a tiny hollow, quite invisible but with a perfect view of the action, in the space between the roots of two shrubs. They watched Marius arrive with the other players and then, a little later, Raisley Conyngham arrive with Milo in attendance just behind him, and Tessa behind both of them: the Lord of the Manor of Ullacote, thought Jakki, with his senior esquire and one of his pages.

'Marius and Tessa,' she said to Palairet, 'are going to stay with Raisley Conyngham in the holidays. In his country house. It's called "Ullacote".'

'Stupid name. Who told you?'

'Mr Conyngham wrote to Mrs Malcolm who told my mother who told my father who told me . . . last weekend. I'd already told my father and mother, you see, that I don't trust Mr Conyngham. My mother thinks I'm talking rubbish. My father is more sympathetic, but says that if one gets up a fuss, one only makes a fool of oneself and embarrasses other people. He's quite right, of course. Anyway, as he said last weekend, I shall be having a much nicer time than Marius and Tessa, because now he's earning more money – working for Salinger, Stern & Detterling – he can afford to take us all on a driving holiday to Greece. Mummy and me and Caroline. That's my sister. You haven't met her.'

'No,' said Palairet, 'but Marius used to talk about her.'

'Oh,' said Jakki, 'did he now? And what did he say?'

'Nothing really. He used to talk of both of you as if you were the same person. "Jakki and Caroline Blessington wear proper trousers, like boys," I remember he said once, "trousers which come right down to the heel and the instep – not those damn silly things which flap about showing knobbly ankles."'

'Anything else?' said Jakki, looking with pleasure at her proper boys' trousers (complete with fly) and wishing that Marius had remembered them as hers, and not her sister's as well.

'Nothing much. "Jakki and Caroline said last hols that their father can't afford riding lessons like ours." That,' said Palairet dismally, 'was when we used to go riding together at Oudenarde House.'

'Pretty stuck up of him to mention it.'

'No. He was just sorry for you.'

'Oh. Which one of us said . . . what you said he said we said?'

'He didn't appear to distinguish.'

'Well, at least Daddy can now afford to take us to Greece in a car this Easter,' said Jakki. And then, making a stratagem of necessity, 'So I shall just ignore this whole business of their going to Mr Conyngham's, as there is nothing I can do about it. I shall make my mind a blank (as my mother would say), and see what has happened by the time I get back.'

'But you don't like it, do you?' Palairet said.

'Marius's match is starting. He's the first to throw the ball up . . . I must say,' said Jakki after a little while, 'these Eton boys play very snootily. They're so dainty and blasé they can hardly be bothered to hit the ball.'

'You don't like it, do you?' Palairet insisted. 'Tessa and Marius going off with Conyngham? Anyhow, where are they going?'

'I told you: Mr Conyngham's house: Ullacote.'

'But where is it?'

'Near a place called Timberscombe, which is near a place called Dunster, which is near a place called Minehead. In Somerset.'

'I shall be near there. I spend part of each holidays with my aunt in Burnham-on-Sea. Only twenty-five miles or so from Minehead. I could take a bus to Minehead and call, couldn't I?'

'How would you get from Minehead to Timberscombe? There's probably one bus a month. And anyway, you'd have to take a taxi, which you couldn't afford, out to this Ullacote place . . . Zowiiieee, did you see Marius smash that one off the ledge? . . . and in any case, Pally, what on earth would you say when you got there?'

Another person who was playing Eton Fives that afternoon was Theodosia Canteloupe, but she was only playing by herself, 'knocking up' in the court at the end of the Great Court. She could now keep two balls in play without much difficulty and was experimenting with three. This was demanding work, with a fascination of its own, but, oh, she thought disloyally, if only Canty and Leonard weren't so decrepit we could find a fourth and have a game. A proper game, she thought, as she lobbed one ball off the wall to the back of the court, retrieved the second off an easy ricochet from the top of the buttress and sent it back to join the first, scooped the third up from the bottom of its bounce on the step, sent it high up to give her time, high up just under the roof, and lumbered to the back of the court, too late to catch all three of the balls there but in time to return two of them. A proper game, she thought, a match, what am I doing here now but a sort of juggling act – enough. She killed the two balls still in play, gathered up all three, and turned to go.

'Brava, brava,' said Canteloupe and Leonard, who had been standing near the back of the court and watching her (though she had not noticed them) for nearly ten minutes.

She started to put on her Cambridge Badminton sweater. The weeks are going by, she thought: Canty has kept his promise and will continue to keep it, but he will also expect me to keep mine. He will remain silent: I must go, presently, and rut. As her face came through the neck of her sweater, she saw a little gleam in both men's eyes: a gleam of eagerness in Canteloupe's, eagerness for birth and posterity; and in Leonard Percival's, a gleam of near dead but still inquisitive prurience, all that was left to him of lust.

'So,' said Raisley Conyngham to Tessa Malcolm, as he beckoned her to him from her modest place at the rear of his train, 'our friend Marius has just won a great victory.'

'But unfortunately, sir, his pair was the only one of ours that did win.'

'I doubt if that will worry him much . . . your aunt, you will be happy to hear, is delighted that you will be coming to me for Easter. I have arranged with her to send anything you may need from Buttock's Hotel directly down to Ullacote. You and Marius will therefore be able to accompany Milo and myself straight there on the first day of the holidays, and will not have the inconvenience of going first to London.'

'But . . . won't Auntie Maisie want to see me – and Marius – if only for an hour or so . . . before we go to Somerset?'

'Why? it would only upset you all, Teresa – so short a meeting and so swift a parting.'

'I expect you're right, sir.'

'I detect reservation in your tone. Do not, Teresa, presume too far upon your privileges as one of the weaker sex. A little more manliness, if you please. Now, while we are all at Ullacote we are going to read *Twelfth Night, or What You Will*. We shall all four of us have to take several parts, of course, but your main part will be that of Viola, the girl who has to dress and make her fortune as a boy. Her example should help to toughen you to masculine standards.'

'Except, sir, that Viola falls in love with a man. And marries him.'

'But suppose, just suppose, Teresa, that circumstances had compelled her to remain much longer, for the rest of her life perhaps, in a male role and costume. What of her Duke Orlando then? That is the possibility that I want you to bear in mind during the very careful study of the play which you will make before we all leave for Ullacote.'

Since Fielding Gray had business and pleasure in London, he returned from Broughton Staithe to Buttock's Hotel, where Maisie now allowed him to live and work, even when Tessa was there for the weekend. Since the hotel was half Fielding's in any case, she would always have had great difficulty in keeping him out of it, had he cared to be obstinate. It was only because he did not care to be obstinate (anything rather than a row) that she had managed to exile him for so long in the past. But however all that might be, the old rule had now been resumed (though Maisie remained anxious that Fielding and Tessa should not both be there together for too long), and Fielding was once more established in his bed-sitting room, where he was grinding painfully away at *The Grand Grinder*.

For truth to tell, though the idea had seemed quite a good one when Carmilla and Theodosia had hit on it down at Broughton, the memoir was turning out to be very sticky going. Although there were several entertaining episodes, the people concerned were of little abiding interest: *mutatis mutandis*, it was rather, thought Fielding, like Boccaccio – the racy adventures of cardboard cutouts. This meant that the interest of the thing depended entirely on action, not at all on character; and that said, there simply was not enough action to keep it going. Unlike Boccaccio, who numbered his tales in hundreds, Fielding reckoned his in tens; and many of these (such as Aunt Flo's spectacular death by water when the cistern turned rogue in the Ladies' Lavatory on Market Day at Brampton) were decidedly brief.

There was only one thing for it, thought Fielding, as he surveyed his completed notes on the third morning after his arrival at Buttock's: I shall have to make up a lot of it myself. But of course this was just what he did not wish to do. He had only taken up the idea of a memoir because his own invention was wheezing; and even if he could supply enough additional and spurious incidents in the *genre* to swell out a passable volume, it was fair neither to his family nor to his public to fake what purported, in its humble kind, to be historical fact. Crossly reflecting on all this, then examining, to cheer himself up, the cheque for £878 which had arrived from Piero in part payment for the manuscripts by the first post that morning; thinking what a clever method this was of eluding the tax-gatherers; wondering uneasily whether the tax-gatherers had come across it before (after all, however casual the individual payments might be made to appear, their aggregate would be ungainsayable); deciding that, for the time being at any rate, there was nothing to be done about this; pondering on all these matters and many more related ones, such as Nicos Pandouros's expedition to the Laguna Veneta (was he back yet?), Fielding was jolted nearly out of his wits when two liberal helpings of female bust descended past his cheeks with a swoosh, one on to each of his shoulders.

Maisie.

'Getting on all right, dear?'

'No.'

'Stuck?'

'Not really. Dissatisfied.'

'Well, I've got some good news to cheer you up a bit. Or sort of good news. You'll be able to stay here uninterrupted from now on right through to the end of July, if you want. Tessa's going to be away the whole of the Easter holidays, and after that she'll only be here Saturdays and Sundays for the whole summer term – '

' – Quarter – '

' – Quarter, and not even on Saturdays, I should think, if she gets into the Girls' Under Sixteen Cricket Eleven.'

'Sweet Jesus, Maisie. What's all that got to do with my staying here? I thought that nonsense of yours was done with.'

'Well dear, it is but then it isn't . . . quite. I mean, nothing of that sort is ever really done with, now is it, and a whole *month* at Easter, if Tessa had been here too, might have been a mis – '

' – All right, all right. Thank you for letting me know I can stay. Though how long I'll *want* to be here between now and July is another matter. And now tell me,' said Fielding, crossing his arms and putting one hand up to each of Maisie's bunjy pectorals, 'where Tessa is going.'

'One of the masters at her school has invited her to his country house in Somerset – her and Marius both.'

'What master?'

'Oh, he'd be well after *your* time, dear. A Mr Raisley Conyngham.'

'The racehorse owner?'

'Yes. Tessa hates horses but it'll be nice for Marius. And there's lots of other things for Tessa.'

'How odd of this Conyngham. Why should he pick Marius and Tessa together?'

'I expect he knew they know each other, and often live in the same house in the holidays.'

'Why should he have known all that . . . unless he's been making enquiries?'

'Come off it, dear. You're making too much of the

thing. And no more of *that* just now,' she said, moving his hands off her dugs and taking two almost military paces to the rear.

'Tell me, Maisie. Does anyone – apart from you and me – does anyone at all know that you are Tessa's mother?'

'I think perhaps Gregory Stern knew, dear. Knew or guessed. He'd have remembered that one time he was with me, and what happened, and later on he'd have done his arithmetic – you know how sharp Jews are – '

' – But you disappeared, absolutely, for several months before and after Tessa's birth. And it was several years before she came to live with you as your niece.'

'Not till I retired . . . but you know what Jews are with those long twitchy noses, they have ways of finding things out. But why worry about that, dear? I only said that *perhaps* Gregory knew or guessed – he used to give Tessa presents you see, rather *special* presents – but since he's been dead two years and more in any case, what's the difference?'

'I was only wondering whether it is conceivable that anyone else knows that Tessa and Marius are half-brother and -sister.'

'No, dear. Only you and me. Only Fielding and Maisie. And anyway, what's that got to do with this invitation? You're not suggesting that Mr Raisley Conyngham might be up to something? I hope not, because Tessa's set her little heart on going, and Mr Conyngham's references are quite unimpeachable.'

Maisie knew a lot of long words as she always read Tessa's holiday task books at the same time as Tessa, in order that they might discuss them together. These literary activities were a source of great joy to Fielding, who considered Maisie's critical judgements to be pithy and accurate; but they also prompted much malicious amusement, at the juxtaposition of Maisie's usual argot (that of a whore tempered to become a hotel proprietor and an 'aunt') with her grandiose and polysyllabic gleanings from Shakespeare or Burke. Normally he would have relished Mr Conyngham's 'unimpeachable' references, but today he was too concerned with Mr Conyngham himself and his intervention in the lives of Marius and Tessa.

'There was some story about a horse,' he said, 'a horse which Conyngham owned and didn't have gelded even when it started to run in steeplechases.'

'And what's that got to do with anything?'

'It is . . . unusual. He seems to be rather an unusual man, don't you think? A schoolmaster with a country house and rich enough to run racehorses . . . picking out Marius and Tessa together from hundreds of boys and girls . . . asking them to stay, not just a few days but nearly five weeks. It is possible that he might have some idea of their real connection?'

'No, dear; how could he? He just knows they know each other. One or other of them probably told him. Use your common sense, and let's not have any more of this silly mystery making. I know what it's all about, of course: you're jealous of this Mr Conyngham because he's taking Tessa away from you.'

'For Christ's sake, Maisie, let's have no more of *that*. See you at lunch.'

Fielding bent his head discontentedly over his notes about the *Grinder* and his manifold cousins, while Maisie closed the door very slowly and softly, which was her way of showing greater displeasure than if she had slammed it.

'The selected play is *Twelfth Night, or What You Will*,' said Milo Hedley to Marius.

Milo was watching Marius while he was having a shower after hockey. Since this was happening in the changing room of Marius's House, to which Milo did not belong, Milo, although he was a School Monitor and therefore highly privileged in many respects, had no business to be there at all.

'We shall all have to take several parts,' Milo went on: 'Your main one will be Olivia – the one who falls in love with Viola, thinking her to be a boy.'

'Who will be reading Viola?'

'Miss Malcolm. For God's sake stop turning your back on me. You're behaving like a little girl.'

Marius turned to face Milo.

'Ah. Something went wrong when you were circumcised, I see. Show me closer.'

Marius showed him closer. Milo put out both hands and adjusted Marius's penis, as deftly and delicately as a doctor, so that he could examine a small scar near the lip of the bulb. He then restored the organ to its owner.

' I was circumcised rather late, you see,' said Marius, 'so that may have made it difficult. It certainly hurt a lot afterwards. Oddly enough, my father had a similar scar – so my mother told me – also from being circumcised. Though of course he was done when he was a baby.'

'And you were done . . . "rather late". How late, Marius? Why?'

'My mother didn't want it done when I was born. She despised Jewish customs and thought . . . that it would spoil my appearance. Please pass me that towel.'

Marius turned off the shower and stepped out. Milo draped the towel round him – or rather, he let it drop on to his shoulders without himself touching him.

'It doesn't . . . spoil your appearance. You know why not Marius? Because your beauty is not pagan – or at least, not pagan in the Greek style. An Apollo or an Eros or a Faun without a foreskin would be quite hideous. But you are something else again. A different sort of deity . . . Egyptian, perhaps. There were tribes in Egypt, you know, that practised circumcision.'

'I thought Egyptian gods had animal heads.'

'Not necessarily the minor ones. But perhaps that is what you need . . . the head of a fox or a hawk. Why were you cut in the end if your mother didn't want it done?'

'It was too tight. So I am to play Olivia. Whom else?'

'The Duke Orlando . . . who also fancied Viola, even before he knew she was a girl.'

'I thought he was in love with Olivia.'

'With her as well, at any rate to begin with. So Marius-Orlando will desire himself as Marius-Olivia. Lest all this should go to your head, you will be sobered up by reading Plato's *Apology* with Raisley, while Miss Malcolm reads Gibbon with me. And lastly, Marius, you will be inducted into the duties of a stable boy in a training establishment . . . so that you would be capable of standing in for another at a need. The actual training at Ullacote is done by a certain Captain Jack Lamprey – ex-Army man, Hamilton's Horse. A sympathetic fellow, you'll find, a sort of extremely coarse-minded dandy. Foul-mouthed and witty with it, like an upper-class – no, a *donnish* – Serjeant-Major.'

'Tessa hates horses,' said Marius. He discarded the towel and began to pull on a pair of elegant Cambridge blue drawers, pausing very briefly to examine the penis which made of him an Egyptian deity.

'Miss Malcolm will be busy with Gibbon, the sabre and the local churches. By the way, I'm going to give you a stallion when we ride to-morrow. You'll need to get used to them. It's a stallion you'll be trained on at Ullacote.'

'Rather rough on an apprentice?'

'This is a very sweet-tempered one. Raisley bought him a long time ago, then sold him, but has bought him back. He's a steeplechaser. Name of Lover Pie.'

'Lover Pie?' said Marius, quivering all over with excitement: 'I won a lot of money on him at Newmarket, nearly three years ago.'

'He don't go on the flat any longer. Fences now.'

'But he's still entire?'

'A stallion, as I said.'

'My word,' said Marius, 'Jeremy will be thrilled.'

'Jeremy?'

'Jeremy Morrison. Friend of mine. He was with me at Newmarket when we backed Lover Pie.'

'Indeed? If I were you . . . Marius the Egyptian . . . I shouldn't go telling anyone about Lover Pie. It's a secret, you see. Raisley is hoping . . . to spring a litle surprise.'

'Goll-liiieee,' Marius said, reverting three or four years in his infatuation; 'then Mum's the word.'

When Nicos and the Greco had finished their report to Ptolemaeos Tunne on how matters stood at Samuele, Ptolemaeos made two comments, the first brief, the second more ample:

'To begin with,' he said, 'let us say that it does my corrupt old heart good to see that instead of being separated from each other for good, which is what I had intended, you two have been re-united in a different and saner fashion. It is an object lesson on the benefits sometimes unintentionally conferred by interference.

'Secondly, it is clear to me, as it must be to you, that if there is any menace to Lord Canteloupe – which we should all deplore – it must lie with this atrocious fellow, Jude Holbrook.

'Now, as to this latter.

'Having studied the documents which Major Gray produced, and being now acquainted with the history of the whole affair, I know that Lord Rollesden-in-Silvis, alias Humbert fitzAvon, debauched in Venice the entire Albani family except the father . . . who, to get him out of the way before anything worse happened, sent him off to hide from the invading forces of Bonaparte in the Albani Villa at Samuele. While there, fitzAvon raped or seduced a little peasant girl, was compelled by the villagers and the priest to marry her when she became pregnant, and was then lynched for vengeance on the evening after his wedding. The child of the Signora fitzAvon, later called Filavoni, was a boy, and from this boy is directly descended the idiot Paolo, whom you have just been to inspect.

'As Albani thought and wrote, when he found all this out, there was no point in revealing that fitzAvon had really been the heir of Lord Canteloupe (at the time still called Lord Muscateer) and that the peasant girl's brat was now, therefore, the legitimate heir apparent to the peerage; nor did he inform Canteloupe of his son's marriage:

'"The family was ancient and noble," he wrote in the second of Fielding's manuscripts. "It was not, in my view, fitting that its line should continue through the coupling of such a vile man as I now knew Lord Rollesden to be, and of such a woman as the peasant hoyden whom he had been forced to make his wife . . . By concealing the fact of Lord Rollesden's marriage, I should be leaving my Lord Muscateer free to assume that his heir was now dead without issue and to make such arrangements as he could for the more proper inheritance of his earldom and estate. The bride, now the widow, knew only that she had married one Humbert fitzAvon . . . There could be no chance, therefore, that she would claim or presume on the place that was now legally hers (and her child's) . . . Some time later I learnt that Lord Muscateer had been raised to the high dignity of an English marquessate . . . This only confirmed me in thinking that I had been right to protect so illustrious a House against continuance through the get of a vicious criminal on a common country bawd.'

'And so say all of us,' said Ptolemaeos Tunne, 'in the very similar circumstances which obtain now. What possible point or use would there be in restoring the marquessate to the right line, and so to that poor idiot in the marshes? And indeed, neither I nor anyone else in the

159

know would dream of trying to do so – except possibly (from your description of the man and his behaviour) this mean, shrivelled, stunted Holbrook, who, bereaved of his mother and now a sick man, has no pleasures or satisfactions left to him save possibly of that of making mischief. Should he finally discover this secret, as he may do if he wishes to persist, then for the sake of making mischief and revelling in spite, Holbrook might just do, or cause to be done, an intolerable injury to our friend Lord Canteloupe.

'It is therefore our duty to find some effective way of silencing Holbrook. *Just in case*. To this end I am already forming a delicate and rather amusing plan, and I shall charge you, Nico, and you, Greco, as the two good and equal friends you have become, with its implementation in due course.'

'Like master, like man,' said Jeremy Morrison to Alfie Schroeder of the Billingsgate Press: 'if I am to come to the true depths of the age old secrets of the soil, then I must first seek the old wisdom of the generations that have laboured on it since the beginning of time. This means, first, immersing myself in their manner of life.'

'So up with the lark and to bed with the bee,' said Alfie, 'and hey presto! The wisdom of the peasant will be upon you – as they used to say of the Holy Ghost.'

'Something of the kind. "Hey presto" is rather optimistic. It could take a very long time.'

'And how long have you been at it so far?' said Alfie.

He watched the two photographers, whom the paper had sent with him, as they made forty-seven finicking photographs of a Georgian dovecot. Could have done it better myself, he thought, with my old box brownie, God bless its remains wherever they are. Could have done it much better at a hundredth of the cost. But, of course, they've got a very powerful union these days. They have to be allowed everywhere, whole squads of them. The photographers moved on, to make seventy-nine more finicking photos, this time of the ivy over the ogival arch of one of the downstairs windows. Any minute now, thought Alfie, they'll be taking about a million arty poses of Piers Ploughboy here, and then there'll be no peace for anyone; so I'd better get on quickly.

'How long have you been at it?' he repeated.

'Just a few weeks,' said Jeremy.

'And what exactly is your regimen?' said Alfie. 'I mean, you don't seem to be living in a peasant hovel or anything.'

'No one on this estate lives in a peasant hovel,' said Jeremy sternly.

'Sorry.' This boy's pa, thought Alfie sadly, or Tom Llewyllyn, or any of the old gang, would have seen the joke (such as it was) and laughed. Heigh-day, he said to himself, then aloud:

'I meant, you don't seem to be living in an ordinary farm-worker's accommodation. You're still up here at the Hall.'

'That is expected of me. I am the 'Squire; I live in the 'Squire's house. In every other respect, I live the life which has been lived by an apprentice farm-worker since . . . since . . .'

'. . . Since the beginning of time,' suggested Alfie wearily.

'No. We've had that phrase already.' Was there a glimmer of humour here? thought Alfie. Would God there were.

'Since man first tilled the earth,' Jeremy said. 'Yes,' he said with some satisfaction: 'my life is the life of all those that have been dedicated to the land and its service, since man first tilled the earth.'

'I see,' said Alfie. 'And in this way you are going to become saturated in the primeval wisdom of the soil? Or would you prefer "atavistic" for "primeval"?'

'I think "primeval" will do very well,' Jeremy said.

Was there, oh dear God, was there just a trace of merriment in his eye as he said that?

'And how long do you expect to go on with this?' Alfie enquired. 'As you've just remarked, it could be a very lengthy business.'

'Indeed it could be. Or perhaps,' said Jeremy, 'just perhaps the whole thing might come to one in a flash. The old rhythms might suddenly find a true response in my mind – after all, I come from a line of farmers that goes back to a vassal of Queen Boadicea – yes, the old rhythms and the old routines might begin to fill my being with the old wisdom sooner than I originally hoped.'

'So it's going to be a matter of "hey presto" after all,' said Alfie, losing patience. 'One morning, not a week from now, you're going to wake up knowing the whole fucking thing backwards, and there'll be no more need of wailing about "the mystic knowledge that goes back to the grey dawn of history" – I think I have you right,' he said, consulting his notebook, 'or getting yourself up,' he said, looking at Jeremy's clodhopping boots and hitched trousers, 'to look like a People's Hero of Agriculture on a bloody propaganda poster.'

Jeremy grinned, very briefly, then gazed straight on

Alfie's red and blue square face with his white and round one.

'My father warned me that you enjoyed your little joke,' he said; 'but I think . . . don't you, Mr Schroeder . . . that you'd better take me seriously.'

Before Alfie could ask why, one of the photographers had tapped him on the shoulder, said, 'Come on, grandad, our turn now if you don't mind', pushed him briskly to one side in case he did, and started ordering Jeremy into a series of affected and contorted postures, which he willingly endured as the price of being finished, at such a very opportune moment, with Mr Alfie Schroeder.

'You see,' Jeremy said to Carmilla, who had come over from Cambridge for the night, as they lay in bed at Luffham-by-Whereham, 'he can't be sure that I was bluffing and so he won't dare call the bluff. Can we please do it properly this time instead of just coming all over each other?'

'No,' said Carmilla, who had been saying this ever since the resumption (at his request and to her delight) of their sexual rendezvous – 'Anyhow, I'm not ready to do anything again just yet,' she said. 'Why won't this Schroeder dare to call your bluff?'

'He knew my father in the old days. He knows that my father once provided a confidential service – parliamentary information of a very special kind – for his employer, Lord Billingsgate. He knows, too, that I am immensely rich – multiply three thousand acres by two thousand 'pounds an acre, and see what that gives you.'

'Six million,' said Carmilla.

'Right you be. Alfie boy knows that, and he also knows that we – that is, I – now have a great deal more in the funds. Enough to ring a lot of noisy bells that might embarrass him. All ways round, he may reckon that he'd better not chance his arm.'

'But if he does . . . chance his arm . . . and makes you look a fool?'

'His text has to have my *imprimatur* before it can be printed – '

' – Clever boy – '

– So if he starts knocking my ideas or making bad taste jokes, the thing just gets torn up. His paper wouldn't like that – time and expenses wasted. So the odds are that he will produce something which I like, and then his paper can print it, and everyone will be happy.'

'Except, perhaps, Mr Schroeder.'

'Who will soon recover his spirits when he receives a nice letter of thanks with a cheque inside, made out for him to endorse and pay over "to his favourite charity", a face-saving formula which he will interpret as meaning himself. I've got a huge thing on. Want a feel?'

'Did you ever let Fielding Gray have a feel?'

'He never asked for one.'

'If he had?' said Carmilla, having one herself.

'I don't know. At the beginning, perhaps; but not if he'd asked recently. For some time now I've been getting ready to say good-bye to him.'

'What a swine you are.'

'Can *I* have a feel now?'

'Yes . . . Yes, like that. Just lately it's started to go stiff. Like a little boy's. Erectile, I think they call it.'

'How *very* exciting.'

'Careful, it's not quite like a boy's, even more tender and hates being bent. Good . . . good . . . nice Jeremy. Clever Jeremy. Tell me, nice, clever Jeremy: why did you have to ditch Fielding Gray quite so savagely? Everyone at Lancaster is very hurt on his behalf. Me too.'

'Yet here you are with me.'

'That doesn't mean I approve of your behaviour. I'm just using you,' said Carmilla, 'in the same way you are using me, as flesh to assuage lust.'

'That's not supposed to be moral,' Jeremy said.

'It's quite all right if we are both honest about it, to ourselves and to each other. Stop evading the issue. Unkindness to Fielding; and disloyalty to the College at the same time. Your sudden departure hit Tom Llewyllyn, and Len, and others, very hard. After all, you're the son of one of Tom's oldest friends, and they'd bent over backwards to do you favours. As well you know, Tom has never been himself since those elms died two years ago, and what with your desertion of the College *and* of Fielding Gray – another old friend of Tom's, remember, you've really put the boot in.'

'The farm-worker's boot?' giggled Jeremy.

'What time do you get up?' said Carmilla, abandoning any attempt to get Jeremy to treat seriously his hateful conduct. 'What time do you begin your daily charade? Not *too* early, I hope. I don't need to leave for Cambridge until ten o'clock.'

'I'm letting myself off to-morrow. I sometimes do, though I didn't tell Mr Schroeder.'

"Fraud. But *this* is genuine enough,' she said, laying her cheek along the length of it.

When Lord Luffham of Whereham went down to his old school to address the staff and the Sixth Form, and then be gowned in Royal Purple as *'Domus Huius Alumnus ita Honorabilis ut Honoratus'*, Jeremy decided to go too, officially to support his father but in fact to escape, more or less legitimately, another day on the soil, and to take a look at Marius.

'So how is the land?' his father said, as they drove up the School Hill. 'I notice that you are deserting it to-day.'

'In your honour, my lord.'

'Yes . . . well, I shouldn't absent myself *too* much, if I were you – at least not until that article of Schroeder's is safely published.'

'A proof came yesterday. As I hoped, Father, a very flattering article . . . which will certainly annoy them all at Lancaster. I don't think Schroeder will withdraw now; but as you suggest, after to-day I shall continue my zealous apprenticeship uninterrupted.'

'Until the day after the piece appears, I suppose?'

'Until two or three days after. To cease on the very day of publication would be cynical.'

'And then?'

'I expect to discover that the almost mystical experience which I am undergoing, requires to be undergone again, and so affirmed, in other lands. It will need *extending*, sir. India might be one country in which to extend it.'

'You'll hate the bloody place. Nothing but beggars and

filth when I was there – except in our own cantonments. And you won't find much left of them.'

'Very cheap to live in, sir.'

'What's that to you? You don't need to live cheaply.'

'I dare say not. But it will do no harm if people think I am . . . as an extension, let me repeat, of my endeavours, about to be much advertised by Mr Schroeder, as spiritual liegeman of the soil. Yes: India might be a very plausible and appropriate place to continue my apprenticeship.'

The chauffeur drove the Rolls over a bridge and under an arch, and both men's eyes flickered as the tears pricked.

'Green,' said Jeremy, as they drove along a terrace past the First Eleven Cricket Ground.

'Yes,' said his father spitefully: 'all we need is to see Fielding Gray standing in the middle of it. He made a lot of runs there in his day.'

'And you, sir?'

'One or two. At the age of fifteen I scored eighty-nine not out in a House Match final on Green. When I reached fifty, I turned my bat round and played with the lumpy side, to confuse the opposition. Alas, I never quite lived up to my early promise . . . Am I to take it, Jeremy, that you're coming to the ceremony, or have you got your own little fish to fry?'

'I have one or two things to attend to, sir. I shall hope to see you in your Gown of Honour before we leave.'

Since only the masters and the Sixth Form would be hearing Lord Luffham's address and assisting at his gowning, the rest of the school had an afternoon off. Jeremy, having surveyed the new Pottery Studio (which had been erected during the seven months since last he had been there) and having found it to be more horrible, both inside and out, than he would thought it possible for the most malignant architect in the kingdom to make it, decided to begin his search for Marius in the Junior Fives Court. On the way there he overtook a loitering boy, whom he recognized from one of his visits to Oudenarde House, and said:

'I think I saw you with Marius Stern a couple of years back. You were grooming your horses after a riding lesson.'

'Yes, sir,' said the boy sullenly.

'I'm now going to the Junior Fives Court to look for Marius,' said Jeremy.

'So am I.'

'Not very fast, it seems.'

'He won't want to see me when I get there,' Palairet said.

'He may want to see me,' said Jeremy, 'so if you'll excuse me, I'll go on.'

'As you wish, sir.'

When Jeremy reached the Fives Courts, Marius ran out of one of them to greet him.

'Jeremy, how super, why didn't you ring up to say you were coming?'

'I don't approve of telephoning people at school. They should be altogether removed from the world of telephones and anger.'

'You could have written.'

'Last minute decision to come down, old thing. They're gowning my pater.'

'I know. Aren't you going to watch it?'

'I'd sooner watch you playing Fives. Now finish the game without any rush, and we'll talk afterwards.'

While Jeremy was watching the Fives, Palairet sneaked up to him.

'I remember that day at the riding school,' Palairet said: 'out at Birchington. We'd just finished riding and were waiting for the school bus to come and take us back to Sandwich. You'd come to say good-bye to Marius.'

'And *you* interrupted.'

'I'm sorry. I know . . . now . . . how you must have been feeling. Something had gone wrong, by the look of you, and you wanted . . . to say a proper farewell . . . before you went wherever you were going.'

'Yes. It was a low time with me. Over now, though. But *your* low time,' said Jeremy, 'is not over, I think.'

'That evening out at Birchington, Marius and I, we were – well – together. And for a long time after. Not now, sir. This game of Fives. It's not an *official* practice, because all the beaks and the Fives Bloods are at this ceremony for your father. You *are* Jeremy Morrison, aren't you?'

'The same.'

'But although it's not an official practice, they still wouldn't find a place for me, because I'm not good

169

enough. I came down in case one of them had to fall out and they needed me after all.'

'You told me . . . when we met just now . . . that you were coming to see Marius.'

'That as well. To look at him. To wonder whether he can be the same boy I went riding with, that afternoon at Birchington.'

'Look,' said Jeremy, 'if you want Marius back, you'll do a smart about turn, march away from these Fives Courts, and keep right out of Marius's way, not even letting him get the tiniest glimpse of you, for the next six months. By that time he'll get worried, he'll think that *you* have finished with *him* (which may very well be true by then) and since this is not what he is used to, he will come looking for you.'

'What do I do then?'

'Behave with the indifference which you will, as I say, by then quite probably feel. Marius will fall at your feet. He will be yours in whatever way you want him.'

'But if I am indifferent, I shan't want him in any way at all?'

'Precisely.'

'That would be horrible. I don't believe you. I won't.'

'Then try it for yourself and find out. You've nothing to lose as things are.'

'Very well,' said Palairet. He turned and ran from the Fives Courts.

'I saw you had poor old Pally Palairet with you,' Marius said when the match was over: 'he's rather a mess these days.'

'Do you remember the lecture you gave me, on the wicked way I was treating Fielding Gray?' said Jeremy. 'On Boxing Day, on the golf course at Broughton?'

'I do. What of it?'

'Let me spell it out, sweetheart: what I have done to Fielding, you have done to Palairet. It is the same with you as with me, you see, as I told you it would be.'

'But it wasn't my *fault*, Jeremy. Pally just couldn't measure up, and got left behind.'

'Like enough. I'm not blaming you. But from now on, don't you go blaming others. Time and chance,' said Jeremy, 'happeneth to us all.'

Milo Hedley came towards them, wearing a dark grey flannel suit with an enormous pink flower, which looked rather like a rhododendron, in his buttonhole.

'Introduce us,' he said to Marius.

Marius introduced them.

'I've just been present, sir,' said Milo, 'while they gowned your father. A memorable occasion. He wept.'

'He was always a sentimental man,' Jeremy said: 'it goes with that generation.'

'I cut the bun fight, said Milo, 'because I wanted to be sure of catching Marius. We have a special ride arranged,' he said to Marius, 'for tomorrow at half past two.'

'But I can't – '

' – Half past two, Marius,' Milo said. 'You will excuse yourself, in Mr Conyngham's name, from any other engagements.' Then to Jeremy, 'Has Marius told you, sir, that he and I are to stay with Raisley Conyngham – one of our beaks – for the Easter holidays?'

'Mr Conyngham owns horses,' said Marius, thinking to himself with pleasure that he would now be able to get out of hateful House Gardening, the following afternoon. 'Racehorses, Jeremy,' he said. He was about to add that among them was Lover Pie, whom they had once backed together at Newmarket, when he remembered Milo's recommendation of secrecy in this matter and said

171

instead: 'We shall read Plato's *Apology*. And *Twelfth Night*.'

'That reminds me,' Milo said. 'Marius, I want you to take a message from Mr Conyngham to Miss Teresa Malcolm.' He handed Marius an envelope. 'A list of books she'll need from the School Library,' he said. 'Off you go.'

'But surely, I needn't take it to her this very minute,' Marius said.

'Now,' said Milo.

'Do as your friend says,' said Jeremy: 'I see from his buttonhole that he is a School Monitor. Therefore to be instantly obeyed, Marius. I was a School Monitor. You will be one before very long. You are a member of an *élite*, Marius . . . and as such must obey a senior member without any question. I should be interested,' he said to Milo Hedley as Marius reluctantly departed, 'to hear a little more about this holiday.'

Jeremy looked carefully at Milo, and Milo looked carefully at Jeremy. Both saw in the other what neither saw in Marius. Jeremy saw a certain smile which was wanting in Marius's beautiful but taut, tense face, the smile of the Archaic *kouros,* enticing to all and contemptuous of most, yet not contemptuous of Jeremy; and Milo saw a promise of smooth, warm and ample limbs, not the narrow thighs and spare calves he had seen on Marius under his shower.

'There used to be a hayloft,' said Jeremy, 'above a barn. Just along Pioneers' Path round the ridge.'

'It's still there, sir.'

'A pleasant way to walk . . . while we talk of Marius and the way he will spend his Easter.'

'Raisley Conyngham?' said Lord Luffham to Jeremy in the Rolls as it went down the School Hill.

'A beak in the school. Marius Stern is going to him for the Easter holidays. Did you meet him, Father, during your bonanza?'

Bonanzas for all, that afternoon, Jeremy thought: his father gowned and weeping; himself prone in the hayloft while Master Milo had his wicked way. Funny, thought Jeremy: I've never let anyone do that to me before, I've always loathed the idea; but when Milo asked so politely, 'Please, sir, may I bugger you, sir?', the request was irresistible . . . and the performance painful at first but later very agreeable. There was, he had heard, a gland situated in that region, which if properly stimulated . . . as evidently it had been by Milo . . . 'Now,' he had said to Milo in the hayloft: 'now, boy, now. . . .' 'Oh Christ, sir,' Milo had said, 'I'm coming, sir, oh Christ.'

'Are you listening, sir?' Jeremy's father said.

'Sorry, Father.'

'Raisley Conyngham. Not a good man, I thought. Rich. Pleased with himself. Devious. Rather like Somerset Lloyd-James used to be, but physically more wholesome. Yes: a prettier and prinked up version of Somerset.'

'Somerset Lloyd-James. Your old and very dear friend?'

'Old, certainly. As for the rest of it, dead.'

'A reading party with Somerset Lloyd-James would surely have been rather a memorable experience?'

173

'So it's a reading party that Conyngham's getting up?'

'With diversions.'

'I'm sure . . . that it will all be very plausible.'

The word that Milo had used was 'respectable'. 'Raisley Conyngham,' Milo had said, as they walked back along Pioneers' Path towards the school, 'sets great store on the *respectable*, on turning his pupils into unexceptionable members of whatever world they elect to enter. Marius, of whom we are both fond, sir, to use no stronger word, can come to no harm this Easter.' Amen to that, Jeremy thought, and said aloud:

'You looked splendid in your gown, father.'

'You were late enough coming to see me in it. Where were you?'

'Talking to Marius and some friends of his.' Now: now, boy, now.

'All that time?'

'And listening to what they had to say about things.'

'Oh? What things?'

'School life, sir, and matters appertaining.'

Oh Christ, sir, I'm coming, sir, oh Christ.

'So that's my plan for Holbrook,' said Ptolemaeos Tunne to Piero, Nicos and the Greco. 'Agreed?'

'Are you sure,' said Nicos, 'that Holbrook will react in the way that you describe?'

'If he doesn't, we go back to the laboratory and think of something else. Meanwhile, no harm done.'

'And if he does so react, and things do go the way you

see them,' said Nicos, 'I shall be very glad. He insulted me, he insulted my Greek manhood.'

'Don't be such a bore, Nico dear,' said Piero. 'You musn't take all that silly Greek rubbish so seriously. God save us from this "Greek manhood" . . . all of you strutting about in your bankrupt villages, insisting on marrying virgins and killing anyone who fucks your sisters. So *extreme*. Who the hell do you Greek boys think you are?'

'Get off your hobby horse, Piero,' said Ptolemaeos Tunne. 'Do not discourage Nicos from seeking his just recompense. And you, Greco? Are you going along again for the ride?'

'For company. Nicos says that I may.'

'And most welcome, *kyrie*,' Nicos said.

'What is your view of my scheme, Greco?'

'Ingenious as always, Ptoly. But how does Nicos go about procuring the . . . agent . . . of all this? Not so easy, these days.'

'What is needed,' said Piero, 'is someone like Baby Canteloupe. No longer, alas, available. Or a drug addict who will risk anything for money. Look,' he said, 'when I lived in Venice with Lykiadopoulos and Max de Freville, we had a major-domo for the Palazzo, a man called Simone Fontanelli. He was kind to me, and when Lyki set him to spy on me he would always report what he knew would make Lyki content, because he was from Sicily, like me, and Lyki was a putrid Greek. This Fontanelli, he is retired now in Sicily, he wrote to me from there when I was in my convent once, and I have his address – that is, I think that I remember it. He was for ever boasting that he knew every bordello and every *puttana* in Venezia; not altogether falsely, as I think, for some marvellous creatures came to the Palazzo while Lyki and Max were out; and although that was a long time ago, he may still be able to help you now. Or maybe he no longer knows such things of Venezia, but knows them instead of Palermo, where he lives.'

'Down to Sicily is a long diversion,' said the Greco.

'We shall try the telephone and the telegraph,' said Piero. 'One can at least enquire. Simone would perhaps like an expedition to serve you.'

This is exciting him for some reason, thought Ptolemaeos: he always slips a bit towards an Italian idiom when he is excited.

'Don Simone, I remember he said he was called in Sicily,' Piero said. '"Don" is usually for priests, or landowners, or lawyers – it is a title of courtesy accorded, without precise regulation, to important men . . . not always honest ones. But who wants an honest man in this affair? If Fontanelli is big enough to be Don Simone in Palermo, he may serve our turn.'

PART THREE
Master Cesario

Enter Valentine, and Viola in man's attire

VALENTINE: If the Duke continue these favours toward you, Cesario, you are like to be much advanced. He hath known you but three days, and already you are no stranger.

VIOLA: You either fear his humour or my negligence, that you call in question the continuance of his love. Is he inconstant, sir, in his favours?

VALENTINE: No, believe me.

Enter Orsino, Curio and attendants

VIOLA: I thank you. Here comes the Count.

ORSINO Who saw Cesario, ho?

VIOLA: On your attendance, my lord, here.

ORSINO (to Curio and attendants)
Stand you awhile aloof. (To Viola) Cesario, Thou knowest no less but all . . .

Shakespeare: *Twelfth Night, or What You Will*: I 4 11.1 to 15

'". . . I have unclasped,"' said Marius, reading the part of Duke Orsino:

> '"To thee the book even of my secret soul.
> Therefore, good youth, address thy gait unto her.
> Be not denied access; stand at her doors,
> And tell them, there thy fixed foot shall grow
> Till thou have audience."'

'"Sure, my noble lord,"' read Tessa in the part of Viola (Cesario):

> '"If she be so abandoned to her sorrow
> As it is spoke, she never will admit me."'

> '"Be clamorous and leap all civil bounds
> Rather than make unprofited return."'

'Stop,' said Raisley Conyngham, who had a way of imposing arbitrary intervals. 'Let us be sure we have the situation quite clear. Teresa: why are you at the Court of the Duke and dressed as a youthful male?'

'Because I wished to serve the Duke,' said Tessa, 'and to present myself as a page or a boy singer seemed the easiest way of gaining admittance.'

'Very fair. Now, in the previous scene but one (i.e. Act One, Scene Two, line fifty-seven), you have suggested that the Captain present you at the Duke's Court as a eunuch. And how, Marius, would you interpret the use of the term?'

179

'At that time,' said Marius, well pleased with himself, 'boys with promising voices were often castrated. Viola proposes to be presented to the Duke as a *castrato*.'

'For a small boy you are woefully worldly,' said Raisley Conyngham, 'and for a Scholar Emeritus of the school, you are woefully imprecise.'

They were sitting on a terrace which looked south over the coloured counties of Somerset and Devon, and west to Exmoor and Dunkery Beacon. This was their second night at Ullacote. Their first had been spent in what Raisley Conyngham oddly called 'Interior Economy', which was unpacking and settling into quarters; and now, after a day of 'recuperation' (walking, resting and private reading), they were launched into *Twelfth Night*.

'I don't know about Scholar Emeritus,' said Marius, wishing to *épater* the company: 'my mother is having a fit of five-star meanness and may well start claiming the actual purse that usually goes with a scholarship.'

'Then she won't get it,' said Raisley Conyngham, resenting the attempted diversion but wishing to kill the point raised by it. 'When you received the award two years ago, she agreed that your family was too rich to take the money with a clear conscience; and you were therefore not called "Scholar Esuriens", a needy scholar, but "Scholar Emeritus", a scholar, that is, by Merit or Desert . . . a title which you will in any case forfeit if you continue in such mental slackness as you have just displayed. You have read this play carefully, as instructed?'

'Yes, sir.'

'Then you should be aware that at no time does the Duke or anyone else assume that Viola is a *castrato*. In a speech that is soon to come, the Duke treats Viola, whom he knows as Cesario, as a growing boy with an unbroken voice. In a scene that comes somewhere later, Olivia falls in love with Cesario as with any young man. Both presume that he is entire – immature, no doubt, but entire. How, then, could he have been presented as a *castrato*?'

'If he wasn't,' said Marius, 'why did he ask the Captain to present him as a "eunuch", and why did the Captain agree to do so with the words "be you his eunuch"?'

He turned to look over the valleys in the evening, heedless of Conyngham's pedantry.

'Listen to me, boy,' said Conyngham. 'I am engaged in, among other things, training you and Teresa in exactness of thought. Later on I have an amusing little exercise for you both which will require absolute precision of timing and action. And conception. These must therefore become habitual with you at all times and in all pursuits, literary or other. Only if you are exact in all things can I depend upon you to be exact in the enterprise which I have in mind for you. So now, Marius: if the Duke treats Cesario as a boy who is growing towards the pains of manhood, and if the Lady Olivia treats him as a youth already capable of loving in the full sense, it is clear that Viola/Cesario was not presented, at Court or anywhere else, in the capacity of a "eunuch". This being the case, now answer your own question: why the use of the word "eunuch", twice, in Act One, Scene Two?'

'Either the use was figurative, sir,' said Marius, who had realized that he was expected to wrangle the question as tirelessly as a schoolman, 'in reference to Cesario's treble voice; *or* it was a private joke between Cesario and the Captain, both of whom knew that Cesario had no male parts whereas the Duke and the Court could not know this; *or* they did indeed intend to pass off Cesario as a *castrato* but changed their minds before he was introduced.'

'Better,' said Raisley: 'but your last suggestion necessitates an unwarranted intrapolation; and you have failed to render what is perhaps the most obvious explanation of all. You provide it, Teresa.'

'Confusion of thought, sir, by Cesario and the Captain. Or simply slack usage.'

'Nearly. Set her right, Milo.'

'Confusion of thought, sir, and/or slack usage, *not* by Cesario and the Captain, but by Shakespeare himself.'

'Good. Do not let your reverence for the Master conceal from you, Marius and Teresa, that inconsistency and sloppiness in Shakespeare's characters as often as not reflects the inconsistency and sloppiness of their creator . . . which we may charitably explain and excuse on the grounds that he laboured under the grinding and immediate pressures of the commercial theatre, and was often much disordered by drink, jealousy, disease or lust.'

'This is Lover Pie,' said Raisley Conyngham to Marius the next morning. He pointed into the stallion's stall, from which the incumbent looked back with blasé disdain. 'Bring him out, Jack,' he said to Captain Jack Lamprey, a short, chunky man, bald under his cap.

'Bring the old bugger out, Jenny,' said Lamprey to a loitering stable lass.

Jenny brought him out. Lover Pie stood quiet and bored by her side in the yard while Marius, Raisley Conyngham, Milo Hedley and a lowering individual who had been introduced to Marius as 'Major Glastonbury', politely and studiously examined the pair of them. The stable lass was messy, busty and lusty. Lover Pie was grave, grey, rather plump, well muscled in the behind, wide and handsome between the ears, and very strong in the chest.

'Jenny will be over you, young Marius,' said Jack Lamprey, 'and old Leery Whelks will be over Jenny, and I'll be over the whole bloody lot of you. Since the forms have been signed and passed and all that sort of shit,' he lilted like a professor quoting poetry in his inaugural lecture, 'we'd better begin the way we mean to go on, and no time like now. I'll take the Lover, Jenny,' he said, doing so, 'and you take Master Marius and find him some clobber. Then bring him back here and we'll give him a few bloody horrible fatigues. And Jenny,' called Lamprey, as she seized Marius by one arm with both hands and led him zestfully away, 'don't try to feel him up while he's changing. He's a little bit shy. His friend, Mr Conyngham, your employer and mine, wouldn't like it at all; and anyway I want him fit and up to his work.'

Jenny grinned, showed a gap where one front tooth should have been, and whistled gaily through it.

'That horse needs a race, Raisley,' Major Glastonbury said.

'I know, Giles,' said Conyngham. 'I have one in mind. Two, in fact.'

'At clappy Regis Priory in early April,' piped Lamprey, 'and poxy Bellhampton Park a few days later. Smelly little courses, both of 'em' – to Lamprey the only proper course in England was Cheltenham – 'but they've got nice, comfy park fences which we hope he won't whack his knackers on. Two three mile 'chases, or just over. The Paignton Trophy and Hamilton's Cup.'

'Ah,' said Glastonbury, 'my cousin Prideau has a mare in those two races.'

'I know,' said Conyngham: 'Boadicea. When are you going on to Prideau?'

'After luncheon.'

'So soon? Why not stay the night? As you see,' said Conyngham, as Jenny emerged leading by the hand a cloth-capped, polo-necked, tightly jeanned Marius, 'we have interesting company.'

'I dare say. Tempting,' said Glastonbury, 'but no. This is a quick stage, as I said on the telephone: lunch is all I asked for and lunch is all I'll have.'

'Why the hurry? Prideau Glastonbury – with respect – is not the most beguiling company in the world.'

'And so say all of us. But I'm fond of him – '

' – So am I, ever since Cambridge, but I wouldn't exactly hurtle from here to Hereford to be with him – '

' – No more would I,' said Giles, 'were it not that he's specially asked me to hurry. I have something to report.'

The two men walked away from Lover Pie, who was now receiving the attentions of Marius, under the immediate instruction of Jenny and the more aloof supervision of Jack Lamprey. 'At least,' Jenny was saying, 'it don't smell as gungy as a mule's.' Milo paused, amused by Marius's discomfiture, uncertain whether or not he was required to leave this entertainment and attend on Conyngham. A nod from Conyngham summoned him to his side but now as ever he halted between six inches to a foot behind him.

'The thing is,' said Giles, 'that Prideau's boy, Myles, has got trouble. When he was Captain of Royal Tennis at Cambridge a couple of years back his second string was a girl called Theodosia Salinger – very remarkable, a female getting a Royal Tennis Blue – '

' – Half Blue at Cambridge,' said Milo, 'full Blue at Oxford – '

' – Theodosia Salinger,' said Glastonbury, ignoring the interruption, 'who later married Canteloupe. Now, Myles met Theodosia's twin sister, Carmilla, and fell for her like Humpty Dumpty. But Carmilla, who likes short, sharp romps, it seems, thought Myles was much too stodgy, and wouldn't touch him. So Myles began to pine away. For two years he went on pining until it was getting rather hairy; at which stage I was deputed, as an old friend of Canteloupe, to try to persuade Canteloupe to persuade his wife, Theodosia, to persuade her sister, Carmilla, at least to give the lad a chance. Prideau expects a full report on how all this is going on. Why are you listening?' said Giles to Milo.

'So that I can ask him later if I wish to remember exactly what you've said,' said Raisley Conyngham. 'My memory is fair, but Milo has almost total recall. And what have you to report to Prideau?'

'That Carmilla has reluctantly agreed to invite Myles to Lancaster College, where she's a don, and to try to be decent to him . . . at least to the extent of explaining kindly why he don't fit her bill.'

'The trouble with Myles,' said Conyngham, 'is that he is nine times as boring as his father, without any of his father's amiability.'

'Right. But I must still go to Prideau and give him what comfort I can. The real reason,' said Giles Glastonbury, 'that I asked to stop off for lunch was to see how Lamprey's getting on. After all, I was responsible for recommending him to you.'

'He is coarse but capable.'

'Delighted to hear it. When he was one of my subalterns,' said Giles, 'in Germany in the early 1950s, he was about the worst officer in the world . . . though funny with it. But I think he has a hand with horses.'

'And with sluts like that Jenny. She'd eat out of his navel – and wouldn't need asking twice.'

'But I wonder,' said Glastonbury, 'whether he will be all right with your little *protégé*, Marius Stern?'

Milo Hedley coughed discreetly.

'Milo?' said Conyngham.

'Captain Lamprey will be just right for Marius,' said Milo. 'Marius the Egyptian, the pampered godling – he needs to be made to jump about . . . to obey orders on the spot instead of first addressing his fastidious intelligence to finding fault with them . . . and Captain Lamprey and Gat-Toothed Jenny will certainly see to that.'

He pointed to the group round Lover Pie, who stood majestic and courteous while Jenny clawed the air above the head of the kneeling Marius and said, 'You'll get it fucking right, if we stay here till the moon goes down.'

'And that's as true as turds come out of arseholes,' fluted Jack Lamprey in his immaculate Cambridge/Bloomsbury.

Fielding Gray walked across the golf course, towards the dunes and the sea.

He had now finished the first part of *The Grand Grinder* and sent it off, under recorded cover, to Salinger, Stern & Detterling. There his work would be examined by Ashley Dexterside, who would send copies on to Carmilla and Theodosia, his self-appointed but most acceptable editors.

Fielding felt confident that he had done the thing well, that it was suitable in style and tone, that the ironies had been neatly implied rather than clumsily underscored, that the provincial splendours and miseries had been deployed in all their bravura and pettiness. Only two considerations now troubled him. First, he knew that he was going to be very hard put to it to produce a second part, of length enough to make the book an economic publication, without padding or lying. Secondly, he knew that in one respect at least, he had already been false: while giving full play to his genuine admiration for his grandfather, the grand grinder, and his quasi-heroic achievements, he had concealed the fact that he remembered the old man to have been, during his last days, a self-opinionated and philistine bully . . . who for his part made no secret of his distaste and contempt for his 'soppy and soapy' little grandson.

But as he passed the second of the rotting gun emplacements, he suddenly saw how these two embarrassments could be made to cancel each other out. A large section of Part Two could surely be devoted to confessing that he had hitherto concealed his grandfather's nastier qualities and the mutual mistrust and misliking which had existed, in Fielding's boyhood and just before the old man's death, between them. He could turn the glittering medal and show the green and tarnished copper on its reverse. By so doing he could legitimately fill many pages and also spring a salutary and entertaining surprise on the reader, who would have come by now to regard his grandfather as improbably and rather tediously immune from the human frailties which attached to everyone else in the book. When it was demonstrated that the grand grinder, like all the rest, had his faults and these less amiable than those of many, a proper balance would have been struck in the matter. He would also, thought Fielding, confess, by way of sales-making self-immolation, that his grandfather's detestation of himself ('a snobby, snoopy, funky boy') had been well merited.

And of course the old man would have found his judgement amply confirmed by later events in Fielding's career. The trail of seduction and shabby evasion which had led to his dismissal from school; the relish of gay trappings and the shirking of plain duties which had marked his military progress; the perverse and treacherous ingenuity which had made him such name as he enjoyed as an 'unwholesome' novelist – all this the grand grinder had, in general terms, foreseen and, by licit extrapolation from his stated views, predicted. How the old Yeoman would have sneered at the dainty uniforms of Hamilton's Horse, at the pretty little dress spurs worn at dinner by those that would run a mile sooner than mount a horse . . . though this, thought Fielding, going off at a tangent, was not quite fair to his old regiment. Some of his companions in Earl Hamilton's Light Dragoons had been expert horsemen . . . Giles Glastonbury for one and Jack Lamprey, worthless officer as he was, for another.

Jack Lamprey, thought Fielding, as he walked by the sullen waters of the Wash: Jack Lamprey, who had now, after nearly thirty years, suddenly cropped up again, not an hour since, in amazing connection with Raisley Conyngham.

It had happened like this. Dissatisfied and irritated by Maisie's account of Ullacote expedition, brooding uneasily about the purpose and purport of this alleged 'reading party' and the roles which might be thrust on Marius and Tessa in the course of it, Fielding had eventually decided to open the matter up and by way of doing so had telephoned, first of all, to Ptolemaeos Tunne, once a very keen follower of horse racing and still knowledgeable in the field – certainly knowledgeable enough, thought Fielding, to be informative about an owner as unusual in type and occupation (a *schoolmaster*, for Christ's sake) as Raisley Conyngham.

Ptolemaeos had sounded rather truculent on the telephone, deposing that Piero was tiresome insisting that they should take a holiday in the North as they both badly needed a change of air. 'What rubbish,' Ptoly Tunne had said: 'all this fuss and bother to get a few hundred yards higher up.' All the same, he seemed pleased, beneath the surface of his complaint, that someone was taking the trouble to think of his health and well-being, and after a while he consented to spill what beans he had in stock about Conyngham. Raisley Conyngham, he had told Fielding, was old blood (as blood went nowadays) and new money (his father married a chainstore heiress, both now dead). He had for some years been an owner of horses which raced with pretty fair success but only in National Hunt events. He currently owned some nine or ten horses, which were trained for him on his estate at Ullacote in Somerset by a private trainer, a certain Captain Jack Lamprey, formerly of the 49th Earl Hamilton's Light Dragoons, commonly known as Hamilton's Horse, under either title now defunct. *My* Regiment, Fielding had reminded Ptoly: Jack Lamprey was once a subaltern in my Squadron (the 10th) and was the most disgraceful officer in the entire Army List. Be that as it might, Ptolemaeos had pursued, it should be noted that to be allowed a permit as a private trainer was a rare privilege, accorded by the Jockey Club only to persons strongly recommended who would be training for men, like Conyngham, of affluence and fair repute. Was it all above board? Fielding enquired. What else should it be? responded Ptoly. The very facts that Lamprey held a permit, and that Conyngham was allowed a private trainer at all, guaranteed that.

But who on earth could have recommended Jack Lamprey to the Jockey Club? Or to Conyngham? Fielding wanted to know. Jack Lamprey, when he had known him, was an idle, septic-mouthed, sottish, fornicating – Very likely, said Ptoly, but there had since been ample time for amendment of Lamprey's life. He was said to have an almost uncanny knack with horses, and in any case he had a well placed ally in the Jockey Club, a man of almost royal connections, called Giles Glastonbury – also one of Hamilton's Horse. Giles Glastonbury, whinnied Fielding: a duellist, nearly a murderer. That was in another country, said Ptolemaeos blandly, almost in another world. In this country, in this year of grace 1981, Giles Glastonbury called cousins with the Queen (more or less) and was liked and esteemed in the Jockey Club – few members of which were likely to think the less of him because he had once carved a juicy slice with his sabre out of an ex-Nazi braggard called von Augsburg. And that, my dear Fielding, must really be that for to-day, as Piero wants me to make a list of the things I need packed for Scotland and Cumbria.

Jack Lamprey, Fielding thought as Ptoly rang off: *dear God*. Still hankering for evidence (as evidence there must surely be) of disrepute or impropriety, Fielding had next telephoned to Giles Glastonbury at his Club, the Melbourne. Both Giles and he had been in the same Sabre Squadron as (the then) Lieutenant Lamprey in Germany in 1952; but whereas Fielding had been out of touch with him since leaving the Regiment in 1958, Giles, he thought, had clearly kept in touch with Jack and had, on Ptoly

Tunne's showing, absolutely advanced him. This being so, explanation was called for. Lamprey had been an atrocious young man: louche, insolent, perpetually insolvent, and in every way indecorous. Some account was needed to explain why and how such a horrible goose should have grown into so seemly a swan as to find favour extraordinary with the Jockey Club. So, braving the possibility that Giles might be playing backgammon and be strongly resentful of the interruption, Fielding had rung the Melbourne – only to be told that Major Glastonbury was not there and was believed to be out of London.

Trail dead. No, not altogether. What was wrong with telephoning Lamprey himself? Why not? Fielding had been both Second-in-Command of the 10th Sabre Squadron while Lamprey was in it and then, after Giles Glastonbury's temporary disgrace and eclipse, over that matter of the duel, Officer Commanding. Lamprey had 'served' under him for several years and had been much indulged by him: the episode of the cheque, for example, and the NAAFI Manageress – had it not been for Fielding's tactful intervention, in exceedingly tricky circumstances, *that* would almost certainly have led to Jack's being drummed out – a procedure on which Hamilton's Horse still insisted (although the rest of the Army had long since praetermitted it) down to the tiniest and most humiliating *minutiae*, such as the snipping off with the Regimental Barber's scissors, by the latest arrived recruit, of the cashiered officer's fly-buttons. The memory of his rescue from this appalling rite, thought Fielding, must surely incline Lamprey to candour if it was asked of him; so why should Fielding not get hold of him now and request a little straight information in exchange for assistance rendered (albeit rendered nearly thirty years before)?

With considerable persistence, Fielding had then

discovered from Directory Enquiries that Lamprey lived in the Villa Nestor-Juxta-Ullacote and had two telephone numbers: a private one which could not be disclosed and an official or public one which was presumably in his office. In any event, application to it overnight went unanswered, but at nine o'clock the next morning (*this* morning) Lamprey had responded promptly and in person).

'Fielding Gray? You don't sound like him.'

'Some time since we met, Jack. I was blown up in Cyprus, just after you left the Squadron, and that changed my appearance . . . and my voice.'

'Yes. I heard a bit about that. Rotten luck. Not but what you've done a bloody sight better scribbling porn than you would if you'd stayed with that pox-ridden whore, Auntie Army. What is it you want? Don't think I'm not pleased to hear you, but I've got a busy old morning on, and I can't imagine you've rung me up over this distance of years just to ask if I can still get my prick up a hole.'

'Can you?'

'Given a co-operative filly, preferably a many times deflowered sixteen year old, I can just about feed it in like a hose-pipe. What is it you want, Fielding?'

'What are Marius Stern and Tessa Malcolm doing with Conyngham at Ullacote?'

'Not my business, all that. Reading suitable books, I expect.'

'What else?'

'Playing suitable games. Tennis, fencing, cricket. Going walkies.'

'Anything else?'

''Pon my word, Fielding, you're demned inquisitive.'

'Answer up, Jack. There's something else, isn't there?'

'And if there is, why should I tell you?'

'*Res Unius, Res Omnium,* Jack. Our motto in the old mob. Remember?'

'Yes. But only because I've got a long memory. That was a quarter of a century ago.'

'That motto is subject to no statute of limitations. The affair of one member of the regiment is the affair of all, if he wishes it to be, twenty-five years ago or *now*. And assistance given, of which you, God knows, had more than enough from me, must be reciprocated.'

'All right, cobber. But first tell me why you're so interested. Fancy one of them, perhaps?'

'Marius is the son of old friends. Tessa is the – niece of a partner of mine.'

'You could still fancy one of them – or both.'

'Tell, Jack.'

'Nothing much to tell.'

'Then why the reluctance?'

'I was brought up to mind my own business and leave others to mind theirs. So I don't like it when buggers get nosy. However, it is certainly true that I owe you, so I'll give you what return I can . . . which isn't, I warn you, very much. Marius is spending three or four hours a day, apart from all his other activities, learning to be a stable lad.'

'Indeed? Does he like it?'

'He's fond of horses and he has a way with them. Nice, kind pair of hands, as well. I fancy he finds some of the instruction a bit rough, but he likes the lass he's working under and she likes him . . . though she swears at him like a Connaught Ranger, which he don't mind one bit. One more thing: I've told this lass and the rest of 'em to keep their hands off his tassel – in case that worries you.'

'Not much, no. It's Raisley Conyngham that worries

193

me. You must admit that the whole arrangement is peculiar. Will Marius ride?'

'He'll exercise the horse he's in charge of. He's too young to ride in a race, if that's what you mean.'

'You're not telling me much, Jack.'

'I told you just now: nothing much to tell.'

'Try. Remember how I helped you pay back that money you stole from the Squadron Mess. Or the dud cheque you gave the NAAFI Manageress. Or what you tried to do – '

' – I've turned over a lot of new leaves since then. Giles has helped me. I went to pot but then Giles found me and put me here. I've been all right here. It's my last chance, Fielding. Don't go raking up the past. Leave me be.'

'Just remember that money you stole from the Squadron Mess, and try to tell me something to square the debt. Then I'll leave you be.'

'All right. It isn't much but I swear it's all. Conyngham has some scheme afoot. He says it's little more than a joke, and it certainly seems harmless, the little I know of it, but sometimes I wonder. It's to do with the stallion which Marius takes care of – Lover Pie. Some mare of Prideau Glastonbury's is also involved. Now, Prideau lives in Hereford. Giles made a diversion over here on his way there to stay with Prideau. He used to own horses in partnership with Prideau, and I think he might be interested in a leg of this very mare I've just mentioned – Boadicea. The other thing is, there's some trouble about Prideau's son, Myles, and Giles is going round picking up the shit and taking samples off to Prideau. That's the reason he gives for being there now.'

'All rather muddled, Jack.'

'I'm a muddled man.'

'Does Giles know about this scheme? After all, if you

194

think he might be interested in buying a leg of the second horse involved – '

' – I think not. I think that Giles is being left out of this joke.'

'And where does Marius come into it?'

'Walking on part. Stable lad under instruction in charge of Lover Pie. He'll walk Lover Pie round the paddock the next time he races . . . with Gat-Toothed Jenny on hand in case anything goes wrong.'

'Gat-Toothed Jenny?'

'Lass who instructs Marius. Head travelling lass as well. The head lad here is pretty well past it, only kept on because he's got nowhere to go, and Jenny handles the bulk of it.'

'But what is this joke, this scheme?' Fielding asked.

There was a kind of gobbling the other end.

'I'm not sure, Fielding, truly I'm not,' Jack Lamprey fluted down the telephone. 'I just know that Conyngham has warned me that he's getting up some harmless little trick, or trying some experiment, which involves Lover Pie and Boadicea, *with* Prideau's consent, the next time they both go out in the same race. Or the next but one.'

'But Conyngham's a highly respected figure on the turf, or so everyone says. If he weren't, he wouldn't be allowed to have you as his Private Trainer. Now respectable owners, Jack, shouldn't be playing little tricks – not even harmless ones.'

'I told you. This is my last chance. It's not for me to question what my governor's up to.'

'Ringing? Doping? Stopping?'

'A harmless little scheme, he said. A trick or an experiment. But harmless.'

'Let's hope so. Otherwise Conyngham might be seen

off, and your last chance vanish with him. How can I be sure Marius is not in some kind of danger?'

'Because they're both potty about him. Raisley Conyngham and his right-hand man – right-hand boy, I should say – Milo Hedley he's called, one of the boys at Conyngham's school, you know the kind, so important he's almost a master. Neither Conyngham nor Hedley want to *touch*, I think, but they both absolutely dote. As does Tessa – Teresa, as Conyngham calls her. If any harm came to Marius, Teresa would raise the poxy dickens from here to John O'Groats. So there can't be any risk to him.'

'But surely . . . Conyngham must have given you *some* instructions? So you must have *some* idea of what's up?'

'Not really. My instructions are to have Marius ready to lead Lover Pie round the paddock immediately before his next race and probably before the one after. He's got all his documents, the identikit they all have to have to get into racecourse stables and all that – and he's just got to be taught by Jenny and me how to go on with a horse in the paddock before a race. Regis Priory, the first race, Bellhampton Park the next. I must also see that he's taught how to manage or manipulate Lover Pie while taking off his blanket out on the course just before a race, and putting it on again when the race is over. Nothing in the least extraordinary about that. And that's the lot, Fielding. I've done my best for you. Please let me go.'

'All right. One condition: you telephone me if you find out any more.' He gave Jack his telepohone number both at Broughton Staithe and Buttock's Hotel. 'It's true, Jack, that it's a very long time since you put your hands in the Mess funds, and I dare say it's also true that you've turned over lots of new leaves since. But I still think the story would do you no good with the Jockey Club. You know how those sort of chaps feel about Clubs and Messes and all that. So if I ever find that you've been holding out on me . . .'

' – If there's anything more to hear, Fielding, you shall hear it. *Res Unius, Res Omnium,* as you say.'

All the same, thought Fielding now, as he turned back past the gun-sites and towards the golf course, I can't imagine that Jack will shop Raisley Conyngham in a hurry, to me or anyone else. From what they all say, Raisley Conyngham is not the sort of man that anyone shops: for how can you betray a man who rouses, as Conyngham has clearly roused in Jack, both the warmth of loyalty and the chill of fear?

'So old-fashioned, darling,' trilled Ashley Dexterside down the telephone to Theodosia Canteloupe; 'it absolutely creaks. The only thing it's alive with is death-watch beetle.'

As Managing Director of Salinger, Stern & Detterling, he was reporting to Theodosia on Part One of *The Grand Grinder*.

'You'll forgive me, Mr Dexterside,' said Theodosia, 'but I'm not at all sure that you are entitled to be so critical here. I don't think sporting and military achievements are quite in your line.'

'Dear me, no, darling. But one *is* a judge of prose.'

'Is one? I thought one was a judge of advertising material. But never mind that now. I think, and my sister Carmilla thinks, that *The Grand Grinder* has great charm and is shaping very well. We want the provisional

arrangements for publication in January absolutely confirmed, and we should like to know, not later than the
end of July, your exact plans for promotion.'

'If you say so, darling.'

'We say so. And we also say that you know neither of
us well enough to call us "darling".'

'If you say so, dar – Lady Canteloupe.'

'That's better. And another thing. If, as I suspect,
Major Gray is rather short of material for Part Two and
there is a significant falling off in quality, then we shall
simply publish Part One by itself. It will stand quite well
alone.'

'The book would hardly be economic to publish at that
length.'

'Then it will have to be uneconomic, won't it? Its
literary excellence will compensate for that.'

'But the Board –'

' – The Board consists of my husband, my sister, myself,
Isobel Stern, widow of the late Gregory, Colonel Ivan
Blessington –'

' – All of whom will support you. But it also consists,
Lady Canteloupe, of myself and five members of the old
Board of Salinger & Holbrook as agreed at the
amalgamation.'

'If you are about to say, Mr Dexterside, that your party
outnumbers mine, I should go on one side first, if I were
you, and do a little quiet counting of shares. Leave alone
my holding and my sister's, my husband and Isobel Stern
between them –'

' – Point taken, Marchioness. No need to come it so
heavy.'

Theodosia giggled. 'Anyway,' she said, 'I dare say he'll
make as good a job of Part Two as he has of Part One.
And if he doesn't, it won't be altogether his fault. As I

say, material must be getting thin. There's a limit to the amount of scandal and eccentricity that one can squeeze out of one family. But then again, he's a very ingenious writer, and I dare say he'll find a way out of the difficulty.'

'Let's hope so, Marchioness,' intoned Ashley.

'"Marchioness" is a ridiculous form of address.'

'You said I mustn't call you "darling".'

'What was the matter with "Lady Canteloupe"?'

'So frowsty. I know, I shall call you "milady", like your maid would. That way,' cooed Ashley, 'I shall feel deliciously *close*, as if I was brushing your hair or something. And while the mood is so *intime*, milady, let me just repeat: I think *The Grand Grinder* is a load of cold semolina.'

'What do you think of the first part of *The Grand Grinder*?' said Theodosia on the telephone to Ivan Blessington. 'After all, you've known Fielding longer than any of us.'

'What's that got to do with it?'

'Nothing. I'm just rather desperate that somebody should agree with Carmilla and me that it's jolly good stuff.'

"Who told you it wasn't?"

'Ashley Dexterside. He said it was cold semolina. And Canteloupe isn't very keen either. He says it's "mannered". It would have been all right coming from someone like E. F. Benson fifty years ago, he says, or even from J. B. Priestley in the 1960s, but coming here and now it smells of mothballs.'

'Look, my dear,' said Ivan Blessington. 'Men like Fielding's grandfather, who win races and ride away to wars, are not, these days, considered entirely proper. They are thought to be "competitive" or "chauvinistic" or "aggressive". Guts and success do not appeal to the mealy majority who have neither. Or again, when Fielding takes for granted that his great-grandfather had maidservants or that the women and children did whatever they were told at the double, he offends almost everyone under forty. Now, as for Ashley, he is simply bored by the book because he is an old queen who does not begin to understand what it's about; but it's Canteloupe's reaction that is our real worry, because he has spotted that its attitudes and premises are dangerously *dated* – "mannered" is the wrong word, I think.'

'But do *you* like it, Ivan?'

'I do. So does Betty. So do the girls.'

'But the girls are under forty, so surely they ought to be offended . . . according to what you've just been saying?'

'And so they would be – so would you and Carmilla be for that matter – if you'd all gone to a state school. The very idea of anyone's winning anything, of an individual who comes first, would have had you all snarling with resentment. As it is, you and they have been brought up to appreciate effort and courage, so you raise a cheer, along of me and Betty, when Fielding's grandfather comes in by a neck on his chin-strap, and we none of us give a hoot when one of Fielding's great uncles puts his women in their place. But these sort of goings-on will be very unpopular in many other quarters, I can tell you that.'

'But surely,' said Theodosia, 'there's still enough of the old gang around for Fielding to have a large audience?'

'Yes . . . if they get to hear of the book. But Ashley

and his kind will try to kill it . . . not by damning it but by ignoring it, by quietly letting it die the death. And all those knotted up women of either sex who edit or write for the weeklies – they'll see that it never gets more than a scruffy mention at the bottom of a column, two or three lines on "the total deterioration of Mr Fielding Gray's always dubious talent".'

'I've told Ashley to lay on a five-star advertising campaign for just after Christmas.'

'Then we'll both have to breathe on him like Drill Sergeants, or he'll somehow contrive to slide out of it. We'd better get together about this very early, make sure all the foundations are properly laid some months ahead. I'll telephone as soon as we're back from the Balkans. We're off on Thursday. Betty and the girls can hardly wait. They've mapped out every yard of the drive from here to the tip of Taenarus.'

This picture filled Theodosia with such pleasure that she started sniffing heavily into the telephone.

'Thea? Thea? What's the matter, sweetheart?'

'Nothing, Ivan, nothing. Have a lovely. Have a beaut,' she said, a curious formula which she reserved for her most rare and especial blessings.

'The thing is, darling,' said Len to Carmilla Salinger, as they walked on the lawn of the Great Court of Lancaster, 'that you like this stuff of Fielding's, and I like it, and Tom likes it, and Ivor Winstanley likes it, and the Greco likes it – or so he said yesterday before leaving for Italy –

and even Nicos likes it in so far as he can understand it, because we all of us still believe in outmoded concepts such as honour, rank, merit and reward. Since we believe in them, we can admire and applaud those who attain to them, and we can also see the absurdity, the tragedy or the wickedness of those who *should* attain to them but either fall short of them or deliberately reject them. Believing in honour and appreciating its exercise, we can also believe in treachery and appreciate *its* exercise, whether as matter for moral disapproval or merely for a grim smile. We see *the point*. When Fielding's great uncle sells the formula for the meat pies, we know that this is treachery, albeit of a mildly comic kind, and we can evaluate and relish the whole affair. But most people in the world can no longer do this. They do not know that honour or treachery even exist. To them the sale of the secret of the pie filling is not a gross betrayal of family confidence but simply a natural thing to do if you happen to be low in luck or money. To them there are no obligations, only gratifications to which they all have a "right": and as for rewards, the whole idea is obscene to them as they think that anything or everything available to reward one person should be shared, as of "right", between them all. It follows that this book of Fielding's will go straight up the nose of the great British public, who will be annoyed and made envious by instances in which merit brings reward, while they will simply not understand the humour, sadness, evil or irony of instances in which the code is accidentally or otherwise flouted. No distinctions will be drawn, no judgements made, no jokes seen or savoured. The universal response will be: so bloody what?'

'Thea tells me that both Canteloupe and Ivan Blessington have been saying the same,' Carmilla said.

'Not that it matters much,' said Len: 'who cares about the groundlings anyway?'

'We all used to,' said Provost Llewyllyn, who for some time had been pursuing them from behind; 'but I for one have found that their appeal diminishes with the years.'

Len and Carmilla turned to look at him, then halted until he came up to them. They then secured him between them, one arm apiece, and carried him slowly onward.

'I have had an idea,' said the Provost, merrily vibrating his now unneeded stick a few inches above the grass, 'which I am going to convey to you both. Shall we invite Fielding to come and write the second half of his book here in Lancaster? He could have one of the best guest suites – the Orde or the Bevis. It's not good for him to be skulking alone at Broughton, and I have always doubted the desirability of that woman with whom he consorts in Buttock's Hotel.'

'"Desirable" she was and still is,' said Len, 'if rather plump. I think you mean her "suitability", Provost.'

'I suppose so. She has a vulgar mind. Yet I believe her to be honest,' he muttered, casting his mind back to his one private encounter with Maisie Malcolm some eighteen years before.

'If you think she's unsuitable for Fielding,' said Len, 'why did you sell her your share of Buttock's?'

'Because at that time I wished to be rid of it,' said Tom Llewyllyn, 'and because the money was good. Now: shall we or shall we not invite Fielding to come and finish his book in the Bevis Guest Suite? I for one could relish a dose of him just now. I am in the mood to be refreshed by his pithy contempt of humanity. What do you say, Carmilla Salinger?'

'By all means invite Fielding,' said Carmilla, as the trio stopped to survey Holy Henry in the middle of his pool, 'but don't expect me to help you entertain him. Or not for the next few days. I have another cross to bear.'

'Darling?' said Len.

'You remember Myles Glastonbury? Captain of Cambridge Royal Tennis the first year that Thea played?'

'A dull young man and not even physically appetizing. Hardly, indeed, wholesome.'

'It appears he has a passion for me. Thea and Canteloupe have persuaded me to let him come here and state his case. I feel like Portia or Olivia, besieged by unwanted men.'

'And quite as rich as either of them,' remarked Tom.

'Rather more so,' supplemented Len.

'Though let us not forget,' said Tom, 'that in both cases Mister Right emerged from the distasteful ruck – to share the lady's great possessions.'

'Myles Glastonbury,' said Carmilla, 'has his own possessions. His father, Prideau, owns an estate near Hereford and many racehorses. Thea went to stay there once.'

'Why didn't he get keen on Thea?' asked Len. 'She was the one he played tennis with.'

'He is said to admire my mind,' said Carmilla.

'Well, if you need a respite from him, you know where to find your old friends,' said Len. 'In the old place,' he said, gesturing over the lawn in the direction of the Provost's Lodging. And then to Tom, 'I'll go and summon Fielding, Provost. You'd like that, wouldn't you, dear?'

'Please, Len,' said the Provost, as if he no longer cared very much.

My God, thought Carmilla, he's crumbling daily. Just for a few minutes the prospect of inviting Fielding Gray gave him back something of his old vigour and gaiety; but already that stimulant has ceased to act.

'Carmilla will bring you back to your Lodging when

you've had enough of your walk,' said Len. 'The sooner I start telephoning Fielding, the better. He can be very slippery.'

'I'm not sure it's worth it, after all,' said Provost Llewyllyn.

'Nonsense, darling,' said Carmilla: 'you'll be delighted when he gets here.'

'Yes. No. No. Len, Len . . .'

But Len was already out of earshot of the thin old voice. For a while the Provost continued to survey King Henry; then he began to cry.

'What I have done,' he snivelled, 'is as bad as if I removed or desecrated this statue.'

'What have you done?' said Carmilla, who knew what was coming.

'I have destroyed the elms of the Avenue.'

'Nonsense. That was a decision of the College Council which had to be taken. Those trees were diseased.'

'What of the tree-nymphs?'

'Either they are dead and at peace,' said Carmilla, who had had this conversation with Tom many times, 'or they have gone elsewhere and are happy there. If they were not happy, they would have returned to haunt us.'

'They never went. They stayed. And they did not die when the trees died. They lurk in the meadows and the wilderness and in the Fellows' Garden, by the Judas Tree. I hear them calling in the night wind.'

'No one else does.'

'Then all but me are deaf. They say that they will soon find a way into my garden, the Provost's Garden. This they cannot at present do, because my garden is enclosed on all sides by the Lodging and other buildings, and dryads cannot move through human habitations and under a roof. The moment they have a roof between them and the sky, they do indeed die. So they are waiting until somehow a path is made for them, and then they will enter my garden to take their vengeance.'

Carmilla began to propel the Provost slowly back across the lawn and towards the path that led to his Lodging. As they went, she saw, out of the corner of her eye, a young man come through the Gate Arch from King's Parade and enter the Porter's Lodge; a young man who was wearing a dark blue overcoat with velvet lapels and was carrying two hundred and fifty pounds' worth of suitcase; a young man with a pasty complexion, close eyes, and a turned down mouth: Myles Glastonbury. He'll go to my rooms, thought Carmilla, and just wait. However long I take getting Tom back to the Provost's Lodging, however long I loiter there with Tom and Len, Myles Glastonbury will wait. It's really too bad of Thea and Canteloupe to make me have him here, thought Carmilla. How long did I say he could stay? One night, I think: but they stood out for three: 'Give him a fair run,' they said. Well, if he's got any decency in him he'll very soon realize that he isn't wanted and take himself off to-morrow.

Maisie Malcolm had been looking forward, now that Tessa was safely out of the way, to a companionable few weeks with Fielding Gray in Buttock's Hotel. She was therefore very annoyed when he telephoned from Broughton Staithe to say that he was about to leave Broughton, not for London, but for Lancaster College.

'Len rang up,' he said.

'Bugger Len.'

'He says that the Provost is out of sorts and needs cheering up by his old friends.'

'Bugger the Provost and bugger his old friends.'

'Bugger me in fact?'

'Yes. I hope your balls drop out and bounce and knock your silly head off.'

Fielding laughed and hung up. Maisie meditated for a while on the perversity of men who were always strewn about the place when not wanted and would not come when they were. She decided to telephone Fielding and say would he, after all, come fairly soon to Buttock's, as she rather – well – missed him. When she dialled Fielding's number at Broughton there was no answer: Fielding had already gone.

Jack Lamprey, having learnt a little more (if not much) about Raisley Conyngham's scheme with Prideau Glastonbury, decided he would ring up Fielding Gray and tell it to him. The more people one had on one's side the better, Jack reflected, and he was eager to demonstrate his good faith to Fielding in case Fielding should indeed keep his threat and go telling nasty tales of Jack's army youth to the Jockey Club (not that Fielding would have much pull there, thought Jack, but he might raise a bit of a smell). What Jack had discovered, from overhearing (not by chance) a telephone conversation between Raisley Conyngham and Prideau Glastonbury, was that Tessa, or Teresa as Raisley called her, was to be kept absolutely out of the way on the occasion of Lover Pie's race at Regis Priory, but was to figure, in some unexplained but clearly important role, in whatever was planned for the meeting at Bellhampton Park. Of her function there, Jack could gather only that it depended on the fact that she disliked horses and they disliked her.

Jack tried Fielding's Broughton number first and drew blank. Then he tried the London number he had been given, and got a voluble female who declared she was sick of the entire male sex, himself included, and that as for Fielding Gray she hoped his bowels would seize up and swell until they burst asunder, that she had no idea where he was to be found but hoped it was in Hades, and that was all about that.

Some time later she realized how childish she had been and fretted to make amends; but she had not heeded when Jack spoke his name, and had not the slightest notion who, what or where he was. So she could not get back to Jack and though she could have been in touch quite easily with Fielding Gray at Lancaster, she decided not to be: first because she disliked the oily tone in which Len, the Provost's Private Secretary, always addressed her on the telephone, and secondly because she had nothing of substance or certainty to tell Fielding except that she, Maisie, had behaved like a silly, malicious old cow.

'Well, young 'un,' said Gat-Toothed Jenny to Marius during the five minute break which she allowed him at mid-afternoon, 'how do you like being a stable lad?'

Marius looked at her huge, hanging breasts, then down to her vast hips, then up again to the kind, common, eager face.

'Know me if you see me again, will you?' said Jenny. 'Answer the question, my pretty gentleman: how do you like your new work?'

After a long pause Marius said:

'It is dirty, disgusting and exhausting. Each day I long for it to be over. And yet there is nothing more satisfying in the whole world than learning from somebody who really understands and loves what he is doing. What *she* is doing, in this case. Will that do for an answer?'

'Pretty well, me darlin',' said Gat-Toothed Jenny, 'it'll do pretty well.'

So far from taking himself off, Myles Glastonbury showed every sign of staying, if he could manage it, for ever. On his second night in Cambridge, after Carmilla had spent three hours explaining to him, or rather repeating to him, that she could not possibly respond to his infatuation (for such she insisted it must be), and after she had then bidden him Godspeed, excusing herself from seeing him off in the morning on grounds of work, he had primly pursed his face and solemnly informed her that he had a 'head cold' coming on and that he must therefore remain in the College at least until the day after next and possibly far longer.

Before Carmilla could recover from this piece of information, he had wished her good-night and gone. A few minutes later she had got enough of her wind back to telephone Len in the Provost's Lodging and seek his assistance in dislodging her importunate guest. Len said he would visit Glastonbury in his guest room early the next day and try what he could: would Carmilla mind if the fellow were quite simply expelled by order of the Provost? No, Carmilla would not: but let the use of courtesy, if possible, prevail.

Later on, while discussing this problem with Fielding Gray (now happily installed in the Bevis Guest Suite and dining nightly with Len and Tom in the Provost's Lodging – for it was seldom, these days, that Tom went to High Table), Len discovered that for many years, off rather than on, Fielding had known one Major Glastonbury, who appeared to be some kind of cousin to Myles's father, Prideau. After Fielding had entertained Len to an account of the duel which Giles had fought with the Graf von Augsburg in the ruins of Hanover, Len proposed that Fielding should accompany him on his visit to Myles the next morning, as Fielding's acquaintance with Myles's family might help (though exactly how, neither Len nor Fielding was very clear) to keep Myles's dismissal from the College precincts as quiet and friendly a matter as possible.

However, when Len and Fielding arrived in the Adcock

(Bed-sitting) Guest Room at nine-thirty the following day, they found that Myles Glastonbury was, beyond doubt, an ill man. He was still in pyjamas, sitting huddled in a blanket within millimetres of the electric fire; his face was chalk; his teeth rattled every few seconds; his 'head cold' had evidently turned, overnight, into a virulent dose of flu.

Len immediately departed to summon the College Matron, as he said, and also, as he didn't say, to warn Carmilla of this tedious development. Fielding was left to amuse Myles, in so far as the wretched youth was still amusable, and could think of no better way of doing so than repeating the story, which he had told Len the previous night, of how Myles's Uncle (or would it be Cousin?) Giles had tricked the Graf von Augsburg into over-confidence, at a late stage of the duel in the ruins, and then nearly sliced his head off his shoulders.

'They had to get your uncle out of the way *instanter*,' Fielding said. 'I'm not quite sure how it was done. Canteloupe – Detterling, as we called him then – happened to be passing through Germany at the time, and I remember he had a hand in it. He pulled rank as an MP and drilled us all in the same lie about how Giles's foot had slipped and turned an intended feint into a lethal lunge. The end of it was that Giles was whisked away to Hong Kong and I became OC of the 10th Sabre Squadron, which Giles had been commanding. But that is another, and very long, story.'

Fielding's narrative had clearly engaged Myles's interest and to some extent mended his condition, for the time at least.

'Did you ever know,' he asked, 'what Cousin Giles did when they got him to Hong Kong?'

'Not really. I saw very little of him between the duel

211

back in fifty-two and last Christmas at Canteloupe's. I don't suppose I saw him a dozen times in the interval – and then only at regimental jamborees.'

'Well,' said Myles, in a deep and beautiful voice somewhat blurred by accretion of phlegm, 'they employed him as he'd been employed in India in the 1940s. Unofficial executioner. He was good at that. Did you know that there's a vicious streak in our family? A killer instinct?'

'I know that during the war, Giles once shot one of his own men out of hand, because he was asleep on sentry duty while in action.'

'That was unpremeditated: the venial if rather extreme reaction of an officer who must ensure absolute discipline in time of crisis . . . and has hundreds of men in his care. But Uncle, or Cousin, Giles was quite good at *planning* murders too – murders which came out as "accidental death" with watertight explanations. I think you know Peter Morrison, now Lord Luffham?'

'Intimately . . . once.'

'Did he never tell you how Uncle Giles masterminded the assassination of an annoying Muslim in 1946? The whole thing was perfectly arranged so that the killers – young officers in the Wessex Fusiliers, which was Morrison's regiment – should appear to have been carrying out their difficult duties in irreproachable fashion, in the face of intolerable provocation and violent physical threat by the Muslim. Then there was an "accident" – the equivalent of Uncle Giles's foot slipping during the duel – and there lay the Muslim, conveniently dead, and nobody to blame except himself. Champagne and medals all round.'

'How do you know all this?'

'My father told me. Uncle Giles and my father are great confidantes. So are my father and I.'

Myles began to look pale and unhappy again.

'Look,' he said to Fielding. 'I've heard a lot about you. You're the sort people talk about. There's your novels, for a start, your wounds, your hotel . . . and your friends. Not the least of these is Canteloupe – whom, as you say, one used to call Detterling . . . and in whose house you last met Uncle Giles . . . at Christmas. But you've known him . . . Canteloupe . . . for a very long time before that –'

' – Since 1945 – '

' – Which means you must have known his first wife, Baby, and her cousin, Marius . . . the son of your publisher, Gregory Stern, now dead. You've known all these people, Major Gray?'

'Yes. I have.'

'Well, look . . . I'm rather ill, I think. What I'm saying may not make much sense to you and it may be coming out in the wrong order, but I beg you to take notice.'

'Speak as you find.'

'My father, Prideau, has always envied Giles's exploits, and wants to show how he's capable of the same sort of thing himself. But my father does *not* want to kill or to inflict the slightest harm on anybody: he just wants to show that he can *plot* as well as Giles . . . exercise the same sort of cunning with the chess pieces. All right so far?'

'All right so far.'

'Now, my father, Prideau, has a friend called Raisley Conyngham, a rich schoolie who runs horses. He was up here with my father, not at this college, it doesn't matter which, they've known each other for many years. As for me, Major Gray, I've hated this Conyngham ever since I can remember. Smooth and smarmy. Dangerous with it. He used to pat my head when I was seven or eight, and I always used to shrivel up with horror because I *felt* that

213

he would just as soon have been slitting my windpipe and was quite capable of it. He knew he inspired this loathing in me and used to pat my head more and more often in consequence . . . I was once beaten by my father for hacking at Conyngham's shins. You understand so far?'

'I understand so far.'

'Now listen, sir. I think something rather funny's happening to me and I want to tell someone what I know while I still seem sane. I *do* seem sane?'

'Eminently.'

'Conyngham knows about my father's ambition to emulate Uncle Giles's plots – *harmlessly*, as I said. So Conyngham has proposed a plan to my father – it's to do with some horses they own – which will serve very well and by which Uncle Giles will be much impressed when it is applied. Uncle Giles, for once, is *not* in the secret: my father aims to surprise him. The plan makes use of that young Marius and also the girl who's staying at Ullacote. I know all this because my father told me.'

Myles stopped and coughed with a rasp.

'*What* then, is the plan?' Fielding said.

'Tell you in a minute. But first I want you to understand that I feel – I can't prove but I feel – just as I used to feel, he'd happily cut my throat if it met his purpose – that Raisley Conyngham's real plan is not what my father thinks it is.'

'Not harmless?'

'Dangerous at least. Perhaps lethal.'

'To whom?'

'I don't know. It could be any of the people involved, except Conyngham.'

'Deliberately so?'

'Perhaps not. But taking what Conyngham must know to be a horrible risk.'

'And since you only *feel* all this, you cannot be precise?'

'No. But I know my feeling . . . my intuition . . . is not at fault, because the last time I saw Conyngham at my father's home – quite accidentally, I only came home for the night by chance – I not only *felt* that something was wrong, and that I ought to warn my father, but I felt Conyngham feeling me feel it, as he always had when he patted my head as a boy. So he patted my head this time too, and he said, "Do you remember, Myles, how I used to do this to you when you were small?" Just to let me know he was on my wavelength, you see. And now I am not well. Do you know that novel of Balzac's, a short story really, one of those about the "Thirteen", and the Arch-Crook, not Vautrin but another arch-crook, pats a young man's hair, and the young man falls into a hideous decline – '

' – Stop it,' snapped Fielding. 'I do know the story: Balzac at his silliest. Now collect yourself, and tell me what I must know: what is this plan as your father conceives it? Never mind just now how Conyngham may aim to pervert it. What does your father *think* is intended?'

'It's to do with the horses. There are to be two races, one at Regis Priory and one at Bellhampton, 'chases of three mile odd, in which Conyngham's stallion, Lover Pie, will be opposed by, among others, my father's mare, Boadicea. Now, as you may know, Marius Stern is being instructed as a stable lad by Conyngham's Private Trainer, Captain Jack Lamprey. When it is time for the race at Regis Priory, Marius will go there with Lover Pie and with nominal charge of him – though both of 'em will be carefully watched by Lamprey's head travelling lass, Jenny, Gat-Toothed Jenny. Now, while Marius is leading Lover Pie round the paddock – '

– Len came in with the College Matron, who looked at Myles Glastonbury, at first with concern and then with mounting dismay. She put a thermometer in his mouth; examined his neck and arm-pits; and then, unembarrassed by Myles or the audience, his groin, and then his feet. She took the thermometer out of his mouth, read it, primmed her mouth, shook down the thermometer, put it away in her huge bosom, opened a black bag, produced a Heath Robinson type of syringe, shot some liquid into the air, injected Myles on the inside of his elbow, and said to Len:

'Case for Sick Bay. Tell Wilfred to send a stretcher and bearers. I'll go ahead and make up the bed.'

'I can walk,' said Myles Glastonbury.

'Indeed you'll do what you're told.'

'Right,' said Len, sorting everybody out. 'Matron to the Sick Bay. I myself will telephone Wilfred in the Porters' Lodge. You stay here with Glastonbury, Fielding, till the stretcher party comes.'

Good, thought Fielding; now for the rest of it. As soon as they were alone together, he said to Myles Glastonbury:

'And then, while Marius is leading Lover Pie round the paddock at Regis Priory . . .?'

'What is the man's name?' muttered Myles, thick and very low, 'The one that touched the young man's hair? *Not* Vautrin. By way of benediction everyone thought, but – '

' – Myles. Back to Regis Priory. Your father thinks there is a plan. What is it?'

'Ferragus. Ferragus the Twenty-Third. Why the Twenty-Third?'

'I told you. Balzac's monstrous silliness. Please, Myles.

I thought there must be something wrong about Conyngham too. Everyone else said "no". But I'm on your side.
If he's really up to anything seriously wrong, you *must* tell
me his plan.'

'Conyngham. Don't know his plan.'

'But you know what your father thinks his plan to be?
They worked on it together.'

'The Comte de Marsay worked for a "demon". The
devil, I suppose, or one of his assistants. De Marsay was
another of the "Thirteen". It can't be much fun working
for the demon or the devil and *knowing* that things will
go right for you. For the time being at least. No sense of
personal achievement, if the demon does it all.'

'MYLES. Please.'

Myles stirred, and looked at Fielding, as if understanding him. 'My father's plan?' he said.

'What your father thinks the plan is. Please.'

Four porters entered, arranged the debilitated and now
almost unconscious Glastonbury on a stretcher, and carried him away to the College Sick Bay.

When Rosie had Oenone in her charge (which was most
of the time) they went either to the meadows near the
chancel in which they lived, or more often, into the old
part of the churchyard, where Oenone liked to clamber
on the sunken box tombs and hide from Rosie behind the
broken stone coffins. On one occasion, Oenone went right
into a coffin and lay flat. It took Rosie a long time to find
her, as it had not occurred to her that Oenone might hide
in this way, and when she did find her she came nearer to

217

scolding her than at any time since she had arrived in Saint-Bertrand-de-Comminges at the beginning of the holidays.

'You must never lie in there again,' she said.

'Why not, Rosie?'

Unwilling to give tongue to the irrational and atavistic fears which moved her, knowing, in any case, that Oenone would not understand the concept of death or the dangers of aping its postures in its own place (and thus perhaps inviting it to regard one as its own), Rosie had recourse to traditional nursery discipline.

'You must not lie in there because I say you must not,' she said.

Oenone's face twisted.

'Oenone likes those old stone boxes,' she said.

'You can like them: you can touch them: you must not lie in them.'

'*Why not?*'

Clearly, thought Rosie, something more than a simple 'nanny knows best' is required of me.

'Because an angel might fly over and shut you up in one of them for ever.'

Oenone was impressed by this speech. She came and held Rosie's hand and snuggled into her thighs.

'But Rosie will take care of Oenone,' she said.

'Yes. If she does not lie in those boxes. The angel might not like it, and Rosie cannot help Oenone against an angel.'

She had a vision of the angel in its passing. It was female and carried a torch as it flew, although it was travelling through broad daylight. It had Tessa Malcolm's gentle face and auburn hair, though this was much longer than Tessa's. Like Tessa, it had a very slight lump on one of its shoulder-blades. I wonder whether she's having a

218

nice time in Somerset with Marius, thought Rosie: whether she's having a nice time or not, she's doing what she thinks she wants to, and there's an end of it.

She prised Oenone away from her fork and said:

'Now we shall walk up to the square of the cathedral and have ice-cream in the café of the hotel.'

'Rosie will carry Oenone.'

'No. Oenone is big enough to walk.'

'Twelve-thirty, dinner time,' Gat-Toothed Jenny said. 'That's it for today, heart. You're improving. I've talked to Jack, and we've agreed you can have the afternoon off.'

'Thank you, Jenny.'

'What shall you do with it?'

'First of all, I shall have a bath.'

'I wish I could give you your bath. Scrape the dirt away. Soap your legs and arms and wash them. Dry you off afterwards. Would you like that?'

'My mother used to bath me when I was little. I think I am too old to be bathed now.'

'Not if you fancied the person that did it. Did you fancy your mother?'

'I suppose so. Without really knowing,' Marius said.

'Where is she now?'

'In France with her lover.'

'What's he like?'

'He's a woman. A girl.'

219

'Oh,' said Jenny, unshocked, unsurprised, uninterested. 'Do you miss your mother?'

'Sometimes. But not much. In a funny way, you make up for her. Being so kind, yet so fierce and bossy. Using such foul language – my mother is a great one for foul language. But there are a lot of differences.'

'I expect there are.'

'For instance, I can never quite trust my mother. She doesn't always tell the truth. I can trust you, Jenny.'

'I'm too stupid to make things up, you mean.'

'Too decent.'

'Give me a cuddle, sweetheart,' Jenny said. 'I won't muss you up at all, I promise. Just a cuddle.'

Marius rested his cheek on her right breast and nuzzled the left with his nose and chin.

'Christ, I wish you were my own,' said Jenny, pressing his head more tightly against her with her thick, brown fingers. 'Tell us a word.'

'A word?'

'You know.'

'I like being with you like this,' said Marius. 'I used to be like this with my nanny sometimes. And once with the matron of my school, when I was ill in the sickroom. Warm and safe. Thank you, Jenny. And now it is time I went and had my bath.'

The Blessington family were having a picnic by the River Acheron, prior to paying a visit to the necromanteion in the village on the hill above.

'The necromancers drugged their clients,' said Jakki,

who had been reading up on it in the guide book, 'and sent them down in a kind of lift. Then, when the clients thought they had descended to the underworld, they were told prophecies by out-of-work actors who were pretending to be ghosts. The priests extorted a lot of money from the customers, because the ghosts always faded away just as they were getting to the interesting bits, and the customers had to come back again the next day and pay for another trip.'

'It reminds me of night clubs in Berlin,' said Ivan, 'in the late 1940s. Strip shows. You never quite saw what you wanted, but you were told it would be revealed in the next act. So you stayed another half hour and drank a lot more disgusting champagne at God knows what a bottle.'

'What a good thing you married Mummy,' said Caroline, 'if *that's* the kind of thing you used to do before.'

'Far worse things than that, I promise you,' said Ivan. 'Yes. I think it was a good thing I married Mummy.' He put a finger over one of Betty's, where it lay on her thigh. 'Do you remember the day I asked you?' he said. 'In that boat-house, in the rain?'

'Get on with your nice taramasalata,' said Betty, eyes brimming, 'and allow me to get on with mine.'

She yanked her finger from under his.

'All right. Let's be unromantic,' said Ivan. 'Now then: family vote. After the necromancy place, we can either backtrack a bit and spend the night in the Xenia at Arta, which is listed as very comfortable and is inside an old castle and apparently has an adequate restaurant; or we can advance to the shores of the Corinthian Gulf and try Naupactos, famous for its sea battles, where there will be another and more prominent castle and uncertainty about hotels and dinner.'

'We mustn't forget Nike,' said Jakki: 'there's time for

that after the necromanteion *if* we decide to sleep in Arta.'–

'What's at Nike?' said Betty.

'A whole ruined city: walls, theatres, Byzantine churches, and a museum, noted for its mosaics.'

'You seem to have gone into just about everything,' said Ivan: 'I hope you're keeping a diary.'

'What for?'

'So that you'll remember all this.'

'How could I ever forget it?'

'A diary to show your friends,' said Betty: 'Rosie and Tessa and Marius.'

'Rosie might be interested,' said Jakki. 'Tessa and Marius have rather moved on. They'd be polite, of course, if I showed them a diary – particularly if there were photos as well. But they'd soon put it down and start talking to each other about something else. It's as well to be clear about these things. When we were two or three years younger, we were all terrific friends, and when we're a few years older we probably will be again; but while we're going through adolescence, a year or two in age makes such a difference that there are bound to be cracks and gaps.' She gulped, but, 'Hiatuses,' she concluded firmly, and helped herself to a great deal more taramasalata than she meant to.

'Leave some for me,' said her father, and blew her a kiss.

Pally Palairet, staying in a house called Sandy Lodge because it was in the dunes at Burnham and almost in the sea, went to his jolly spinster aunt (who had built it there) and showed her the Four Day Declarations for Regis Priory, as listed in that morning's *Sporting Life*, which paper alone the old girl had delivered daily, seeing no point in any other.

'I particularly want to watch a horse called Lover Pie,' said Palairet.

'A stallion which goes over fences,' remarked Auntie from memory: 'unusual. Though there was always good old Rubor . . . Of course we'll go if you want.'

The reason why Palairet wished to watch Lover Pie was the horse's association with Marius: *not* because Marius was its stable boy (for Palairet was as yet entirely ignorant of this last, which on Milo's insistence had been kept an absolute secret at school) but because Marius had once told him that he had made a lot of money on Lover Pie when he had won a flat race at Newmarket some years before.

Although Palairet was determined to follow Jeremy's advice and keep absolutely away from Marius for the next six months, he felt that he could not live without some occasional reminder of his friend (a place they had visited together, or a film they had watched), and a sight of Lover Pie would serve very well. Palairet, thought Palairet, could watch Lover Pie in the paddock at Regis Priory (some two hours' drive from Burnham) and think of Marius as he had been when two and a half years younger, as he had watched the horse in the paddock at Newmarket and then cut away to back it; and this would make him (Palairet) quite happy in a melancholy way. Whether Palairet would still have wished to see Lover Pie had he known that its owner was Raisley Conyngham and that there must therefore be at least a chance of Marius's being present as Conyngham's guest, is a nice question. He had sworn that Marius should not get even a glimpse of him (and *vice versa*) for half a year, and he meant to keep his oath; on the other hand he might have thought that a coincidental meeting on a racecourse (should such occur) need not really count. The truth is, however, that Pally did not know that Lover Pie was Raisley Conyngham's horse, did not know that Marius was being trained as Lover Pie's stable boy or indeed had ever set eyes on it since the Newmarket bonanza two and a half years before, and did not know that Marius would be present at Regis Priory. He had asked his old Auntie to take him there simply because he would get an emotional pleasure out of backing and watching a horse whom Marius had once backed and watched; and his old Auntie had agreed to take him because she was (though poor these days) a kind, sporty, energetic woman, who loved her nephew and was only too glad to give him any treat that she could conceivably afford, particularly just at this time when he was looking (so she averred to herself) very peaky and low.

Milo Hedley sat with Tessa Malcolm under a plover cut from yew, in the garden of Montacute House. Tessa was reading aloud from Gibbon about the translation of Theodora from whore to empress.

'That will do, sweetheart,' Milo said: 'you read it very nicely.'

'Thank you, Milo,' said Tessa, and blushed fiercely. God make him hold my hand, she thought; God make him touch me in any way he likes.

'The point is,' said Milo, 'as of course Theodora discovered, that virtue is much more rewarding, amusing and generally agreeable than vice. Although vice has marvellous, even ecstatic moments, these are heavily paid for by bankruptcy, disease and ostracism. Virtue, on the other hand, if not exaggerated by excessive abstinence or perverted into martyrdom, can offer comfort, entertainment and excellent livelihood: bishops' palaces, the right to censure mankind, a plenitude of tithes, or, as in Theodora's case, an imperial crown.'

God make him touch me, make him put his knee against mine.

'Didn't she become a saint?' said Tessa.

'Yes. She altogether overdid it . . . She took religion seriously, went in for inquisitions and persecutions, and became a monster of bigotry and zeal. Though even that,' said Milo, 'tiresome as we may find it, must have been more fun for Theodora than being a creature of the common pleasure . . . in which role she was equally extreme. Do you read Greek, sweet Tessa?'

'I'm afraid not, Milo.' Sweet Tessa . . . thank you, God.

'Then I shall translate these footnotes for you. Or give you the gist of them. It seems that Theodora used to lie prostrate and have pieces of grain scattered in and round her groin.' Very lightly and for a split of a split second, he touched Tessa's lower belly. 'In the hair . . . just there. You have hair there, Tessa?'

She nodded.

'What colour?'

She pointed to the hair on her forehead.

'How charming. I doubt whether Theodora's was such a pretty colour. Anyway, after the grain had been scattered in it, two geese were let loose, who came and pecked the grain out of Theodora's crutch, thus driving her and her audience – for this was a public performance, you understand – into frenzies of pleasure. What do you make of that?'

'Nothing much,' said Tessa. 'Oh Milo, please kiss me.'

'With pleasure.'

He kissed her gently on the forehead.

'Raisley Conyngham,' Milo continued, 'says that there used to be a prostitute in London – retired now – who sometimes gave the same kind of exhibition. Mandie, or Marilyn, she was called, I forget the exact name just now: Marie or Myra, something rather like that; she was famous in her day. Raisley went to one of her performances. Very dull work, he told me, except for one moment when Muriel or Maida or whatever opened up her legs and put the goose's head and neck into her – '

'Milo, please stop. Why are you telling me all this?'

'As part of your education. And to see how you react.

Quite admirably. No silly prudishness, but politely urged objection when the thing grows tasteless.' He stood up. 'Come along,' he said, 'we have a long drive back to Ullacote. If you were over seventeen, we could stick up an L-plate and give you driving lessons. I should like to see those delicious legs of yours straddling the controls. I'm glad you're wearing a dress to-day. I get dreadfully fed up with those boring, impregnable jeans.'

'Milo. Say something *nice* to me.'

'Very well. If you will say something nice back.'

'You first.'

'Sweet Tessa, adorable Tessa . . . I love your elbows, little one, and I love your knees. It is my wish to kiss the inside of your elbow . . .' He held her arm, which was bare to the upper part, and kissed the fold of it. '. . . And also to kiss you one day, not now, just above the top of your stocking, behind the knee . . . and between the sinews. May I?'

'Yes. If you will only believe what I am going to say to you. I love you, Milo; love you.'

'Good. Then from now on you will do whatever I ask you? It will not be to give me your maidenhead, I promise you that: unless, that is, you wish to. But curious things may be going to happen to us all before very long, and I must be assured of your absolute obedience above all else.'

'You always were.'

'Even if it meant . . . harming Marius?'

'Surely you cannot wish to harm Marius?'

'No. But he may be required to take risks. If so, you must not dissuade him.'

'I shan't . . . if he is willing.'

'He may not know he is taking risks. But you, being

227

female, might see the risks where he does not. If so, you must not tell him.'

'Oh Milo. I love Marius.'

'You just said you loved me.'

'I do, I do. But Marius is like my brother, something I never had . . . just as his sister Rosie is like my sister. I cannot see him take risks without warning him.'

'You decide,' said Milo coldly. For the first time that afternoon he ceased to smile.

Looking at Milo's blank face, Tessa felt the ice creep into her soul. 'Oh Milo, Milo . . . Very well. If you will do as you say, and kiss me behind the knee . . . not now, but later . . . I shall obey you in this too. But Milo, you must smile again.'

'Of course. And you must not displease me ever again as you have just done. You will find that it is very easy to extinguish the smile on someone's face but sometimes very hard to rekindle it. In this case, there is no trouble.' Milo resumed his Archaic smile. 'But later on there might be,' he said, 'if you should disobey me at some difficult moment.'

'"τοῖς δὲ ἀποψηφισαμένοις ἡδέως ἂν διαλεχθείην,"' read Marius to Raisley Conyngham: 'But with those who voted for my acquittal I should like to converse about what has happened, while the authorities are busy and before I go to the place where I must die."'

'Very good,' said Conyngham.

They both looked down from Dunkery Beacon across the moors.

'When I was doing my National Service,' said Raisley Conyngham, 'we spent two days and three nights on a manoeuvre on these moors. Although it was midsummer, I have never been so cold and utterly miserable in all my life. I acquitted myself so badly that I very nearly didn't get my commission. In fact, I should not have done, had not Giles Glastonbury done some fiddle on my behalf through a friend in the War Office. I knew Prideau at Cambridge, you see, and through him I'd met his cousin Giles, and I suppose Giles thought I might be useful one day and so was worth a substantial favour. And so I was. He has claimed several favours in return, from time to time, one of them being my appointment of Jack Lamprey as my Private Trainer. Do you get on well with Jack?'

'I think so, sir. I like him, and I do my best to please him.'

'Good. Everyone seems to enjoy trying to please Jack. Rather odd, if one thinks about it carefully, but undeniably the case.'

'A question, sir, if I may?'

'You may.'

'From what you say, you must have been at Cambridge, where you met Mr Prideau Glastonbury, *before* you did your National Service. Rather unusual, sir?'

'But not unheard of. I'd hoped that if I went to Cambridge straight from school – as one was allowed to do if one's college could take one – *something* might turn up or be got up to get me out of National Service later on. No such luck. Not even Giles could manage that – he could arrange promotion but not exemption. The only way I could have avoided it would have been by switching to science or medicine, which was unthinkable. I am for the Classics, as you know. Which brings us back to the *Apology*. And so, Marius the Egyptian – as Milo would say – you have read the passage that follows the one you have just translated?'

'"ἀλλά μοι, ὦ ἄνδρες, παραμείνατε,"' said Marius from memory: '"But wait with me, my friends; for nothing prevents our talking together while there is still time."'

'Good. Very good. You learnt it because you liked it?'

'Yes, sir.'

'And what follows that?'

'Socrates says that the state of death will either be an eternal sleep, and therefore painless, *or* the habitation of another world, where he will meet Orpheus and Hesiod and Homer, so that either way he has nothing to fear.'

'And your verdict on this prediction?'

'I do not think,' said Marius, 'that even the company of Orpheus and Homer could make an eternity of consciousness tolerable.'

'So for Socrates' sake . . . and our own . . . we must hope that after death there is only sleep.'

'Unless,' said Marius carefully, 'one's sojourn in the afterworld were limited strictly to a span during which it was still of interest. But I do not think that this is proposed here.'

'It isn't. Plato posits either absolute and immediate death *or* an immortal soul. Elsewhere he writes of the possibilities of transmigration or metempsychosis; but not here. Socrates would have been stuck, on the showing of the *Apology*, talking to Homer and Co. for ever. Just imagine, that dismal Hesiod drizzling on and on at one *ad infinitum*. There is a question in your eyes, boy.'

'Yes, sir. Why have we started the *Apology* at the end?'

'Because it is the best part, and we shall not have time

for any more. Just as well: all that boring squabble about whether Socrates did or did not corrupt the youth of Athens. It didn't matter then and it certainly doesn't now. There were and are in the world weak people, who will sooner or later be corrupted however carefully they are guarded, and strong people who will not – unless, of course, they want to be. That is all there is to be said in the matter. We can take the *Apology* as read.'

'As I understand you, sir, We shall not in any case have time to read it. Why not?'

'Other work, boy. Time is going on and we must step up your hours in the stables. Only two days to Regis Priory.'

'All I have to do is travel with the horse in its box, and lead it round the paddock.'

'Yes. That is all you have to do . . . at Regis Priory. But you must be practised in holding the horse as the jockey mounts . . . and in leading the horse on to the course, where you must go with Lover Pie, if the day is cold, and remove his blanket at the last moment. None of this is quite as easy as it sounds. Jimmy Pitts, the jockey, is a sharp-tempered fellow – gets it from his father, Johnny Pitts, who was always too keen to go for the whip. If you annoy Jimmy by Leading Lover Pie too quick or too slow on to the course, or by removing the blanket clumsily, you'll certainly regret it.'

'Perhaps, sir, I shall regret even more not having read the first seven-eighths of Plato's *Apology*.'

'"I could be round with you were the occasion different,"' said Conyngham; 'but just for once I shall let that pass. Attachment to your book and to your author is no light matter. But there will be time for Plato, Marius, I promise you that. Sour winter will be the time for Plato. Now it is spring, beloved of sweet lovers and merry fellows and, not least, of gentlemen adventurers.'

Marius's skin tingled.

'I understand you, sir,' he said: 'we have great matter afoot.'

'Aye, lad.'

'And what part in it for Tessa?'

'Teresa's part is to hate horses. For Regis Priory she will stay home and play at chess or the sabre with Milo. Later on . . . her part will be, as I say, to hate horses – and to be hated by them.'

'Time for a romp,' said Jeremy on the telephone to Carmilla: 'a farewell romp. I'm off.'

'Where?'

'All over the place. First stop India, for a bit more devotion to the soil, and then Polynesia, Oz, New Zealand . . .'

'What on earth do you want with Oz?'

'I find Australians irresistibly comic. What about this romp? Can I come to Lancaster *now*?'

'No. It isn't suitable.'

'Then you come here.'

'That isn't suitable either. The thing is, Jeremy, I have a guest here who has been taken very ill. He wished himself on me in the first place, but here he is and ill he is, and I must concern myself with him.'

'What's up with him?'

'He's in a deep coma, and no one knows what's caused it. He should be in hospital, but one of the Fellows is so fascinated by the case that he's begged the Provost to keep him here.'

'There'll be a nasty row if he dies on you.'

'I wish to hell they'd got him out. But this is a place of science and learning, and I must say his symptoms are rather fascinating . . . even from the layman's point of view. So here he stays. And you know as well as I do, Jeremy, that whatever happens there won't be a nasty row. Inside Lancaster, the Provost is Coroner, Judge and Lord of Appeal. If Myles Glastonbury dies in an embarrassing way, the Provost will sign the death certificate and the body will be put away under the Chapel, and nobody from outside will ever be allowed to stick his nose in or ask one single question.'

'All right. Here's this chap, whom you never wanted anyway, having a deep coma. So why can't we have a romp?'

'It would be tasteless. Anyway, Fielding Gray's in the College. Wouldn't that embarrass you?'

'I think I'd better ring again in a few days. But time is running out, remember: I want to be off. That piece of Alfie Schroeder's will be appearing at any minute, and after that there's nothing to hold me. Tell me, did you actually do it with that chap in the coma?'

'I told you: I never even wanted him here.'

'He might have bored your knickers off, all the same. It has happened.'

'Well, it didn't.'

'But you were close to him? At meals and so on?'

'I suppose so,' Carmilla said.

'Well then: is this coma thing catching? I mean, a fellow can't be too careful these days with all these frightful diseases going round. So what has he got?'

'I told you. Nobody knows, but an expert on blood conditions is fascinated by whatever it may turn out to be. Fielding says that Myles said, just before he went into his coma, that some enemy of his has touched his hair and infected him that way.'

'Which has to be ballocks.'

'Fielding says it happened somewhere in Balzac.'

'And what does this blood expert say to *that*?'

'He says that some types of poison, e.g. arsenic, could, just *could*, act through the follicles in the hair or lesions in the scalp.'

'Well, well, well, well, *well*. I'd better have a few hand jobs and be in touch with you later.'

'Jeremy . . . don't sail away to India without seeing me.'

'I should think not, old girl. I couldn't bear to go, not without hearing you make that noise of yours one more time. Do you rmember how you bellowed in Bishop Alcocke's Chantry in Ely Cathedral? Like the Minotaur, it was. I've always wondered why nobody rumbled us . . .'

'"In this age of remote control and bureaucratic central-ization,"' Alfie Schroeder had written in GLOBE-2000, the weekly colour supplement of *The Daily Globe*, '"it is refreshing to find a proprietor who strives to share the physical labours and mental attitudes of his employees. THE HON JEREMY MORRISON, second son but in practice sole heir of Lord Luffham of Whereham, has undertaken to lead the working life of a farm apprentice until, as he puts it, 'the ancient lore and vibrancy of the soil enters into my bones, until the primeval bond between man and the land from which he lives (like the bond between nurseling and mother) has bound me for ever and inescapably to my Norfolk fields. In this way I shall achieve oneness, not only with the Good Earth but with the Good Men who till and tend it by my side.'"

'And so on,' said Len, who had been reading all this aloud to Provost Llewyllyn and Fielding Gray. 'There is rather a fetching picture of Jeremy milking a cow, and another of him dining alone in his mansion and being waited on by a manservant.'

Len passed the magazine to Fielding, who looked glumly at a picture of Jeremy, seated beneath a portrait of his grandfather, at the head of a table as long as a cricket pitch. About halfway down the table, under a portrait of Peter Morrison's – Lord Luffham's – dead wife, Helen, stood the Chamberlain, holding a pitcher of (presumably) Adam's Ale and looking with adoration towards Jeremy. This picture carried the caption 'Lord of the Manor Dreaming Dreams' while another, of Jeremy behind a plough and a pair of huge shire horses, one of whom was copiously defecating, was entitled 'Son of the Soil Faces Facts'. Fielding was too depressed to look for the picture of Jeremy a-milking and see what they had called that.

'Carmilla tells me,' said Len, 'that before very long he's taking off for the Far East. His excuse for leaving his holy soil in Norfolk will be that he wants to establish a similar *rapport* with the paddy-fields and peasants of the Orient. You see what his game is? To become an internationally recognized dispenser of sanctimonious drivel about "rituals of nature", that kind of thing. He's started here with what he calls the "lore and vibrancy of the soil". No doubt he will soon extend his range to include fisheries, forests and wildlife sanctuaries, public parks, commons and beaches; from which it is an easy jump to recreation and health, and so to medicine, welfare and paediatrics, until he'll end up delivering world-wide sermons on every aspect of existence from the Big Bang to the Great Pox. In time,' orated Len, prancing about in front of the Provost, 'we might even have to make him an Honorary Fellow.'

'Thank God I shall be dead before that,' Tom Llewyllyn said.

'I wouldn't bet on it,' said Fielding. 'Popular success these days is a very swift process.'

'So, mercifully, is popular neglect. You have to have *durability* to be made an Honorary Fellow here. And in any case,' said Tom peevishly, 'I don't see that this grubby little write-up constitutes a foundation for popular success.'

'Let us change the metaphor,' said Len, who was being deliberately annoying, 'and say that a seed has been sown. It could grow to heaven like the Beanstalk, overnight. Have we a set of rooms free in case Jeremy wishes to come into residence? Yes. The single storey E. M. Forster Set, which stands on one side of the Provost's Garden, joining the Lodging to the West Cloister. Like Forster himself, the E. M. Forster Set has got both wet and dry rot, but restoration will be completed in about three months – by which time Jeremy's meteoric career as Gnomic Spolesman will doubtless have reached its apex. In a mood at once of pride and humility, the College Council will invite its charismatic alumnus to accept a Life Fellowship and life tenure of the Forster Set.'

'Did you say,' said Tom, 'that the Forster Set is being restored?'

'It has to be.'

'Which means dismantling its walls?'

'I imagine so, what with the state it's got into.'

'And its roof?'

'They already have, Provost. Half of it had to come right off. You can see it, if you crane your neck, from the Withdrawing Room window.'

'The dryads,' said Tom.

'What about them?'

'They'll have a way through to the Provost's Garden. They cannot walk through buildings inhabited by men, but they can go through empty and roofless ones.'

'Then you must make them welcome,' said Fielding, trying to humour the obsession.

'I fear,' said Tom Llewyllyn, 'lest they prove unamenable guests.'

'It's a job for Tiresiana,' said Don Simone Fontanelli to Nicos and the Greco, as the three of them examined Fra Angelico's Annunciation in the Diocesan Museum in Cortona. 'Very sickly, all this pink and gold,' he said, and turned to inspect Signorelli's Pièta.

Piera had followed up his own suggestion that he seek out the former major-domo in his place of retirement at Palermo, and arrange for Nicos and the Greco to meet him. Fontanelli had been easy to trace and quite willing, once he fully grasped who Piero was and had been reminded of their old association in Venice, to be of specialized assistance. When roughly apprised of what was in the wind, he stated quite categorically that he would meet Nicos and the Greco at Cortona (no, nowhere else would do), and that he was to be paid full expenses and a fee of one million *lire*, half as soon as they all met, and half on production of the goods. To this, Ptolemaeos had assented, and the first meeting had now been effected at the agreed rendezvous, in front of the Angelico Madonna in the Cortonese Museum.

'You will notice,' said Don Simone, prodding his fat nose at the Peita, 'that one of the women is taking an interest in the physical attractions of the Madonna, at the same time as Mary Magdalene is quite definitely relishing the naked attributes of the dead Christ. Such sexual references or jokes are quite common even in the most serious painters' treatments of the most sacred subjects. You will find that the theme of the Madonna's appeal to Sapphists is repeated, quite blatantly, in the reredos of the chapel downstairs. Another entertaining example of such a diversion is to be found in several paintings of the Adoration. An esquire of one of the Three Kings gives an insinuating glance at a much younger page in the retinue of another, and receives an inflammatory look in return. I think,' said Fontanelli, 'that you have something for me.'

The Greco passed over seven hundred-thousand *lire* notes. 'Half your fee of a million in advance,' he said, 'and two hundred thousand on account for expenses.' '*Va bene*,' said Don Simone. 'Now then. Why, you ask, are we meeting in Cortona? Because Fontanelli enjoys the pictures? No, my friends: but because near here is the off-duty villa of the celebrated Tiresiana. Tiresiana is the person you need for your enterprise – as I understood that enterprise from the *Signorino* Piero.' He gave a brief account of Piero's account, whereupon both the Greco and Nicos confirmed that this was a pretty good summary of the plan devised by Ptolemaeos.

'So,' said Fontanelli, 'that is your scheme and the intent of your mission?'

The Greco and Nicos nodded.

'*Dunque*,' said Fontanelli, 'the agent whom you need is undoubtedly Tiresiana. Let me explain. You have heard, of course, of Le Cascine, the infamous gardens in Firenze, much frequented by whores both female and male. Some years ago it occurred to an ingenious whoremaster that there would be a magnificent market for those who combined male and female in one sex – in a word, since genuine hermaphrodites are rarely procurable, for transvestites. The reasoning was as follows. Italian men do not like to be seen picking up other men; and they get a very rough time of it when confessing, since homosexual sin is held by the priesthood to be far worse than mere fornication. Very well then: present them with a creature brilliantly arrayed as a woman and they need have no shame in accosting it; and as for confession, they can very plausibly claim that they thought they were going with a woman until at the last moment they found a peego – that is your splendid English word, yes? – until at last they found a peego where they should have found the other thing, by which time they were too aroused to desist. Thus, face is preserved in public and a passable defence is put up in the privacy of the confessional – and indeed in their own minds as well. I am not really queer, they can tell themselves: I was tricked.

'The theory worked brilliantly. The cars in the Cascine all thronged to the grotto where gathered the transvestites, who were swathed in fabulous furs and displayed huge thighs above silk hose, huge smooth thighs as of warm marble. Now, of all these transvestites the most famous was Tiresiana, a beautiful student of noble but impoverished family, who was disgusted by his medical studies, filled with loathing by all the common left-wing students, and much bored and irritated by shortage of pleasure-making money. He therefore decided to sell his beauty, to offer it in the now highly fashionable transvestite style, and to take as a *nom d'amour* a feminine version of Tiresias, who, as you will remember, had been both male and female in his day. To cut a long and eventful story short, Tiresiana prospered from the very beginning of his new career, very soon attracted the attention of two influential cardinals and a film producer, and is now as rich as anyone can be who lives under our invidious fiscal code. He is at present having a holiday on his country estate, which marches with that of the Contessa Passerini (doyenne of the local aristocracy), and whither we shall now proceed.'

'Will he wish to interrupt his vacation?' Nicos enquired.

'I think the bizarre nature of the case will amuse him. His fee will probably be five times my own. *Va bene, signori?*'

Yes, they said, it went well. Ptolemaeos had anticipated a request for some such honorarium and had amply provided them.

'Very well. I shall talk with him first. Although he has never met me, I have been sending him rich clients from Sicily ever since his talents were first rumoured through the channels of our trade, and so he will be well disposed. Then I shall call you in, *signori*, to agree the contract. The arrangement will take the same form as my own: fifty per cent down and fifty per cent on performance.'

'Well, old girl,' rumbled Jeremy down the telephone line to Carmilla, 'how goes it? Is the coast clear?'

'Very far from it. Fielding is still here. Myles Glastonbury is still in a coma. The Provost thinks he is going to be torn to pieces in his own garden by hysterical woodnymphs. One of our students has just hammered out half the West Window of the Chapel, as a protest against the presence in the College Library of a signed photograph of George VI and Queen Elizabeth, presented during their visit in 1952. It's all happening, Jeremy. Don't come here. Don't ask me to come to Luffham.'

'That's all very well. I'm suffering from permanent tumescence.'

'And I'm suffering from permanent liquefaction. We shall just have to be patient until things tidy themselves up.'

'Righty-ho. I'll go to London and arrange for all my tickets. Want to come? To the East, I mean.'

'No. I've got a book and several papers to finish.'

'Talking of all that,' said Jeremy in a complacent voice, 'did you see that piece about me in GLOBE-2000?'

'Yes. It was more loathsome than I would have thought possible,' Carmilla said: 'and so say all of us in Lancaster.'

'I see. You're all getting jealous, just because *I've* had a little attention at last. Fielding and Tom can't expect to hold the stage for ever, you know. They're both crumbling into their grave already. Mine is the modern way. People want charisma, the odour of sanctity: they want a guru.

But of course what they really want more than anything is to be forgiven for their foulness, to be told that nothing is their fault. I'm working on how to get round to that through the Oriental Connection. Isn't there some Hindu sect which believes absolutely in predestination? *That* lets everybody off the hook. Hullo? You there, Carmilla? Hullo?'

'Yes, I'm still here, Jeremy. Pundits . . . prophets . . . professional mongers of forgiveness and compassion . . . never prosper, in the end, unless they believe in their product and their powers of production. Your irony does you credit, in my eyes, but it makes of you just a faker, a fabricator. You'll be caught out, Jeremy.'

'Not before I've made a fortune, like that guru johnny who scarpered from his ashram with a Rolls Royce and five million.'

'Why do you want to make a fortune? You already have one.'

'I want to be sure I can do it for myself. So much more satisfying. Money is rather a bore if it's just given to you. To appreciate it properly you must have made it, or gambled for it, yourself.'

Marius was leading Lover Pie round the paddock before the three-fifteen race at Regis Priory. Although Regis Priory is a charmless course in all but its name, the paddock (so Marius thought) was neat and agreeable, having trees in blossom round two-thirds of its circumference. 'Wearing white for Easter Tide,' thought Marius, remembering one of Rosie's favourite poems:

> 'Now of my three score years and ten
> Twenty will not come again;
> Take from seventy years a score,
> It only leaves me fifty more:
>
> And since to look at things in bloom
> Fifty springs is little room . . .'

How was Rosie? wondered Marius. He pictured her in a meadow in the Midi, coloured flowers growing separately round her feet (at uniform distances from one another, as in early Italian paintings), with Oenone trotting at her side. And as they went across the meadow, the Madonna, throned, appeared at the other end: Mother of God and Queen of Heaven, O, Ave Maria, *gratia plena* . . . Stop it, he thought. No time for reverie. He must not get all vague and make some horrid mistake. True, Gat-Toothed Jenny was watching him, in case of accident, from the entrance to the ring, and Jack Lamprey was keeping a kindly eye open from his place by Raisley Conyngham in the middle of the grass; but it would be shaming, it would be disastrous, it would be the end of his favour with Raisley, if either had to come to his rescue. No more poetry or fantasy: he must concentrate absolutely on the matter in hand before Raisley spotted his mental dereliction, which please God he had not done already.

There were, thought Marius, pulling himself together, nine entries for this race (the Paignton Trophy), a 'chase of three miles, two furlongs and eighteen yards. Lover Pie, not surprisingly, was the only stallion entered; seven of the rest were geldings; the remaining runner was Prideau Glastonbury's mare, Boadicea. Although Marius had known very little of handicapping, he was now, under Jack and Jenny, beginning to learn; and he knew that on an informed estimate neither Lover Pie nor Boadicea was expected to win at the weights. Even so, Jenny had promised to pop a fiver each way on Lover Pie at tote prices for both of them (for old times' sake, of course, Jeremy at Newmarket that summer, oh, Jeremy, it would be nice if you were here with your soft hands and huge round face – stop it, Marius, stop it, or Raisley Conyngham will catch you out); and what with the grateful sun, the white blossom ('And since to look at things in bloom' – stop it, stop it) and the fresh grass, what with excitement and hope and gambler's infatuation, what with the knowledge that many of the public were regarding both himself and Lover Pie with approval, Marius, all vagaries now vanquished, entered into a titillating and almost triumphant condition of euphoria.

A bell rang somewhere. Nine jockeys filed into the ring. The two last, who were walking almost, but not quite, side by side, were Conyngham's jockey, Jimmy Pitts, wearing the Conyngham colours (magenta with Cambridge Blue Maltese Cross on back and magenta cap) and a scrawny, hooky youth of about twenty-two, who sported a cherry jacket with Cambridge Blue skull and cross-bones on the back and a cherry cap, and was, as Marius knew, Prideau Glastonbury's jockey, Danny Chead. It occurred to Marius that a casual observer, watching in bad light or at a distance, might easily confuse the two sets of colours. On the other hand, thought Marius, there was no chance of confusing the horses the two men would be riding; for leave aside their sex and size (Lover Pie somewhat the taller), Prideau's mare, Boadicea, was chestnut while the stallion was grey.

Jimmy Pitts, who had been muttering back over his

shoulder to Danny Chead, paused a second at the edge of the paddock as Marius walked past with Lover Pie.

'Don't forget, sonny,' he rapped at Marius: 'don't take that blanket off until I give the word.'

Marius nodded and passed on with Lover Pie. Jimmy Pitts, still muttering back at Danny Chead, strutted towards the centre of the grass. Danny Chead peeled off towards Prideau Glastonbury, who was standing with his trainer, an urbane six-footer called Phil Loche, and his cousin Giles. Jimmy Pitts, having given a perfunctory Wolf Cub salute of two fingers to Raisley Conyngham and snarled more or less amicably at Jack Lamprey, stood in total silence, slapping his right boot with his whip, while Lamprey spoke intently into his left ear. Marius was conscious that the kindly spirit which had filled the paddock only a few minutes before, had abruptly departed with the arrival of Jimmy Pitts and Danny Chead. His euphoria had ebbed and gone. The sun, though still shining, pleased him no longer. The white blossom was now speckled and grubby, the trim, green grass was yellow grey and full of weed. Any eyes that still rested on him and Lover Pie, Marius felt, were indifferent or even hostile. He broke into a muggy sweat all over. He remembered Pitts's order about the blanket but trembled with fear lest he should somehow mismanage even this very simple operation.

The loudspeaker system commanded jockeys, and requested gentlemen, to mount immediately. Jack Lamprey beckoned to Marius. He led Lover Pie over the grass, passing quite close to Prideau and Giles Glastonbury, and was agreeably surprised, though by no means totally restored, when Giles raised his hat to him, as to a gentleman of his acquaintance; and Prideau, whom

245

Marius had not met, nevertheless followed Giles's example.

Milo Hedley and Tessa Malcolm were in a summer-house on the ridge of a slope which rose from the edge of the lawn at Ullacote, and from which they had a view of the sea between Minehead and Watchett. They were playing chess. During the intervals between his own moves, Milo was reading selections from *Twelfth Night* to Tessa, while she pondered hers.

'Come boy, with me, my thoughts are ripe in mischief.
I'll sacrifice the lamb that I do love
To spite a raven's heart within a dove.'

'That is the Duke threatening Cesario,' said Milo, 'because Cesario has won the heart of the Lady Olivia. That is, it is Marius as the Duke Orsino threatening Tessa as Cesario because Tessa/Cesario has won the heart of Marius as Olivia. Which is to say Marius is angry with Tessa because she has won the heart of Marius.'

'Don't be silly, Milo. I have not won the heart of Marius. I tried once, some years ago, but did not succeed. We are just good friends, as the papers say.'

Tessa castled on the Queen's side.

'Just as well, perhaps. Tell me, little one: did you ever know your mother?'

'Auntie Maisie says she died giving birth to me.'

'Do you never feel curious about her?'

'Sometimes. Auntie Maisie discourages me. She says my mother was a bad lot.'

'Suppose . . . Raisley could find out more about her for you?'

'How?'

'Raisley has knowledgeable friends.'

Milo castled on the King's side.

'Why should they be knowledgeable about someone as unimportant as my mother?'

'Perhaps she wasn't as unimportant as your aunt makes out.'

'I think I'd rather not know any more about her, thank you very much. There's no possible point, after all this time. I'm very happy with Auntie Maisie, who's done everything for me all my life. I wonder how they're getting on at Regis Priory.'

'Marius is being rehearsed. Next time you'll be there too. At Bellhampton Park. But your part is so simple that it needs no rehearsal, which is why you don't need to be there to-day.'

'I don't want to go to Bellhampton Park either. I hate horses.'

'You won't have much to do with them.'

'I hate being anywhere near them.'

'Nevertheless,' said Milo, 'after your promise of obedience, you will do whatever is asked of you. Otherwise I shall never kiss you behind your knee.'

'I had hoped you would do that this afternoon.'

'This afternoon is not the proper time. The proper time will be after you have been to Bellhampton Park.'

'Very well. But I don't think you quite understand – about me and horses, I mean. I might actually faint or be ill, if I came too near to them. Or they might be disturbed. There was a time in Kensington Gardens – '

' – Nevertheless, you will come to Bellhampton Park,' said Milo. 'Otherwise we might start telling you about your mother, Raisley and I, and you wouldn't like that at all.'

'Let my mother rest in peace.'

'As it happens, your mother ended up very respectably. But before you were born . . . oh dear me. You remember what we were reading about the Empress Theo – '

' – Be kind, Milo. Let her rest.'

'Very well, little one. But you won't make any more difficulties about coming to Bellhampton?'

'None. But don't say I didn't warn you about what might happen. About my fainting and the rest.'

'Would you like to hear more of *Twelfth Night* while you think about your move?'

'No. We'll be reading it with Mr Conyngham and Marius all these holidays.'

'Not for quite that long. I rather think reading is almost at an end on this particular reading party. There are only a few days more until the race meeting at Bellhampton, and they will be very busy days.'

'After that there should be time.'

'After that you will find that everything is different. Not disagreeably so, but still . . . different. You will no longer be interested in playing the part of Master Cesario.'

'I'm not particularly interested now. Cesario/Viola is in love with Marius/Orsino and is loved in turn by Marius/ Olivia. This situation would have intrigued me some years ago, when I could have identified myself with Viola because I wanted Marius . . . as a brother, I told him, but really as a lover, young though we both were. But now such a situation is no longer of the slightest interest to me – unless *you* will step into the part of Orsino.'

'I prefer Sebastian and Malvolio. Malvolio was right, you know. He detested stupidity and drunkenness and extravagance . . . But even if I did become Orsino, you would still cease to be interested in this play.'

'Why?'

'Your move, Tessa.'

'Why should I no longer be interested in *Twelfth Night*, after I've been to Bellhampton? As I say, I'm not mad about it now, but I do think it's a very pretty and melancholy piece, and if, as I say, you were to be the Duke Orsino – '

' – It would still not be of the slightest importance to you.'

'Why not?'

'Because you will have been made to confront certain realities. For a long time, if not for ever, this confrontation will ruin your taste for fictions, even for those of the high quality of *Twelfth Night*, and no matter who may be playing the part of Orsino.'

Pally Palairet and his jolly, purple aunt watched Marius as he led Lover Pie round the paddock. Palairet had come to see Lover Pie because the stallion was linked in his mind with Marius and the wager which Marius had made, years ago, at Newmarket; he had neither expected nor wished to see Marius himself, whom he intended to avoid for the full half year of denial on which, at Jeremy's suggestion, he had determined. When, however, he learnt from his racecard that Lover Pie was one of Raisley

Conyngham's horses (a fact omitted in the Four Day Declarations which he had read in his aunt's *Sporting Life*), he at once realized that Marius, being Conyngham's guest, might well be present at the meeting; and when he saw Marius actually with the horse in the paddock, he formed a pretty good notion of what must have happened.

'That boy with Number Four, Lover Pie,' he told his aunt: 'he's at school with me. He was at Oudenarde House too.'

'What a nice looking boy,' said his aunt with enthusiasm. 'Let's go nearer and wave.'

'No. It would only put him off if he saw me.'

'Nonsense. Let's show him we're on his side. What's his name?'

'Stern. Marius Stern.'

'The one that hit you in the throat?'

'Yes.'

'Well . . . I do see he might be embarrassed. We'd better stay put and not shove ourselves forward.'

Palairet, who was determined not to be seen by Marius until his absence and the passing months had made Marius's heart once more grow fonder, did not trouble to clear up his aunt's misunderstanding in the matter, but steered her to a special alcove for the disabled which combined an excellent view of the ring with discreetly contrived immunity from the prying or contemptuous eyes of those sound in wind and limb.

'Can't you see the notice?' said a whining and self-righteous voice.

'Perfectly well,' said Pally's aunt, and at once produced a heavy limp and a clever illusion that she was crook-back.

'What's 'e doing then?'

'My nephew is taking care of me,' said his Auntie,

leaning with great pleasure (for she seldom had such a good excuse) against his sturdy body.

'Now then,' she whispered to Pally, 'let's have a good look at this near-assassin of yours. Ah. He's taking the horse over to the owner. Two tall men have raised their hats to him. Why, I wonder? Princely manners, I must say. And now that snake Conyngham – I've hardly ever met him, but I've never liked the cut of his jib – is giving him his usual slimy smile, and that sot, Jack Lamprey, is saying something conspiratorial to Jimmy Pitts . . . and . . . and this is surely *most* peculiar, darling . . . can you see what I can see? All of them are looking at Master Stern . . . just looking at him, as if he were on probation or being inspected or interviewed or something . . .yes, they're just like that Board I was put in front of during the war when I was in for a commission in the ATS – just looking at me in silence to see if I was up to the mark. What's more, those two men who took their hats off – one of them *has* to be Prideau Glastonbury – are also staring at him. And Phil Roche, Prideau's trainer, and that little dung rat, Danny Chead. They're all looking at your Marius Stern as if they expected him to expose himself or something. The only one who is looking rather differently is that one with Prideau, even taller than Prideau, looks like Prideau's cousin Giles, now I come to think of it, who used to own horses with Prideau: Major, or was it Colonel, Giles Glastonbury: did something quite *horrid* with the Army in India and then butchered some Hun in a duel, and good for him, of course I don't see these people as often as I used when I still had all my money, but I knew 'em all once . . . Now the interesting thing is that *Giles* is only looking at young Stern because the others are looking at him in such a funny way, and Giles don't know why and he's trying to work it out, and he can't. Ah. I see that Master Stern is to lead Lover Pie on to the course. Let us follow unobtrusively . . .

'. . . I wonder what they're all up to,' she went on in some excitement, forgetting her limp and provoking spiteful hisses from the malingerers all round her, as they left the 'disabled' section of the paddock. 'Whatever it is, it don't look as if Giles were in on it . . . though it wouldn't have surprised me if he was, because Giles first produced Danny Chead to be Prideau's jockey . . . Danny Chead being the son of an old NCO of his, or something . . . so that if Giles *had* been in on whatever it is, he *could* have helped by putting pressure on Danny if needed, if you follow my train. But it's clear that Giles *doesn't* know what's going on, and it's also clear that little Stern doesn't know either. He's a study in bewilderment, and I don't blame him, all those huge men looking him up and down as if he were being auctioned off in a market. See? He's quite white with puzzlement and worry, that little Stern. And now Jimmy Pitts is saying something to him, not too kindly by the look of it . . . and little Stern is taking off Lover Pie's blanket. Why on earth, I wonder, does Lover Pie need that atrocious, thick blanket on a warm and beautiful spring day like this?'

Raisley Conyngham and Marius were home in time to join Milo and Tessa just before dinner.

'Well?' said Milo.

'Fifth. Not a bad show at all – very much what we expected this time out.'

'And Boadicea?'

252

'Danny Chead tried to produce her just before the third out, but she wasn't having any, not this afternoon. She was sixth, two lengths odd behind the Lover.'

'Also much what we expected. How . . . did other arrangements go?'

'Marius made an admirable stable boy, and was accordingly much admired on his *début*. Jimmy Pitts snapped at him about the blanket when they got on to the course, but it seemed to me that Marius managed the whole thing pretty well, always allowing for beginner's nerves.'

'A very heavy blanket' said Marius, accepting Raisley's encomium as the truth, forgetting the faces that had peered from all angles and the cold sweat in his crutch. 'Yes; a very heavy blanket to handle on a hot day.'

'Lover Pie likes his blanket like that,' said Raisley: 'hot or cold, he finds it reassuring. Now then: dinner. And after dinner we'll have another go at *Twelfth Night* . . . Sebastian and Antonio in Act Three, Scene Three. We shan't have much time for literature during the next few days, and it would be a great pity not to have read that.'

As soon as Palairet's sporty old aunt, full of fresh air and booze, had retired (very early) to bed, Palairet went to work on the telephone. Although economy was the order of the day with this instrument, as it was with everything in Sandy Lodge, Palairet felt that in the circumstances, he had no choice but to make what was going to be very expensive use of it, even at evening rates. He would explain to Auntie later what he had done, give reason and ask forgiveness; meanwhile, since he could not run the risk of her denying him, he found the deceitful patience to wait until she withdrew and the prudence to put an extra powder in the sleeping draught which (according to their custom when he was staying at Burnham-on-Sea) he mixed for her every evening before she went upstairs.

Having consulted *Who's Who*, he dialed the number of Peter Morrison (for as such he was still listed in Auntie's edition) hoping to speak to Jeremy.

Yet what shall I say? he thought, as the number rang. 'I'm Palairet, you may remember me from the riding school at Birchington, from the Junior Fives Courts, *please* remember me, because Marius, our friend is in trouble, such deep trouble – no, I can't easily explain, it was a peculiar feeling I had at Regis Priory Races, my aunt had it too, I know it sounds ridiculous, but – '

'Chamberlain to the Barony and Household of Luffham-by-Whereham,' said a deep and scarcely sane voice.

'Mr Jeremy Morrison, please.'

'You mean the Honourable Jeremy Morrison?'

'No, I don't. That's only for envelopes.'

'Are you contradicting me?'

'I'm sorry. I didn't mean to be rude. Can I please speak to him? It's urgent.'

'Since you sound,' said the Chamberlain, 'an honest and excellent sort of boy, I shall tell you what I can. Mr Jeremy has gone, *via* London, to Lancaster College, Cambridge, where he should be arriving, any time within the next thirty-six hours, for a stay of two or three days.'

'The next thirty-six hours?'

'He may be there already, sir.'

'And supposing he isn't? Where do I find him in London?'

'You don't, sir. Mr Jeremy keeps his own counsel about his haunts in London.'

'But this is urgent.'

'So you have already said. This cannot alter the fact, sir, that I am not in his confidence about where he may be in London. All I can do is save you trouble by giving you the number of his next destination, which, as I say, is Lancaster College.' The Chamberlain dictated the number of Lancaster.

'Thank you,' said Palairet, 'for being so kind.'

'My pleasure, sir. Please telephone whenever you like. It can be lonely here when Mr Jeremy and his lordship are away. Mr Nicky, you see, has gone for ever. But I can tell that you are busy, and I shall not keep you now.'

'"I could not stay behind you,"' read Jack Lamprey, who with the assistance of half a bottle of cognac had been conscribed as Antonio:

'"My desire,
More sharp than filed steel, did spur me forth,
And not all love to see you" – This Antonio is as queer as a cardboard box,' said Jack. 'Why have I got the part? He reminds me of that bugger in our Regiment, Fielding Gray, sort of way he'd carry on.'

'Major Gray is a friend of Tessa's and mine,' said Marius.

'So *that's* why he's sticking his nose in. Come to think of it, he said so himself.'

'Let us discuss this later,' said Conyngham gently: 'please carry on with the reading, Jack.'

When Pally Palairet got through to the Porter's Lodge in Lancaster and asked for Jeremy Morrison, the Porter on duty hesitated, then put him through to Len in the Provost's Lodging.

'Please may I speak to Mr Jeremy Morrison?' Palairet said.

'And who may you be?'

'Nobody much. I just want to speak to Mr Morrison.'

'I want doesn't get,' said Len, who was in a foul temper because of the absurd way in which Tom Llewyllyn was carrying on about the dryads in the Provost's Garden. 'Mr Morrison hasn't arrived yet. When? How should I know? There's enough going on here without him.'

'Sorry. I didn't mean to be a nuisance.'

Pally put the receiver down and rang up Enquiries for Jakki Blessington's number in London.

'"I am not weary and 'tis long to night,"' said Milo Hedley as Sebastian without looking at his text, which lay closed on the floor beside his left foot:

> '"I pray you, let us satisfy our eyes
> With the memorials and the things of fame
> That do renown this city."'

'"Would you pardon me,"' carolled Jack Lamprey:

> '"I do not without danger walk these streets.
> Once in a seafight 'gainst the Count his galleys
> I did some service – of such note indeed
> That, were I ta'en here, it would scarce be answered.'

'And that reminds me,' said Jack. 'He threatened me.'

'Who did?' said Milo.

'Fielding Gray. He said that unless I tipped him off whatever I knew, he'd rake up some old Army scandal.'

'And did you . . . tip him off?'

'No,' said Jack, omitting to mention that he had telephoned in order to do so but had drawn a blank.

'Then that's all right. Forget him.'

Marius and Tessa exchanged looks. Marius hesitated for a moment, then nodded. Tessa said to Milo: 'If you like I'll ring up Major Gray and tell him what a super time we're having.'

'Not a bad idea,' said Conyngham: 'that should finally rid us of this particular pest, whoever he may be.'

257

Tessa bit her lip and was about to say that Fielding was a very well known author and Mr Conyngham should be ashamed not to have heard of him. But then she realized that Mr Conyngham was almost certainly only pretending to ignorance, for some reason of his own, and that she would do much better to let the thing pass: and so when, a second later, Milo smiled at her, as if to say, 'Whatever you do, don't take the bait,' she simply smiled back and went quietly to the telephone.

After about twenty minutes (or so it seemed) Palairet got through to Enquiries, and was instantly given Colonel Blessington's number. When this had rung twice, a mannered and recorded voice of Colonel Blessington 'had the honour to inform his correspondent that his family and he had left for a month's holiday in the Balkans', as indeed, thought Pally, I should have remembered for myself.

'"Haply your eye shall light upon some toy,"' lilted Jack in his best Bloomsbury.

'"You have desire to purchase; and your store,
I think, is not for idle markets, sir."'

'You see?' said Jack. 'A real *fruit*, this one. Much fruitier than Fielding.'

'Major Gray is not with Auntie Maisie at Buttock's,' said Tessa, coming away from the telephone. 'She sounded quite cross. I think she hoped he'd be there with her for Easter. She says he's at "that College", by which I imagine she means Lancaster.'

'Full of fruits, Lancaster,' said Jack Lamprey. 'I expect he's having a marvellous time there – all those fruits being fruity together. There was one of those fruits from Lancaster I met once, Daniel Mond he was called, friend of Fielding's. We came across him in Germany, place called Göttingen, where we were playing at soldiers and he was researching into some high-powered sort of arithmetic. We had to dress him up as a Dragoon for some reason – I expect he got some sort of fruity kick out of it.'

'I think that's enough of *Twelfth Night*,' said Raisley Conyngham. '*Good*-night, Jack. It's been a long day . . .'

'Shall I try Lancaster?' said Tessa to Milo and Conyngham, after Captain Lamprey had fallen out for the evening. 'Get hold of Major Gray there?'

'Please, darling,' Milo said: 'get the thing out of the way for good.'

The next person whom Pally Palairet telephoned was Ptolemaeos Tunne. He had heard a lot of him from Marius, enough to know that Ptolemaeos, if not exactly Marius's friend, had nevertheless been an important factor in his life at one time and might well turn out to be an abiding one. What was more, Pally had the impression that Ptolemaeos would be prepared to listen carefully to what he, Pally, had to say, and would not be scornful of his fears and suspicions simply because they were conceived from a fleeting impression rather than founded in hard fact.

Having asked Enquiries for Ptolemaeos's (ex-directory) number and been turned down flat, Palairet had had an inspiration: Mr Tunne, he remembered hearing from Marius, had once been a regular racing man like his own aunt. Palairet therefore applied himself to the address book on his aunt's desk, in the hope that she and Ptolemaeos had been acquainted; and was rewarded by the discovery of Ptolemaeos's Fenland number and address, which were written in mauve crayon under the entry TON, Tolymius, and were followed by the comment, 'Greedy fat fruity sod, amusing shit.'

At this stage Pally's luck ran out. The telephone was answered by a female voice, clearly much the worse for drink (Pally was familiar with the noises of women in drink because Auntie sometimes overdid it), which said that it was called Mrs Statch and what the fucking hell was anyone ringing it up for.

'I'd like to speak to Mr Tunne.'

Mr Tunne and his pansy secretary were away for a few nights, which was why Mrs Statch was there guarding the place, which she wouldn't be never doing again 'cos Mr Tunne, or more likely the fairy secretary, had locked up all but two bottles of the cunting gin.

'Aren't two bottles enough?'

This question elicited a magnificent curse in Fenland vernacular, followed by a prolonged liquid noise.

'Hallo?' said Pally.

'That was me being sick,' said Mrs Statch.

'Oh. Well, good-night.'

The next person whom Palairet decided to appeal to was Fielding Gray. Major Gray, he remembered, had often been spoken of as taking Marius to watch racquets, cricket and royal tennis, also as someone given to close inspection of Marius's physique or person and liable to hand out fivers in an equivocal manner. However, it had always been clear to Pally that Major Gray was regarded by Marius as an amicable if disreputable figure, and there was no difficulty, in this case, in raising the number of the novelist's Norfolk hide-out from Enquiries (for although the number had once been ex-directory, Fielding had begun to find himself so lonely in Broughton that it was now a pleasure to him to answer the telephone, no matter who turned out to be on the other end of it). Once again, however, Pally was out of luck: thirty rings brought no response.

So perhaps, thought Pally, he's in London, at the hotel where he often stays: Buttock's. Having rung Buttock's and asked the operator there for Major Gray, he was put through to Maisie Malcolm, who told him her name (which he remembered from Marius's account of the place) and briskly asked him his business.

'My business is with Major Gray.'

'You're the second person in ten minutes who's rung up for him,' Maisie said: 'what's UP? And what's someone of your age wanting with Fielding Gray?'

'Literary advice?' said Palairet, at a venture.

'At this time of night?'

'It's only ten o'clock.'

'Too late for literary advice. He's always drunk by this time. Anyway, he's not here. That's what I told Tessa when she rang just now. You know who I mean by Tessa?'

'Your niece.'

'Right. Well, she's no more business than you have to be ringing up Fielding at this hour of the night or any other, and she doesn't want literary advice, only to talk dirty, I wouldn't wonder. Nevertheless I told her where he was, bless her heart, because she said she simply wanted him to know what a marvellous time she and Marius were having in Somerset. Know who I mean by Marius?'

'Yes. I'm at school with them both, you see.'

'Oh. Then you'll be pleased to know they're having a lovely holiday. Or that's what Tessa says.'

'Have you any reason to doubt her, Mrs Malcolm?'

'I know when she's up to something. There's something not quite straight going on.'

'In Somerset?'

'Perhaps. Though it could be she just wants to talk dirty to Major Gray, like I said.'

'Where do I find Major Gray?'

'That bloody college, Lancaster. I'd hoped he'd be here with me about now. But he's not. Nor he's obliged to be, of course. I'd just hoped he would be, that's all. Know what I mean?'

'Yes, I do. I am very sorry, Mrs Malcolm.'

'You really sound it.'

'I am. Good-night.'

Dreading the idea of telephoning Lancaster again and getting the same beastly man as he'd spoken to before, whom he could hardly expect to be any more civil just because he was asking for Fielding this time and not for Jeremy, Palairet tried a number which he knew by heart: the Sterns's London house, the number and address of which he treasured in his breast with much the same emotional compulsion as had sent him to Regis Priory to see Lover Pie. Here he hoped to find Isobel Stern, Marius's mother: surely *she* would listen to anyone who feared for Marius.

And perhaps she would have done. But Isobel was not there, being hundreds of leagues away in her chancel under the Pyrenees, and Pally was answered by someone else.

'I'm Mavis, the cook,' said a man's voice. 'Or call me Ethel if you prefer. What's in a name?'

'I hoped to speak to Mrs Stern, Mavis.'

'Bless your little heart, duckie, none of them have been living here, except for odd nights, since poor old Clarabelle Stern went up to be with Jesus two years ago, and then some. They let me stay on out of kindness . . . to keep the place warm just in case.'

'In case of what, Ethel?'

'Well, one of 'em might want to come, one of these nights. Dame Isobella might get sick of her dykey arrangement in France; and then little Rosie's been given the birdie by her best chum, Tessa, so she might not fancy being at Buttock's any more when in London; and Marius may feel his oats one day and decide he needs somewhere private to have it off with whatever he fancies, and choose here, knowing that old Ethel won't spoil his sport or tell tales to Mummy; and so on.'

'But no one is there now, Mavis?'

'No one here now, except me. Ring any time, if the fancy takes you.'

'Thank you. Good-night.'

Nothing for it, thought Pally: I shall have to ring 'that college' again.

This time Len was more civil.

'Sorry I was so stroppy when you rang just now, sweetheart,' said Len. 'We've been having rather a trying time, but that's no reason to bite *your* balls to pieces. Now: it was Jeremy Morrison you wanted?'

'Yes, but you said he hadn't come. This time I want Fielding Gray.'

'Boy oh boy, are you low in luck. The thing is, Fielding went this afternoon, because Jeremy, although he hasn't come *yet*, is very soon going to come. Neither of them wants to see the other just now, you understand?'

'I think so. Where has Fielding gone?'

'His home in Broughton, I'd say, or else Buttock's Hotel.'

'I've tried them both. He's at neither.'

'Then he's gone off in a sulk, and you'd better give him up.'

'I suppose so. When does Jeremy arrive?'

'Not for a day or so. Carmilla Salinger, whom he's coming to see, has had to put him off. A guest of hers has just died in one of the guest rooms.'

'How very awkward.'

'Isn't it? What a sensible boy you sound. Most people would have gone all sanctimonious and said "how dreadful" or "how tragic" or "how sad". "Awkward" is much more to the point. Anyhow, I'm afraid I can't really help. If you still want Jeremy, ring again to-morrow evening and then just keep trying.'

'I rather wanted one of them . . . Jeremy or Fielding . . . *now*.'

'Then you're not being a sensible boy. I told you: they're just not here.'

'I know. I was being silly. Thank you for trying to help.'

And now, desperation mounting, Pally sat down in a chair and began to snivel, then bethought him of just two sources of hope: Mavis (or Ethel) and the Chamberlain, both of whom had invited him to telephone again, both of whom would be lavish with time and good will and advice, if requested. Mavis, thought Palairet, would perhaps be the shrewder; the Chamberlain, despite the undertone of madness in his voice, the more experienced and the sounder. He would try the Chamberlain first.

'The thing is,' he was saying, as to an old friend, some two minutes later, 'that I *think* something is wrong, even if he himself does not know what is wrong, with Marius Stern, who is Mr Jeremy's friend. Mr Jeremy has not arrived at Lancaster and you say you don't know where he is in London. So I need someone else who will listen to me and who will not laugh at me for imagining things.'

'Here I am, sir.'

'I know, and I can't tell you how grateful I am. But you cannot leave Luffham. I need someone who can come.'

'I understand, sir. Mr Jeremy you cannot find, nor anyone else, because, by the sound of you, you have telephoned everyone you can think of and have found only silence.'

'Yes.' He told the Chamberlain the names of all the people he had telephoned. 'Is there,' he concluded, 'anyone else at all? You may know.'

'Oh, I do. Master Marius had a cousin called Miss Tullia Llewyllyn, "Baby" to her friends. She married Lord Canteloupe. They are both very attached to Marius. Her ladyship is somewhat volatile; his lordship, whom I served for many years, as a soldier and a friend, is totally reliable in personal matters – though he was often less than dutiful in military ones. Telephone their house in Wiltshire.' He gave Pally the number. 'And say . . . say to his lordship . . . *Res Unius, Res Omnium . . .*'

'. . . Res Unius, Res Omnium,' Palairet said.

'Ah,' said Theodosia Canteloupe, 'the old motto. You want my husband. I'm afraid he's out to dinner, a stag party with the MFH, so he won't be up to conversation when he comes back.'

'Then can I speak to you, Lady Canteloupe? It's about your cousin.'

'My cousin?' said Thea, illegitimate and adopted.

'Marius. Marius Stern. You are . . . "Tullia"? "Baby" – please excuse me – to your friends?'

'Tullia is dead.'

'But the Chamberlain at Luffham –'

' – Is an old man, who wanders and forgets. Tullia, "Baby" to her friends, is dead in Africa. I am Theodosia Canteloupe.'

Somehow this piece of intelligence upset Pally more than any of the evening's disappointments or frustrations so far.

'Oh, Lady Canteloupe,' he said, 'I have rung up so many people to ask them to help. Jeremy Morrison and Mr Tunne and Marius's mother and Fielding Gray, and none of them are there. My aunt will be so upset about the telephone bill,' he blubbered, 'she's asleep now, but she'll find out, and then she'll pretend not to mind because she loves me, but I know she can't aff –'

– 'What is your telephone number at your aunt's?' said Theodosia, crisp as a Colonel of Horse.

Pally told her.

'Then ring off at once. I shall ring back.'

This she did within ten seconds.

'Now,' she said, 'let us get a few things straight. You rang my husband, and when you got me, you thought I was Marius Stern's dead cousin, Baby.'

'Yes. You see, I didn't know – '

' – Never mind that. You had something to say about Marius. *What* did you have to say about Marius?'

'There is something horribly wrong with Marius. There is some trouble . . . which I do not yet understand. I cannot prove it, I cannot say what it is, but I know there is something.'

'*How* do you know?'

'Because . . . because I like him rather a lot. Oh, Lady Canteloupe, because I love him.'

'As good a reason as any, I suppose. Details in a moment. But first: you are talking from your aunt's house in Burnham-on-Sea. This I know, but I do not know your name.'

'Palairet. I am at school with Marius.'

'I have heard your name. He half murdered you at Oudenarde House.'

'By accident.'

'And you remained his friend. Indeed you did. You rang up all these people, risked ridicule, risked distressing the aunt you love, because you thought Marius might need help.'

'I knew he did.'

'Very well, Mr Palairet. What is your Christian name?'

'Everyone calls me Pally.'

'How horrible. What is your real name?'

'It's silly. Galahad.'

'Not silly. But I'll call you something else, even Pally, if you prefer.'

A long silence.

'No. You may call me "Galahad".'

'I am Theodosia. My friends call me "Thea". You call me "Thea" . . . Galahad Palairet. And now: tell me exactly how you came to know that Marius needs help, and what sort of help it must be . . .'

When Piero and Ptolemaeos returned to Tunne Hall, they expected to find the guardian Mrs Statch ready to render her report and serve their luncheon. Instead they found her unconscious in a flood of unspeakable liquids under the kitchen table.

'One sees the perils of absenting oneself,' said Ptolemaeos, 'even for only three days.'

'It was worth it, sir. You look much fitter.'

'I feel much fitter. And I much enjoyed those Cumbrian castles. How clever of an Italian to plan such a trip in England.'

'Always ask a foreigner if you want to see the most beautiful and curious things in your own country. The natives take them for granted. Familiarity breeds blindness. I shall now start working on our next expedition, sir, if you please.'

'Not till after your examination at Cambridge. You'll need to work on *that*.'

'It's not for nearly two months, sir.'

'You'll still need to work on it. I want to see your name on that list,' said Ptolemaeos, 'with stars clustering all round it. And when we do go away next,' said Ptoly, surveying the supine Statch, 'we will leave no watch-dog.'

'We must, sir. The terms of the Insurance Policy for the books and artefacts in the library require a caretaker in your absence. But let us negotiate that barrier when we reach it. You go and look at the mail, and I shall cope with the *Signora* and make the lunch.'

After Ptolemaeos had rumbled off to his office, Piero raised Mrs Statch's heels to rest on a chair, poured a bucketful of hot water heavily laced with Jeyes Fluid between her legs, and slapped a pint of cold water on to her face. As she whined her way back into consciousness, she was told to clear up and get out, either for good, or, if she wished to retain her job, to return the next day only on the absolute understanding that she ceased to make spells against Piero behind his back.

'How d'ye know I does that? Canst prove?'

'My dear, abominable Mrs Statch, I have lived in countries where witchcraft is of a far higher standard than it is in your English Fens. You make one more spell against me, and not only are you dismissed from Mr Tunne's employment – '

' – That be for Mr Tunne to say – '

' – No. It be for me to say, for so he has charged me. One more spell out of you, Goody Statch, and not only will you be sacked, you will receive a bigger and better spell up your own apertures – all seven of them.'

Half an hour later, when he limped into the office with a tray of light luncheon for Ptolemaeos and himself, he found Ptolemaeos in a rare frot of excitement, apparently caused by a letter from the Greco in Tuscany.

'". . . Tell Piero",' Ptolemaeos read out, 'that his idea of consulting Don Simone Fontanelli was quite brilliant. Fontanelli has engaged, as our "agent of reaction" in the business ahead, a Florentine who calls himself Tiresiana or sometimes La Tiresias. When in full drag he is a magnificent blond with three Viking plaits, flashing green eyes, a rapier nose, and a wide, red mouth, like Dracula's. He has lovely, long, smooth legs which he dresses in purple stockings gartered three inches above the knee, a bottom which beggars all description encased in lederhosen which conceal his sex, a bare midriff with a devouring navel, and a subtly folded sash of gauze over the bosom which simulates mammary formations at one moment huge and succulent, the next *petites* and poignant.

'"Fontanelli, who sends the 'Signorino Piero' his compliments, has returned to Palermo. Nicos and I are off to Venice, where we shall be joined by Tiresiana this day week – by which time we shall have set everything up in Samuele . . ." '

'I hope they don't get too clever,' said Piero. 'In essence your plan is simple and had best be left so.'

'Whatever happens,' said Ptolemaeos, 'they should have an amusing tale to tell on their return. What an excellent soufflé, Piero. Now tell me something, dear boy: when you do have time to turn your mind to our next little jaunt, whereabouts had you thought of taking us?'

'How about a cruise in a private yacht, in the wake of Odysseus? Or following the voyage of Jason to Medea and the Golden Fleece?'

'A sea journey? I have always been shy of them. But if you, my dear Piero, are making the arrangements and accompanying me, I shall be shy of them no more.'

'When are you leaving?' said Canteloupe to Theodosia.

'Almost at once. I must meet Master Galahad in Taunton this evening. We shall go on from there.'

'Go on where from there?'

'Ultimately, Bellhampton Park. From what Galahad tells me, the affair at Regis Priory must have been in the nature of a dummy run. Marius was being observed and, up to a point, rehearsed . . . and the Glastonbury set were in on it, as well as his own lot. Now then, Canty. This morning came news from a distraught Carmilla: Myles Glastonbury, whom we persuaded her to accept as her guest in Lancaster, has died in a coma there. Before he went into the coma, he told Fielding Gray, who later told Carmilla, that his father, Prideau, has some scheme on with an old friend of his, Raisley Conyngham, a master at Marius's school. This scheme has to do with horses. It so happens that this Raisley Conyngham has Marius – and his chum, Tessa Malcolm – staying with him for the Easter hols in Somerset, and that Marius is being trained by Conyngham's people as a stable lad. According to Myles, Marius is involved in the scheme, whatever it is, which is being got up by Prideau and Conyngham. Although Myles went into his coma and died before he could reveal what the scheme was, he said two things of interest about it first. One: as far as Prideau is concerned the scheme is a harmless joke or trick, undertaken for the fun of the thing and to show how clever Prideau can be when he tries; but Myles suspects that for Raisley Conyngham the thing is

271

very different – that Raisley Conyngham plans to engineer some occurrence at the best risky and at worst definitely "evil".'

'Why did Myles suspect that?'

'He just felt it, he told Fielding. And this brings us to the second interesting thing he said. He said that Raisley Conyngham somehow *knew* that Myles felt suspicious; and that he laid his hands on Myles's hair (just as he used when Myles was a little boy) and had thus infected Myles with the illness from which he was already beginning to suffer.'

'What nonsense.'

'I agree, and so does Carmilla. But the real point of all this, Canty, is that though we don't know what the scheme is, we do know that the second part of it will operate at Bellhampton in two day's time, when Conyngham's horse, Lover Pie, runs against Prideau Glastonbury's mare, Boadicea, in the Hamilton 'Chase.'

'But how do we know this?'

'Because that far Myles *did* get before he became unconscious. Lover Pie and Boadicea, he said, were major factors in the whole affair. They were running against each other at Regis Priory and then soon after at Bellhampton. Something preliminary was to happen at the meeting, now over, at Regis Priory; and in the light of Galahad's report, we can now guess that this was some kind of trial or rehearsal. A few days later, something final, so Myles at any rate implied, was to occur at Bellhampton Park, something which would arise from, or during, the race for the Hamilton Cup.'

'This is sheer romancing.'

'So I would have thought – had not my Master Palairet, thinking no evil, just out for a spree with his Auntie, watching independently and from a totally different angle

272

– had not my Master Palairet, I say, witnessed such very peculiar behaviour at Regis Priory, which bears out everything said by Myles Glastonbury.'

'This Master Palairet. How did *he* come to be telling *you* what he saw – or thought he saw – at Regis Priory?'

'That is a long and complicated story; but the nub of the matter, Canty, is that Galahad's instinct told him that his friend was in trouble, and he was not going to rest, no matter how many people scoffed or rejected him or just weren't there when wanted – *he was not going to rest*, Canteloupe, until he had found his friend help. In the end, never mind quite how, he found me.'

'Very well. As you know, I have business with the lawyers for the next few days, so I suppose you may as well join this boy at Taunton, if that will amuse you.'

'Whether it will or not, I am going to Taunton.'

'Will you be gone long?'

'I have not forgotten our agreement and the time limit set on it, if that is what you mean.'

'In part, yes. I also meant, how long are you going to bear with this silly schoolboy fantasy of imbroglio and plot.'

'I thought you cared for Marius. You have come to his aid in the past.'

'For good reasons, responsibly presented. Not because some hysterical boy with a pash on Marius was trying to draw attention to himself.'

'There is also Fielding's account of what Myles Glastonbury said.'

'Fielding is another hysteric.'

'Carmilla believes him.'

'All right: so let us concede that Myles Glastonbury said what Fielding alleges he said. That does not mean that any of it is true. Myles was (a) much disordered by calf love and (b) about to disappear into a terminal coma.'

'Canty. Whether the whole thing is merely imagination and hysteria, or whether it is not, will be made abundantly plain in two days' time at Bellhampton Races. That is where it is to come to crisis. So to Bellhampton Races I shall go, with Galahad, to watch for foul play.'

'And if you spot any? What would you do then?' sneered Canteloupe. 'Blow a whistle?'

'I shall tell you all that I have done when we meet again, after you return from your grand confabulation with the lawyers.'

Giles Glastonbury was still staying with his cousin Prideau on the afternoon during which Prideau received the news of his son's death, this having been telephoned from Lancaster by the Provost's Secretary, Len. When Prideau gathered from Len that Fielding Gray had been the last person to talk to Myles before he fell into a coma, Prideau expressed a wish to talk with Fielding. Len told him that Fielding had now left the College. He gave Prideau the telephone number both of Fielding's house at Broughton and of Buttock's Hotel, but warned him that he had reason to suppose that Fielding could not be found at either. Then where could he be found? Len, who hated not knowing things, had to confess that he did not know this. Fielding, he said, had just gone off somewhere – anywhere – to brood and sulk.

When Prideau reported this to Giles, Giles said that when he and Fielding had been soldiers together, Fielding used to do his not infrequent brooding and sulking in his London club, then, as now, the Thackeray. At Prideau's request, he rang up the Thackeray Club, found that Fielding was indeed there, and had him summoned to the telephone on a plea of extreme urgency.

'Why are you sulking?' said Giles as soon as Fielding came on to the line.

'A lot of people don't like the book I'm writing. Even those that do think it's too hopelessly old-fashioned to have any appeal to the reading public.'

'Well, here's another load of trouble to take your mind off your own. Was Myles Glastonbury dead when you left Lancaster?'

'No.'

'He is now. My cousin Prideau, who is rather cut up, wants a word with you – about what sort of thing Myles was saying before he fell unconscious. I am appointing myself as censor before you tell him. So what *did* Myles say?'

Fielding told Giles what Myles had said about the scheme which was being hatched by Prideau and Raisley Conyngham. He also told him that Myles thought Conyngham was exploiting Prideau, in order to bring about something a good deal nastier than Prideau was reckoning on. Finally, he told Giles that Myles thought that Conyngham had guessed at his (Myles's) suspicions and for that reason, was bidding to kill him by his laying on of hands.

'All of which fits very well,' said Giles, 'with the shifty and sinister way in which they were all of them behaving at Regis Priory the other day. Why have you kept it quiet so long?'

'I told Carmilla Salinger.'

'Why only her?'

'Because I didn't think it was anything very serious. I'd

275

had my doubts when I heard that Marius was to spend Easter with Conyngham, so I dug out Jack Lamprey and enquired of him. He said there was some jape in hand, nothing dangerous, and solemnly promised to report to me at once if things did, after all, look like getting rough for Marius or Tessa. Then, having heard Myles's tale but having heard nothing more from Jack, I assumed that Myles's rigmarole was a sick man's fantasy, a distorted version of what Jack had originally told me – and as for Myles's idea that Raisley Conyngham had poisoned him by touching his hair, it was simply preposterous. What was more, Myles gave no details or hard facts, despite my repeated requests, he only referred to "instincts" and "feelings" and "suspicions"; so I decided, on balance, that there was no reason to do or say anything more, unless, and until, Jack got in touch again after all and corroborated Myles's highly coloured conjectures.'

'Jack could have had his own reasons for keeping quiet. Anyhow, you can take my word for it that the story Myles told you, however fantastic it may have seemed to you, squares with everything I've seen down here.'

'So what's to do? Surely, Prideau will take his mare out of the race now Myles is dead? That could stop the whole thing. I mean, though we don't know exactly what part Boadicea was to play, we do know she had a part, and an important part at that. The whole thing, Myles said, depended on the horses.'

'A very good point. Look, old thing,' said Giles: 'as I said just now, Prideau wanted to talk to you in person. But that don't suit at all, not with things as they are, so I'll tell him it's just a waste of time, that you've nothing to report to him except that Myles was more or less delirious. Right?'

'Right.'

'And then I'll ask him what he means to do about this race, now that Myles is dead. If he does take Boadicea out of it, then our troubles are probably over; but if he doesn't – '

' – Surely there can be no question. He can't run his mare before his son is even buried.'

'How very old-fashioned you are. Just like what they're saying about your book.'

'But in this case, common decency – '

' – Common decency, my dear Fielding, died with George the Sixth. In any case, if Raisley Conyngham is up to something as serious as Myles implied, he probably won't allow Prideau to scratch Boadicea.'

'But how can he prevent him?'

'For God's sake stop asking silly questions and put the receiver down. I'll telephone you again as soon as I possibly can.'

'So at last I've got here,' said Jeremy Morrison to Carmilla Salinger, as they walked by the River Cam, 'and you have to go and have the curse.'

'Sorry. I was looking forward to seeing you so much. And now you're going away . . . for a long time, it seems. To India, the Far East . . .'

'Australia. America – both halves. I've got a lot to see . . . if I'm to speak for all of us in the world who till the soil and tend the earth.'

'It hasn't taken you long . . . to get sick of tilling your sacred soil in Norfolk.'

Jeremy chuckled.

'Norfolk is just a tiny bywater,' he said, 'compared to which the area over which I must work my mission is like the ocean.'

'You're a fake, Jeremy Morrison.'

'Am I? You'd be surprised how many admiring letters I've had since the appearance of that article by Alfie Schroeder.'

'From gulls. Strictly from gulls.'

'Most of the world consists of gulls, Carm. Gulls who listen to big-mouthed politicians or revivalist preachers or quack doctors or crook fakirs. Gulls who think that here at last is something different, something to give them comfort or hope. So there will be plenty of gulls to listen to my message . . . and to take comfort from it.'

'What is that message to be?'

'If you work on or with the land, you are part of nature. If you fall in with the rhythm of the soil and the seasons, you will also be absorbed into the greater rhythms, of the solar system, of the galaxies, of the universe itself, which is God.'

'Only you don't believe a word of it.'

'It'll do as well as anything else, I think.'

'Very impersonal. But then of course you have ceased to be interested in people.'

'What nonsense,' said Jeremy. 'I have come all the way from London to see you.'

'Only because you wanted a body to play with.'

'A body which I couldn't have. But I'm still here talking.'

'Because you have been brought up as a gentleman,' said Carmilla. 'You do at least have manners. But how deep does it go? Do you have any loyalties? Let us

278

examine your record with your friends. You've ditched Fielding Gray for a start.'

'Fielding was my mentor. After a time we grow beyond our mentors.'

'That doesn't mean you have to ditch them. Then . . . you deserted this college. In particular, you deserted the Provost, who was fond of you and did his very best for you.'

'Only in memory of my father.'

'Well then. What about Marius? Marius Stern?'

'Marius is all right. Quite all right. I can't see him before I leave England because he's down in the West Country; but I shall write him a letter, wishing him luck, telling him where I'm going and when I expect to be back.'

'Marius is not all right, Jeremy. Marius is in danger.'

'What danger?' scoffed Jeremy.

'No one knows. There have been only . . . indications. Myles Glastonbury, before he died here, babbled to Fielding Gray of a plot. There has been a boy telephoning, wanting you, then wanting Fielding, finding neither. Finally, I don't know how or why, he found Theodosia. The boy is called Palairet, she has told me, and he is convinced that Marius is threatened by no trivial threat. Theodosia takes the boy Palairet so seriously that she has gone to join him in Somerset.'

'This is sheer madness.'

'Is it? Dying men tell the truth. The instincts of adolescent boys are often sound.'

'I've met this boy. He is in love with Marius and has been rejected by him. Perhaps this is some desperate attempt to force his way back into Marius's notice.'

But even as he said this, Jeremy remembered how Palairet had run from the Junior Fives Court, determined to renounce Marius, to see him and be seen by him no more. Palairet, he remembered, was a sincere and seriously minded boy. If he had changed his policy towards Marius, if he was now in the field to save him from some danger, either the danger must be real or there must be very good reason for Palairet to think it so.

'No,' he said to Carmilla. 'That was unfair. If the boy Palairet has spoken to Thea in this way, there must be a cause. An imagined cause, very likely, but a cause nevertheless.'

'Do I glimpse a glimmer of loyalty here?' A light wind hovered in the willow which wept nearby on the river bank. 'There must be a cause, you say. So shall you go to your friend Marius, who may be in danger?'

'Very probably a danger imagined by somebody else.'

'Thea thinks not. When she telephoned me before she left for Taunton, she said the boy's voice was the voice of truth.'

'How could she tell?'

'Shall you go to Somerset, Jeremy?'

'My plane leaves to-morrow afternoon. I have a complicated schedule.'

'You can afford to change it.'

'I suppose so. Shall *you* go to Somerset, Carm?'

'No. I have pupils who have an imminent and important examination. Their schedule is unchangeable. Theodosia, my twin, can stand for me too. Only you can stand for you.'

'Yes . . . What should I do? Of course I can change my schedule, but it will mean great expense and trouble and the remaking of appointments, made only with great difficulty, with over-worked and important men. All this . . . just for some alarm which may well be imaginary? What should I do?'

'Ask the river,' said Carmilla, 'the river by which you lived so happily and for so long.'

'Yes, the river. The kindly river. Oh, Father Cam, old Camus, tell me, what should I do?'

'Smelly,' said Giles Glastonbury when, after about half an hour, he telephoned Fielding at the Thackeray for the second time: 'very smelly. I asked Prideau what he was going to do about running Boadicea in the Hamilton, and he asked me to ring up Raisley Conyngham and tell him that in the circumstances, Boadicea would have to be withdrawn. "What's it got to do with Raisley Conyngham?" I said. "If you want to take Boadicea out of the race – and it's really the only right and proper thing to do – then take her out and be done with it. No need to consult Raisley." But he begged me to telephone Raisley for him, so I did.

'"He can't do this," Raisley said.

'"He can't do anything else," I said. "I'm not much of a mourning man myself, but I do know you can't run a racehorse while your son and heir is lying on a slab ready to be fitted for his box."

'"Outmoded convention," drawled Raisley. "Put Prideau on the line."

'"He's in a bad way," I said: "you talk to me."

'"All right," said Raisley, "go and ask Prideau if he still wants to be picked for Sheriff of the County."

'So I went and asked Prideau, and he shambled about groaning, and at last he said, "Ring up Raisley Conyngham again and tell him that Boadicea will run. But say that I can't be there myself and you'll be standing in for me."

'So all this I told Raisley, who seemed satisfied but said it was a pity Prideau wouldn't be there. However, he wasn't going to make a point of *that*, he said, and he looked forward to seeing me at Bellhampton.'

'So,' said Fielding, 'we deduce that Raisley Conyngham has a hold over Prideau . . . the nature of which need not detain us just now. Far more to the point is this, that it was obviously essential for Conyngham's purpose, that Boadicea should run in the Hamilton.'

'And secondly,' said Giles Glastonbury, 'while it was clearly of great importance to Conyngham, it was of very little to Prideau – otherwise he would have been all for running Boadicea let Myles have been never so dead. This supports your theory, or rather Myles's theory in origin, that as far as Prideau is concerned, the whole thing is merely an ingenious jape, got up to amuse and amaze his friends, some utterly harmless spoof or what not . . . which, however, Raisley Conyngham was going to pervert into some far more sinister form, for some far more sinister purpose.'

'So what,' said Fielding, 'now?'

'We take our places as near the stage as possible,' said Giles Glastonbury, 'and see what comes out of the conjuror's hat. I shall be doing piquet in the paddock, in a pretty good position to act if needed. It would be nice to know that you were hanging about somewhere. *Res Unius, Res Omnium*, you know.'

'I shall be there.'

'That's my boy. See you at Bellhampton.'

When Fielding telephoned Canteloupe in Wiltshire (which he did as soon as he had finished tallking to Giles), he was told by Leonard Percival that Detterling was spending a few nights in his London club, and that her ladyship had departed for the West Country.

'Something's up,' said Percival, 'and whatever it is she's not letting me in on it, because she don't care for me one little bit.'

'One thing I can tell you,' said Fielding: 'if anything happens it'll happen the day after to-morrow at Bellhampton Races, probably before or during the 'Chase for the Hamilton Cup.'

'Too far for Leonard Percival this time,' Leonard Percival said. 'My ulcers are tearing me apart.'

Having done his best to commiserate, Fielding crossed Pall Mall, walked round St James's Square, and so up St James's Street to Canteloupe's club.

'Hamilton Cup at Bellhampton,' he said to Canteloupe, who was hanging about morosely in the library, there being no takers for backgammon. 'We ought to be there.'

'Why ought we?'

'The Cup was first given by the founder of the Regiment. In the old days, there were always two or more officers of the 49th riding in the race. In 1933, it was won by a corporal of ours, up on a gelding owned by a Troop Leader in the 10th Sabre Squadron.'

'That was when soldiering was a pukka profession,' Canteloupe said. 'There won't be any of ours riding this year or ever again. So why go to Bellhampton just to be reminded that the Army these days is a mob of greasy mechanics?'

'This year, as it happens, there *is* a connection with the Regiment. Corporal-Major Chead's boy, Danny, is riding Prideau Glastonbury's Boadicea.'

'As a pro?'

'As a pro. Even so . . .'

'Look,' said Canteloupe: 'don't try to pull the wool over my eyes. I know why you're interested in Bellhampton Races: there's something up there to do with Marius Stern, or so they say. Theodosia's off already. In my view, the whole thing is mere moonshine, and one Canteloupe is enough to cut capers in it. Anyway, I have important discussions in London. I have to see that all the Sarum entails, about the house and the land, are arranged as . . . as flexibly as possible.'

'Entails are never flexible.'

'I'm afraid that's turning out to be the case. So the flexibility,' said Canteloupe sullenly, 'will have to come from another source.' He emptied a glass of port and pressed a bell. 'Tully,' he said, 'has money in trust, in America, from Max de Freville. That would be quite enough for him.'

'But as things stand,' said Fielding, 'Tully will have it all, house, land and Cant-Fun, unless you break the entail?'

'Right.'

'But of course you can't break the entail?'

'Right again.'

'Then why not give up what can only be a futile attempt, and come with me to Bellhampton?'

'No. There could just be some chink somewhere. I must go on talking with the lawyers.'

'Whatever chinks there are, Tully must have the title.'

'Unless I challenge his paternity.'

'Too late. You'd wind up on a charge of conspiracy. Besides, you'd be dishonouring Baby's memory. Not kind, Canteloupe. We did our best for you, Baby and I, and such as it is, you're stuck with it.'

'Am I?'

'Yes; so give up all this jabbering with lawyers at a thouand guineas a minute and come with me to Bellhampton.'

Silence.

'*Res Unius*, Canteloupe, *Res Omnium*.'

'That cock don't fight. Not with me. Not any more.'

'I see. "Detterlings do not serve."'

'Who told you that?'

'You did. You told it to another, years ago, who told it to me.'

'Second hand.'

'You told me first hand, just now . . . albeit in different words. So I'll be off, Canteloupe,' said Fielding. He steered his way past an old and tipsy waiter, who was bringing Canteloupe port in what looked like a goldfish bowl on a stem, and left Canteloupe's club, more depressed than he had been for a very long time.

That Canteloupe, as foreseen by Leonard Percival at Christmas, was evidently thinking of using lethal or at best underhand means to remove Tullius, did not much surprise or shock Fielding, even though Tullius was his own natural son; for Fielding now knew Tullius to be grossly deficient and although he had attempted a token defence of the boy, he cared little what fate might be spun for him. What did upset Fielding was Canteloupe's threat to challenge Tully's paternity in order to disinherit him, as this would amount to breaking an absolute oath of secrecy which had been binding on all three people concerned: Canteloupe, Baby Canteloupe, and himself. But he'll not do that, Fielding thought: he'd have to admit to sterility, and then any son whom Theodosia might bear would also be disqualified from the inheritance. No, thought Fielding: he'll keep quiet, wait for Theodosia to be safely delivered of another man's son (whose?), and then dispose of poor Tully: perhaps fake his death and arrange for him to be somehow and somewhere maintained in secret from the funds left by Max de Freville (which would probably come under Canteloupe's control after Tully's 'demise'); perhaps send him to Doctor La Soeur to 'catch pneumonia' and die in good earnest; possibly a combination – an apparent 'death' in La Soeur's nursing home, followed by a shadowy afterlife either there or in some sister establishment on the continent or in the United States.

But whatever Canteloupe might or might not be going to do about Tullius, he had already committed one crime which wounded Fielding so deeply that he could never, he thought, forgive him: he had refused the Regimental appeal, when Fielding had made it to him, for a comrade's assistance in need; he had repudiated, he had scorned ('That cock don't fight') the plea of *Res Unius, Res Omnium*, and had thus shamed every man that had ever carried the motto on his cap-badge, the old skull and cross-bones, of the 49th Earl Hamilton's Light Dragoons.

'Myles Glastonbury, Provost,' said Len to Tom Llewyllyn: 'here is his death certificate for your signature.'

'What did he die of?'

'No one really knows,' said Len. 'Some virus, I suppose. Whatever it was was so fascinating that Balbo Blakeney begged for him to be kept in College and not sent out to a hospital.'

'I didn't know Balbo still bothered with science.'

'From time to time. If he finds something really succulent in what used to be his line. Unusual conditions of mammalian blood were very much in his line, and there was a really macabre condition for him to investigate in poor, young Glastonbury. Quite beyond analysis, Balbo says.'

'Beyond Balbo's analysis, I dare say. Did Glastonbury have no other care?'

'Matron and Doctor Grampion.'

'The whole thing sounds quite Dickensian.'

'Precisely, Provost. Which is why you must exercise your powers as Coroner within the College, sign this certificate, and have him put away under the chapel crypt *pretty damn quick*. His father is happy for him to be buried here,' said Len, 'so all should be well; but despite the undoubted validity of your jurisdiction inside these walls, some prying do-gooder or life maniac may get up a fuss at any second, unless we whisk that interesting cadaver to the other side of the Styx.'

'Where is it now? The cadaver?'

'In the reserve meat safe. But that will be wanted very soon for the baby lambs for the Feast of the Resurrection, so please, darling Provost, will you sign that damned certificate and authorize instant burial?'

'All right. You don't suppose the wood nymphs, the dryads, had a hand in all this?'

'No, I do not.'

'Well, what *do* we say he died of?'

'Doctor Grampion, who has, after all, been in practice for seventy years and so sought to know a thing or two, has already filled in the cause of death as *Corruptio Carnis*, i.e. Decay of the Flesh or Body.'

'Rather . . . rather a *general* diagnosis?'

'Yes, but accurate enough in its way, as you'd see if you looked in on the reserve meat safe. So please, lovely Provost, will you sign that fucking certificate?'

Theodosia had met Palairet, by arrangement, in The Castle Hotel at Taunton. She knew him at once – the solemn, clean-cut boy sitting stiffly on a chair in the hall.

'Galahad Palairet?' she said.

He shook hands firmly but shyly, releasing her hand after a split second, as if afraid lest he should crush her bones or offend her by physical contact.

'My car is outside,' she told him. 'I could have driven straight to Burnham-on-Sea and spared you the trouble of a train journey. But there are some things we have to discuss before I meet your aunt. She can put me up?'

'She is very excited about it.'

'Then I'll just make one telephone call, and we'll be off.'

'*Écoute bien*, Galahad,' said Theodosia, fifteen minutes later, as she drove him by the long way round over the Quantocks. 'I have found out much that you know nothing of.' She then told him the full substance and detail of Myles Glastonbury's story as told by Myles to Fielding, then repeated by Fielding to Carmilla and by Carmilla to herself. 'So you see,' she said, 'you were right to suspect that Marius was in trouble – '

' – I didn't suspect, I knew – '

' – And right to flog your aunt's telephone account in order to get in touch with someone. I am glad,' she said, looking straight ahead over the wheel, 'that in the end it turned out to be me.'

'So am I, my lady.'

'Thea . . . my friends call me "Thea". And now you see how we are placed. Something is planned, almost certainly, for the day of the Hamilton 'Chase at Bellhampton. We have no idea what, except that it involves Marius, as an ostensible stable lad, and the two horses, Lover Pie and Boadicea. On Myles's showing, this plan is of comparatively little interest to Prideau Glastonbury; but as far as we know, Prideau has not withdrawn his horse from the race, despite the death of his son, so he must be under some kind of pressure to run it. And that is about all we have to go on. I think that what you saw at Regis Priory was almost certainly some kind of rehearsal or dry run of the first part, or at any rate *a* part, of the plan for Bellhampton. So can you remember anything particular about that scene in the paddock which you might have forgotten to tell me on the telephone?'

'I told you that Giles Glastonbury took his hat off to

Marius? And Prideau did the same. My aunt was very impressed.'

'Giles Glastonbury is not involved. He knows nothing about any of it,' Myles said. 'So anything he did would be entirely by the way.'

'I see. There is one thing. The blanket.'

'Blanket?'

'The hindquarters of Lover Pie were covered by what looked like a very heavy blanket. It was a warm day, my lady, even hot. But they left the blanket on until Lover Pie was out on the course. Jimmy Pitts, the jockey, then spoke to Marius – rather sharply, by the look of it – and Marius at once took the blanket off.'

'And then Lover Pie went off to the start?'

'Right.'

'Did you notice anything in particular about the running of the race?'

'No. I'd had some money on Lover Pie, but he never looked like winning. Auntie said he needed the race.'

'What about Boadicea?'

'Very moderate.'

'No dramas on the course or after the race?'

'None. Marius went out to meet Lover Pie, put on his blanket, and led him back. Jimmy Pitts took his feet out of the irons and hung his legs down. He looked a little thoughtful but fairly contented. The race was won by Pearl Barley at six to one, and I'm happy to say that Auntie had a tenner on it. But she shouldn't really be betting,' said Palairet in a worried way, 'in tenners. I hope it doesn't become a habit.'

'Neither Pearl Barley nor any of the other runners at Regis Priory are going in the Hamilton 'Chase. Only Lover Pie and Boadicea. But there are,' said Theodosia, 'seven other runners declared at four days – luckily my husband takes *The Sporting Life*, so I was able to check back. That means that there will be nine runners in all, as at Regis Priory. All except Lover Pie and Boadicea are geldings – again, the same pattern as at Regis Priory.'

'I have to tell you something rude,' said Pally Palairet, going vermilion.

'You want to stop for a pee?'

'No, thank you. It's something I've just remembered. Something Auntie said at Regis Priory. About Boadicea. "That mare," she said, "is going to be in season at any minute." '

'My darling boy. Nothing rude in telling me that.'

'I'm so glad you think so, my lady. I think I'd die rather than upset you after you've been so kind, listening to me like you did and coming all this way to help me.'

'Sweetheart . . . no, don't cry. I'm enjoying every minute of it. I know I shouldn't be, I know I should be thinking of poor Marius and what they might be planning against him, but I'm not made like that, I just like to enjoy things as they come – . . . except for one thing, which I don't think I'll ever enjoy, although one day very soon it'll have to come – but never mind about all that. So . . . Boadicea, by now, is in season. What do we think about that? Can a horse run when it's in season?'

'Oh yes. I said to Auntie at Regis Priory, "What happens if it comes on now?" "If it comes on now," she said, "it comes on now. She can still run – and go on running." I'm afraid I've got to tell you something else rude, my lady.'

'Thea . . . I am not easily shocked.'

'"Sometimes," Auntie said, "when a mare in season is running, the boys get all horny . . . which would be a pity in this case, as Lover Pie would have trouble with the fences – would probably have to be withdrawn. Whacking great peegoes, these stallions have." '

'Was that last bit you or Auntie?'

'Auntie.'

'I thought so. Funny old-fashioned word, peego. You find it in Victorian pornography.'

'Ullacote is near here,' said Palairet: 'I looked it up on Auntie's Ordnance Survey. Shall we drive past?'

'No. They might see us and recognize us – or you at least – and wonder why we were taking so much interest . . . It's not Ullacote that matters, Galahad, but Bellhampton Races. This trip is for discussion and general planning, not for reconnaissance.'

'We don't seem to have planned very much.'

'Do you wonder? What have we to go on? A heavy blanket on a warm day, and Boadicea in season. So where does Marius come in? As a stable boy. He's fond of horses and he's being trained, during his holiday, to look after them. What could be more suitable and natural? So what can *they* possibly be up to, and why indeed should they be up to anything? Yet up to something they must be, or else that dismal Myles Glastonbury, who hadn't an iota of imagination and was as honest as the day is long, would never have said they were.'

'Ought you to call him "dismal" when he's only just dead?'

'Dismal he was. But we had some marvellous games of tennis together. He was a brilliant player and a real sportsman with it. He could have won the Aberdare Cup, you know – he *had* won it, but then he said his last stroke hadn't been up, he'd taken it on the half volley of the second bounce, he said. Nobody could believe their ears. But he insisted that the marker declare "deuce" instead of "Game, Set and Match" in his favour, and his opponent won the next two points and the next two games.'

'I like that story.'

'I thought you would. Anyway, sweetheart, if Myles said there was something up, there was something up, and since Prideau is keeping his mare in the race despite his bereavement, then there still is. The best we can do is go home to your Auntie, sit tight, ask her everything she knows about the race game in general and mares in season in particular, and then go to Bellhampton ready to jump if the bell rings. I think,' she said, 'that others may be there too.'

'He has a friend called Jeremy Morrison. If *he* knew – '

' – He does. My sister Carmilla will have told him by now. It was her I telephoned from Taunton, and she said Jeremy was going to arrive at Lancaster this very afternoon.'

'And then she will tell him about Marius? Then he must come.'

'There are no "musts" with Jeremy Morrison. What is this place?'

'It's called Roadwater. It has a pretty cricket ground with a stream running past. There it is now.'

Thea stopped the car. Palairet pointed over a gate in a hedge. On the far side of the narrow cricket ground, a ridge rose almost sheer.

'It must be marvellous in the summer,' said Theodosia, 'when the leaves are out all the way up that ridge, hiding it, making a huge, green shield . . . Where is the stream?'

'Hidden under a bank, with the bottom of the ridge on the other side of it. The ridge rises vertically from the very edge of the water.'

'Let's look.'

Theodosia ambled over the ground, her long, twilltrousered legs making such enormous strides that Palairet had to trot to keep up with her.

'You're like the giant with the seven league boots,' he said, and for the first time since he had met her, a smile came into his thin, prim, serious face.

He ran ahead of her, turned and capered backwards, still smiling. Theodosia smiled back, her wide mouth angled like a boomerang under her kind, brown curving nose.

'Thea,' called Palairet softly, 'Thea,' as she smiled yet wider.

Very near to them now, the stream rattled down its deep and stony channel. Palairet ran up a bank at the edge of the ground. Thea slipped on her way up the bank and extended her arm with fist clenched, so that Palairet might grasp her wrist and help her. They stood side by side, looking down into the stream, Palairet's fingers still round Thea's wrist.

'According to Auntie's Ordnance Survey,' said Palairet, 'this stream has its source in the hills and runs through the Ullacote estate in its descent. It is called the Ull.'

'Ah,' said Theodosia: 'what message to us from Ullacote, little Ull?'

A hedgehog floated past, belly swollen and burst, entrails spread and writhing in the wake of it like the snakes of the Medusa's hair.

'I think you should not have asked,' said Palairet, taking his fingers from Theodosia's wrist.

'To-morrow,' said Milo to Tessa.

They were in Tessa's bedroom in Ullacote. Milo was carrying a large parcel which he dumped on the bed.

'This is what you must do,' he said.

He ripped open the parcel.

'Take off that skirt you're wearing,' he said, 'and put on these.'

He threw her a pair of corduroy trousers from the parcel. Tessa turned her back on Milo and took off her tartan skirt.

'Don't turn your back on me. I want to see you.'

Tessa turned to face him and picked up the trousers.

'I once said that to Marius,' said Milo. 'He let me see him. Will you?'

'If you like.'

'Ah. Ginger is it, or auburn? Soft, not bushy, like mine. I wish you were a boy, Tessa. I am going to dress you as a boy. Put on these trousers.'

'I will do whatever you ask; but please ask kindly. When shall you kiss me behind my knee . . . as you promised?'

'To-morrow, when everything is over and our time has come. Now, put on those trousers and you will get all the kindness that is coming to you . . . to-morrow. Then take off that shirt of yours, and your bra, and bind your breasts as flat as you can with this' – he threw her a sash of grubby towelling – 'and then put on this' – a ragged khaki shirt.

'We shall both,' he said, 'be dressed like this to-morrow.'

He passed her a battered pair of blue 'trainers' and a foul cloth cap.

'Can you get all your hair inside?' he said.

'Yes.'

'Now my turn.' He produced from the parcel a shirt and trousers similar to those in which Tessa was now dressed. 'You can see *me*, if you wish. There. Absolutely soft. It's not that you don't excite me, Tessa – I've often got excited when looking at you, though I've been careful not to show it – but until to-morrow, you understand, there can be nothing between us. But if all goes well to-morrow . . . then *"Cras amet qui nunquam amavit, Quique amavit cras amet* – He that has loved let him love to-morrow, let him love to-morrow that never has yet." Let *her* love to-morrow that never has yet. You.'

He began changing into the second pair of corduroy trousers.

'Brother and sister,' he said: 'Sebastian and Viola . . . or rather Cesario. With Jack Lamprey as Antonio and our dear little friend, Marius, as Olivia . . . *and* Orsino.'

'I don't understand.'

'You don't need to. Just obey. You go to bed dressed like you are now. So do I. To make the clothes even more awful than they are already. There will be an early start in the morning. No breakfast, so bring biscuits or choco-late. I shall come for you at six. You must be ready to jump out of bed, dressed in that lot, boots and all, and come with me there and then. No washing or gargling or brushing or combing. The cap will cover your hair anyway.'

'Milo. These clothes stink.'

'They're meant to. Sebastian and Viola . . . And Cesario . . . gone gypsy.'

'Where are we going in the morning?'

'You'll see. No questions. No comments or complaints, whatever your distaste or discomfort. Just obedience. All right?'

'All right.'

'And then, to-morrow night, when it's all over, we shall have the transformation scene. I, that was a gypsy, shall be your prince, and you shall be my princess.'

'Milo . . . ?'

'Yes, little one? Not frightened of your gypsy prince, I hope?'

'No. Not really. But . . . well . . . my Auntie Maisie. You must promise me, Milo, to be careful. I cannot bear the idea of hurting, of shaming, Auntie Maisie. I will adore you, worship you, serve you and grovel before you. But you will be careful?'

'Yes, little one. I shan't even pop your maidenhead if you don't wish it. And so I always said.'

'Why do you speak so coarsely? I want you to do everything you want to do . . . if only you will be careful.'

'What an old-fashioned girl you are. Abortions are ten for tuppence these days, or hadn't you heard? Raisley would fix you up in no time with his old friend, Doctor La Soeur; you could have it on the house, little one, with a complimentary box of liqueur choccies thrown in.'

'Oh, Milo. Why will you talk like that?'

'Well, I see what you mean. You don't want Auntie Maisie to think that anyone has spoiled you. Very well, little Tessa. Have no fear: all will be well to-morrow if you will only obey. "*Cras amet qui nunquam amavit, Quique amavit cras amet.*"'

'I want you and Lover Pie looking your best to-morrow,' said Raisley Conyngham to Marius Stern.

'Yes, sir,' said Marius, who was sitting to the right of the fireplace in the long, low library at Ullacote, while Conyngham stood with his back to the flame, sipping at a small tumbler of calvados.

'So Jenny will be responsible for the Lover's appearance,' said Raisley, 'and you will manage your own.'

'What do you want me to turn up in, sir?'

'Grey suit and school tie. Black shoes, highly polished.'

'But at Regis Priory – '

' – Never mind Regis Priory. Although to-morrow will be the same in many ways, it will be different in others. Suit and school tie. Black shoes polished like a guardee's. Those brogues of yours will do very well.'

'Any other instructions, sir?'

'Just carry on as you did last time.'

'But some things will be different, you say?'

'You'll know how to deal with them when they happen. You're not a fool: no need to cross "t"s and dot "i"s. But one thing: when you've removed Lover Pie's blanket and seen him off down the course, take it straight to the horse-box, where you will find that Jenny has prepared a large bucket of disinfectant solution which will be in the far left-hand corner. Put the blanket in the bucket to soak. Then return to the course as quickly as you can and watch the rest of the race from the paddock gate. You should be back there about the time the horses start the second of the three circuits. Do not stir an inch, Marius, unless instructed by Milo or myself, until all the horses which are still running have passed the winning post. Then go to meet Lover Pie and Jimmy in the usual way, but of course without his blanket. If one is needed, Jenny will come out with a fresh one ... or one of Jenny's assistants.'

'So it doesn't seem very different after all, sir, except for the bit about the blanket.'

'Just you wait and see, and keep your wits about you.'

'I hope you'll let me come with you both,' said Palairet's Auntie (Flo), who had been explaining that mares were sometimes brought into season by the mere proximity of stallions and (unlike bitches) were unpredictable in the matter. 'Sounds like an interesting old day out.'

'Of course you must come,' said Theodosia. 'From what Galahad tells me, it was you rather than he, that spotted something odd in the first place.'

'Rather more than odd I think,' said Auntie Flo, taking a swill out of a bucket-sized tumbler of whisky. 'Years ago, I remember, I saw rather a good film about a coven of witches and warlocks in New England. Valentine Dyall was in it, with that lovely deep voice of his. They all lived together, the witches and warlocks, in a remote village on the sea-shore – where there was nobody else except them. Then along came the hero, quite by accident: his car had broken down along the road and he wanted a garage. As he came into the charming little square at the centre of the village, he realized that he was being watched. All round the square, the witches – though we didn't yet know that's what they were – were standing in pairs, man by woman, witch by warlock, and staring at him, quietly and intently, as if they were adding him up and getting his number. I was reminded of this film by the scene in the paddock. Although in this case there were only some six or seven people looking at Marius Stern, it seemed much more, it seemed as if everyone, all round the paddock, had suddenly stopped what they were doing and were standing stock still and stone silent, all turned towards young Stern, all deliberately staring at him.'

Theodosia remembered the hedgehog which Palairet and she had watched as it went past them down the Ull, and rubbed her hands together and shivered.

'And yet,' she said, 'it's all so respectable. A rich schoolmaster with a string of horses and a Private Trainer . . . a pupil who likes riding, being trained to groom one of them and allowed to exercise him . . . for the rest just an old-fashioned reading party, with sword practice, tennis, walks on the moors . . . What *can* be wrong?'

'Milo Hedley, for one thing,' said Palairet, 'and Raisley Conyngham for another.'

'What have you got – what has anyone got – against either?'

'Milo Hedley never stops smiling. Raisley Conyngham's fingernails look as if they've been manicured.'

'Neither morally nor personally offensive,' said Theodosia; 'you must do better than that.'

Palairet thought.

'I once saw Hedley swimming in Baths,' he said: 'he is as white as a corpse and he has no hair on his legs or his chest – but he does on his back. A thick tuft between his shoulder-blades.'

Theodosia shivered as she had when she remembered the hedgehog.

'At least we shall be spared a view of that,' she said.

'He may not even be there. He wasn't at Regis Priory.'

'Where was he?'

'I expect he was looking after Tessa Malcolm. Marius always used to say that she couldn't stand horses – and horses couldn't stand her.'

'A little girl who hates horses,' said Theodosia; 'a stallion brave enough to run over fences – not just hurdles but fences; a mare in season – quite possibly brought into season by the presence of the stallion at Regis Priory; a man with manicured nails; and an ever smiling boy with hair between his shoulder-blades. Trainers and jockeys staring like gorgons. Prideau Glastonbury – why is he running his horse when his son lies dead? Poor Myles. He did not deserve what happened to him.'

'What did happen to him?' Aunt Flo asked.

'He fell into a coma and died.'

'What of?'

'Nobody really knows.'

'Sickly, I expect,' said Aunt Flo; 'like his mother. She went off pretty quick . . . when Myles was about ten. Raisley Conyngham was mixed up in all that as well. It seems that Prideau's wife – Konya, she was called – didn't like the way Conyngham used to put his hands on little Myles's head. Neither did little Myles. Konya asked Conyngham not to, and although she was perfectly polite, Conyngham resented it. They quarrelled at some dinner party – or it might have been at a race meeting. Then she got a bad cold, either at the race meeting or coming home from the dinner, got weaker and weaker . . . then fell unconscious and died.'

'What did the doctors say?'

'Dicey heart,' said Aunt Flo, 'weakened by incipient pneumonia.'

'After running foul of Conyngham,' said Theodosia. 'Like poor Myles. We know,' she said to Aunt Flo, 'that Myles tried to or intended to warn his father against Conyngham, and so constituted a threat to Conyngham. And now we hear that Konya Glastonbury constituted a rather similar threat. Presumably, she implied that Conyngham's attentions to Myles were those of a pederast. Is he a pederast?' she said to Palairet.

'He's neuter,' said Pally with loathing, 'neuter as a gelded toad.'

'But not a man to cross, it seems.'

'All eunuchs are spiteful,' said Aunt Flo, 'but Raisley Conyngham is far too canny, from what I've heard, to commit casual acts of spite, let alone criminal ones. Raisley Conyngham, they used to say in my London days, never did anything without a sound and serious reason.'

'A heavy blanket on a warm day . . . the choice of Marius as groom . . . round we go in circles. What sort of chance,' Theodosia asked Aunt Flo, 'has Lover Pie got in the Hamilton Cup?'

'Better than the last time out. He badly needed a race, and this time the handicap is slightly in his favour. He'll start at about seven or eight to one.'

'With a lot of money on him?'

'Raisley never had a bet in his life. Some of the public will have a bit of a punt. Nothing out of the way.'

'So no one will have any reason worth mentioning to dope the horse either to win or to lose?'

'Not the teeny-weeniest, my dear,' said Aunt Flo. 'The trophy is silver gilt, of feeble design (if one considers its provenance and period), and the prize money wouldn't

302

keep a cab-horse in rations from Michaelmas to All Hallows.'

'I give up,' said Theodosia. 'Bedtime, chums. An early start to-morrow.'

Jeremy Morrison leaned over the white railing and watched Marius lead Lover Pie round the paddock. By contrast with most of the stable lads and lasses, who were informally if not scruffily turned out, Marius was wearing a well pressed dark grey suit, his school tie (dark blue with narrow pink stripes) and a pair of brilliantly polished black brogues. When, as was bound to happen and as Jeremy intended to happen, Marius spotted him on the rail, Jeremy smiled and waved and received a diffident grin in return. There doesn't seem much the matter with him, Jeremy thought, and God alone knows why he's got up for Speech Day. He would follow Marius's progress through the afternoon, he decided, and take the first opportunity of talking to him. Since it had cost a lot of money, effort and ingenuity to arrange the logistic alterations in his plans that had made his presence at Bellhampton possible, Jeremy was keen to get good value; and the very least he could do now that he was here, he thought, was to say a proper farewell to Marius.

Although he had come in response to Carmilla's grave prognosis that wickedness was brewing, a prognosis which, knowing how level-headed Carmilla usually was, he had been inclined to believe, he now found himself lulled by the warmth of the spring sun, the good humour of the crowd and the comfortable normality of the proceedings. What wickedness could possibly be brewing here? All that was happening – all that could conceivably be happening in such a place – was that those concerned were making leisurely but punctual preparation for the big race of the afternoon (an unimportant race as races went but the principal offering of a modest card), on a pleasant country racecourse in West Sussex.

Marius came past again with Lover Pie and again grinned at Jeremy. Jeremy blew a kiss back. This was noticed by two men who were standing on the grass: a scrawny man and a sleek man. *Honi soit*, thought Jeremy, *qui mal y pense*. The sleek man, he knew, was Raisley Conyngham, by whom he had been taught while at school and who would probably recognize him. Either way, thought Jeremy, no harm done and no harm in prospect. What harm could possibly be wrought or intended, here under the trees in this homely little paddock? Now he came to think of it, thought Jeremy, Milo Hedley had quite definitely assured him, as they walked back along Pioneers' Path after their pleasing bout in the hayloft, that Marius would not come to harm while in the care of Conyngham. Of course he wouldn't. Whatever was Carmilla thinking of? She should have had more sense than to listen to some fantasy of that silly old woman, Fielding Gray, a fantasy based on a sick man's babbling. He should never have come, thought Jeremy; but come he had, and now he was here he would enjoy the 'Chase for the Hamilton Cup, put a pony or two on Lover Pie for old times' sake, seek out Marius that they might exchange civilized blessings, and then go forth on his Oriental travels to gather the experience and to secrete the wisdom that were to make him a voice among mankind.

Fielding Gray, loitering near the paddock in a huge panama hat with the 49th Light Dragoons's riband round it, decided that the best thing he could do was to keep his one eye firmly on Jeremy Morrison. Jeremy was as likely as anyone was to lead him to any action there might be, and while he, Fielding, had him in sight, he could indulge himself in dreams of protection and rescue. For although he bitterly resented the manner in which Jeremy had deserted him, he still loved him as his own.

Milo and Tessa hung around in the park for horse-boxes. Identically dressed from head to foot, both having their hair hidden beneath voluminous floppy cloth caps, they might have been two gypsy brothers, elder and younger, both up to no good. Whereas Marius had travelled with Lover Pie and Gat-Toothed Jenny in the horse-box, Milo and Tessa had been ferried to the course by Jack Lamprey in his Ferrari.

'Christ, you both pong,' Jack had said: 'I'll be glad when this business is done with.'

'What business?' said Tessa.

'You'll see,' said Milo. 'Just obey my orders and keep

your eyes open and you'll have a front seat view of everything.'

'No horses, I hope.'

'Not near enough to matter.'

But now they were in among the horse-boxes, and Tessa was becoming uneasy.

'Not long now,' said Milo, sensing this. 'Christ, you look attractive, dressed like that, with your lovely face and that putrescent smell.'

Giles Glastonbury, in correct racecourse order of dress, stood on the grass in the paddock with Phil Loche, waiting for Danny Chead. Here he came now: cherry jacket, light blue skull and cross-bones on his back, cherry cap. These colours, thought up by Giles in the days when he used to share ownership of horses with Prideau, were based on the rig of the 49th Earl Hamilton's Light Dragoons, who affected tight cherry trousers, light blue tunic and a skull and cross-bones as their badge. Really quite appropriate, thought Giles: the son of a Dragoon (fat Corpy Chead) riding in the Regimental Colours for a Cup originally put up by the founder of the Regiment.

Ex-Corporal-Major 'Corpy' Chead hated his son because he was mean and ratty. He had come to this meeting, not to watch Danny, but because he always attended what he regarded as the 'Regimental' steeplechase. For many years there had been little or nothing of the Regiment about it; but this year, thought 'Corpy' Chead happily, there was Major Glastonbury (they didn't come like *him* any more) standing as representative of the owner of a horse which would be ridden by his own son (ratty or not) in what was to all intents the Regimental insignia; there was 'Sozzler' Jack Lamprey, who had trained another horse in the race; and this year, too, by all the powers in hell, was Major Gray, and wearing the Regimental riband at that.

Corpy Chead waddled up to Fielding and raised his brown trilby the regulation nine inches from his head.

'Good afternoon, sir.'

'Ah, good afternoon, Corporal-Major,' said Fielding, and raised his panama a precise three inches. 'Quite a turn out of the old gang.'

'Yes, sir. It's a long time since I've seen Major Glastonbury. Or Captain Jack. Or you.'

Captain Jack, thought Fielding: Jack Lamprey. He hadn't been in touch. He had sworn that he would be if there were any danger to Marius. *Res Unius, Res Omnium.* So if he was a man of his solemnly given word, his silence meant that there could be no danger to Marius.

'I hope you're free to watch the race with me, Corporal-Major?'

'Here on my own, sir.'

'And I hope you won't mind helping me to keep an eye on that young fellow there.'

Fielding pointed to Jeremy, who was still leaning on the paddock rail. 'Jeremy Morrison,' he said. 'Son of an old friend.'

'What's he up to, Major Fielding?'

'I don't really know. There's a story going round that something's going to happen here this afternoon. He's here looking into it, I think. So am I.'

'*What* is going to happen, sir?'

'Whatever it is, Lover Pie and Boadicea are mixed up in it. You've heard no word from your boy Danny of any jiggery-pokery?'

'Danny don't confide in me, Major Fielding. We live many miles apart – in every sense. But I wouldn't put anything past him if the price was right. What do we know about that Jimmy Pitts?'

'Very little. I once saw a horse die under his father, Johnny. At Whereham Races. Funny thing. The horse belonged to Jeremy Morrison's grandfather. Tiberius, he was called; a stallion, like Lover Pie. Do you believe in echoes, Corporal-Major? Echoes in time?'

Jimmy Pitts (pink jacket, light blue Maltese Cross on his back, pink cap) padded towards Raisley Conyngham and Jack Lamprey.

'No need to snap at the boy this time,' said Conyngham: 'he'll be under enough pressure without that . . . just about the right amount, I think.'

'What's he doing,' yapped Pitts, 'dressed up for a bloody wedding?'

'At my request, Jimmy. Where's your sense of occasion?'

Marius led up Lover Pie, who seemed entirely calm and at ease, despite the heavy blanket over his hindquarters.

'Good luck, Jimmy,' said Jack Lamprey. 'Remember to keep well clear of Boadicea until after the second from home. Just in case.'

'He don't seem to be bothered by her yet,' said Jimmy Pitts, bending to peer under the blanket at Lover Pie's private anatomy.

'Nor he shouldn't be neither,' said Jack Lamprey. 'He's never been bothered by a mare yet, in or out of season.'

'Like 'is owner,' muttered Pitts, quite audibly. 'Question is, is he still interested in running?'

'As to that,' said Conyngham affably, 'you have your instructions. Off you go with 'em, Marius.'

Aunt Flo, Theodosia Canteloupe and Pally Palairet were watching the events in the paddock from a side-balcony in the stand.

'So Jeremy Morrison came,' said Palairet.

'So did Fielding Gray,' said Theodosia.

'Who's that fat man with him?'

'Danny Chead's father,' said Aunt Flo, unexpectedly.

'Come to watch his son?' asked Theodosia.

'He hates his son. But he always comes to this meeting because he was in Hamilton's Horse. I was here once with Giles Glastonbury – long time ago, before I went broke – and he introduced me to him.'

'I must say,' said Theodosia, 'I never saw a scene so proper and peaceful.'

'Agreed,' said Aunt Flo: 'but God always reserves his nastiest jokes for the nicest occasions. Remember Dickie Mountbatten two years ago? Or Abe Lincoln? Or Julius Caesar, come to that? Boadicea is behaving very decorously,' she continued, 'if one considers that there is an attractive grey stallion in the company. Perhaps she don't like grey. I wonder how many people in all this crowd know she's in season? The geldings are a grotty lot . . . except for number three . . . Alfie Boy.'

'Favourite,' said Theodosia, 'according to the board. Even money. With Jack Spratt at two to one, Forceful Horsfall at fours . . . Boadicea at six to one . . . and Lover Pie at tens.'

'Marius is taking Lover Pie's blanket off . . . out on the course there. He's hurrying away with it somewhere. Last time,' said Palairet, 'he just hung about in the enclosure. Do you think we ought to follow him?'

'No,' said Theodosia, 'someone's coming to meet him . . . two other stable lads, by the look of it.' She raised her binoculars. 'Beautiful faces but villainous kit. I hope they don't start resenting Marius's pretty clothes. No. All is well. One of them has taken the blanket . . . and Marius has gone to stand by the entrance to the paddock, between the paddock and the course. I should have thought he might be needing that blanket at the end of the race but the two other lads are taking it away to the

310

horse-boxes. Not that it can be of the slightest importance.'

'And now Jeremy Morrison has gone to talk to Marius,' Palairet said. 'I'm beginning to think I've been very silly, my lady. Nothing's going to happen at all.'

That was what Fielding Gray thought as he stood in the enclosure with Corporal-Major Chead and watched Jeremy approach Marius, take his hand briefly, and begin to talk.

And that was what Giles Glastonbury thought, as he studied Jeremy and Marius through his binoculars from the Owner's Box in the stand, whither he had come from the paddock as soon as Danny Chead had ridden Boadicea out on to the course.

'They're under Starter's Orders.'

Giles switched his binoculars to the line of horses on the rim of the downs.

'THEY'RE OFF.'

On the left-hand corner before the approach to the first fence, Forceful Horsfall takes the lead two lengths clear of Jack Spratt and the mare, Boadicea. All safely over the first fence, though Lover Pie slow in jumping in fifth place and moves back to seventh as they run down the hill towards the second. Forceful Horsfall by three lengths from Jack Spratt, who is in turn a length clear of Boadicea; a gap of three lengths, then Alfie Boy (the four to six favourite), Lack Lustre, Simon Magus and Lover Pie all in a bunch, with Nicholas Christopher (fifty, five-o, to one) three lengths behind them and Japhet (twenty to one) already five lengths behind him. Over the second (a much better jump by Lover Pie) and on downhill towards the third, same order, but fallen at the second Lack Lustre, and Alfie Boy making good ground to come upsides with Boadicea, Nicholas Christopher quickening to join Simon Magus and Lover Pie, Japhet not wanting to race and already tailed off.

The water jump at the bottom of the slope. Forceful Horsfall at a steady pace in the lead, four clear now from Jack Spratt (the five to two second favourite), nothing to choose between Boadicea and Alfie Boy both a length behind Jack Spratt, Nicholas Christopher over with Lover Pie, Simon Magus sheds rider, Japhet refused. Round the bottom right-hand corner to the next plain fence, Forceful Horsfall still leading by four lengths, Jack Spratt following, two back to Alfie Boy and Boadicea, Lover Pie and Nicholas Christopher three lengths behind them in the rear. Round the bottom left-hand corner, same order, over the open ditch, starting up the hill again, Forceful Horsfall a violent faller at the next fence (opposite Tattersalls) almost bringing down Jack Spratt, who swerves cleverly round the fallen horse but loses three lengths to Alfie Boy and Boadicea, these two still neck and neck. On up the hill past the Members' Stand and the winning post: two complete circuits still to run. But on the corner at the top of the hill Jack Spratt shows lame and pulls up, leaving only four horses in the race. As they run along the skyline towards the eighth these are: Alfie Boy (four to six favourite) by half a length; Boadicea (six to one) three lengths clear of Lover Pie (eleven to one in the final betting) who leads Nicholas Christopher (fifty to one) by a neck . . .

Raisley Conyngham had watched with satisfaction while the gypsy boys, Milo and Tessa, relieved Marius of Lover Pie's blanket. Marius will think, thought Raisley, that they will take it to the horse-box and put it in the bucket of disinfectant which I told him would have been prepared by Gat-Toothed Jenny. Then he will start to wonder if he was right to let them have it, as he was ordered to take it to the horse-box himself and return to the entrance of the paddock in time to see the horses run the last two circuits. He knows I require precise obedience, and he will wonder whether even the presence of Milo excuses the change of programme. Also, he will soon begin to wonder who will bring him a second blanket in case of need, and when. In short he will be very jittery indeed.

At the moment of the 'Off', Conyngham put these reflections aside and began to watch the race, with interest but without binoculars, relying on the commentator (Mr J. B. Budden, whom he knew to be a particularly succinct and accurate performer) and on the pithy interjections of Jack Lamprey, who was by his side.

'So far, so fucking good,' said Sozzler Jack as the four contestants ran past the start on the second circuit and turned the corner at the top of the slope: 'all we need now is for both of 'em to stand up.'

As Tessa and Milo walked away from the paddock into the park for horse-boxes, Tessa started to vomit.

'It's that blanket,' she choked: 'keep it away from me.'

As she fell on her knees and went on spurting vomit, Milo flapped air at her with the blanket, much as a second in the corner of a boxing ring flaps air at his principal, save that the blanket, even when folded, was far larger and more cumbrous than the conventional towel.

Jeremy Morrison had come up to Marius by the entrance to the paddock, and had there started to talk to him, early during the first circuit. At first Marius was very pleased to see him; but then he remembered that he was meant to be watching the race alone, and indeed wasn't even meant to be watching at all just yet, as he should have been taking Lover Pie's blanket to the horse-box. •

'India,' Jeremy was saying: 'perhaps you'll join me there in the hols. I could send you a ticket.'

'Gosh,' said Marius, beside himself with worry about his dereliction of duty. 'Oh, Jeremy, gosh.'

By the time the horses still in the race were rounding the top left-hand corner for the second time and were going towards what had been the first fence in the first circuit and was now the ninth, anyone who cared to take his eyes off the course for a moment to look at what was happening by the paddock would have seen a very beautiful fair-haired boy in a dark suit, school tie and black brogues (by which tokens he might have recognized the stable lad who had had charge of Lover Pie before the race) obviously very anxious (presumably about the fate of his horse) in conversation with a large, moon-faced man of about twenty-three years old. Apart from any member of the general public who may or may not have paid attention to this couple, certain interested observers were watching them closely, and were thinking or reasoning or speculating much as follows:

Fielding Grey, while he saw nothing actually amiss, was

315

surprised by the extreme agitation displayed by Marius.

Corpy Chead briefly admired both the boy and the young man, with the tender eye of a part-time (because married) pederast of long standing, who had, however, retired from practice because he considered it ridiculous, in a man of his age, and no longer worth the trouble. Having paid his tribute of theoretical appreciation, the Corporal-Major went back to watching the race, rather hoping that his son Danny would break his neck at the tenth fence, which the survivors in the race were just about to jump.

Giles Glastonbury, though aware that the conversation was in progress, thought little of it, being much preoccupied with the behaviour of Boadicea, who had suddenly become fretful, pecked badly at the tenth fence and was sharply 'reminded' (or so it seemed) by her jockey.

Theodosia Canteloupe, seeing that Marius was clearly embarrassed and getting no enjoyment from Jeremy's company, was sad for both of them, because she had once loved, still did love, Jeremy, and thought that such a dismal, jerky conversation was a terrible waste of opportunity. What would she not have given to be standing there talking to Jeremy?

Aunt Flo had forgotten all about the mission of her party and was concentrating on the outsider, the little chestnut gelding Nicholas Christopher, on whom, unknown to her nephew, she had had a tenner each way on the Tote, having slipped away to do so on the pretext that she was 'busting for a pee'. Lucky, she thought, that Theodosia hadn't been busting for a pee too, or she might have accompanied her and fucked up her chance of making the wager. This would have been a pity, because Nicholas Christopher, who had shown a light step and an honest eye in the paddock, was now running very much to the purpose.

Galahad Palairet, seeing the tête à tête by the paddock in progress, was divided between a wish that nothing would happen (as now seemed likely) and a fear of losing face with Theodosia Canteloupe for having raised a false alarm.

Raisley Conyngham, who had not allowed for the possibility of anyone's engaging Marius in conversation, was irritated by his lack of foresight but not badly worried: it should not, he thought, make any difference.

Milo Hedley, having left the prostrate Tessa for a while to spy out the ground and having duly noticed Jeremy's presence, opined to himself, as Raisley Conyngham had done, that this would make no difference to the planned sequence of events. He also resolved to take any chance that might show itself of retiring somewhere private with Jeremy before the afternoon was done. ('Now, boy, now.' 'Christ, sir, I'm coming, sir, oh Christ.') He then turned his attention to the race, saw that all four horses still in it were approaching the open ditch at the bottom of the hill, and went back to attend to Tessa. Although it was some while since he had desisted from fanning her with the injurious towel, she was still vomiting in little gobs. Just about right, Milo thought.

Jack Lamprey, switching his binoculars from Alfie Boy, in the lead, to Lover Pie, now second, and then to Boadicea, a flagging third, chuckled at the skill with which Danny Chead was delivering his deliberately futile reminders. Lover Pie, he thought, would have no difficulty in keeping well clear of Boadicea; and although there was really very little chance of Lover Pie's suddenly being afflicted with lust *en courant*, a nice wide gap between the pair was what everybody wanted.

. . . And now the runners are halfway up the slope for the second time and over the fence opposite Tattersalls, Boadicea fourth and last, pretty well tailed off, Nicholas Christopher running easily just behind Lover Pie, Lover Pie tracking Alfie Boy and slowly closing the small gap between them. Alfie Boy past the winning post and starting the third circuit . . .

As Alfie Boy went past the entrance to the paddock, Jeremy and Marius were still standing there, awkwardly talking. Jeremy was determined not to leave Marius until he had made some sense of their interview, but he was making no progress – indeed Marius was becoming more jumpy and inconsequent by the second. He cast a frenzied glance at the horses as they passed, realized that Lover Pie was a very promising second and might well take the race, and then said anxiously to Jeremy:

'But what shall I do without his blanket?'

'Blanket?'

'He was wearing one before the race. He'll need it again at the end. Mr Conyngham said that somebody would bring me one, but they haven't.'

Boadicea, now over twenty lengths behind the three leaders, went past Jeremy and Marius in a despairing lollop.

'Where did you put the original blanket?' Jeremy said.

'I was meant to take it to the horse-box and soak it in disinfectant; Mr Conyngham said that Milo was going to bring me another if it would be needed, but he hasn't and I think it will be. I suppose that if I'd gone to the horse-box myself as I was told to, I might have found another blanket there.'

'Well, you'd better go now,' said Jeremy, seeing action as the only cure for this potty babble; 'I'll come too.'

'Oh, thank you, Jeremy.'

As they passed from the paddock and into the park for horse-boxes, Milo met them.

'Why are you dressed like that?' Jeremy asked.

'Makes a change,' said Milo; and to Jeremy, 'I expect you've come for another blanket?'

'Yes, Milo.'

'You'd better take the original one. I haven't soaked it yet, as there don't seem to be any more, for some reason.'

'Where is the original one?'

'Lying on the ground over there, near Tessa. She's just been sick.'

'Oh God.' Marius walked over to Tessa, who was still lying on the ground and seemed to be dozing. Best left alone, thought Marius. He picked up the blanket, which was flecked with blobs of sick, and started back towards the paddock.

'It's in a horrible state,' he said to Milo, as he passed him and Jeremy.

'No time to do anything about that now. You'll have to make the best of it.'

'I suppose so . . . Well, good-bye,' Marius said to Jeremy.

'Good-bye, Marius,' said Jeremy, who was looking hard at Milo, who was looking hard back. 'I'll be in touch one way or the other,' Jeremy muttered, without taking his eyes off Milo; 'you'd better get on now, Marius, your horse will be needing that blanket pretty soon.'

Marius marched miserably away. He had let Jeremy down, he knew that, but he couldn't help it, he'd been full of the worries of the occasion, particularly of the nagging problem of Lover Pie's blanket, and unable to concentrate on what Jeremy was saying. Things had not been improved by the manner of their parting; for although Marius had been delighted when Jeremy had

319

offered to come with him to collect the blanket, the whole business had turned rotten when they were met by Milo. Marius, wondering what was going on in the horse-box park, wondering why they hadn't even looked at him when he said good-bye, decided that he had better think of something, of anything, else. He came to the paddock entrance, hung the blanket on the rails, and turned his eyes to the bottom of the course, where Lover Pie and Alfie Boy were now taking the water jump together, with Nicholas Christopher some three lengths behind them.

'We can go into the horse-box,' said Milo to Jeremy. 'Jenny – the head travelling lass – she's off boozing.'

'Why is Tessa Malcolm lying there like that? Why are you dressed like that?'

'I wanted to see her like that. Filthy and smelly. I wanted to be with her like that.'

'What's going on, Milo? What's the matter with Tessa?'

'The smell of a horse blanket has made her sick. Come on, sir: we've no time to waste.'

Giles, having given up watching Boadicea, had set his binoculars on Alfie Boy, who moved very easily over the plain fence in the bottom stretch, turned the last corner neatly, sailed over the open ditch, slipped and crumpled on the far side of it. The race was now between Lover Pie and Nicholas Christopher . . . who was half a length behind Lover Pie at the open ditch but began to gain inch by inch as they went uphill towards the last plain fence, after which there would be a run in of one hundred and forty odd yards to the winning post.

Well, thought Aunt Flo, I'm certainly getting a run for my money.

Never mind which of 'em wins, thought Raisley Conyngham, so long as they both stand up and Boadicea comes past the post a safe third, however distant. With the entire course empty but for the three of them, surely they can manage that.

Jeremy seems to have given up piquet duty, thought Fielding Gray: he's left Marius on his own. He started to move across the lawn of the Members' Enclosure, ostensibly to be opposite the winning post, in fact to be near the Winners' Enclosure and its entrance. Corporal-Major Chead moved with him, looking back, as he went, to the bottom stretch, where Danny and Boadicea were now clearing the plain fence, very slowly but absolutely safely. Two more chances for him to break his fucking neck now, thought Corpy Chead, the open ditch and the last, some fucking hope . . .

'Never mind,' Theodosia was saying to Palairet; 'you did the right thing to get hold of me. You *thought* your friend was in danger, even if it turns out that he wasn't; better safe than sorry.'

'Thank you, my lady.'

'Thea . . . and it's been a splendid day out. I think . . . that outsider is just going to do it.'

Sod it, thought Jack Lamprey: I know it don't matter to Raisley whether or not the Lover wins, but it would have been a nice little *coup* for the stable – and for me, with two hundred on him at ten to one.

As Lover Pie and Nicholas Christopher approach the last fence, there's nothing in it between them (though informed spectators, like Jack Lamprey, have sensed that Nicholas Christopher is gaining the advantage). And so to the last and over together, but Nicholas Christopher jumps the better, a huge leap for such a small horse, and begins to go clear . . .

Goody gum drops, thought Aunt Flo, as Lover Pie came under pressure but failed to make up any ground, hoorah for Nicholas Christopher, started at fifties, with luck he'll pay sixties or even seventies on the Tote.

Tessa, walking unsteadily towards the horse-box, checked her stride (what there was of it) when she saw the tail was up.

'Christ, sir,' came a squeal from within, 'Christ, sir, I'm coming, sir, oh Christ.'

Nicholas Christopher, first past the post by two lengths, went on up the hill gradually easing his pace; the grey Lover Pie followed, in vain passed Nicholas Christopher, and like him slowly pulled up. Both horses turned to come down towards the paddock and the Winners' Enclosure which lay just beside it. Marius was about to go to meet Lover Pie on the course when he remembered Raisley Conyngham's orders. 'Do not stir an inch, Marius,' Raisley Conyngham had said, 'unless instructed by Milo or myself, until all the horses which are still running have passed the winning post.' Which was not yet the case. Boadicea still had the last jump to take and then the run in.

So Marius, who had already taken Lover Pie's blanket off the rails, stood waiting with it on the grass between the entrance of the paddock and the entrance on to the course.

'If we want to see the finale, sir,' said Milo to Jeremy inside the horse-box as they both adjusted their clothes, 'we'd better be quick.'

'Finale?'

'You asked what was going on, sir; now you're going to find out.'

Tessa, standing at the rear of the horse-box, heard all this. She turned and ran for the paddock.

Thus Marius was standing by the gap in the rail which led on to the course; Fielding Gray and Corpy Chead were approaching him round the paddock rail; Jack Lamprey was walking round the other side of the paddock from Fielding Gray, on a route which would avoid the crowd and eventually bring him to the enclosure for the winner and the placed horses; Aunt Flo was already dashing for the nearest internal TV Tote screen, on which the dividend to be paid by the winning Nicholas Christopher would shortly be displayed; Theodosia and Palairet were thoughtfully coming down from the stand by the open stairway on its side, which overlooked the paddock; Tessa was emerging from the horse-box park on the far side of the paddock from the stand; and Milo and Jeremy were walking briskly behind her when the following scene took place:

Boadicea at last passed the winning post with a very weary and galumphing motion, came to a halt, and made a group of three with Lover Pie and Nicholas Christopher, who had now come back down the course.

Marius approached this group, intending to put the blanket on Lover Pie, and spread it in order to do so.

All three horses started rearing violently and neighing as if from extreme terror.

Marius, now surrounded by the three horses, who were kicking and lunging more viciously than ever, put the blanket over his head for protection and sank on to his knees.

Fielding Gray and Jeremy Morrison both ran (from diametrically opposite positions) towards the entrance on to the course (through which Marius had gone with the blanket), there met and stopped, confronted each other briefly, turned towards the course, and began to shake and sweat, some fifteen yards short of the mêlée and within full sight of it.

Tessa Malcolm dashed out on to the course and made straight for the horses but was cut off and forcibly restrained by Milo Hedley, who had darted under the rails a little higher up.

Galahad Palairet leapt down the last few steps from the stand, hurtled past the rail of the paddock with a thin, high wail of love and grief which was to haunt all present until the day they died, slipped through the grasp of the not very nimble Corpy Chead, sprinted on to the course, running zigzag to avoid any who would stop him, and was felled instantly by a flying back kick in the throat.

Gat-Toothed Jenny, who had seen the end of the race from just outside the bar, then swallowed the rest of her

Guinness in one and had been well on her way to assist Marius with Lover Pie by the time that the horses erupted – Gat-Toothed Jenny, all breast and hips and jaw and guts, charged through the mêlée, snatched the blanket off the cowering Marius and carried it ten yards away over the grass; then returned towards the horses (who were already quiet and obedient to their jockeys) bent down over Marius, who was vibrating with terror, calmed him by the touch of her thick, brown, loving fingers, and raised him to his feet.

Raisley Conyngham, having observed with complacency the outbreak and its consequences, vaulted the fenced rail between the enclosure and the course, walked lightly across it, ducked under a plain rail, and came to two St John's Ambulances which were parked on the other side. One of these was already starting up the side of the course towards the recumbent Palairet. Raisley climbed into the co-driver's seat of the second and ordered it to proceed (as by previous arrangement with the driver) towards the vehicle-crossing just beyond the winning post.

Meanwhile Gat-Toothed Jenny, making for the Winners' Enclosure and Jack Lamprey on the other side of it, was escorting Marius through the crowd, which divided like the Red Sea in the legend to let them pass and then, seeing the beautiful, shivering boy still alive in his pathetically crumpled grey suit and observing the well rigged motherly woman (with her arm around his shoulders) who had passed through the whirling hooves of death to his rescue, broke into a warm and throaty English cheer, much to the puzzlement of Aunt Flo by the Tote TV screen, which showed that her dividend would be £97.40 to a £1 stake for a win, and £11.50 for a place. One thousand and eighty sovs and the odd pence, she said to herself: not a bad afternoon's work.

As the Tote would not actually be paying out until Nicholas Christopher had weighed in (which would not be for some minutes yet), she walked along the back of the stand and round the end of it, making for that part of the enclosure (adjacent to the paddock) from which the applause was rising. This was changing in quality as she approached. Having started as an expression of conventional approval (jolly good show), it next became apprehensive in tone, then affectionate, then boisterous and rather embarrassed, and at last sentimental. As Aunt Flo came round the end of the stand, she began to understand why.

Jenny had sensibly taken Marius well to one side while the three horses which had so nearly killed him in their recent fury passed Jenny and Marius, bound for the Winners' Enclosure. Marius, still fearful of them, slunk into Jenny's arms as the animals passed, at which juncture the crowd's apprehensive tone showed that it shared Marius's reaction. As he clung to Jenny, and as she responded with more than mere maternal warmth, the crowd started joshing; as the pair clung yet closer, the spectators cooed with vicarious pleasure; as the look on both Marius's and Jenny's faces become intent yet dreamy (lips slightly parted, eyes spread wide), the witnesses, scenting the onset of sudden heat, shouted and boomed to disguise their fear and their hope that Eros would make himself manifest under their very eyes; and as Raisley drove up in the ambulance, and with the assistance of the driver coaxed the now inseparable couple into the back of it, the populace, reassured, disappointed and on the whole congratulatory, bade a gushing good-bye to Jenny and Marius, as if to say: 'Only the Brave, Only the Brave, Only the Brave deserve the Fair.'

'Galahad shall make my child,' said Theodosia Cante-loupe aloud as she walked over the course towards him.

The team of the other St John's Ambulance, two fat and jovial women and two skimpy young men with the insignia of full lieutenants on their shoulders, ran past Theodosia towards the supine Palairet.

'He is very young,' said Theodosia: 'but I shall be kind to him and he will be kind to me; we shall be very gentle together. He is the only man I could bear to touch me. He was among those that showed courage this afternoon; Fielding Gray, the old soldier, and Jeremy Morrison, the would-be prophet, both shook right down their worthless shanks, having no stomach for this fight.'

She turned to look for them, but they had slunk away into the crowd.

'Galahad,' she called as she neared him. 'You were so quick in need, so true.'

But already the two skimpy lieutenants were pulling up one end of a brown blanket over the deaf ears of Galahad, the true knight, who lay upon the field.

Unlike the ambulance in which Pally was removed, Marius and Jenny's contained, of its official personnel, only the driver, who was driving. Raisley, who had vacated his original place in the front, was now riding with Marius and Jenny in the back.

'We shall go on moving until I make the driver a signal,' Raisley said, 'and there will be no interference. First, then, the cleansing.'

With occasional help from Jenny, Raisley began, deftly and gently, to strip Marius of his ruined suit, his sweat-drenched shirt and his silly tie, his scuffed shoes and clinging socks, and his horribly soiled pants. Then he took from a kind of aumbry, which was under a fitted couch, a basin and ewer and a flask of lavender water. He poured lukewarm water from the ewer into the basin, laced it liberally with the lavender, and with his hands washed Marius clean from his feet to the top of his thighs, from his head down to his navel, and then from his navel to his crotch, being particularly careful of his tumescent penis.

'What a pretty little scar,' said Jenny, bending to kiss it.

Raisley Conyngham rapped on the wall behind the driver. The ambulance stopped.

'It will take you back to Ullacote,' said Raisley. 'You will be alone until then.' He went to the back of the ambulance, unfastened the door, and climbed down. 'This is my gift to you both,' he said; 'that having been a little chastised you shall be greatly rewarded; for I, Raisley

Conyngham, have proved you, and found you worthy for myself.'

'So what was Raisley up to?' said Giles Glastonbury to Jack Lamprey.

The three horses had been taken from the Winners' Enclosure, and Giles and Jack had crossed the course, for privacy, to the meadow at its centre.

'He never really said. Mind you, we all knew something was up. Raisley told us something was up. Something which was going to earn us all hefty bonus payments – with the money right up front. It was nothing bent, he said, nothing to get anyone warned off; he was just interested in conducting some psychological tests, for a treatise which he was writing, on young Marius – on any boy of his age, come to that, Raisley said – but Marius was easily available and was a particularly good sort of subject, being intelligent and responsive and whaah, whaah, whaah. In short, he wanted to know how, in certain circumstances, the boy would behave. It might also be interesting, he added, to watch the reactions of the crowd to Marius's behaviour. So Marius was to be put in charge of Lover Pie in the paddock at one meeting, when nothing at all would happen, though he'd thank us to scrutinize him very carefully for his form, and to report our opinions. And then the boy would be put in the same situation at a second meeting – but this time he would be faced with something unexpected.'

'And no one enquired what form the unexpected would take?'

'The basic plan was that three or more horses had to congregate at the end of the race, and that Marius would then be confronted with some difficulty or confusion due to crowding or ill temper or whatever. That was why Boadicea and Danny Chead were important. Raisley could be almost certain that Lover Pie and at least one more would finish, and he needed to be sure that Boadicea would also be there to make up a minimum complement of three at the end of the race. If the worst came to the very worst, Raisley said, two horses would have to do, so the Lover and Boadicea *must* stand up, and the best way of ensuring they did was to let Boadicea, who is totally reliable if not pushed, take it very slowly, and to allow Lover Pie, who likes having a crack, to have his crack.'

'Mightn't that have been fatal to the scheme?' said Giles. 'I mean, if Lover Pie had gone, and Boadicea had finished alone, or even with something else, Marius wouldn't have been there at all. He would have been somewhere down the course looking after the fallen Lover.'

'The old Lover has never fallen yet,' said Jack, 'provided he's been allowed his own way. That's why Raisley bought him for this stunt. For the rest, well, in this sort of game there had to be chances, and Raisley had made as sure as he could of having Marius in the right place by instructing him not to move until the last horse still in the race had passed the post. In any case, and as you saw, the scheme worked. Three horses were duly assembled near the exit from the course, and there was Marius going to put that blanket on one of them. Perfect . . . from Raisley's point of view.'

'Did no one ask Raisley any questions about the

"difficulty" to which he proposed to expose Marius when he went out with the blanket?'

'Everyone was far too busy counting their bonus payments,' said Jack.

'Even you? A gentleman? An ex-Officer of the 49th? Did you feel no concern for the boy?'

'I did, oh yes, I did,' tooted Jack in his Bloomsbury accent, 'and when I began to suspect, some little time ago, that Marius's test might perhaps be dangerous, I tried to warn Fielding Gray, whom I knew to be interested. But I couldn't find him at the crucial moment, and then I thought, oh well, I'm probably making a fuss about nothing, everyone else seems quite happy. Why shouldn't Raisley, who is a highly respected schoolmaster, be conducting a perfectly *bona fide* if rather weird experiment in the psychology of adolescence, *et cetera, et cetera*. None of us had the faintest idea – except perhaps that sly little beast, Milo Hedley – what a hideous affair Raisley was in fact planning. Now we do know, the jockeys will be furious at what he let them in for – but they're both the kind that can be easily bought off for ready money. As for Prideau, he's too cut up about his boy to mind anything.'

'Phil Loche?'

'No names, no pack drill, is Phil's philosophy: just button your lip. Phil just don't want to know, let alone to talk. No, Giles. An accident it looked, and an accident it will go on looking.'

'Anyway,' agreed Giles, 'after a pig's breakfast like that, nothing can ever be known for certain. But I'm fascinated by the mechanics of the thing. What about Boadicea's being in season? Did that have anything to do with it all?'

'Nothing. No one, not even in her own stable – knew

she was coming into season – no one ever does – until Regis Priory. Possibly the state was brought on by her seeing a stallion there. Anyhow, she was still allowed by the rules to run here at Bellhampton, and it made no difference to the plans whatever.'

'It might have done if Lover Pie had got excited.'

'Lover Pie ain't the excitable sort, and anyhow Danny kept Boadicea out of Lover Pie's way. You see, it didn't matter where Danny and Boadicea finished so long as they *did* finish.'

'How much did that stable lass know?' said Giles. 'Was she told to go in and rescue Marius?'

'If so, she never let on . . . though she'd do anything for Raisley, if he asked her. He picked her out of some Borstal, or whatever they have for girls. Years ago now, but girls like Jenny don't forget.'

'You're saying she would have risked her life for Raisley?'

'And the next life too, good Catholic as she is – or tries to be. But my view is that Raisley left that last act up to chance. It was to be a far stiffer test of Marius than Raisley dared tell anyone – far more than a test of how Marius would behave if confronted with some nasty little local difficulty, or how the crowd would carry on if he wet his knickers. It was to be an ordeal of death itself, trial by battle. Would he save himself, and if not who would?'

'An initiation?'

'That's it,' said Jack: 'an initiation.'

'He told me,' said Jenny as she held Marius in her arms on the couch in the ambulance, 'that I could either save you or leave you. But I never thought it would really work out like he said. I never thought those horses would really create like they did. So I didn't decide what to do; I just waited. When the race was over I went to meet you – and then the horses *did* do what Mr Conyngham said, and so I went in after you. Without thinking. Which is what he wanted. Or so I think. He wanted to see what would happen if I saved you.'

'And did he know it would be this?'

Although they had separated their bodies not many minutes before, Marius now showed a renewed readiness, taut and curved and glistening.

'I think so,' said Jenny as she caressed him. 'That scar,' she said, and lowered her head to kiss it. 'I think that he knew, or guessed, that what happened would make a special sort of excitement . . . a kind of madness . . . which we felt there by the paddock . . . a kind of frenzy which very few people ever know. That was his present to us: his gift, his reward. There will only be this one time,' she said, 'this one time, here in the ambulance. He will find other uses for both of us, and other prizes, but for this . . . this . . . we only have till Ullacote. It's your first, isn't it?'

'Yes, Jenny. It's almost too much to bear. It's so strange with you like this. Wonderful, but somehow too . . . dangerous . . . ever to be allowed again.'

'Go on. Say it, Marius.'

'I feel as if I were being shown this . . . the finest of all things . . . by someone who has nursed, cherished, protected and saved me just for this one hour. I feel as if I were being shown . . . this great secret . . . for the first and only time that the gods, or God, permits . . . by my mother. Cupid with his mother.'

'Jesus Christ, how fucking marvellous,' cried Jenny, and pressed her open lips on Marius's scar.

Theodosia and Aunt Flo went with Galahad Palairet to the place where he was being taken.

'I missed it all,' said the old woman, broken but not irreparably broken. 'I was finding out about my divvy. Over a thousand. I'd sooner have you, my darling,' she said, stroking the brown blanket, 'but two monkeys is some kind of consolation . . . How did it all start?'

'The three remaining horses came together after the race. Marius Stern came up to them with a blanket and got it all ready to put on to Lover Pie – and then there they were, all rearing and raging, like the horses of Diomedes.'

'And two might they be when they're at home?'

'Evil horses of legend. First Tessa Malcolm tried to come to Marius's rescue. She was prevented, and so she is all right. Then Galahad came. He is not all right. And then, somehow or other, a girl, a woman rather, some stable lass – she dashed in and took away that blanket, and the whole thing died down.'

'Brave,' said Aunt Flo. 'But there's a lot here don't smell quite right.' She paused, stroked the brown blanket beside her rhythmically and without attending to her action, and said:

'That blanket, the one on Lover Pie. Too thick, too heavy. But what do we know of it? Nothing. And that's all we shall ever know. Except that it seems to have been right at the centre of the trouble . . . I find myself thinking of Myles and his mother, Konya, Prideau's wife, both dead of inexplicable illnesses, having first incurred Raisley's displeasure. But the connection between all that and what happened here to-day – it isn't clear, girl. It never can be. All too vague. Best just let it go. As for Galahad, it could be a blessing in disguise. His father died of cancer last year and his mother is full of it, like a partridge stuffed with chestnuts. Soon there will be no money, only mine, and that's little enough these days. It'll run to Sandy Lodge and a few bottles a week: not to that school. He didn't know it, I hadn't yet found the courage to tell him, but he was going to be taken away from that school this July. Simply not enough money, girl. But he didn't know it, thank God, and now he'll never know it. Are we there?'

'Yes. Time to say good-bye.'

'I shall ring up those people,' said Aunt Flo, 'the Humanist Society or whatever they call themselves, and have them pick up the remains. They'll get rid of him without fuss. What do we want with white coffins and unctuous voices?'

'Isn't he a little too old for a white coffin?'

'You know what I mean, girl. Smelly old men pretending to grieve for the death of one so young and pure, but revelling in it, full of glee that their cracked and pallid limbs still move while his sweet flesh is already rotting.

337

No; we'll have no banners and no bugles for young Galahad; let the Humanists and the worms take him to themselves in silence.'

Jeremy, since he was about to go abroad for a very long time, had put his car up for sale in a garage and had come down to the course by train. (He would have had a chauffeur driven car, had he not been anxious to get out of England without being spotted by the press or the public in any instance of luxurious behaviour not consonant with his professed role as disciple and pilgrim of the soil.) Having learnt this while they had a restoring drink together, Fielding offered Jeremy a lift back to London, where he, Fielding, wished to spend one night (only) before returning (as he then thought) to his guest suite in Lancaster College, there to go grinding on at *The Grand Grinder*.

'You know,' said Fielding as they drove towards Lewes, 'Tessa hated horses and they hated her. Something almost chemical, her Auntie Maisie once said. Now, at one stage Tessa got near that horse-blanket – when she and that boy took it from Marius.'

'Later on, Marius went to fetch it back again,' said Jeremy, 'and I went with him. Tessa had been sick near it. On it, too. She was lying on the ground asleep. So Marius took the blanket away . . . while I . . . while I talked with that boy, as you call him – Milo Hedley.'

'You stink, Jeremy. You stink of gypsy – like that boy

was dressed. So while Marius was walking to his doom, you were fucking Master Milo.'

'Master Milo was fucking me.'

Fielding began to laugh. He laughed so much that he had to pull into a lay-by.

'Not that I was any more use than you,' he said when he had at last ceased gulping and choking with merriment. 'Marius loved you. He knew and trusted me. But when he was in trouble . . . for his life . . . we both stood about like a pair of fairies. Cowards. Poltroons. Two of a kind. May I share your shame, Jeremy? May I come with you to the East? I've got enough money to be going on with, and you'll need company, and if you ever start feeling grand or important, I'll be there to remind you that you're just a pusillanimous pathic who stood about quaking with terror, as indeed did I myself, while the little boy who loved you was in hazard for his life.'

'I loved you,' said Tessa to Milo. 'I should have let you do whatever you wanted with me . . . starting with the kiss, which I longed for between the sinews behind my knees . . . as soon as we got home to-night. I shouldn't even have made you bathe first or throw away those horrible clothes. I should have been your – odalisque. But you couldn't wait. You had an itch, and you waggled yourself at that Jeremy thing – it must have been him, I saw you together just afterwards – and you both climbed up into the horse-box, and started frotting and squealing like two little pigs. I heard you.'

'So what are you going to do? Go home to Auntie in a pet?'

'Yes. And then go to my friend Rosie in France.'

Shall I tell her? he thought. Shall I tell her what Raisley discovered (along with all the rest, like her providential allergy to horses), that her 'Auntie' is an ex-whore and her mother? That her 'Auntie' used to give exhibitions in front of chosen gentlemen, sometimes by herself, sometimes assisted by one or more members, male or female, of her own profession, on at least two occasions (at one of which Raisley himself had been present many years before) partnered by a dog? Shall I tell her all this for a fine and mighty revenge for her sneering about Jeremy? No; I shall not tell her. It would poison for ever the sweetness of what little we have had and of the vision of the kiss behind the knee. That kiss will never now be given nor received: but if we part in relative kindness I can still remember, *con amore*, how I kissed her in the crook of her arm and had been promised, eagerly promised, a kiss behind her knee.

'I'm glad you have someone to go to,' he said. 'You know that Marius is now Raisley's – and mine, if I want him – for ever?'

'That remains to be seen. It may not be long before he realizes that he has been tricked. You used me for that, Milo. There was something about that blanket.'

'A smell of horse, which you didn't like. It made you sick. And when Marius took it out on the course, it had a smell of Tess – of Tessa's sick – which the horses didn't like. It drove them wild. Is that what you are thinking?'

'Very roughly, yes.'

'And to whom are you going to tell *that* story? To whom are you going to say, "Horses don't like me, so when they smelt my sick, on a blanket which Marius had been tricked into taking among them, they started to go mad?" To whom are you going to tell that tale, little Tessa?'

'I'm going to tell no tales to anybody. You needn't worry, Milo. There's a lot I don't understand and nothing at all that I can prove. I can't make trouble, and I wouldn't if I could. After all, I once loved you all, and I still do, in a way. So no trouble, Milo. It's a shame about that poor little Palairet, of course, but he was born to die in a dud cause, so why make a fuss about him? I'm going now. Say good-bye for me to Marius and Mr Conyngham.'

'Going? Dressed like that?'

'Why not? I'll take one of the race trains to London. There'll be a lot of people on that who will smell even worse than I do.'

'Got the fare . . . little one?'

'Don't be silly. Of course.' Tessa passed a filthy sleeve over her face to wipe away a drop under each eye. 'Good-bye, Milo. Please send my things on from Ullacote to school.'

'So Greece was a success?' said Carmilla to Ivan Blessington.

'Yes. Greece was a lovely. As your sister would put it. Greece was a beaut.'

'You've heard that Fielding Grey has gone off to India with Jeremy Morrison? He says he'll get on with *The Grand Grinder* there, but somehow I doubt it. Something has happened to Fielding, Ivan: he's seen right through himself; he's found himself wanting. I don't think he cares any more what he does, what he writes. He's gone with Jeremy to kill time. That's all he'll ever do now: kill time until time kills him.'

'Well . . . we can always print the *Grinder* as it stands. Although it's the wrong length for commercial ends, it has the makings of a minor classic.'

'Yes. What a pity that Fielding should write something pretty near a classic, and should no longer know nor care.'

'At first,' said Nicos to Ptolemaeos Tunne, 'this Holbrook was suspicious. But eventually he agreed that poor Paolo should have some opportunity of sexual experience (other than what may or may not happen between him and his aunt), and he accepted our offer to produce a suitable lady at our expense and to allow her to appear, in Paolo's eyes, as a gift from his patron, Mr Holbrook.'

Nicos and the Greco were at Tunne Hall, reporting back to Ptolemaeos on events in Samuele.

'And so,' the Greco took up the tale, 'on one pretext or another, Paolo's aunt was got out of the way one afternoon – I think Holbrook sent her into Oriago on a shopping expedition, saying that he himself would supervise Paolo – and we produced Tiresiana.'

'Tiresiana,' said Nicos, 'liked the prospect. Paolo was big and beautiful and docile. He greeted Tiresiana in the way he greets most strangers, by exposing himself, and what she saw she found very promising. It was agreed that the *kyrios* and Holbrook and I should go outside and walk in the vicinity while Tiresiana and Paolo amused each other on the mattress which Paolo usually shared with his aunt in the kitchen – the only room – of their cottage. In consideration of her huge honorarium, Tiresiana was quite happy to lie roughly, and all was well set, except that Holbrook would keep popping back to peep, to make sure, as he said, that everything was in order and Paolo was behaving himself. At last the *kyrios* and I restrained him; and the three of us listened from about fifty yards away from the door of the hovel while the noises of pleasure – from both parties – mounted within.

'Now your plan, *kyrie* Ptolemaeos, assumed that Paolo would so resent the fact of Tiresiana's masculinity, when it was finally uncovered, that he would take vengeance on those who had cheated and deceived him, and with a little skill might be persuaded or induced to concentrate that vengeance on Holbrook.'

'It was, of course, always an outside chance,' said Ptoly Tunne. 'But I remembered a passage in Defoe, in which two whores seduce an idiot but find his prick so huge that they take fright and deliberately toss him off without letting him fuck either of them. The idiot first wept, then sulked, then turned murderously violent. I was hoping something of the kind, when Tiresiana or whomever you employed turned out to be unfuckable, might happen here.'

'Well, it didn't,' said the Greco. 'According to Tiresiana, later on, Paolo was delighted with her prick, thought it was the most splendid plaything he'd ever had . . . so splendid that when the time came for Tiresiana to go, he wouldn't let her. He thought that she had come to play with him, and be played with, for ever. And he *loved* Tiresiana. When she called us all in after the performance was over, we found Paolo sitting with her, hand in hand, making little coos of tenderness, kissing her gently on her brow and cheek. When Holbroook offered Tiresiana his hand to help her rise, Paolo slapped it down and held Tiresiana to him. She had more sense than to struggle, indeed she pretended to be grateful to Paolo, thus rendering Holbrook's role even more invidious. He addressed some brusque words in dialect to Paolo, made to disengage Tiresiana from his clutch . . . whereupon Paolo, eager to keep, and to defend from harm and insult, his new-found love, lifted Holbrook off the ground by his hair with one hand, so that he was dangling like a dolly, put the other to his throat, and there and then throttled Holbrook to death while Nicos and I made token gestures of prevention. What can two men do against a lunatic in a rage of sentimental passion?'

Ptolemaeos, envisaging the scene, began to laugh, rather as Fielding had laughed when Jeremy confessed to being buggered by Milo.

'And so,' said Nicos, 'Paolo is now confined to an island in the lagoon where there is a prison for the criminally insane (and doubtless has as full a life there as ever he did with his aunt in the marshes), while Holbrook lies unlamented beneath the church on San Samuele, and his secret with him.'

Ptolemaeos, red and then black in the face, went on laughing. 'So that's the way it turned out,' he spluttered: 'Paolo turned murderous, as we hoped, but out of love and chivalry, not out of frustration and disgust.'

He went on laughing; the Greco and Nicos joined him; the laughter became infectious, self-fuelling, uncontainable, so that even when Ptolemaeos slumped heavily in his chair and rolled to the floor, Nicos and the Greco continued to howl with merriment.

'You see,' said Theodosia to Canteloupe, 'that boy would have loved me, in his gallant, childish way. Although chaste by nature, he would have done what had to be done because I asked him to, showing no reluctance or disgust (however he might have felt), not presuming it was his male right, demanding or claiming nothing in return. He would have been considerate and respectful and unfailingly kind. But now . . . now I must take the person I most closely associate with him. Marius. I must explain that I am asking him to do what his dead friend cannot, and to do it in the same way as Galahad would have done it . . . if, that is, you still wish me to go on with this enterprise for you.'

'I do,' said Canteloupe.

'Marius is now Conyngham's,' said Theodosia. 'But Conyngham will wish him to keep up his connection with your sort of people, so he will let him come if you or I invite him for a few nights. Let one of us do that, Canteloupe, before he goes back to school, and I shall . . . go to him . . . while he is here. He will be full of all the arrogance and presumption of which Galahad would have been innocent, but because Galahad loved him I think I shall be able to go through with it.'

'A good, strong, healthy, intelligent boy,' said Canteloupe with relish, 'with a salutary strain of Jew in him. An excellent choice, if only there were no doubts about his mother's side. But it's no good trying to be too careful. We thought there was no doubt about Fielding and his heredity, Baby and I – that was perhaps the main reason we chose him – and look how poor little Tully has turned out.'

'So Marius has gone for good,' Tessa said to Jakki and Caroline Blessington as they all walked in Hyde Park. 'We shall see him again, of course, and he will know us, and be polite, even friendly. Nevertheless he has gone from us for ever.'

'Where shall you go now?' said Jakki.

'I shall be with Auntie Maisie at the hotel.'

'You know what I mean. Marius has gone, you say, and Milo was never really there. So to whom shall you go now?'

'I wanted to go to Rosie in France until school starts; but there came a telegram which said there was no room.'

'Her mother sent this telegram?'

'It was signed "Rosie". "Best wishes, Rosie." '

'Come with us now,' said Caroline.

'Yes,' said Jakki; 'come with us and we will show you our photographs of Greece, of Dodona and Delphi and sweet Argos, of sandy Pylos and Olympia and Thebes . . .'

'Kind of Ptoly to leave so much of his money to the College,' said Len to Tom Llewyllyn.

'Only proper. His niece Jo-Jo has got plenty already, and he has no other relatives. Come to that, he needn't have left Jo-Jo anything at all . . . which would have meant more for us.'

'Don't be greedy, Provost. I'm very glad Piero has come out of it so well. Now that his loyalties need no longer tie him to Tunne Hall . . . except by way of maintaining the place . . . he will make an admirable Fellow of this College.'

'Yes. Of course, he'll be very preoccupied with arranging Ptoly's last rites – and his rather onerous duties as executor. I hope it doesn't affect his Tripos results.'

'We can smuggle him in whatever happens.'

'Yes, I suppose so. I must have him in as soon as Term starts and ask his advice about the dryads in my garden. These Sicilians know a thing or two about all that.'

'We have failed with Teresa,' said Conyngham to Marius and Milo. '*Milo* has failed with Teresa. But you, Marius, will stay?'

347

'For as long as you will have me,' Marius said.

'I see . . . now then. You are invited to spend two nights with Lord Canteloupe in Wiltshire,' said Raisley Conyngham, passing Marius an opened envelope which had been addressed to Marius. 'I think you should go. People say Canteloupe and his kind have had their day, but the fact is that they are still here. Would you like to go?'

'If you think it is for the best.'

'Write and accept. We must get you a new suit. Your dark grey one is ruined.'

'I shall never forget,' said Marius, 'how you stripped it off me and washed away the filth underneath.'

'An act of corporal charity, as they say in the Roman Church. And a pleasure, my dear Marius. Beautiful things like you should not be handled lest they lose their gloss; but if there is, just for once, a valid and even an exigent excuse for handling you, who would not take it? You were in no condition to clean yourself; you had to be cleaned; you had to be handled and washed and wiped and touched. A great occasion, never to be repeated. You might almost regard it as a baptism, as a laying on of hands. There are many ways, Marius, in which hands may be laid on, to kill or cure, to corrupt or cleanse, to excite or to soothe, to pervert . . . or to dedicate. Mine were laid on you to dedicate.'

'To dedicate me to what?'

'You will understand as time goes on. Now go and write to Lady Canteloupe, accepting their invitation.'

Marius rose. 'What about . . . what about Jenny, sir?' he said. 'Was she too a dedication?'

'An initiation and a reward. I told you at the time. And a lesson. You may choose to remember Jenny when you are with Lady Canteloupe.'

'What can you mean?'

'You will find out. Now tell me. Did Jeremy Morrison speak to you, when you met at Bellhampton, about his future plans?'

'Yes, sir. But only vaguely. He is going to be a long time in the East, and he said he might fly me out there for a visit.'

'When?'

'He didn't say. During one of the school holidays, I suppose.'

'I think we should encourage him to be more precise. Jeremy Morrison, with his money, and his land, and his father . . . to say nothing of his own winning ways . . . could be a great asset to us in what lies ahead. You will be our messenger to him. Our angel.'

'You will find that he likes to be buggered,' said Milo, jealous of Raisley Conyngham's concentration on the younger boy, and wishing to show off. 'I asked it at first as a favour, but he was not slow to accommodate me a second time.'

'Jeremy has been very kind to me.'

'And now you know how to be kind to him.'

'The papers say that Fielding Gray has gone with him,' said Marius, turning from Milo Hedley to Raisley Conyngham. 'Have you . . . any use . . . for Fielding in what lies ahead?

'None.'

'If I asked you to be good to him, sir, as a favour to myself? To see that he is not just cast away?'

'Don't try to make conditions,' Raisley said.

'I wasn't. I was asking a favour.'

'You will receive many,' said Raisley Conyngham. 'They will all be chosen, as Jenny was, by me. I transformed her into something rich and strange for you. I shall not do that again – '

' – She doesn't expect it, sir, and neither do I – '

' – *Do not interrupt.* As I was about to say, Marius: I shall not transform Jenny again, but other favours, similar and dissimilar, and other rewards, there will certainly be. Of my choosing. Now go and write that letter to Lady Canteloupe. Then bring it to me, unsealed. I must insert a little note and introduce myself. After all, you are a guest in my house with your mother's permission. That makes me responsible for you, Marius. It is as well that the Marchioness Canteloupe should be clearly reminded of that . . . before you have the honour of waiting upon her ladyship.'